Pengu

Barbed Wire and Roses

Peter Yeldham's extensive writing career began with short stories and radio scripts. He spent twenty years in England, becoming a leading screenwriter for films and television, and also wrote plays for the theatre, including the highly successful comedies *Birds on the Wing* and *Fringe Benefits*, which ran for two years in Paris. Returning to Australia he won numerous awards for his mini-series, among them *1915*, *Captain James Cook*, *The Alien Years*, *All the Rivers Run*, *The Timeless Land* and *The Heroes*. His adaptation of Bryce Courtenay's novel *Jessica* won a Logie Award for best mini-series. He is the author of nine novels, including *A Bitter Harvest*, *Against the Tide* and *The Murrumbidgee Kid*.

For more information please visit
peteryeldham.com

Also by Peter Yeldham

The Murrumbidgee Kid

PETER YELDHAM

Barbed Wire and Roses

Penguin Books

PENGUIN BOOKS

Published by the Penguin Group
Penguin Group (Australia)
250 Camberwell Road, Camberwell, Victoria 3124, Australia
(a division of Pearson Australia Group Pty Ltd)
Penguin Group (USA) Inc.
375 Hudson Street, New York, New York 10014, USA
Penguin Group (Canada)
90 Eglinton Avenue East, Suite 700, Toronto, Canada ON M4P 2Y3
(a division of Pearson Penguin Canada Inc.)
Penguin Books Ltd
80 Strand, London WC2R 0RL England
Penguin Ireland
25 St Stephen's Green, Dublin 2, Ireland
(a division of Penguin Books Ltd)
Penguin Books India Pvt Ltd
11 Community Centre, Panchsheel Park, New Delhi – 110 017, India
Penguin Group (NZ)
67 Apollo Drive, Rosedale, North Shore 0632, New Zealand
(a division of Pearson New Zealand Ltd)
Penguin Books (South Africa) (Pty) Ltd
24 Sturdee Avenue, Rosebank, Johannesburg 2196, South Africa

Penguin Books Ltd, Registered Offices: 80 Strand, London, WC2R 0RL, England

First published by Penguin Group (Australia), 2007
This edition published by Penguin Group (Australia), 2008

1 3 5 7 9 10 8 6 4 2

Cover design by Jo Hunt © Penguin Group (Australia)
Text design by Debra Bilson © Penguin Group (Australia)
Cover images: Photolibrary
Typeset in 11.5/17pt ITC Legacy Serif and ITC Legacy Sans by Post Pre-press Group, Birsband, Queensland
Printed and bound in Australia by McPherson's Printing Group, Maryborough, Victoria

National Library of Australia
Cataloguing-in-Publication data:

Yeldham, Peter.
Barbed wire and roses / author, Peter Yeldham.
Camberwell, Vic. : Penguin Books, 2008.
ISBN: 9780143007913 (pbk.)

A823.4

penguin.com.au

To my daughter Lyn and my son Perry,
and in loving memory of their mother

Part One

Stephen

1914

Chapter One

It was the last day of August when Stephen said his farewells and left the cloistered quadrangle, pausing only at the main gates for a last nostalgic look. The familiar sight of the green lawn and sprawling university brought a brief moment of regret. The Gothic sandstone building with its famed clock tower was a landmark, both in this city and in his own life. It was a place to which he had aspired, an existence he'd enjoyed all year and would greatly miss. While he felt excited at what lay ahead, he hoped he could keep the promise he'd made himself to return here when it was over.

The winter afternoon was cold and gusty, and billowing sheets of newspaper were among the litter being blown across Camperdown Road. As Stephen ran for an approaching tram he managed to grab a section of the *Herald*, by good fortune capturing the centre page that contained the major news stories. He paid his fare and settled in the open tram, struggling to fold the paper against the flurrying wind. Today the normally sedate broadsheet was more like a tabloid with its shock headlines: BELGIUM CRUSHED. CIVILIANS SLAIN. HUN ATROCITIES. An editorial expressed outrage at

German brutality. Cartoonists were already following the trend, depicting them as bestial subhuman figures.

Dispatches from European correspondents reported the cities of Liege and Brussels had fallen to German cavalry. There were allegations of nuns being raped; children brutally bayoneted. In Flanders the French and British were in retreat. The battle of Mons was a disaster, where both sides made the bizarre claim of having seen the vision of an angel above the battlefield. Whether fact or fantasy, this Angel of Mons did not save the Allied armies from a humiliating rout that threatened the loss of Paris.

Stephen was stunned by the litany of disasters. Only one column had cheerful tidings: in New York the United States had lost the Davis Cup tennis final to a combined Australian and New Zealand team called Australasia. Meanwhile tucked away in small news paragraphs and deemed of less importance were reports of German shops in Adelaide and the Barossa towns being vandalised. Stained-glass windows in German churches were targets for rocks and hooligan missiles. Music stores were banning Beethoven, while Steinways and all other German pianos had been hastily removed from sight. It was hard to believe, he thought, that the war was just three weeks old.

As his tram reached the city, loudly clanging warnings at the street intersections and forcing motor traffic to give way, Stephen began to hear the stirring sound of a military band. In Martin Place, where he and most other passengers alighted, a huge crowd had already gathered to fill the entire square. It was a spectacular response to the national recruitment day, the start of a campaign to raise a volunteer force of twenty thousand. And when that quota was filled the next objective was to recruit and send another twenty thousand, to meet the offers of assistance so readily pledged to Britain.

Flags were flying in the breeze. Buildings draped with massive banners bore persuasive messages. JOIN UP AND KEEP AUSTRALIA SAFE! proclaimed one. FIGHT FOR GOD AND COUNTRY IN THIS WAR TO END ALL WARS! exhorted the largest sign of all. Below it on a rostrum a politician stood waiting with a loud hailer. When the band finished playing 'Men of Harlech' he made a short speech, his voice echoing up and down the concourse as he told his audience not to forget that their government had sworn loyalty and support to our kinfolk across the seas. 'As our prime minister has famously said, our duty is quite clear – to gird up our loins and remember that we are all Britons . . .'

Someone close to where Stephen was standing shook his head in dispute and sniggered. A large woman carrying a furled umbrella whacked him with it, and told him to have some respect and be silent. On the rostrum the politician plunged on without a pause.

'And remember, my fellow citizens, the PM also spoke for us all when he declared: "We will stand behind the mother country to the last man and the last shilling."'

This brought a loud cheer of approval and sustained applause. Stephen had heard many such emotional sentiments in the recent weeks. Beneath the flags, outside the head offices of banks that occupied this section of the city, he could see long lines of men queuing at dozens of trestle tables where a recruiting centre had been set up. Behind the tables uniformed officers sat waiting. The cheering crowd had come to encourage and vicariously participate in the process.

'Going to be in it, mate? Good on you, son,' a fit-looking man in his early thirties said to Stephen.

'God bless you, darling.' A smart young woman patted his arm as he walked past. Her smile lingered on him, following the progress of his tall figure as he moved easily through the crowd.

Others noticed him too: the clean-cut features, tanned face and deep brown eyes, his thick fair hair ruffled by the wind.

The queues were starting to increase. The very young as well as much older men – some in work clothes, others in business suits as if they had just come from an office – stood waiting their turn. The band began to play 'Rule Britannia', and the patriotic fervour reached fever pitch as the crowd sang with them.

Stephen, having a week ago made the decision to give up his first year of law and enlist, had a strange moment of uncertainty. The song felt false, he thought; it was another country's song. The flags that flew so proudly were all Union Jacks – there was not a single newly gazetted Australian ensign in sight. On the tables in front of the row of officers were sheafs of forms to be filled in and signed, together with Bibles on which oaths would be sworn: all this before even a medical examination. It looked preconceived, a show for the public, he felt, and in his indecision he hesitated and became aware of a redheaded figure who also stood watching it, and had not yet joined a queue. They exchanged a nod.

'G'day,' Stephen said. The other nodded again and nervously cracked his knuckles. He was thickset and moved like a bushie with a sure but leisurely gait.

'Fair-sized mob,' he replied at last.

'Big rush to join up,' Stephen said, and for want of anything else asked, 'you from round here?'

'Nah,' the other looked incredulous at the thought. 'Not me, mate. From the bush. Walgett. Ever heard of Walgett?'

'Yes. It's up north, on the way to Lightning Ridge.'

This brought a more careful scrutiny. 'You from the country?'

'Hardly. Strathfield.'

'Where's that?'

'A suburb about ten minutes by train from here.'

'Not many kangaroos there, eh?'

Both smiled. The band switched to a rousing military march by Sousa. Stephen indicated that the queues were increasing to the lure of this martial music.

'What do you reckon?'

'Dunno,' the other replied, 'not too sure.'

Stephen agreed. 'Once you sign, that's it. No going back.'

'Oh, I'm gonna sign,' the boy from Walgett said, 'but I ain't sure if the legal age is eighteen or older. So I reckon to be on the safe side, the best thing is to tell 'em I'm twenty-one, or else we might have to get our parents' permission.'

'How old are you really?'

'Nineteen. Nearly twenty. Well – I'll be twenty next year.'

'Me too,' Stephen replied, and as if in celebration of their shared youth, they grinned and shook hands.

'Good on yer,' the other said. 'Well, wanna give it a go?'

'Righto.'

In the end it was as simple as that. An immediate rapport, the pair joining a queue with other hopefuls, and Stephen's moment of doubt was dispelled. Not only the right thing to do, it was going to be an adventure. The two of them, with a once-in-a-lifetime chance to see the world in the process.

While they waited in the line Stephen learnt more about his new acquaintance, whose name was Jack Watson. But he didn't answer to his given name.

'Forget Jack. Only me mum calls me that. I'm Bluey to me mates, on account of the red hair.' He was a shearer, had been since his first job as a fourteen-year-old tar boy. His team travelled all year; to Stephen whose knowledge of the country did not extend beyond his own State boundary, it seemed they covered immense distances.

'We work the sheds from up north in Queensland – around Emerald, then down to Cunnamulla on the Warrego, on to the Murrumbidgee, and end up as far south as Gippsland in Victoria. Sort of follow the seasons. We load up and travel by horse wagon between the big sheep stations. Not a bad sort of life.'

'Will you go back to it – afterwards?'

'You bet,' Bluey said. 'As soon as we've beaten the Huns. Unless something goes wrong.' He smiled at Stephen's expression. 'I don't mean *that* sort of wrong. I mean if it ends by Christmas, before we can be in it. Some silly buggers are trying to put a spanner in the works by reckonin' that with Britain and France too strong for Germany, the war won't last very long.'

'Don't jinx us, Blue! We'll get there.'

'Hope so, mate.'

The queue moved slowly, and it was an hour before they reached the head of it. At adjoining tables they were each allotted an officer who asked their names and addresses. Then came a series of personal questions: married or single? What religion? Any criminal record? And finally, what age?

'Twenty-one,' Stephen heard Bluey say with an air of casual confidence, and observed his new friend's interviewing officer nod and note this down.

'Twenty-one,' he also replied when asked, and moments later he was holding the Bible and swearing to 'do his duty, to fear God, and honour the King.'

'Medical exam tomorrow at nine,' they were told, and given provisional identity cards. After passing the medical they would be officially registered as members of the Australian Imperial Force, or as it was already being widely called, the AIF.

'But what happens if we fail the medical?' Stephen asked, still bemused by the army's way of doing things in this order.

'Fail? Son, you're nudging six-foot tall – you look strong and fit. We need troops, so you won't fail,' he was promised.

It was almost dark by this time. Despite the chill of the winter evening the crowds remained, singing one song after another. Their massed voices in ragged but enthusiastic chorus rang around the square:

On land or sea, wherever you be,
Keep your eye on Germany!
Should auld acquaintance be forgot?
No! No! No! Australia will be there.
Australia will be there.

Stephen and Bluey, gratified by the success of their deception, went to have a beer.

'After all,' Bluey said, cracking his knuckles – in triumph this time – 'we're not only soldiers of the King, but now we're twenty-one as well. We can stroll into any pub in town!'

They both passed the medical exam the next day as predicted, after which they and hundreds of new recruits were issued with pay books and allotted army numbers. They also received metal discs stamped with their name, religion and regimental number. These, attached to a thin leather lanyard, were to be worn around the neck at all times from then on.

'Known as meat tickets,' a grizzled sergeant – a Boer war veteran – told them unsparingly, 'so the stretcher-bearers can identify you. Now line up at the Q store, get your kit, and for gawd's sake, try to look like soldiers.'

Looking like a soldier was not easy. The rush of volunteers had taken the army by surprise. Not only were recruits being forced to train using broomsticks as make-believe rifles and bayonets, but factories were on round-the-clock shifts to provide enough uniforms. Stephen and Bluey spent the rest of their first day at Moore Park showground, in one of the huge exhibition halls recently converted into a quarter-master's depot, just two of many young men trying to find uniforms their size and, more importantly, boots that fitted them.

The winds of August gave way to a mild September as the rush to enlist continued. After the big enrolment drives in the major cities came the country marches; small towns were denuded of young men determined not to be left behind. As everyone knew, it was unpatriotic not to go.

There was an electric excitement in the air. The long-anticipated conflict was at last a reality, and Australia was to be a participant! The war, a newspaper editorial declared, was 'a shining moment in our history, the country's first great test as a nation', and it predicted glory when the troops finally set sail to engage the enemy.

But behind the excitement lurked anxiety: a concern that the distance from Europe would delay the AIF's arrival: after weeks of training, there would be more weeks at sea and in the meantime who knew what might happen? A cease-fire? Surrender? Not quite fourteen years since Federation, the collection of colonies now a nation called Australia felt a need to prove themselves to the world. Which they assuredly would, it was considered certain.

Provided – and this was the disturbing spectre in everyone's mind – that the war did not end before they could take part.

Chapter Two

Stephen's parents, Stan and Edna Conway, took the news of their son's enlistment with equanimity. They had sensed his restlessness in the first few weeks as he had watched other friends join up. They were reassured on finding out he had requested a year of leave from the university and this had been granted, for it meant their expectations and his rare achievement of obtaining a scholarship place in the law school would not be wasted. In a year the war would almost certainly be over, and he could return to finish his degree and marry Jane.

Stephen and Jane had grown up together. At the age of eighteen she was slightly built, with silky blonde hair and friendly blue eyes. The families lived a few minutes away from each other in the same street, and the pair had been unofficially engaged since they had left their local high school. Even before that, in fact, for when Stephen was eight years old he had asked Jane to marry him, and saved his pocket money to buy her a ring at a local trinket shop. The ring cost him a shilling – several weeks of savings – and Jane had worn it until they had a quarrel, when she threw it into a rubbish bin. On making up two days later they had gone to retrieve it, but the rubbish had been collected and the bin was empty.

They no longer needed a ring to know they loved each other, for each day in the past year it had become more difficult to control their feelings. It was now impossible to have a simple goodnight kiss; it always lengthened into a passionate and ultimately frustrating event. They could hardly bear to part, but to go any further was equally impossible. After these encounters Stephen was left with bruised lips and aching genitals, a condition he knew from dirty jokes in the schoolyard as 'lover's balls'.

It was no joke to him. Ever since his enlistment, when leave passes were infrequent and his ache for Jane more extreme, it had become far worse. Mutual lust was intensified by the realisation he might soon be gone; within a month, was the current rumour, so that Australia would not miss the show. Stephen began to sleep badly, he dreamt of her, and while he wondered what desire did to Jane and if she suffered in a similarly cruel way from sexual frustration, he dared not ask. Instead he asked her to marry him.

They went hand in hand to her parents and then to Stephen's to announce the news. If either family had reservations, the sight of Jane's face convinced them. Her blue eyes sparkled, her animation was so overt it was irresistible. Both sets of parents agreed: the war had changed things. There had always been an expectation of this happy event once Stephen graduated; it was merely taking place a few years earlier than anticipated.

He asked Bluey Watson to be his best man, and applied for compassionate leave.

'Someone die?' the same veteran sergeant asked, and when told it was a wedding he frowned and used his rank to express some highly personal views. He considered it downright bloody stupid, young blokes rushing off to the altar just because there was a war on. 'A hasty hitch never tied a proper knot,' he declared with a chuckle, aggravating Stephen, who rashly replied his marriage was not a subject for anyone else's opinion.

'Is that so?' The sergeant gave him a withering stare and demonstrated his power by refusing a leave pass for Bluey Watson to be best man. 'Next you'll want the whole bloody platoon to have the day off to be wedding guests. Well, I've got news for you, mate. We're an army, not a fucking marriage bureau.'

The application was forwarded to battalion headquarters and it took a week to be returned. Leave was granted, but because of the uncertainty of future troop movements only four days were permitted.

'Four days?' Jane was shocked by the army's rigidity. She tried to conceal it but her disappointment was palpable. *Four days for a wedding and a honeymoon?* Both the families were equally dismayed.

'I know there's a war on.' His mother, who rarely grumbled, felt it most unfair. 'But I'm sure they could manage to defend Australia without you for a bit longer than that.'

It was Jane's mother who posed the question of a postponement, adding hastily that it might be sensible, just until things sorted themselves out. Why rush into marriage, if it couldn't be a proper one with a proper two-week honeymoon? Her father, an insurance broker, had always found it good policy to agree with his wife, and suggested they have a family round-table on the matter.

Jane rejected this and wrote to Stephen at the army camp, telling him how much she loved him – and not to listen to anyone, especially her mother. Four days would be four better than nothing; they should think of it as the start of their life together, and they would have the rest of the honeymoon later on when the war was over and he was not beholden to the rules of anyone's army.

Stephen agreed, but despite the odds against him he did seek another meeting, making a plea for a few extra days. He was firmly told by the intractable sergeant that an appeal was pointless; once battalion HQ made decisions like this they were irreversible. In fact, he would risk having the leave cancelled if he carried on with any more fuss over such a trifling matter. Either accept what he was offered, or call the whole thing off.

No, Stephen said resolutely, he was definitely not calling the whole thing off.

In that case, the NCO replied, he would be issued with a four-day pass after reveille next Tuesday morning, and must be back in camp before lights out on Friday or be considered AWL. And just in case Private Conway did not know it, being absent without leave would mean an appearance before the brigade major with loss of pay and privileges, and a bad start to his life in the army.

'So be sure you're back on time, laddie. Four days marital leave,' he concluded, 'is ninety-six hours by my reckoning. Time enough for whatever you have in mind.'

Stephen's mother took over arrangements. A regular church-goer, she went to see the local priest, Father Geraghty, who promised a splendid nuptial mass. He would call their names in the ritual way from the pulpit three times, beginning next Sunday. Edna Conway explained the war would not wait for this fine Catholic tradition. Nor, much as it pained her, would there be time for a nuptial mass.

Her son and Jane must be married without delay. As short a service as possible. Otherwise, she told the priest, Stephen and his childhood sweetheart might feel tempted to commit a mortal sin and break a commandment. There was no need, she felt sure, to tell him which commandment . . . For the good of their eternal souls, she needed the church's help.

For the good of their souls, Father Geraghty agreed, he would do whatever she asked. An early service, and a short one.

Cars were rare in the district and the family did not own one, but Stan Conway borrowed a friend's motorcycle. He was waiting outside the barracks on Tuesday morning at dawn. As the gates opened and Stephen ran out, his father kick-started the machine. It sped away through the early streets, with the groom riding pillion.

The ceremony was held at eight o'clock. Jane wore a simple ankle-length white dress bought off the peg at the local Bon Marche emporium, and instead of the long bridal train she had envisaged, settled for a short tulle veil. The truncated service was followed by a hasty celebration at the bride's family home. There was just time for a cake to be cut and toasts to be drunk. After she threw her bouquet to her youngest sister they were taken in a friend's motor car on a rushed trip to Central Station before the departure of the morning express to Katoomba.

Stephen had reserved a room at the Valley View Guest House, but his father handed him an envelope just before they boarded the train. In it was a note to say Valley View had been cancelled, and they were to go to the Carrington Hotel where the bridal suite awaited them. All expenses had been settled in advance.

The newlyweds hugged each other in delight. The Carrington was prestigious; it was a wonderful surprise, and being alone in a box carriage they kept hugging each other all the way to the first stop at Penrith. Passions they had kept at bay since puberty were unleashed; Jane spread her skirt as she sat on his lap with her legs tucked on either side of him, and her eyes widened as she felt his instant response. She had taken his hand and put it inside her dress to caress her breasts, while their lips locked and grew hot with longing.

In this state of bliss two stops safely passed. At each station they held their breath as adjacent carriage doors were slammed shut and platform whistles blew departure, but no one came to disturb their privacy. The rhythm of the train made them passionate; when the engine slowed to tackle the mountain ascent their fervour seemed to become deeper, more intimate. Stephen began to feel deliriously and utterly out of control.

'I don't think I can wait for the Carrington,' he whispered, freeing his mouth from hers for a moment to confess it.

'Nor can I,' she said softly, an invitation which prompted him to place his hand inside her new silk underwear to the hitherto forbidden zone there. Her moistness immediately responded to him, her body accepting his fingers and beginning to thrust as he was struggling to unbutton his trousers, and they were on the verge of their wildest fantasy as the train pulled into Emu Plains station. When it stopped the carriage door was flung open.

A well-dressed elderly couple saw vacant seats and promptly entered to claim them. It gave Jane a moment to slide from his lap and rearrange her skirt, although there was little she could do about her flushed face. By the time the couple stowed their luggage and settled opposite, Stephen and Jane were attempting to look relaxed and normal. He nodded to the couple who did not respond, except with a critical appraisal. In particular the woman's sharp eyes studied them until her gaze fixed on Jane's new wedding ring. It appeared to make her less judgemental, but she shifted her righteous scrutiny to Stephen. Too late he realised his face was smeared with Jane's lipstick, and he had not fully done up his fly-buttons.

The rest of the journey seemed endless. It was a relief to reach their mountain stop and escape the disapproving elders, whose attitude by now seemed to suggest the wedding ring might, after all, be no more than a cheap camouflage.

Katoomba was busy with holiday-makers. Still in a state of arousal they took a taxi to the Carrington with indecent haste, only to discover it was just a two-minute walk from the station. The unique hotel, known as 'the grand old lady of the mountains', was a vast Victorian building set in landscaped gardens. Guests strolled on the trim lawns or took tea on marbled verandahs dwarfed by a row of colonnades. At first glance it felt the perfect place for three-and-a-half glorious days in which to consummate their new marital status, and consummate it as frequently as possible. Stephen's eager imagination preceded their progress into the foyer; he could hardly wait for them to be alone.

But closer acquaintance proved daunting. There was a delay when they announced themselves at reception. Were they quite sure, an immaculately groomed desk clerk asked them, that they actually meant the *bridal suite*? His polite air of doubt created an impression this was improbable; such a reservation was more likely for officers rather than a youthful private soldier. Since the foyer was crowded the enquiry was overheard, prompting the interest of other guests. By the time an assistant manager had been summoned, the matter confirmed and apologies given, speculative glances followed them and their luggage across the lobby to the gilded lift cage. They were assigned a pert bellboy who, to their disbelief seemed to be whistling 'Here Comes the Bride' between his teeth, and who lingered until Stephen fumbled for a tip, then bestowed a knowing wink at him before leaving them alone.

The boudoir itself was spacious, an elegant chamber of some

splendour – almost too much splendour, was their first impression. The four-poster brass bedstead with its ornamental lace canopy seemed to dominate the room. Stephen had a moment of regret for the discarded Valley View, which he was sure would have been a cheerful guest house where they could've felt more at home.

'What do you think of it?' Jane asked him, and he made her laugh when he indicated the bed and rolled his eyes.

'I preferred the train,' he said.

'Me too!' she agreed. The formidable bed, like the embarrassment of their arrival, did not inspire the thought of hot-blooded afternoon consummation.

'Tell you what,' he suggested, 'let's unpack, then get some fresh air. Why don't we go out for a walk?'

Jane kissed him on the cheek and declared it a lovely idea.

At the lookout on Echo Point they bought mountain devils from a festive stall, then joined a crowd to admire changing colours on the famous rock configuration called the Three Sisters. Three beautiful young ladies, according to the Dreamtime legend in the tourist brochure, were turned into stone after illicitly falling in love with three brothers of the rival Nepean tribe. Jane and Stephen smiled over this – it seemed a good day for romantic allegories – and later they held hands as they took a ride among happy and shrieking children on the scenic railway.

It was a wonderful afternoon that ended too swiftly. They decided to linger as sunset lit the breathtaking vista of the Megalong and Jamieson valleys, while the battlements of Mount Solitary and the granite face of the Ruined Castle were bathed in crimson. They were the last to leave Echo Point. When they were entirely alone Stephen cupped his hands to his mouth and shouted into the gathering dark.

'Hello, you sisters of the mountain, my name is Stephen!'

'Stephen . . .' the echo replied, 'Stephen . . .' it repeated far down the valley, a fading reiteration of the echo, like a ghostly whisper. As it evaporated in the distance, Jane pirouetted and raised her arms to the sky.

'I'm Jane, and I love him!' She took his hand as the reply came back: 'love him . . .' then a more distant reverberation 'love him . . .' and once again very faintly but still the words intact, as if the echo seemed determined to pass on the message to anyone who would listen, no matter how far away.

After this they walked slowly back to the hotel, arms around each other, ever slower and pausing frequently to tightly embrace the nearer they came to the grandeur of the Carrington.

'Gritted teeth,' Stephen said at the entrance, and she kissed him again. They went past the reception desk, through the now-empty foyer, aware from a hubbub that the dining room was crowded for dinner, but neither of them feeling the least tempted by the thought of food. In the bridal suite they locked the door, hurriedly took off their clothes and made silent love for the first time in their lives. When Jane cried out as he entered her he tried to stop, but she begged him not to. They hardly slept that night; time was too precious and their needs too urgent.

Three more days would never be enough; they knew that as they woke in happy exhaustion and made love again in their grand and gloriously romantic bed all morning.

In the first week of November Stephen's platoon and the whole battalion left Melbourne aboard a crowded troopship. They had arrived the previous night at Flinders Street Station following sudden orders for embarkation. Stephen, like the rest of his company, had not been given any final leave. It was, they were told, a matter of high security. The German cruiser *Emden* was still somewhere off the coast of Western Australia; a lone-wolf raider, she had already sunk almost twenty vessels, and therefore a secret departure was essential.

Because of this he did not spend any more nights with Jane. Since their return from Katoomba they had seen each other only twice, but these were 'open day' visits by relatives to the infantry training camp where picnics took place and social intermingling was encouraged. The army felt it an enlightened step forward. A number of ardent young married couples, having tasted so few precious days of love, would have preferred more private ways to convene.

So it was with incredulity that he saw a big crowd gathered at Melbourne's docks to farewell them. No secret and secure exodus; this was a very public departure with local people – all of whom were strangers to him and to the battalion – cheering and throwing streamers, so it was more like an ocean liner embarking on a world trip than a stealthy covert exit to war. Stephen was moved by the emotion of the occasion, even though he would've swapped the lot of them for a sight of Jane on the wharf below. He spotted a slimly built girl with blonde hair who looked slightly like her, and waved with one hand while blowing her an extravagant kiss with the other. The girl saw him, waved eagerly and blew profuse kisses in return.

When the troopship began to move and all the streamers broke the crowd started to sing. Massed voices were raised in a familiar chorus: 'Now is the hour when we must say goodbye.' The same girl waved until she became a tiny figure among the dispersing people left behind.

A small flotilla of tug boats, ferries and private yachts followed them, tooting and waving, as they sailed down Port Phillip Bay.

'Well, we made it,' Bluey said, watching the land fall away.

'We made it,' Stephen agreed. It was barely two months since the day they had met, but they felt as if they had known each other all their lives.

It was exciting to be on our way at last, he later wrote in the diary Jane had given him, *but we were such innocents. We had no idea of what lay ahead.*

Chapter Three

Early that day a hard north wind began to lash the coast. The sea gave warning as the water of the bay grew turbulent with rolling whitecaps. The horizon contracted, the clouds took on a different hue - one they had never seen before - and towards evening it began to snow.

In the night the wind grew stronger; it howled across the Gulf of Saros, the snow turning to missiles that whipped at their faces and stung their eyes. Their forward trench was open to the sky and long before dawn they were drenched and chilled, for wet-weather gear and winter uniforms had not arrived, reportedly lost aboard a transport ship. Lost, or else carelessly left behind - they were unsure what to believe after the constant blunders of the past few months that had put this campaign and their lives in such jeopardy.

With daylight came a lull in the gale and a singular moment of radiance, for the ground was buried by a thick mantle of white that erased familiar landmarks with their scars of battle. The snow lay deep in Shrapnel Gully, it covered Lone Pine and The Nek. Bomb craters vanished, and sharp ridges where the snipers hid became soft like alpine mounds. A stand of fir trees on the distant hills added to this rare illusion of tranquillity.

It was Stephen's first sight of snow, and he was astonished at the difference it could make. 'I can't believe it. The bastard of a place looks almost beautiful,' he whispered.

'Wait till it thaws,' Bluey warned. 'The bastard of a place'll be horrible as ever, but a bloody sight wetter and colder.'

'You see much snow back home, Blue?'

'Heaps when we worked the Monaro, down Kosciuszko way. Real icy there at times. If the sheep had balls they would've froze right off. Like mine might, any time now.'

Stephen grinned. Eight months now since the April landing, both equally terrified and seasick in the dawn convoy, the pair of them still waking each day to wonder if they would survive until nightfall . . . Australia felt like another life, a long way away. In the intervening time they had become as close as brothers.

A weather forecast arrived, sent along the lines from the snug warmth of the officers' dugout. More arctic winds and a prolonged blizzard was predicted. Bluey went to join a game of two-up. Stephen sheltered beneath his ground sheet and tried to write a letter home.

My darling,

A few months ago we cursed the summer heat, and before that we cursed the sand in Egypt. But one thing we never thought to experience in Gallipoli is this freezing cold. Snow is falling and the wind must be coming from Siberia. Huge seas are making it impossible for the hospital ships to take off the wounded. We haven't got warm clothes for this weather – but winter gear is just one of the things we lack here. Ammunition is running low for the guns, and for months we've had to make our own bombs. It sounds mad, but it's true! We're short of everything, even medicines. When the censor reads this he might use his heavy black pencil, but he's a friend of mine – our company commander, Eddie Cavanaugh – and Eddie might go easy on these comments because I'm sure everyone knows how hopeless the situation is here. Or else they're not telling you the truth at home.

We're in an open trench trying to keep warm and dry. I have an hour's break, as I was on watch since dawn, using a trench periscope, one of our own clever devices that means we can see the enemy but we avoid sticking our heads above the parapet. Johnny Turk's a dead-eye shot, so that wouldn't be a smart move. You'd be surprised how inventive we've become; we had to be, the odds were so much in their favour we needed a bit of Aussie know-how.

With this freeze it's hard to imagine it's late November at home. Almost summer. The cicadas will be singing. Yachts will be out on the harbour, and you might be taking Richard to the beach. How I miss Australia, and you – and of course the baby son I've never seen.

There's talk we might be leaving here soon. The grapevine says the generals are arguing – it feels to us they've been arguing ever since we landed – but this time it's all about whether Gallipoli should be evacuated. It's one of those army secrets that nobody is supposed to know, but everyone does.

It would be good to go, although we haven't won anything here, not that we ever had much chance to do that. It was a dreadful mess right from the start. If we go, it will have been for nothing. Which is sad, because we'll leave good mates behind, who died for some vainglorious and impossible strategy. I'll write again soon.

My love to you and the bub. Give him a big hug for me,

Stephen

Later he re-read the letter and tore it up. He wrote instead that all was well; things were working out fine; they were winning the battle of the Dardanelles. He told her how much he loved and missed her.

He tried to sleep, but it eluded him. It was wrong to tear up the truth and invent falsehoods, but it was done because the reality was unbearable. Letters were the one link they had: an eagerly awaited lifeline no matter how many months they took to reach her, but his thoughts expressed in them had to be circumspect to spare her feelings. It was not possible to write otherwise - blunt honesty could only be confined to the diary she had given him, kept safe in his sodden kitbag. It was preserved in oilskin along with his paybook and the treasured letter from Jane that had come while they were still training in Egypt. He took it out now, noticing the paper was starting to fray, but the writing on it was still clear.

The doctor says it should be at the end of May. Her hand was a neat copperplate. She had been a trainee teacher before their sudden decision to marry.

> *So I've been doing lots of calculating, and it's my belief it happened on our very first lovely night. If he's a boy I'd like to call him Richard, and if a girl then perhaps Emily. Write and tell me what you think. How does it feel to know you'll soon be a dad, and how I wish you were here instead of wherever you are. And please, dearest, take care. Come back safe to me.*

Dearest. Just re-reading it evoked fond memories. She was the only one who had ever called him that. The only real girlfriend he'd had. Stephen put her letter carefully back inside his diary for safekeeping. He'd written to express his joy at the news, agreeing it had surely been that wonderful night, their first love-making on that enormous bed in the bridal suite, and perhaps one day they could revisit Katoomba and spend a night there again to commemorate the event. He said Richard was a nice name for a boy. He felt sure it would be a boy, but if she should turn out to be a girl he also liked the name Emily.

As he was to be a dad, one other matter required attention. On joining the army they'd had to make a will. It was not something he'd told Jane – it would unnecessarily alarm her – but he had been to see the orderly-room sergeant and amended it. In the event of Jane's death his estate should go to his son or daughter.

'That's a bit vague,' the sergeant had said.

'It has to be,' Stephen replied, 'since I won't know if it's a he or a she until the end of May.'

Six weeks before the expected birth he was on a troop transport in the Aegean approaching the Dardanelles; after that in the dawn convoy, wading ashore onto a shingled beach – he and Bluey, thoughts focused on how to scale the steep hillsides, fearful of Turkish snipers and the machine guns whose deadly hail of bullets would surely kill them.

In the weeks that followed there was no word of her progress. It was not until the middle of May – when there was a one-day truce so both sides could bury their dead – that a telegraph from his father found him. A medical orderly brought it to the hospital tent, where he was being treated for a shrapnel wound in the arm. He'd been lucky – a grenade exploding perilously close – but unlucky enough for it to be classified a minor casualty. Not even a day's rest, just a bandage and back to the trenches.

Stephen was startled by the message. He had read it aloud and laughed happily at the news, although he was conscious of the ironic date. 'Listen to this: "Congratulations! A son born on April 25th. Premature but Jane and baby Richard both well."'

A few months later, after the unit had been pulled back for a brief rest, there was a long, happy letter from Jane, which made him realise that as he waded through the shoal water to the beach during the landing she must indeed have been giving early birth. The east coast of Australia was eight hours ahead, and her letter said Richard had arrived just in time for a late lunch, so by his calculation it could have happened at virtually the same moment.

Often since then he wondered if he could have continued up that hillside into the Turkish gunfire, had he known it.

The silence was disturbing, so unfamiliar it felt threatening. The night was cold but clear, the sky luminous with stars. Providentially there was no moon as they made their way in small groups with not a word spoken and without even the sound of footsteps, for their boots were wrapped in hessian stripped from sandbags. In the pitch dark they followed a trail of white flour marking the path that led down to the beach.

Alongside the jetties the ancillary lighters and barges waited. Over a period of several days, aware they were under the scrutiny of Turkish field glasses, these same craft had approached the shore laden with what appeared to be huge quantities of supplies from the transport ships anchored in the bay. Their arrival did what was intended: created the impression the Australians were stocking up for the winter ahead.

It was imperative that everything should contribute to this perception. A whole army was to be taken off, and the whole army had to keep the secret. A flurry of trench digging took place to add substance to this. Each day the light horsemen chosen as dispatch riders galloped along the beach as usual, risking fire from the Turkish snipers, while the infantry had their customary bets on whether they would make it through the fusillade or get shot. The classic touch to create a feeling of normality was the staging of a game of cricket on Shell Green.

'Steve.' Lieutenant Cavanaugh found him in a trench and sat with him while they ate their sparse rations. 'I hear you played for the second eleven at the uni?' Before Stephen could answer, he was told he'd been selected to open the batting for Australia A in the forthcoming match against Australia B.

'Raving bloody mad,' he'd pronounced it, but scored twenty runs and took two catches while an array of armed guards stood ready to protect players from any unsporting snipers. Afterwards the twenty-two relieved cricketers shook hands, declared the game an honourable draw and even waved to distant Turks who'd watched the performance of this strange Anglo-Saxon pastime.

Meanwhile in empty trenches, rifles were set up to fire long after their owners had departed. Inventive minds used a system of weights made from water cans, punctured so that when the water dripped out a trigger was released and the gun operated. Other homemade controls were manipulated from the beach by wires that set unattended machine guns firing. In this way, as the transports departed with troops packed in their holds, a façade of normality was kept constant. Many thousands had now been lifted off and carried to safety in Lemnos.

Before leaving Stephen had been among those who had paid a last visit to the burial ground originally called God's Acre, and later renamed God's Square Mile. He had gone there to say an awkward goodbye to mates, to straighten flimsy wooden crosses and try to tidy the graves. Over half his platoon were buried there. He'd attempted some kind of prayer, but was unable to find the words. In the end he had simply said sorry to them – sorry he was alive and leaving them; sorry it had been such a mess, a botched campaign, and that they and eight thousand other young volunteers who'd come here to fight their first battle would not go home again.

Ironically, the evacuation was succeeding brilliantly. The first pessimistic forecasts in London had predicted half the army could be killed in the attempt to leave; so far there had been not a single casualty. But each day the pressure increased on those selected to be the rear guard. Fewer men remaining had to create the same volume of gunfire, the same impression of full trenches, while also destroying the supplies they could not take with them.

A squad of sappers set mines and booby traps in fading daylight on the final day. The sappers were the last group to leave for the beach, together with Stephen's platoon. Bluey led the way with the loquacious Duggie Chandler, tall and skinny as a beanpole. Ever since training camp he'd been known as Double-Trouble, a nickname acquired from his compulsion of saying everything twice. This habit of repetition, comical until now, almost became a disaster.

On the steep slope his foot slipped. 'Bugger,' he said aloud, and 'bugger,' he automatically repeated before he could prevent himself. They all froze, aware how far the slightest sound could carry in the night air. There was still half a battalion on the beach below, waiting to be taken out to the ships. One blunder even now would alert the Turks, some of whom in forward dugouts were only a few hundred yards away. Discovery of the empty Anzac trenches could lead to a massacre of those remaining.

'Fucking drongo,' Bluey hissed ferociously, and taking a rag from his pocket, stuffed it into Double-Trouble's mouth that was about to issue an apology. For the next hour he kept a tight grip on the other's arm as they followed the flour trail to the beach.

They were safely on the last barge, muffled oars moving them away from the shore, when the pre-set mines began to detonate. The sappers with them had set the fuses.

'You bloody beauties,' Stephen whispered. The sappers were from another unit; he didn't know them, but knew they had primed the unstable devices and were heroes.

'Beauties, beauties,' Double-Trouble echoed.

The whispers went around the craft.

'Wait till the really big Christmas cracker goes off,' one of the sappers murmured.

It began to rain. Soft, like tears. Their barge reached the last transport ship and they climbed on deck. The land was lit as the promised blast exploded like a thunderclap. The soldiers on board, freed from hours of imposed silence, cheered this last defiant gesture.

Stephen stood at the stern rail looking at the silhouette of the Turkish cove, with its rugged terrain above it. Perhaps some day in peace it might have its own sort of beauty, he thought, but to them it was an awful place. So many dead. No matter what anyone might try to say, it was a dreadful and costly failure. Except for this escape. He had a strangely ambivalent feeling about that. If the landing had been as well planned as the retreat, there would surely not be so many graves or such a bitter taste in his mouth . . .

At last the ship began to move. The rain grew heavier and the land behind them disappeared from view.

January 1916

My darling,

You will have heard, I'm sure. It seems that in the early morning the Turks began to wonder why everything was quiet. They decided to attack, and soon after dawn they reached our trenches to find no one there. An entire army had been evacuated almost in front of their eyes. Despite predictions of disaster, there were only two casualties. We're now in Lemnos, which is a Greek Island in the Aegean Sea. We reached here on Christmas Day, and all your letters were waiting for me as well as the photo of our baby. It's hard to realise we now have a nine-month-old son. I promise I'll be careful. I know you worry, but please don't fret, I'll survive and come home to you both.

The latest rumour is we're headed for England, where we all wanted to go in the first place. In the meantime, we're made to train and go on route-marches as if we've just joined up. We're serving under British officers here, who seem to think we're an undisciplined lot. We don't salute enough for their liking. They reckon we're a rabble because we don't kowtow and refuse to be subservient. But that's the army for you. I'd hate to be a regular, and have to put up with all this drill and saluting for a living.

Remember how people said the war would be over by Christmas 1914, and foolishly you and I believed them? I can only hope now it will be over by Christmas 1916. Then I'll finish my law degree, become a suburban solicitor, and we'll raise kids. Send me more photos of our baby, and another of you as well.

We don't yet know when we'll leave here. The army prefers not to tell soldiers anything, but my next letters may come from London. By the way, I've been promoted to platoon sergeant. My pay goes up by three shillings a week. My mate Bluey says that makes me a capitalist.

Your loving capitalist,
Stephen

P.S. We've just heard on the grapevine it is *England, and probably some leave in London. The grapevine is better than official orders. Unlike them, it's hardly ever wrong!*

Chapter Four

In the troop train from Portsmouth they gazed through misted windows as the countryside sped past. Stephen was surprised by the fields and tracts of woodland, so much open space in a land that seemed so tiny on the map. He saw many substantial homes, even a few that looked like small castles or manor houses, and just when he began to wonder where ordinary people lived, the train clattered through a series of towns and past rows of tiny terraced cottages.

They felt the strangeness of this landscape and the way the pale sun was only occasionally visible between intervals of rain, a rain so fine it seemed like mist. It was wonderfully peaceful. The fields were neat, divided by clipped hedgerows, and the lanes that ran beside the railway were empty except for sporadic horsedrawn carts or heavily rugged figures riding bicycles.

As ever, they were unsure of their destination. The brigade bookie was quoting generous odds against London; Salisbury was a red-hot favourite at even money. Salisbury meant further training, the prospect of it filling them with gloom. They had no wish for more of what the Tommies called 'square bashing' that involved being yelled at by ferocious sergeant-majors; they had been given more than a taste of it on Lemnos when all they wanted (and felt they had rightly earned) was some rest and relaxation.

Bluey insisted their objective would be London, and to bolster his optimism put half a crown on it. He, Double-Trouble and Stephen were invariably together now, for they were among the only twelve survivors of their original platoon. Despite the relief at their escape from Gallipoli, the memory of heavy losses had left them dispirited. Thus it had been a surprise when the troopship docked at Portsmouth. There was a crowd on the wharf, and as they disembarked came the sound of cheering and the realisation these people had gathered to greet them.

'Strewth, don't they know we had the shit beaten out of us?' Bluey wondered aloud.

'They're cheering as if we won!' Stephen said, perplexed.

The truth was more prosaic. As they discovered later, the war had become bogged down on the Western Front, and Britain needed symbols to stimulate recruitment. Newspapers were fulsome in praise of the Australians – Anzac was an iconic name that caught the eye – and the slouch hat had become augmented with hero status. In the press they were constantly described as a different kind of soldier, all volunteers, possessed of a breezy irreverence that had begun to appeal to the stratified British society. There was admiration for their courage under fire, and for the daring evacuation.

So when news of their imminent arrival swept the port, crowds gathered. They were garlanded with flowers and offered drinks and cigarettes. Men shook their hands and women hugged and kissed them with what seemed like genuine affection.

'Lovely,' exclaimed Double-Trouble. 'Lovely, lovely,' and in the ensuing hours while others shivered in the cold waiting for a troop train, he sneaked away with a friendly girl who said he had earnt himself a suitable reward and took him home to bed.

'You bastard,' Bluey said on hearing this, cracking his fingers more vigorously than usual, 'you skinny, long streak of shit! Didn't she have a friend?'

'She did, she did – and she was nice too.' He laughed uproariously at their expressions. 'Nice,' he reiterated, 'both of 'em . . . nice.'

'Both?' Bluey was divided between disbelief and outrage.

'Both . . . both,' Double-Trouble confirmed happily.

The light was fading though it was still midafternoon. When the train slowed Stephen saw the spire of a church, and wondered if it might be St Paul's. He hurriedly realised his mistake as steam hissed and the brakes were applied. There was a collective groan when they saw the name Salisbury on the station platform.

My darling,

We're in camp on Salisbury Plain in Wiltshire, along with what seems like half the troops of the British Empire. Thousands of us: New Zealanders, Canadians, Indians, Ghurkhas and South Africans. Between being drilled and forced on route-marches, we've seen Stonehenge, which is only six miles away, and visited Salisbury Cathedral, which has the tallest spire in England, but all we really want is the promised leave in London. The grapevine has really let us down this time. I loved reading all your letters that were waiting here for me . . .

He didn't like to say so, but there had been so many of them, one written every few days, even just a few lines, to tell him their son Richard had managed to stand at the age of nine months and soon might take a first step, which was early . . . She felt sure Stephen would agree it was very advanced. She was confident Richard was going to be clever, because he knew both sets of grandparents on sight when they visited. He was such a bright, happy boy.

There were times when Stephen yearned to hear news of other subjects; for instance, what was it really like at home now? Was there going to be a vote on conscription, so they'd get some much-needed reinforcements? Was it true what they'd heard, that life seemed completely normal there – that the beaches were full and race meetings crowded – and the enlistment rate had dropped off ever since publication of the shocking casualty lists after the Gallipoli landing?

And what about the strike of hundreds of soldiers at Liverpool, who'd refused to drill because they said the camp was dusty and made them thirsty! Had they really walked out, got blind drunk and started fighting and looting all over the town? Was it really true? They'd read it in papers, but he and his mates couldn't believe it. Imagine soldiers complaining that drilling made them thirsty! He'd like to see how thirsty they'd get in dusty Egypt. As for going on a rampage in which some civilians were apparently shot and wounded, what a pity these soldiers didn't volunteer to fight overseas instead of starting their own private wars in Liverpool.

He'd written to ask about this, but when the letters came back they were only about the latest cleverness of their baby son.

Their promised leave came at last, and London was a revelation. When the suburbs first appeared outside the train window they thought they'd reached the heart of the city, but the streets, shops and rows of terraced houses went on for miles, until at last they arrived at Paddington Station. After that came the confusion of the underground tube system, as well as braving the new experience of the electric stairways that were called escalators. Then there were the huge crowds, pavements packed with people, the roads full of motorbuses and, astonishing to them, the realisation that most of the drivers and conductors on these vehicles were women.

Stephen and Bluey went in search of a cheap place to stay. They asked Double-Trouble to join them, but he had a more urgent priority. The reason for army leave in his considered opinion was to latch onto a bit of crumpet, and he'd heard there was heaps of it, willing and available in Piccadilly, Soho or the Strand - in fact almost everywhere in London. He intended to shag himself stupid for the next ten days, and if he caught a dose of the clap, they'd have to send him to the infectious diseases hospital instead of France - which in his opinion might be a better option.

'Hooroo,' he said cheerfully, and walked directly towards a young woman nearby, doffed his slouch hat with a touch of flamboyance, leant down from his great height to admire her and asked politely whether a fuck was out of the question.

'Struth! Mate, did yer hear that?' Bluey asked.

'Incredible! He only said it *once*.'

'Once was enough! Look at 'em! She's took his arm and they're off to the races!'

'Sure you don't want to try your own luck?' Stephen asked.

'My oath I will, but I want a feed and a few beers first. What about you? Mate, I know you're happily married and all that, but it's been a long time.'

'It has,' Stephen said, a touch thoughtful, 'but I'll be okay.'

'You mean the straight and narrow? It'll be ten days of hell,' Bluey predicted.

'It will. Don't let that stop you.'

'Not bloody likely. After we have a grog I'll be off to check the talent. You write to the wife. Tell her you're bein' faithful, while us randy bastards are dippin' our wicks all over town.'

Going back to Salisbury in the train ten days later, Stephen tried not to listen as the others compared notes. Double-Trouble, as usual, had the floor. He declared English women were the goods, and for everyone's benefit described his amorous adventures. He had a notebook with their names, addresses and the intimate details of what best aroused them. Of the eight names listed, he had promised to return and marry four.

'When did you get time to eat?' Stephen asked.

Double-Trouble looked at him pityingly. There was always time to eat, he said. But a chance to bury the bishop in such willing and eager flesh was food and drink combined. Bliss like that would not come again until they returned from France. He'd promised his ladies he'd sort out the Huns and return to take up where he had left off. They awaited him with bated breath.

Since he had so much to report in duplicate detail, the train was past Andover and Nether Wallop before Bluey had a chance to discuss his leave. Not that he appeared eager to do so.

'Come on, Blue,' the others encouraged, 'how did you go?'

Stephen could tell he didn't want to talk about it, but the group, led by Double, were vociferous.

'Had a beaut time,' was all he offered. 'Met this girl first night.'

'Pretty?' he was asked.

'Sort of. Extra nice. Took me home to meet her family.'

'Never mind the family. How many times did you do it?' The others in the compartment all awaited this answer.

'We didn't,' Bluey said, frowning and clearly disliking this interrogation, 'just held hands mostly. Talked a lot about the future. You might have four wives lined up, Double, old mate-mate, but I'm comin' back here to marry just one. Then she'll come home to Australia with me.'

Double-Trouble roared with scornful laughter, and declared it was romantic bullshit. Fancy silly old Blue not cracking it. He'd drawn the short straw! Before they left for France his girl would be holding hands with some other poor deluded drongo. He must be a real dill to think otherwise. It was obvious he'd got himself landed with a prick teaser or a professional virgin.

They had to carry Double off the train at Salisbury. If not, he would likely have remained unconscious until the terminus in Cornwall. Bluey couldn't understand how the great Casanova had been so easy to knock out. Probably sexual exhaustion. It hadn't been a hard punch at all. Just a little tap on the snout, to warn him not to talk that way about another bloke's fiancée.

The fight in the train took precedence over further reports of their leave, so Stephen had no trouble evading queries about his own time in London. In fact, he could truthfully say he had stuck to the straight and narrow. He had spent each day tramping the streets exploring London, trying to absorb himself in the historic past instead of the empty present.

He had visited the Tower, fed pigeons in Trafalgar Square and marvelled at Elizabethan buildings that had been standing long before Australia became a colony. He walked past the newspaper offices that gave Fleet Street their fame, stood on Ludgate Hill and admired St Paul's; he discovered Covent Garden and roamed along the river towpath from Chelsea to the Isle of Dogs. In the process he'd encountered many people, been complimented for being an Anzac, had his photograph taken and his hand shaken, but in reality had met no one for more than a few desultory minutes.

It had been a time of strain. He was committed to Jane, but the solitary days took a toll; he had not envisaged the challenge of being isolated amid so much temptation, and slept badly in his tiny boarding-house room. Late at night, looking out at the clamorous streets, he began to envy his mates their cheerful wantonness. He had no problem ignoring the tarts with their overt invitations; more difficult were the fleeting glances of women who were clearly not prostitutes but just alone, perhaps as lonely as he was, their wistful looks seeming to offer an ephemeral interlude of warmth and love.

Then, on that last day . . . why did it have to be the last?

In Leicester Square he had seen a sight that made him stop. He was confronted by a billboard with the word SUNLIGHT emblazoned on it. Below was a picture of an Australian digger, looking so immaculate it was unreal. With this was a message:

A BOX OF SUNLIGHT IN FRANCE IS
WORTH TWO IN THE BUSH
The Australian is no stranger to Sunlight. The
tan on his cheek, the badge on his hat, his smart
bearing and clean appearance, all proclaim
SUNLIGHT. Clean fighters recommend SUNLIGHT!

'Good God Almighty.' Stephen gazed at it with disbelief. He had already seen a bizarre advertisement for a truck declaring it to be as strong as an Anzac. He felt an increasing unease at the rhapsody of praise in English newspapers, overblown prose making them out to be like Olympian warriors, but this stupid poster using them to sell soap angered him.

'Disgraceful, isn't it?' a voice beside him had commented, and he'd turned to gaze into clear grey eyes and a young face framed by a coat collar and a cloche hat. She had smooth pale skin, traces of brown curly hair the hat did not entirely hide and a well-shaped nose with a tilt. An impish face, he thought, although the word endearing also came to mind. 'I wouldn't have spoken, but I could see you were upset. It's quite wrong, don't you think so?'

'Yes,' he'd said, 'I do.'

She had a soft voice to go with her looks, but being unfamiliar with English accents he could not tell if she was a Londoner. He tried to think of something to say, realising she had only paused to make a friendly comment and was about to move off.

'Please,' he'd said impulsively, 'may I buy you a cup of tea?'

'I'm sorry, sergeant, but I have a train to catch.'

Recalling the moment, he knew he must've looked downcast, for she'd suddenly smiled and said there was always another train. Endearing, he'd decided; that was the right word when she smiled. They had gone to the nearest Lyons Corner House and ordered tea and toast.

Her name was Elizabeth Marsden, and she lived in a small village called Grantchester near Cambridge, where her father was a school teacher. She had been visiting an aunt in London, and had to catch the 2.15 fast train from Kings Cross, now that she'd missed the 1.15.

'I'll make sure you catch it,' Stephen assured her. 'We can get a tube, or walk there along Tottenham Court Road.'

'Then you know London?'

'Some of it.' He told her about his leave and the days spent walking and discovering the city.

'But I thought Australian soldiers –'

'You thought we all got drunk and chased girls?'

'Well . . .' she seemed flustered for a moment, then laughed. It was an enchanting sound, and a man at a nearby table turned to look in envy. If Elizabeth noticed this she ignored him, her eyes remaining focused on Stephen. 'I was obviously misinformed.'

'Not totally misinformed,' he grinned. 'I think some of my best friends are probably doing that right now.' It was then he told her he was married, and had a son almost a year old whom he had never seen.

'But you're about the same age as me,' she said, astonished. 'My parents are always saying I'm far too young to marry.'

'So was I,' Stephen replied. 'Ridiculously young. But the war made us impulsive. It also made me leave university, and rush to join up.'

'University?' She was surprised again, but he'd encountered this before. In the British army few university students were to be found in the ranks; most of them were at least subalterns.

'What did you read at university? Or do you say study?'

'Law,' he'd said, 'I was reading law.'

A pert young waitress brought their tea, and with it a large plate of toast with an assortment of jams. Elizabeth looked surprised. 'My goodness, we are being spoiled.'

'Nothing's too good for our Anzacs. Got to keep their strength up, so they can win the war,' the waitress said with a glance at Stephen, a plainly flirtatious appraisal, then with a cheeky grin had patted the three stripes on his sleeve before hurrying off to another customer.

'No wonder the poor English lads are jealous!' Elizabeth

Marsden observed. 'Extra toast, a choice of jams *and* an overture as well, unless my eyes deceived me. Which they didn't,' she added with another smile.

'It's my exalted rank of sergeant.' Stephen was embarrassed.

'Does that kind of thing happen often?'

'Not to me.' He occupied himself selecting which jam to spread on his toast. After a moment he asked, 'Are the English Tommies really jealous of us?'

'They say you're better paid, and you get all the glory.'

'Such as being made to look like idiots on an advertisement to sell soap. Well, they're welcome to it.'

'I doubt if they'd be jealous of that.' Elizabeth sipped her tea before continuing. 'But yes, there's envy. It's a shame, though understandable. I've heard them complain they were at Gallipoli too, but these days people only talk about what the Anzacs did.'

'None of us should've been there,' Stephen replied, but not wanting to discuss the war he changed subjects and told her about his friends, including a sanitised account of Double-Trouble which had her amused.

'A real Lothario, is he?'

'He likes to think so.'

'Poor thing! He sounds rather insecure. Perhaps that's why he says things twice, so someone will take notice.'

He nodded, impressed by her insight. 'I never thought of it like that,' he said.

'And now you, Stephen.' She'd smiled. 'Tell me about you.'

'Not much to tell.' He had felt strangely inarticulate, possessed by a sudden shyness. In his own opinion his life had been quite ordinary: whatever he might say would hardly be of interest, and could well disappoint her.

'Apart from being married, and dropping law to enlist, there must be more to tell. Will you go back to it? The law?'

'I hope so,' he replied.

'Of course you will.'

'If all goes well. You know . . .'

'Yes,' she said.

'I worry about that. The future . . . and what might happen.'

'I'm sure everyone does. It must be frightening.'

'It is. But we keep reading these silly stories about what great fighters we are, and how fearless. It's not true, Elizabeth. Anyone who says they aren't afraid is lying.'

He was lifting his teacup when his hand began to tremble. He hardly managed to replace it on the saucer. Her hand had reached to cover his.

'Tell me where you live, and all about your family.'

He felt the warmth of her touch, looked into her grey eyes and wished this was not the last day. He no longer felt shy.

'My family goes a long way back,' he began, 'to when Sydney and Hobart were penal colonies. My great-grandfather was a convict.'

'From England?'

'From Ireland. An Irish rebel from Tipperary.'

'Tell me about him.'

'He was a bit of a firebrand, I think. An agitator. When he was seventeen he was sentenced to death for speaking against the red-coat occupation, but they sent him to Botany Bay instead. His name was Jeremy Conway, and seven years later he got his ticket-of-leave – a sort of pardon, but not a real one. More like a parole. He started a printery and married my great-grandmother. She was a convict too. Most people at home don't like to admit to skeletons like that in their closet. But I'm proud of being descended from them.'

'What was your great-grandmother's name?'

'Bess. They had a son named Matthew, and adopted an orphan boy called Daniel.'

He'd told her how the two boys grew up together, his grandfather Matthew to become a journalist and run a tiny news sheet that became an influence in the colony, and how Daniel owned square-rigged ships by the age of eighteen. Both of them successful so young, both proud to be known as Currency Lads and embroiled in the near revolt when England sent out more convicts against popular opinion. While he was telling her, Stephen realised he had never before spoken of this to anyone. She was an avid listener, asking why they were called Currency Lads.

'It was a name they adopted. It meant first-generation Australians. They made their presence felt at a time when local society only approved of free settlers. They helped to change all that. I've read Matthew's editorials and seen pictures of the ships Daniel owned. They must have been great days, exciting times.'

He had barely been aware that the afternoon was half gone and Elizabeth Marsden had missed two more trains. He suggested they find a motor cab, but she preferred they walk together to Kings Cross. She took his arm as they reached Charlotte Street, and their progress slowed as they walked companionably in step. It was because neither of them had wanted to hurry that she was only just in time to catch the 4.15.

He helped her find a seat, and she had impulsively put her arms around him and kissed him goodbye. Train doors were slamming prior to departure. He wanted to tell her how wonderful the past few hours had been.

'I wish we'd met sooner,' was all he'd had time to say before an English soldier deliberately jostled them, barging into Stephen with his kitbag while looking for a seat.

'Bloody colonials,' he'd snapped in their faces, 'all yer do is pinch our girls. I'm sick of the sight of those stupid slouch hats.'

Stephen had been bracing himself to ask for Elizabeth's address so he could write to her, but the Tommy continued his tirade, and he'd taken her into the next carriage away from the abuse. By then the station guard's whistle had shrilled, and there was no time. The train had already begun to shuffle forward as he jumped off.

'Want to get yourself killed?' the guard berated him, and Stephen yelled at him to shut up. Too late he turned back to the train, only managing to catch a last glimpse of her face through the smeared window, her hand waving, then the train – and she – were gone.

Chapter Five

It was midsummer in France, but they shivered despite the heat, for the night was rabid with the sound of gunfire. Tracer bullets made cross-stitch patterns in the dark. A blinding flare lit the desolation of no-mans-land beyond the barbed wire where the dead lay in hideous disarray. Mutilated bodies that weeks earlier had been dismembered by shellfire were strewn like wreckage beyond hope of retrieval, many of them eaten by marauding rats. This was a different kind of war to the Dardanelles – infinitely worse – for the Western Front was a sickening slaughterhouse.

Stephen knew they were changed out of all recognition, himself included, perhaps himself most of all. They were now insensitive to such sights – secretly relieved that the bodies scattered out there were those of others. The tight-knit mateship forged at Gallipoli had been left behind there; thoughts had turned to a longing for home and survival at any cost. Tomorrow would be an anniversary, a gruesome one that no one wished to celebrate; they were about to enter the third year of the war.

His platoon was confined in a forward tunnel where duckboards were laid to protect them from the sea of mud around them. The mud was deep, as dangerous as quicksand; men had vanished into it and been lost within seconds. And not just their own side: Germans were entombed here too, for both armies had occupied these trenches, both had shed blood for this place, both had won then lost it, men dying by the thousands in a single afternoon to regain this small strip of pockmarked ground.

They were here because Field Marshal Haig's grand plan to retake the Somme had failed. The British had fought until an entire army corps was annihilated, when even the unrelenting Haig had been forced to order their withdrawal. As a consequence Australian troops were deployed as reinforcements. Their objective was to regain the town of Pozieres. No one had yet told them the truth: Pozieres was a ruin, a village that no longer existed.

They had marched from Amiens, through countryside once sylvan and now stripped of green, past miles of defoliated trees with blackened limbs like grotesque casualties. For Stephen's platoon it was their first sight of Picardy, trudging the Bapaume Road as the Tommies limped back. The British wounded, too numerous to count, were piled on horse wagons, while those still able to stand were being made to march in step. Their exhausted faces gazed in bewilderment as the Anzacs tramped past, hardly anyone in step, young voices massed in a raucous chorus:

We are the Ragtime Army,
The A-N-Z-A-C.
We cannot shoot,
We don't salute,
What bloody use are we?
And when we get to Berlin,
The Kaiser he will say:

'Hoch, hoch, mein Gott,
What a bloody odd lot,
To get six bob a day!'

But that was over seven weeks ago. The swagger had gone and the incessant day-and-night bombardment of high-explosive shells had wreaked its dreadful effect on morale. Even worse was the impact of the *Minenwerfer*: huge land mines fired by howitzer that ripped craters out of the earth, destroying trenches and the soldiers sheltering in them. Men who escaped death from these massive explosions often suffered concussion and were left glassy-eyed, crying helplessly and unable to control their bowels. Sometimes at night, when he could find a candle in the dugout, Stephen wrote in his diary, attempting to analyse what these past weeks in France had done to them.

We came here too young, too sure of ourselves. We'd begun to believe we were special, like the British papers said. Even their generals praised us, which should've been a warning. Generals sit in safety far behind the lines, they play their games of war and never count the cost. Look, we're as shit-scared as everybody. And why not? Gallipoli was bad, but this is a bloody carnage. There is a dreadful feeling of utter hopelessness here, and we play a game of tag with death every hour of every day.

He often found himself thinking of London, remembering the warmth of the teashop, the grey eyes that watched him as he talked, the laugh that made other men's heads turn. He wondered if this was disloyal to Jane, then dismissed the thought, because it was just the occasion he had enjoyed so much, the few friendly hours with a girl his own age instead of the continuous company of army mates. Nothing more that that. Although . . . he could still feel the touch of her hand and the brief kiss on his cheek, and wondered how different his ten days might've been had they met sooner. Just to walk about London with her as a companion would've made it a different city. Above all, he regretted there was no way he could write to her. She might perhaps have agreed they could meet on his next leave, but with no address that was impossible.

He thought instead of Jane at home, imagining her day as he worked out that the time would be mid-morning there, and tried to envisage his son who must be walking and talking by now. In his diary he sometimes wrote of their fondest moments.

I often lay awake at night, thinking of our few days at Katoomba, Jane's voice echoing down the valley, us hugging each other and dreading all the curious eyes that were trying to calculate if we'd made love yet or not at that smart and snobbish hotel. It was what the English call 'posh'. But after the first night we weren't a bit shy or nervous, and we used to walk through the foyer as if we owned it, not caring how many of the guests whispered about us. We decided they were all old and past it and jealous. We hung a 'Do not disturb' notice on our hotel door all the time, even when we were just chatting or reading. Gosh, it's hard to realise that soon it'll be two years since the last time I saw her.

There was comfort in remembrance of the past; it helped him to forget the horror of the present or the bleak prospect of a future.

The diary was his slender grip on reality. Sometimes he wondered if anyone else in years to come might read it.

The platoon was very different now. So many gone, too many new faces. The recruits seemed younger than ever; they huddled in the trench, alternately shivering and sweating while listening to the roar of the big guns, openly terrified as the bombardment began to find range. The trenches were not deep enough – no real protection against the German field artillery, let alone the weapon the troops were calling 'Minnies', the 100-kilogram landmines against which there seemed no defence. In the sweltering dark they could detect the acrid smell of smoke bombs.

They feared that later there would be gas.

Stephen was about to check his watch, then remembered he had left it behind with his diary, and the final letter written to Jane – just in case. Always, before an impending action, they were told to write final letters to next of kin and were reassured it was only a precaution: all letters would be returned to them after the action, but it was sensible to make these provisions – 'just in case'. This phrase, so often repeated, gave no one the least scrap of comfort.

'What time is it?'

'Buggered if I know,' Bluey replied, shrugging. On their leave he'd had his twenty-first birthday, and his girl's parents had put on a special tea. Now he looked years older; there were traces of grey visible in his red hair. Not surprising, Stephen thought. Before they came to France there'd been twelve survivors of their original platoon, now just five remained.

They had been such kids. So stupidly naïve. It was incredible to recall how desperate they'd been at the prospect of missing the 'great adventure'. In Cairo while fed up with training he'd dreamt of fighting here in France, the cauldron of the war; now he pined for the heat and dust of Egypt, the mere discomfort of a sandstorm seemed like bliss after the time spent here.

'What day is it?' Jerry Tate, one of the five originals, asked.

'Dunno, mate. But I know it ain't a Sunday, or you'd have your Bible out, linin' up for church parade,' Bluey scoffed.

'Why not?'

Both were instantly embroiled in a recurring and familiar argument. 'What's wrong with belief? Everyone must believe in something,' Tate insisted.

'Not me, sport. Not after the things I seen.'

'I've seen them too, don't you forget that.' Tate was thin and nervous, but never afraid to voice his conviction. 'It's clear that God is testing us.'

'He is, eh? Well, when you and 'im next have a chat, tell 'im I failed his test,' Bluey retorted. 'But say not to get upset; don't let it bother 'im. I never passed no tests at school neither.'

'Get off his back, Blue,' Stephen said. 'You know the old motto. No politics or religion in the trenches.'

'Fair enough.' Bluey grinned, cracked his knuckles and slapped Tate on the back while declaring that his disbelief was nothing personal. He had nothing against Jesus. From what they'd told him in Sunday school, he seemed like a fair sort of a bloke. He could rustle up a feed for a crowd, cure the sick and probably even manage a walk across the Somme when it was flooded. And people always reckoned that if you wanted a bit of work done in the house, you couldn't find a better carpenter.

Stephen steered him away before Tate was taunted into the folly of trying to hit Bluey. 'You big ugly bastard,' he admonished fondly, 'can't resist it, can you? Can't help giving the pot a stir.'

'Got no one else to get a rise out of these days, since silly old Double-Trouble forgot to duck.'

'I know,' Stephen said, thinking of how his anecdotes about

their friend had made Elizabeth laugh on that treasured afternoon. 'The four fiancées and all those other women are certainly going to miss him.'

'If they ever existed!' Bluey replied. 'He could come the raw prawn with some of his stories, you know that. Double-fucking-Trouble, strewth I miss 'im. Stupid bugger! Skinny as a skeleton, and the awful thing is he ain't even that now! I keep wishin' that I never hit him so hard on that train ride back to Salisbury.'

They still found it difficult to believe their mate, the chatterbox platoon comic, had been blown to pieces the day after they were ordered here. His was one of the dissevered corpses that lay beyond the wire in no-man's-land, impossible to recover for burial because there was no way to tell which remaining scraps of bone had been him.

'The great nong,' Bluey persisted. 'We told him to piss in the trench. No, not flamin' Double. "I want a bit of fresh air when I take a leak," he says. I must've loosened his brains when I knocked him out . . . Why else would he go up there when the Hun artillery was on target?'

'Take it easy,' Stephen said. 'I nearly went with him.'

'I'm bloody glad you didn't,' Bluey told him.

They walked back along the duckboards to the others. A new recruit was talking to a group near the signals dugout.

'I had a letter from home, about what they call the Anzac landing.' He was the youngest of the reinforcements, looking almost too young to be anywhere near a war. 'Some of you blokes were at Gallipoli, weren't you?'

'Just shuddup,' Dan Ridley said sharply. 'Shuddup about lousy bloody Gallipoli.'

The boy looked taken aback, but Stephen and the others knew the cause of his rancour. Ridley had been platoon sergeant when they landed at Anzac Cove; months later, found hiding, terrified in an abandoned trench, he'd been stripped of his rank and given six months hard labour.

The British colonel who presided at the court-martial had been caustic, describing Dan as a snivelling coward, deserving of the death penalty. An execution, he stated, would set an example. When this was refused, his angry remarks about how these ill-disciplined colonials could be knocked into shape if a few were shot at dawn had given rise to some sympathy for Dan Ridley.

On completion of his sentence, to everyone's surprise Ridley had requested a return to his original unit. To face the mates he had let down was how he put the application, and after some discourse this was eventually granted. He was a private and would remain so, but it created an awkward situation. Stephen, who had become the platoon sergeant, knew none of the survivors were comfortable with Ridley's presence.

As Bluey had put it, 'We're all scared at times. But you don't hide in a hole and let your mates down. That's what I can't forgive, or forget.'

'The bloke was petrified, Blue.'

'So? The same bloke was full of blood and guts when we was in Egypt trainin'. Gave us a real hard time. When some shit starts to fly, he's petrified. Maybe he'll be petrified again tomorrow, when we're in trouble. What I'm tryin' to say is, you can't count on 'im, not when it matters. And that's a real worry, if he's the joker taking care of my back.'

'It could happen to any of us. You can't tell. Maybe happen to me or you.'

'If it did, we'd manage till it was over,' Bluey asserted, 'not run away and hide. You wouldn't, and I don't reckon I would. Truth is, mate, he shoulda never come back to the unit. Been better if he'd made a fresh start somewhere else.'

On that Stephen could only agree. Those who knew of it – the originals – kept it to themselves by unspoken accord. But it was not a good situation. Particularly when a chance remark provoked such a reaction from their former NCO.

'Gee, I wish I'd been at Gallipoli,' the young reinforcement went on, clearly unable to take a hint. 'I couldn't get Dad and Mum to sign the form in time.'

'Half your luck.' Ridley spat on the ground.

'We don't talk a lot about Gallipoli,' Stephen said, trying to end the conversation.

'Why not?' The boy seemed surprised.

'Because it was a proper fuck-up,' Ridley said brusquely.

'They don't think so at home. They celebrated it. Same as in London, when we were there. We took part. There was a dawn service, then a march, and the English people all cheered us.'

'Fancy that.' Ridley's flushed face began to show real anger. 'A dawn service, and a march, eh? And you, who wouldn't have the faintest clue what it was like there, took part. Is that s'posed to make us feel good?'

A flare exploded high above the trench. Stephen glimpsed Ridley's tension, his nerves stripped raw by the accidental comments of this boy.

'Just one good thing about flamin' Gallipoli,' Bluey began, feeling it was time to change the subject, 'there were no rats. At least not great big evil things like here. In winter, the bastards are the size of feral cats.'

'You're kidding,' the boy replied. 'I ain't seen one that big.'

'You will, son,' Bluey assured him, 'if you stick around long enough. But don't try to earn a Victoria Cross, or you'll end up with a different cross . . . a wooden one stuck in the ground, with you stuck underneath.'

'Fair go, Blue,' Stephen protested. 'Give him a break.'

'I am, mate. I'm giving him good advice. The thing is, kid, don't try to be a hero. Keep that in mind. You know why the rats are so big?'

'No.' The boy looked nervous, fearful he was being ridiculed.

'Cos they feed on dead soldiers – either us or the Germans, the buggers ain't real fussy. Mind you, the Huns have more meat on their bones. All that sauerkraut makes 'em tasty.'

Stephen Conway saw shock freeze in the vulnerable young face. It was time to put an end to this. In another hour, perhaps sooner, they would need all their reserves of courage – not tension stretched to breaking point.

'Knock it off, Blue. I need to talk to these fellers.'

The reinforcements clustered around him as if there might be comfort in proximity. He felt a moment of indecision. What was he to tell them? The truth? How they were in such disarray until relief officers arrived that he'd been ordered to take charge of three other platoons as well . . . That by default he was virtually a company commander without any command experience, and when the new officers did arrive, they'd be untrained and useless for this kind of warfare? Should he explain how the losses had become horrendous, beyond belief? That a month ago at Fromelles, another Australian division had lost five thousand men in a *single day*? He wondered himself how many they would lose here at Pozieres.

Beyond the focus of their eyes – these kids hoping for some word to quell their fear – Stephen saw an English major standing outside the signals dugout. He realised the officer, who looked out of place with his polished Sam Browne and spotless uniform, had been lingering there with one objective: to listen to them. Bastard, he thought, annoyed by the arrogance of this blatant intent to monitor their conversation. He turned back to the platoon, knowing exactly what he would say.

'We've got some tough days ahead, don't let me kid you, and what we all need is a few laughs. Cheer us up. Does anyone know any jokes?' When there was no response, Stephen asked, 'Ever heard the story of the general and the sentry?'

The veterans grinned. The newcomers shook their heads.

'It happened in Cairo. A sentry was on duty when a general drove past. A spick-and-span general, wearing a plumed feathered hat. The sentry failed to salute. He just lent against his sentry box and ignored him. So the general stopped the staff car, not at all pleased, telling the sentry to stand to attention. "You're supposed to salute me, soldier. Don't you know who I am?"

"No idea. Sorry, sport," said the sentry.

"I'm your commander-in-chief! I'm General Birdwood."

"Is that right?" the sentry said. "Well, why not shove those feathers up your arse . . . and fly away like any other bird would?"'

There was a roar of laughter. It ended abruptly as the British major approached and snapped an order for them to be silent.

'I want a word with you, sergeant,' he said, walking away with stiff outrage and waiting until Stephen joined him. 'Are you mad?' he asked, fuming with disbelief. 'Are you totally insane?'

'It's a matter of opinion,' Stephen replied.

'What?'

'You asked about insanity. Being here like this, we often discuss if we're mad or not. We could be at home, on the beach or at the races, if we hadn't volunteered. I'll bet the people enjoying themselves back there think we're mad as a gum tree full of galahs.'

'What's your name?'

'Stephen Conway.'

'Rank and number. And say "sir" when you answer me.'

'Sir,' Stephen said, then after a provocative pause, gave his rank and army number. The major took out a notebook and wrote it down.

'No non-commissioned officer in our army would dare ridicule a general with such a derisive and impertinent falsehood.'

'It's not a falsehood . . . Sir.'

'Don't interrupt. I intend to put you on a charge for this.'

'If you insist . . . Sir.'

'Insist? Insist? Where do they get you people? How do they find trash like you? I most certainly insist! I don't in the least care for your attitude, Conway. My name is Major Carmody, and the charge will include your behaviour towards me which amounts to insubordination.'

'When you fill in the charge, major, you should mention the joke was told to us on Gallipoli . . . by the general himself.'

'*What?*'

'General Birdwood told us that one.'

'I don't believe you.'

'Ask the other blokes who were there.'

'I'm hardly going to believe them!'

'Then ask our own brigadier at HQ.' Stephen met his gaze with apparent surprise. Then he added ingenuously, 'I thought everyone knew that was old Birdie's own story.'

They were given a ration of rum at three-thirty in the morning, and tried to steel themselves for what lay ahead. The shrill whistles that signalled the attack came ten minutes later. When they climbed from the trenches and cut the wire to cross no-man's-land without sign of return fire it felt like a reprieve, but most knew this meant there'd be gas. A short time later they began to hear the sporadic thump of mortars, an indication that somewhere in the dark ahead canisters were exploding, not scattering shrapnel but spewing out far deadlier phosgene fumes. The faint stink of rotten fish was a sure warning that chloride gas had been fired. It attacked the heart and bloodstream, and men swiftly suffocated and died from it in agony.

'Masks!' Stephen shouted, and Bluey ran back to convey the message. They could hear him yelling, berating the tardy ones to get the bloody things on, 'Quick smart and *tout*-bloody-sweet, *mes amis*, or you'll soon be pushing up bloody daisies.'

They hated the masks, but there was no option. Devised in haste when it was learnt the Germans were using gas, the masks did not always protect them: gas could seep through the material, and sometimes breathing tubes became so blocked that men choked in their own vomit. The respirators often fogged, making vision difficult. Whatever the outside temperature, even if it was zero, all soldiers sweltered inside the hoods, and audible communication was virtually impossible.

Stephen did his best. It was the first time he had led his own platoon, let alone others. He knew they were unable to see his hand signals; he simply had to lead and hope they could follow. The amount of equipment they were made to carry encumbered them; not only rifles and ammunition, but water bottles, Mills bombs and grenades. Festooned with this ordnance, they were also weighed down with a backpack containing trenching tools and rations.

'Like bloody draught horses, only they get fed better,' had been Bluey's opinion when the kit was issued.

They ran to the opposing trenches hurling grenades, but the lack of response confirmed they were unoccupied. Stephen felt sure the Germans had moved to the high ground towards Thiepval Hill. There were blockhouses up there, well-fortified observation posts that gave them enormous advantage. By now they'd have machine gun placements established; there would be portable searchlights powered by their diesel generators. Any attempt to approach the village and they'd be held like trapped rabbits in those lights.

It would be suicidal; the battle plan they had been given was concocted in a hurry and without detailed knowledge of the terrain; it would surely lead to a massacre. There was only one possibility: use the dark to find their way north to some high ground marked by the ruins of an old windmill. He hoped the brigade major had thought of this, wherever he was, and wondered why the hell the intelligence – if that was the right word for the useless bastards – hadn't latched on to the bleeding obvious.

After dawn the nightmare was complete. Stephen's decision for his platoons to change direction had been followed by hundreds of dislocated troops from other sections of the brigade, and this had briefly confused the enemy artillery whose gunners spent the remaining hours of darkness wasting ammunition. But with daylight came Fokker planes. First was a reconnaissance aircraft that discovered the diversion, and soon after this the sky seemed full of attacking aircraft that flew low overhead, dropping cylinders of gas wherever they could find clusters of Australian infantry. This time the phosgene was combined with a far more lethal mix of chlorine. With those on the ground forced to again don their masks and try to run from the danger, they were an easy target as the biplanes swooped even lower to strafe them with machine-gun fire.

There was no respite even when the Fokkers left to refuel, for the German guns had now been told of their error and began a systematic onslaught. It was a deadly accurate bombardment that lasted the rest of a cataclysmic day in which bodies were blown apart and men deafened, while others were driven insensate or demented by the incessant pounding.

When the shelling ceased they were too exhausted to bury their dead. The three platoons Stephen led, and the hundreds who'd joined them, had been almost annihilated. The remnants loyally followed him, because they hoped he knew what he was doing. Stephen kept going forward because he had to; retreat was no longer an option. Blind instinct made him head in the direction of the ridge between the valleys. Along there must be a way to reach their objective: the village of Pozieres, provided the village still existed, which now seemed doubtful. He was conscious Bluey was always there alongside him, sending back messengers with new reports of their movements, so there was at least some link between the surviving forward platoons. Where the other battalions were that made up the brigade Stephen had no idea, such was the confusion now. When they finally had to rest for a time, Bluey was gasping.

'Why the bloody hell,' he said breathlessly, 'do we always seem to be attacking up a bloody hill?'

'Huns are smart.' Stephen was equally fatigued and out of breath. 'Why do you think they're winning this fucking war?'

'Are they?'

'Bloody oath they are. They live in dry trenches on the tops of hills. We sleep in the mud and shit down below.'

'I'll write to bloody old Haig, complain our accommodation stinks,' Bluey decided. 'And if it don't improve, we're off home.'

'Send a copy to Birdwood.'

Bluey laughed. 'Feathers up his arse, eh? That Pommy was a real prick. I bet he's somewhere safe right now, probably busy polishin' his belt and boots.'

'Or putting me on a report. I expect he will.'

'Stuff him. Forget the bastard. Most Pom officers treat their own mob like dirt. They're the pits. Piss on their troops from a great height, they do. They can't pull that stuff on us. We're a different army.'

'I wish we were. We'd be better off, fighting on our own.'

'Mate, you know what?'

'What, Blue?'

'Much as I'm enjoyin' this chat of ours, I reckon we gotta find somewhere a bit safer from the planes, or we're likely to be in for another real crook sorta day.'

It was almost mid-morning and they were near the crest of the ridge when they found temporary shelter in some abandoned trenches. But there was hardly time for much-needed rest, as the guns found them again. The bombardment, nowhere near as intense as before, was still enough to keep them pinned down. The night brought no relief, for with it came an enemy counterattack across the entire front. All the isolated battalions and groups like their own were outnumbered and in extreme danger.

When this was finally repulsed the dawn brought more German planes with gas canisters and bombs. Sleep was now out of the question. They'd had none since being informed of the battle plan, forty-eight hours before the attack. It was now twice that time, and they were entering their fifth sleepless day.

Fatigue became more invasive than the enemy. Food supplies ran out, and they were short of ammunition. Lice were rampant, infesting their hair, nesting in their clothes and tormenting them. Haggard and filthy, they began at last to lose their optimism. On the fourth night of the actual battle, and into their sixth day without rest, Stephen expressed the wish he'd brought his diary instead of leaving it behind with his watch and letter to Jane. There were things he wanted to write in it, thoughts about how it felt to face death. It was a serious mistake not to have brought it, he kept telling those around him. He needed to record his final thoughts. One day his infant son might want to read what had happened here.

'Jesus,' Bluey said, trying to jolt him out of this perilous mood of bleak depression, 'stop yer bloody laughin', will yer?'

At midnight they heard the brigade major had been killed, and it was rumoured there was a signal from Haig ordering all groups to withdraw to the original trenches.

Bugger that, they decided. Has all this been for nothing?

'It's the way they fight their shitty war,' Dan Ridley complained with customary bitterness. 'A few yards at a time. One step forward, two steps back in a weird and mad dance of death.'

'Put a sock in it,' Bluey told him.

'When we joined,' Ridley continued, 'they all said it'd be over by the first bloody Christmas.'

'Shut yer fuckin' whingeing!' Bluey ordered angrily.

They began to realise he was the strongest man among them. Indomitable, Stephen thought; he should be in charge, not me. He felt Bluey deserved a medal, but knew if he tried to express this opinion, his mate would tell him to stick the medal up his arse and stop carrying on like a headless chook.

Since Haig's signal to retreat could not be confirmed and most of their officers were either dead or out of communication, they debated the issue of what to do. Should they assume the order was authentic and withdraw? Could they even get back without more appalling losses? Most of them would probably be killed in a degrading retreat. They concluded that if there was to be a bullet, it was better to face it in the front than feel it in the back. There was no confirmation of Haig's order. Did they go; did they stay, or – what about surrender?

'Let's vote on it,' Bluey suggested.

So they did. After the vote was counted, a runner went to tell those alive in other groups – if he could find them – what had been agreed.

The next day at dawn, the exhausted remnants of the division gathered together and attacked the German forces holding Pozieres. They left behind their supplies and heavy equipment because it would delay them; they went carrying just their rifles, firing from the hip as they moved forward in the manner they'd made famous. It had been agreed the previous night that if they ran out of ammunition they would use bayonets, and after that if nothing else was left, their fists, then their boots.

Major Carmody had been ordered to attend a staff meeting in Paris, and not wishing to rebuff French hospitality, it was a week before he arrived back at the British Empire Forces headquarters, situated in a large chateau behind the lines at Armentieres. The catering officer, Captain Lacey, was busy supervising crates of fresh food being unloaded from a field ambulance. The Red Cross markings on the wagon were a sure guarantee against attack on this most cherished of cargoes.

'My dear James.' The greeting was prefaced by a smart salute. Despite their friendship, Lacey knew James Carmody was a stickler for conformity. 'Been to Paris, we heard. Some of us have to do the tough jobs in this war, eh? How are you?'

'Flourishing,' Carmody replied as he stood watching medical orderlies unload the ambulance. 'New supplies, Lacey?'

'Nothing but the best. Scottish salmon, lamb, venison – the old chap loves his venison as we know.' He lowered his voice to prevent the orderlies hearing this, for the 'old chap' was Sir Douglas Haig, the British Commander in France.

'Any decent wine?'

'Burgundy. The 1910. Port and brandy as well. Should be a right Royal shindig tonight. You're back just in time.'

Carmody was delighted at the prospect. 'Something special?'

'Things have gone well at the front, so the general's ordered a celebration. Any excuse for a party. How was Paris?'

'Stimulating,' Carmody replied, deciding it was perhaps best not to mention the banquets he'd attended, or the exclusive brothel in the Rue Saint Honore, where he'd been made an honorary member by a French colonel. Being an honorary was a particular delight, since the choicest of the mademoiselles were freely available, paid for by a special fund established for what the French called Officers' Creature Comforts. The OCC club was both elite and restricted. Carmody thought it highly civilised, and was manoeuvring to spend the rest of the war in Paris as a liaison officer.

He went into the chateau where tables were being set in the elegant dining room that tonight would be *en fete*. Passing the first floor that contained Sir Douglas Haig's private quarters, he proceeded upstairs to where the chateau had been converted into a labyrinth of offices. This was Carmody's destination, requesting an urgent meeting with the major-general who commanded the Australian first division.

On being advised the general was touring his troops on the battlefield, he met instead with a senior staff officer, Colonel Bridges, informing him of his wish to lay a charge. Insubordination and offensive behaviour by a mere sergeant, a non-commissioned officer. It was a serious complaint, and he opined these colonial troops were a conceited unruly rabble, having been given far too much adulation after their arrival in England from the Dardanelles. It was ridiculous, the acclaim that had been bestowed on them; marches through London, cheered by crowds, sought after by girls, not to mention the columns of praise in some English newspapers. It had gone to their heads, and their conduct had become intolerable.

He spoke as if unaware, or uncaring, that Colonel Bridges was himself an Australian.

As for discipline, he continued, they rarely bother to march in step, they show no respect, hardly ever salute, and he thought their prowess as fighters vastly over-rated.

Although senior in rank and annoyed by the tirade, Colonel Bridges was not of an aggressive nature or he might have disputed some of this invective. He glanced at the name on the charge sheet with mild surprise, then told the major an Australian division had just pulled off a remarkable victory. Perhaps the news had not reached Paris with its distractions, but the previous day, while vastly outnumbered, the Anzacs had driven the enemy back and retaken the town of Pozieres.

An NCO – the same Sergeant Conway accused here – had been heavily involved, commanding several platoons whose officers had been killed. There was talk of his being mentioned in dispatches. He had led his men in a savage bayonet attack from which the Germans had fled. Despite huge losses, days under heavy bombardment and counterattack, the Australians had prevailed and Field Marshal Haig was greatly impressed. In fact, there was a dinner tonight for staff to celebrate it, did the major know? Sir Douglas had even sent word to all the AIF brigades involved that this was a splendid achievement.

Despite these plaudits, the major showed no sign of changing his mind. He just pointed to the charge sheet.

'Insubordination, sir. It can't be allowed to pass. Without proper discipline and respect for officers, we'll never win this war.'

Chapter Six

There was a gentle splash of water. Stephen thought he was dreaming. It sounded like waves lapping onto a beach, something remembered from the school summer holidays when his family went to Narrabeen, but surely he was mistaken. It could not be a beach. Perhaps it was a dripping tap, but how could there be a tap when there was no village? What they had captured at such cost was little more than a stretch of mud, with the bones of men strewn everywhere: an awful place full of nothing but the stench of death and a pitiless silence.

Then he felt a cool cloth wiping his forehead.

'*Pouvez-vous m'entendre?*' a soft voice asked. He did not know what it meant, and had to be dreaming for the voice seemed to be a woman's. Young, and perhaps foreign. But it was impossible. There was no beach, no taps and no woman within miles.

'*Comment vous sentez-vous?*'

More words he didn't understand. He opened his eyes and saw her. The Angel of Mons, he thought, seeing luminous brown eyes gazing down at him, and recalling the strange story he had read on the tram the day he enlisted.

She was young with dark hair that fell to her shoulders, kneeling at his side with a pail of water and a cloth. He was in some kind of a farm shed, lying on what felt like straw or hay. She wet the cloth again and gently moistened his mouth and face this time. The relief was instantaneous and he smiled his gratitude. Her face that had been grave with anxiety was transformed by an answering smile.

'Who are you? Where am I?'

'*Vous* –' she began, then paused. 'You . . .' she pointed at him, 'your *nomme est* . . . Stephen.'

He nodded, surprised, then felt for his identity disc. It was not around his neck. She took it from a pocket of her shapeless dress and handed it back to him.

'Stephen . . . Con-way. *Oui?*'

'*Oui*,' he said. '*Et vous?*'

She replied in rapid French, too swift for him to understand, which he took to be a reaction to his attempted few words. From his brief acquaintance with the French he was aware they liked foreigners to speak Français. Some insisted. Stephen had often tried to oblige, but his vocabulary of about twenty words, useful for rudimentary moments, rendered any real conversation like this out of the question. He raised a hand to stem her flow.

'*Sil vous plaît*,' he began cautiously, 'my French is very small.'

'*Comment?*' she asked, looking puzzled.

'Small,' he repeated, and then remembered the words from his schooldays. '*Mon Francaise est petit.*' He used both his hands, putting them close together to show how extremely *petit* it was.

'Ah! *Petit!*' The girl laughed softly. It was a nice laugh. He wondered where she came from, and how he had ended up here.

'My name,' she said in strongly accented and halting English, 'it is Marie-Louise.'

'Hello, Marie-Louise,' he said.

'*Bonjour* Stephen,' she replied, and kissed him.

Reports kept coming in confirming that more Australian troops had been killed during the recapture of Pozieres than in any other battle. During the remorseless weeks of attack and counterattack and especially in the ferocious final days, more had perished than during the entire Gallipoli campaign. Casualties already numbered over twenty thousand dead or seriously wounded, and the toll was likely to rise with many still missing and unaccounted for. In the chateau at Armentieres, Harry Norton, a staff captain of the Anzac contingent, was appalled at the tactics and the cost.

'Between us and the New Zealanders we came here with sixty thousand men and have lost a third of them,' he pointed out. 'Field Marshal Haig claims a great victory. Well, too many more victories like that and we'll have no troops left for him to squander.'

'It was tactically essential,' Colonel Bridges argued. 'We had to regain Pozieres to keep the Huns from that high ground. You can tell its importance by the way they fought so hard to hold it.'

The two were friends, and despite the disparity in rank, Norton felt free to air his dissent.

'Maybe, but you can't convince me a few kilometres was worth all those lives. It's his whole battle plan that's wrong. The same sort of catastrophic balls-up we had at the Dardanelles. In my opinion Haig's a deluded old bugger, and the British should get rid of him.'

'And in my opinion, Harry, you better shut up before you get into hot water. Even if some of us . . .' he shrugged and did not continue. 'Never mind that. Have you found Sergeant Conway?'

'No sign of him. Christ, why are we chasing one bloke about a lousy little misdemeanour when we should be giving him a medal, from what I've been told?'

'Because I have a Pommy major hard on my hammer, and the way the charge is phrased doesn't sound the least bit like a 'little misdemeanour'. I've got no choice. I need to clear this up.'

'Maybe Conway's dead?'

'If he is, that would certainly clear it up. If not, Sergeant Conway is in a certain amount of shit.'

Stephen kept thinking about the kiss. It was surely just a gesture of friendship. An impulsive act because in this war they were on the same side. The French, after all, were known to be impulsive. And from what he'd heard they often kissed – even the men kissed each other – so it surely couldn't mean anything that special. Or else she was sorry for him because he was so exhausted. But that didn't seem right, because it had actually felt quite special, that kiss, and he could still taste her lips and feel the unexpected warm softness of them.

He lay on a bed in what appeared to be the only undamaged room of the farmhouse as Marie-Louise brought a basin of hot water from the wood stove and began to wash him. She had undressed him. The mud and blood encrusted on the uniform she'd removed was ingrained in his skin. He had a livid rash from the infectious lice that pervaded the trenches, and painfully swollen feet. Added to this he had not been able to bathe for over a week, and knew that he stank.

Memory had begun to return as disorientation from the five days of continuous bombardment started to recede from his mind.

Instead of chaotic thoughts there was a gradual recollection of the place they had won, a village without any houses or streets, where not even the rubble of shattered buildings was visible any longer. In fields around it where wheat had once grown and cattle grazed, nothing remained except a gruesome moonscape.

Now he could visualise the scene in shocking detail. A mass of enemy dead and almost as many of his own comrades. There had been no time to mourn or bury them as the artillery were brought in to secure the position, the heavy guns being towed by teams of horses and mules. The animals had floundered in the mud, sinking helplessly as the weight of the cannon dragged them to their deaths while taking human corpses with them. To add to the horror came a squadron of ungainly mechanised tanks that slithered without traction, crushing bodies and proving futile in the rain that had turned the land into a quagmire.

But other recollection was slow in returning. While he could recall these images, he had difficulty working out what he was doing at the field hospital. And why was Bluey there with him?

'*Vous sentez-vous mieux?*' Marie-Louise asked.

He smiled and nodded. He was now aware it meant 'do you feel better'. Indeed he did feel better! Someone taking care of him like this . . . his mates would never believe it. Stark-bollock naked, being washed by a French girl who'd even helped remove his stained clothes and the warm water lulling him into a gentle contentment. Marie-Louise softly hummed a song as she worked, her hands as tender as a nurse's.

The hospital? His mind became clearer about the hospital as he relaxed. Bluey had copped a bullet in the leg sometime during their ferocious charge at dawn on the last day, but typically had not said a single word about it until their relief took over. Stubborn as hell, Stephen thought fondly; claiming it was just a scratch and he hadn't wanted to go to the field hospital. Stephen had insisted, had gone with him, waiting there until an orderly told him not to hang about getting in the way, it was only a simple flesh wound – told him in fact to push off because they were busy, his mate would be treated when it was his turn, and then sent back to the unit later in the day.

And the dispatch rider? He remembered him now, and the lucky moment the motorcycle had pulled up alongside him. It was just after he left Bluey at the hospital, heading in the vague direction of where he thought he might find the remains of the division. He was limping badly; hoping it wasn't a renewal of the trench foot he'd suffered a month ago. Bloody awful pain; he knew feet could become so swollen it was impossible to get a boot on, and a bad enough case could get a man invalided back to England. While this was everyone's idea of a good result, a really serious case could mean amputation. Which was a result no one would welcome.

'Where do you want to go, sport?' the rider had shouted over the noise of his engine.

'Anywhere,' Stephen yelled in reply. 'How about London?'

The courier had pushed back his goggles and grinned. How about somewhere local, was his reply. He had some messages in his bag for a signals' group a few miles away at Mont St Quentin. No fighting around there at the moment, as far as he knew.

'Beaut,' Stephen had agreed. Even a short distance from Pozieres might mean a few hours of serenity. He felt an urgent need to be alone for a while, to find somewhere peaceful and away from this bloody war. He had only been on a motorcycle once before, the morning of his wedding day with his dad, who had driven slowly because he was a novice, whereas the dispatch rider was an expert who drove at a frightening speed. Stephen clung tightly as they bumped alarmingly across rough fields and down rutted tracks. Soon there were stretches of open land – now and then the bleak remnants of a shelled house as they sped by. The fighting had been here and left its scars, but after what he had been through this seemed like a much kinder part of France.

It was then the impact of so many sleepless days caught up with him, and he experienced such weariness that he'd almost fallen off the back of the machine. Glimpsing a shed in a field, he'd urgently tapped the shoulder in front of him until they halted.

'You want to stop for a pee?' The dispatch rider switched off his engine to ask this.

'No, this is far enough. Right here is fine.' Stephen slid off the pillion and steadied himself, feeling dizzy after the vibration.

'You sure?' The other was uncertain about leaving him here in such an isolated place; he seemed to be trying to assess if this was a prelude to desertion.

'Positive. Thanks for the ride.'

'Suit y'self.' He shrugged and rode away: the clatter of his engine dwindled and the silence was sublime. Even the sun was warm on Stephen's back as he walked across the empty field. It appeared to be a abandoned farm. He could see a damaged house with most of the roof smashed and broken slates lying on the ground. There were rusty farm implements, an old ploughshare, and some distance away stood a drinking trough. There was little else apart from the derelict cow shed, in which there were no cows. Only a bale of scattered hay, and it was on this he'd gratefully fallen asleep until Marie-Louise had discovered him there and helped him walk across to the farmhouse.

He had thought her just a girl, but she was twenty-three, two years older than him. She was surprised to find he was so young. They managed to learn something about each other, his fractured French supplementing her modicum of English words, and when both these failed, their gestures helped bridge the gap. Her father who owned the farm was a prisoner of war, held somewhere in Germany, she thought; her mother who had never liked country living had moved to Paris. Marie-Louise was engaged to be married, her fiancé had fought at Verdun, and she had not seen or heard from him since then. It was lonely on the farm, she conveyed to Stephen, but if she left here neither her father nor her fiancé would know where to look for her.

There was less discussion now. Having washed his back, his arms and the upper part of his body, she was now heating another basin of clean water. He lay in her bed, realising it was the only room that still had its roof and windows intact. He thought about his clothes that she had left soaking in a tub, and he wondered if there'd be anything to wear until they were dry.

Most of all, he kept thinking about the kiss.

Major Carmody made it abundantly clear he did not intend to let the matter rest. He had already complained to his brigade colonel that a serious charge against an Australian non-commissioned officer, a highly defamatory story about General Birdwood as well as blatant insubordination, was not being seriously dealt with by the staff people of the AIF headquarters at the chateau.

'Australians,' he told his senior officer, 'are not like our army. There's no respect between the ranks. The officers tend to unite in a most indiscreet way with their lower-class countrymen, no matter what difference in status. It seems inconceivable, but it's embedded in their way of life. Well, I don't think we should allow it, and if the man's alive I insist he be charged. I'm not being unreasonable about this; it's a matter of obedience and authority.'

'Quite so,' the colonel agreed, 'but we should remember the chap has apparently done rather well. I'll have a word to their staff. Can't believe they'd deliberately mislead you. After all, old man, we are on the same side.'

Carmody retorted that sometimes he was unsure about that.

It was not until Marie-Louise returned with the basin of warm water, and her attention shifted from Stephen's torso to what lay below the waist, that everything began to change.

Her hands, wet with soap, carefully lathered his upper legs and buttocks, then moved to gently wash more intimate areas. When she fondled his scrotum – at least it seemed to him she fondled it – all senses instantaneously responded to her touch. What had been surprisingly flaccid was suddenly firmly erect. He heard her intake of breath, then her fingers covered in foam wrapped around this and began to stroke and fondle it. This time there was no mistake, it was an undoubted fondle.

His hand reached out and encountered a slim leg, then slid slowly up beneath her dress. To his surprise she was not wearing underwear. She leant down and kissed his chest as she let the dress fall to the floor while climbing in beside him. When she began to kiss him again, this time her tongue probed deep while her hand held him and guided him inside her.

Stephen had almost forgotten what it was like. Three nights of love two years ago had not prepared him for this much delight.

'*Australien héroïque*,' she kept whispering while her hands roamed sensitive parts of his body titillating him, her own slim form pushing against him to match his urgent thrusts. Australian hero, he supposed it must mean, but had no time for translation. Amid her whispers were tiny grunts, a sound so sexually erotic he found himself losing all restraint. It was too intense to last, but just as he felt on the verge of everything it was Marie-Louise, breathless and wildly impassioned, who climaxed first.

'*Mon dieu*, darling *cheri*,' she gasped, 'now I come!'

'Soon,' he urged, 'both of us together, like a great big tidal wave.'

'*Oui*,' she cried loudly and happily, '*Oui!* Like *la grand* tidal wave, I am come!'

'Jesus Christ, me too,' he said, responding to her riotous orgasm in a torrid release unlike anything he had known.

In the depth of night they made love again, this time with soft endearments, slowly and tenderly, as if to prolong the act forever. He lay awake for a long time afterwards, his mind swirling with thoughts; guilty thoughts of Jane that competed with images of the farm girl who slept soundly in his arms, her nakedness so warm and inviting. He tried not to be disloyal, but she was so acutely real in a day when everything else was surreal; their meeting unbelievable. It felt miraculous after all the months of soggy trenches, the rats, the filth and the constant fear. Especially the fear.

He found himself trying to imagine what it would be like not to go back there, his mind tempting him with visions of remaining in this isolated farmhouse, in this room, this bed, with this girl for the rest of the war. Escaping. It felt almost possible. With so many casualties he'd be another of the nameless ones, blown to pieces, listed as missing, believed dead.

He could help her restore the farm and . . . he knew it was just a foolish dream, but at the age of twenty-one nothing in his young life had prepared him for this. Marie-Louise. He mouthed the name silently, savouring it. He'd never forget her. Perhaps he could record fragments – coded in case something happened to him – in the diary he kept so faithfully. In years to come it would be a nostalgic and very private memory.

Outside it was almost dawn now. He tried to be realistic. In all truth he must not stay another day here; if he was not back soon he would be in great trouble, officially absent without leave. Even now it was dangerous. A few more hours, his mates might be able to cover for him – he knew Bluey could and would gladly do it. Good old Blue, he'd be back from the field hospital by now, and he was smart enough to bamboozle anyone looking for him. But noon today was as long as he dared risk.

When he tried to explain this to Marie-Louise her response was a fond smile at the possibility of a hero like her Stephen being in trouble, and she proceeded to provoke him to such heights of passion that nothing outside their room seemed to matter.

'One more night,' he said while she caressed his body, her tongue exploring it, arousing him until all control vanished. He lost any desire to go back to the war. He could no longer even feel guilt for his infidelity to Jane. He knew staying here was perilous and insane, but could not bear to think of leaving.

He promised himself a few more days here.

Just a few more. Bluey would help cover for him.

He had no idea as yet that Bluey was dead.

Part Two

Patrick

Chapter Seven

Patrick Conway found it difficult to concentrate on the glittering ceremony at the baroque State Theatre. The occasion was the National Film Awards; the elite crowd, both decorative and charismatic, contained a mass of famous faces, the most celebrated of whom occupied the best front stalls where the cameras could easily find them. Patrick and his wife Joanna were in the next and less exalted section of the house, but still in prominent seats because she was considered an outside chance for an award. It was the only reason he was here, and while the ceremony progressed slowly and, it seemed, endlessly, his mind kept straying to the events of the past month few months. In particular, to the discovery of his grandfather's diary.

The millennium year that would see the long-awaited Olympic Games take place in Sydney had begun with a family loss. The sudden death of Patrick's father, a heart attack at the age of eighty-four, had come as a shock despite his age, for Richard Conway had always enjoyed good health. He and his wife Katherine were a year from celebrating their fortieth anniversary. He had married late; Katherine was ten years younger, but it had been the happiest of relationships, creating a deeply affectionate family environment for Patrick and his sister Sally.

Sorting through the mass of material in the rambling family home at Northbridge had been a tedious process for Patrick. His father was a careful man, successful in business. On the assumption it might be required some day, he had never thrown any paperwork away; as a consequence there was a glut of letters, bank statements, envelopes of tax returns that went back many years, and even gas and electricity bills from other houses they'd lived in when Patrick was a child. He was astonished at the abundance of debris.

'Good God! I knew he kept a lot of stuff, but look at this,' he said to his mother, who began to recall the different homes and her memories of them. Patrick had heard many such reminiscences lately which troubled him, for this preoccupation with the past was unlike her.

'Ma,' he was patient, knowing she was still in a state of grief, 'do I have your permission to hire a skip, and move this lot to the council tip?'

'Of course, darling. I've been telling him for years it's silly to keep everything. But he had it all so neatly filed in boxes that moved with us whenever we changed houses, which in those days was quite often. I did try to point out it cost us for the extra time the removalists took,' she added, 'but you know what your father's like. He can be awfully deaf when he wants to be.'

'He could,' Patrick said, conscious of her sporadic switches of tense into the past and back again. She can't let him go, he thought, any more than Dad could relinquish any of this disorder. He hugged her with affection, and began the long task of disposing of a lifetime's clutter. It was during this time, covering weeks – for he was forced to check each storage box to ensure he was not throwing away anything of value – that he found the diary.

On the fly leaf, in a neat copperplate handwriting it said: *With my fondest love, Jane.* It looked expensive, leather bound. His grandfather's name, Stephen Patrick Conway, gilt-lettered on the cover, was almost worn away. Time had wrought other deterioration: frayed leather, the spine of the book crumbling, the edges of the paper browning with age, although the writing inside – at times in ink but mostly in pencil – was relatively clear. On some pages there was a trace of mud; another was smeared by what he felt might be blood.

The words were sharp and concise; terse phrases as if there had been little time to jot them down, or Stephen Conway had been too exhausted to write more than notes. There was an abrupt entry for an August day in 1916, under the name Pozieres.

Muddy. Still more rain. An awful day. I've just learned Bluey is dead.

The next page dated three days later was more extensive, and revealed his grief. Bluey had clearly been a deep and bitter loss.

He could be a bugger, Bluey could. He liked a joke, liked a drink, and liked stirring things at times, but he was a good mate. We came from different worlds, but I've never had a better friend. I didn't know he was dead until after I left the farmhouse. I finally had to go, had to leave M.L., who was crying. I tried hard not to look back. It would have been easy to stay with her. It was so hard to leave.

We all thought it was just a flesh wound. I was sure Bluey would be in the hospital tent or at the base. When they said that he'd died – blood poisoning – I asked what kind of lousy doctors they were. I think I shouted that it was just a wound. How could he be allowed to die of a bloody flesh wound?

I could've wept, only blokes here don't. I wish we did. It would've been easier to weep. Or to go back to M.L., but I knew if I did there'd be no way I'd ever leave the farmhouse again. I'll miss her, and God how I'll miss Blue. He wanted to marry his girl in England and bring her home. He was the best and bravest of us, old Bluey. Old? Christ, he was only twenty-one.

That night Patrick stayed for dinner with his mother. With the two of them alone, he took the opportunity to ask about the diary.

'Did the army send it back? When Grandpa was killed?'

'Darling, I haven't the faintest idea,' she said. 'I wasn't born then. And your Dad . . . he was three years old when that war ended.'

'So it must've been sent to the next of kin. My grandmother, along with the rest of his effects, I suppose?'

'Perhaps,' she said vaguely. 'I'm not sure. She didn't confide much in me. She was an old lady when I met Richard. Not so much in years, but she seemed to have retreated into some kind of a shell. A very lonely and rather bitter old lady, that's what I thought. Granny Jane. It's what we called her when Sally was born, but she never showed much interest in you children. She died before your first birthday.'

'Never remarried?'

'No. Poor woman. Apparently her entire romantic life consisted of just a few days' leave the army gave them for a honeymoon. And after the war there'd been so many men killed, there was a surplus of women. A widow with a child . . . not much chance for her.'

'Or much fun for her, either.'

'No.'

'Did she ever speak of her marriage?'

'I tried to talk about it once. She didn't want to discuss it. Quite decidedly didn't want to, she made that clear to me. Your dad said his father was never mentioned at home as he grew up. As if she could not forgive him . . . for being killed, I suppose. At least that's what he and I always thought.'

'What a waste.' He hesitated, then ventured the question he'd been working toward. 'Do you think Grandpa had a woman overseas?'

'Patrick.' She smiled. 'How would I know that? And why the sudden question? Is there a mention of someone?'

'Just initials. M.L.'

'That's a big help, darling.'

'It was a woman. The diary says "her". She was crying and he didn't want to leave her. She was in a farmhouse.'

'The plot thickens,' Katherine Conway replied. 'But do we really want to dig up family scandals when they're all dead?'

'Of course not.' But he added as she glanced at him, 'However, they *are* the grandparents that Sally and I never knew. It's natural to want to fill in blank spaces.'

'And you have a writer's instinct to probe. Some would call it professional curiosity. Others would say you're a stickybeak.'

He laughed, and asked if she wanted to hear the passage.

'Absolutely,' she replied, and he brought the diary, reading her the requiem for the friend named Bluey. There was a brief silence when he finished.

'How awfully sad,' she said, and he realised there were tears in her eyes. 'Stupid of me, but I'm crying for your grandfather, who couldn't weep. And for Bluey, whoever he was, dying so young. Even for M.L. He didn't want to leave her, did he?'

'She didn't want him to go. I wonder if Dad ever read this?'

'He never mentioned it.'

'If he inherited it from his mother, I wonder if she read it?'

'Let's hope not,' Katherine said.

'You think she'd have realised?'

'I imagine she'd have made the same assumption. Which would hurt deeply. So few days of love in her young life, left with a child and no husband. Perhaps that explains her bitterness. I'll be crying for poor Granny Jane in a minute, if we don't stop this.'

She made them coffee. He watched as she stacked dishes and ground the beans. Time had started its healing process. She moved like a woman younger than her seventy years, even appeared to look younger now the initial grieving months were over. She'd had her white hair cut shorter; it made a lively match with her alert hazel eyes. More importantly, she'd recovered her poise, her humour and sharp intellect.

He had always been proud of his mother: at primary school, later in his teens and at university, he always thought she outshone the other mums on speech and graduation days. But he had never been more proud of her than now, coming to terms with the loss, being what she had always been - more like a friend and companion to him and his sister.

She had also been his ally in the family when he had begun to write articles and poetry for *Honi Soir*, the university magazine, and after two years of studying law had come to the conclusion that neither life in a legal office nor combat in the courts had the least appeal for him, and what he wanted to do was write for a living. Her support, in the face of his father's dismay and disappointment at what he called 'this bewildering change of direction', had created a special bond between them.

When she returned with the coffee Patrick had switched on the late news. The immigration minister was on, his cold judicial voice demonising asylum seekers as he made his consistently repeated claim: he had reliable information that many of them were terrorists, and had secret agendas that he was unable to reveal for security reasons . . .

'Darling, please –'

'I'll switch the bastard off.' Patrick knew his mother's political views, and saw her nod as the face of the minister diminished into a spot on a dark screen.

'That's all we can do,' his mother said, 'turn him off. But so many people believe that xenophobic bile. Others are convinced by the talkback ranters on the radio.' She sat in an armchair and put the coffee tray between them. 'I remembered something while I was in the kitchen . . . about the diary.'

'What about it?'

'Your dad *did* mention it. I'd quite forgotten. I don't think your grandmother ever saw it.'

'Why not, Ma?'

'Because someone sent it to Richard. Granny Jane had come to live with us then, but it was sent to him, not her.'

'You mean this arrived when you were married to Dad?' Patrick asked, surprised. 'Not just after the 1914 war?'

'No, about forty years after that war! Sally was a baby. And you, my pet, were just a work in progress.'

'That puts it in the 1960s,' Patrick calculated with a smile. 'And he told you someone had sent him grandfather's diary?'

'Yes. Together with a letter, saying he might like to have it.'

'Did you see the letter?'

'Darling, I never even saw the diary until you found it today. It was just a passing remark. I don't think he ever referred to it again.'

'And you don't know if he read it?'

'He never said so.'

'Or if Granny Jane read it?'

'I doubt that. She certainly never mentioned it.'

'Strange that nobody's read it. Did you never feel tempted?'

'Darling, I was up to my neck in nappies, plus pregnant with you and trying to hold down a job. After all, it was just a war diary kept by someone I didn't even know. I probably assumed your dad had thumbed through and thought it wasn't of great consequence.'

'Or else he *did* read it,' Patrick said, 'and didn't like the inferences he drew about M.L and her farmhouse. So he hid it away without showing it to you or his mother.'

'There you go again.' She laughed. 'Beware of writers in search of stories. How about this for a scenario? He put it aside to read and it got covered by years of tax receipts, all awaiting a dreaded audit that never happened.'

'Ma,' he had replied, laughing with her, 'I suspect you could be right.'

Patrick came back to the present with a start as Joanna nudged him. He realised the nominations for best director of a feature film were being read out.

'You were asleep,' she whispered.

'Not quite,' Patrick murmured.

She shook her head in mock despair, then as the names were announced gripped his hand so tightly that her nails almost cut into his flesh. Hers was the third and last name. It was greeted with moderate applause in which Patrick could take no part because one hand was being fiercely clutched like a lifeline. The pressure increased as the envelope was produced that held the winner's name. There was the customary byplay while the Eminent Person to whom this task was entrusted held it up to the lights as if to discover the name within. Then, perhaps hearing a muted sigh from the illustrious assembly, he set about unsealing it.

No envelope, Patrick thought, has ever taken this long to open. Talk about fumble-fingers! Film industry award nights were inescapably full of this prolonged and counterfeit entertainment: amusing for the audience, highly stressful for the listed trio. He disliked these show-biz carnivals. When the cameras were finally switched off the glamour often deteriorated: jealousy, malice and drunken spats had been known to end many an awards party, providing spice for the following day's tabloids. Patrick, regarded by his peers as a 'journeyman writer' of television series and serials (a polite surrogate for 'hack'), had never been nominated for anything, nor did he expect to be. He was only there because Joanna, despite being a long shot in the betting, could not bear the thought of staying away from this public torment.

'And the winner is —' there was the customary pause to generate more tension as pre-set spotlights picked out the three candidates and television cameras caught the moment of strain as each tried to look nonchalant. In several million homes across the country the mass audience focused on these faces, enjoying the recognition of a nervous twitch on one, a rigid jaw on another and, in the case of his wife, a half smile that tried to suggest it didn't really matter, it *truly* didn't – it was an honour to even be here and be considered. While he admired her composure he knew this was a masquerade; her pulse was racing like a Formula One car, and if the bloody fool with the envelope didn't get on with it either her nails would break or his hand would start to bleed.

'The winner is . . . Joanna Lugarno for *The Next Time We Meet!*'

There was a moment of surprise, then an eruption of delight. She gave Patrick a joyful look and hugged him, while everyone around them cheered. He watched proudly as she walked to the podium, slim and stylish, the best-looking winner of the night (or so the press reported the next day), kissed the Eminent Person and made a short, graceful speech. The applause when she came back with the coveted award was deafening.

They attended several parties, encountered no jealousy or any malice, hardly even a drunk, and went home in the early hours to their flat in Neutral Bay. Floated home, Patrick thought, Joanna on cloud nine all night long, deliriously happy. The rush of phone calls with congratulations and job offers began the following day while they were still in bed, tangled together after a night as ecstatic and fulfilling as their lovemaking had been when they first met.

A month later Joanna signed a contract to direct a new film at Fox Studios. It was a political thriller with a background of the Sydney Olympics, and with the games due in three months' time she was fully occupied with casting and script conferences. Patrick tried to interest her in Stephen's diary, but she was preoccupied. Unlike his sister. Sally was intrigued, posing the question: Why had their father in all these years never mentioned the diary? Growing up they'd always known they had a grandpa who'd died in the First World War. It had sometimes even been a subject at family gatherings. Yet their dad had kept this account of his own father's wartime experiences carefully hidden. Why?

It was Sally who, after reading it, had helped Patrick search through the remainder of their father's files, looking for the letter that had accompanied the diary. While unable to find it, they did discover a folder containing two other letters that confirmed their grandfather's death. Letters of sympathy written to Jane Conway: one from the battalion padre, the other from the medical officer, both simply headed France, August 1918.

'Trust Dad.' Stephen shook his head. 'These must've passed to him after Granny Jane died, and he stored them with all his papers and tax files.'

Sally read the letters. Both were brief and formal, clearly no more than duty required. 'Regret to inform you . . .' She shrugged at the phrase. 'That's cold comfort for the poor widow. Just a few lines and the usual clichés.'

'Maybe it helped her. They said he was courageous.' Patrick pointed out the brevity was understandable, for there must have been a great many of these to be written and sent home.

'At least it tells us when it happened,' Sally agreed, for she had already searched the Commonwealth War Grave Commission web site, and found no trace of Stephen Conway's last resting place there. On another list of the early AIF volunteers she did find his name and army number, but it lacked the details and date of his death. Puzzled by this, Sally had written to the records division of the War Museum in Canberra, but frustratingly received an acknowledgement of her enquiry and nothing else. They discussed it one night over a family dinner Katherine hosted at Northbridge, and decided a personal approach was required.

'Aren't you two getting a bit obsessive?' Joanna remarked, tiring of the subject.

Sally bristled at this. 'Did you ever know your grandfather?' she asked.

'Of course.'

'Well, we're just trying to get to know ours.'

Joanna shrugged and sipped her wine. Katherine refrained from comment. Patrick said they could use another bottle from the cellar and went to fetch it, wishing his wife and sister could at least find some common ground, even if there was little chance they would ever grow to like each other.

It was mid-winter in Canberra and the sedate avenues of deciduous trees were stripped bare of foliage. A chill wind blew off Lake Burley Griffin. On the hill the parliament was in recess, and politicians had fled like migratory swallows to Europe and warmer climes.

Patrick and Sally had an appointment in the building that housed the National Archives. There they were no more successful than she had been by letter or telephone, being passed from one puzzled official to another.

Was it possible, Patrick asked, that a soldier who had fought in the First World War could not be traced? They had records of his enlistment, and he had been killed, the condolence letters proved that; but apparently there was no record of it. Was that possible?

Highly unlikely, he was told.

But was it *possible*, he persisted, and with some reluctance the senior official admitted – using the same emphasis – that under certain conditions, in the confusion of war, anything was perhaps *possible*. It was all so long ago. For instance, this roll was compiled in London, back in the year 1919 from records kept at the Infantry Headquarters, Horseferry Road, Westminster. The sources on which it was based were unknown. Papers may have gone astray. Were they sure they had the right name?

We're sure, Sally told him scathingly. Since it's also our name,

I think we ought to know. Patrick was dogged but more conciliatory, showing officials the cover of the diary. He read out the names of places where Stephen Conway had fought. He even produced some faded photos they had collected from old family albums, including a picture of their grandfather in army uniform.

We'll make some enquiries, they were told, but both felt from the lack of conviction it would hardly lead to anything positive.

What you mean is, it's a big ask, Patrick had responded.

If we're honest, the official said, that's putting it mildly.

They had driven home dismayed.

'Sorry, Sal . . . it was a wasted trip.' He pulled up outside the apartment block in Manly where she had bought a unit after her divorce. It had spectacular views towards the northern beaches.

'Not their fault. I suppose it *is* a big ask,' she said. 'Don't rush off, we rarely see each other lately. Stay for a drink.'

They went upstairs to the top floor. He stood on the balcony, watching the surf roll in on successive spits of sand along the coast while she poured them white wine.

'Bloody marvellous sight.'

'Bloody horrible mortgage,' she answered, handing him his glass. 'But worth it to see Jim's face when he came here. Shaken rigid he was. He and his sweetie-pie are in a little flat at Artarmon. She hates it, complains it's like a rabbit warren.'

'And you're delighted,' Patrick said.

'I try not to be. But I did tell him that since rabbits spend all their time fucking in warrens, he and sweetie-pie had clearly found the perfect patch.'

He laughed. She was a year older than him; after a roller-coaster marriage and several career failures, she had finally found the right niche as a scenic designer.

'Well, here's to our grandfather.'

They sipped their drinks with a sense of regret.

'We tried, Pat. I don't think we can do any more than this.'

'Doesn't seem like it.'

'It bugs me. Not only that, I think it stinks – he volunteered to fight for his country and nobody gives a rat's arse where or how he died. Someone, way back there, slipped up. Which means we'll never know what happened.'

Two months later, a film script Patrick had written attracted the interest of Tim Carruthers, the executive in charge of BBC Films who was looking for a co-production. The story was set in Sydney Town when it was still a penal colony in the 1820s, a costume comedy based on a true story of three convicts who robbed a private bank. As the bank was owned by an unpopular autocrat, the event was hailed with jubilation and the robbers achieved hero status. In Patrick's fictional ending they avoided capture and returned to England where, rich and respectable, they became benefactors.

He had a phone call followed by emails saying that if he cared to consider a joint venture and could agree to terms, they would approach a major distributor like Miramax. If so, they could have a cinema feature with television and DVD sales to follow. If not, BBC Worldwide could consider it as a telemovie. Either way it seemed highly promising.

However (there was always a 'however', Patrick reflected ruefully), they would not at this time agree to an advance payment. This was followed by a more personal letter from Tim Carruthers, explaining the BBC was enduring yet another cost-cutting crusade. He liked the script but was limited on funds. The best way for Patrick to advance his cause was to get on a plane. Meetings in London were essential, and he assumed Patrick would want to be independent and take a 'producer position' at this stage – by paying his own fare and expenses and thus avoiding a servant-and-master relationship.

Crafty bugger, Patrick thought, but knew he'd have to take the risk. It was a complete gamble, but there was no option. This was a real chance to free himself from ten years of writing television series, and join his wife in working on the big screen. Writer-producer: it was something he'd been struggling to achieve for years. The lack of an advance to defray expenses was a blow, but he'd never get anywhere without grabbing opportunity when it beckoned.

He settled for the following month, a few days before the 2000 Games began. Cost wise, it was an ideal time to travel. He booked a cheap seat on one of the flights that would be returning half empty after delivering a planeload of Olympic visitors. Able to save on the fare, he decided to take some extra days in France. Make a brief visit to the actual places where Stephen Conway had fought. Perhaps there he could find out something. Or else, using the diary as a guide, at least retrace his grandfather's footsteps.

If it led to nothing, he would have done his best.

Chapter Eight

Outside the terminal in the blaze of afternoon Patrick could hear loudspeakers summoning the faithful to prayer. In the overcrowded airport transit lounge mobile phones were ringing like a symphony of protest. His plane was delayed; it was to be an hour, then longer; now it appeared uncertain whether it would leave at all that day. Visions of three hundred passengers bussed to an overnight hotel weighed on everyone's mind. Some had become enraged, unfairly threatening those at the transit desk: they were going to miss connecting flights and would never use this airline again. The harassed staff, their apologies met with abuse, became unhelpful and terse. Patrick thought that when modern travel was disrupted like this it was akin to the biblical conception of hell.

Tired and bored, he watched the veiled Arab women, rendered faceless by burquas, all armed with mobile phones on which they held murmured conversations while he wondered to whom they spoke: was it a husband, lover, children or friend? Some in heavy robes looked mediaeval; the tiny handsets they held an odd denial of this illusion. Then his own phone rang, sounding like a badly tuned piano. It was Joanna, calling from Melbourne where she was in the final weeks of shooting studio scenes.

'How was the flight?'

'It's not over yet,' Patrick said.

'But you've turned your phone on. You must be somewhere on the ground.'

'I am,' he confirmed grimly, 'I'm definitely on the ground.'

'Where?'

'Bahrain. Plane trouble. We've been stuck here for five hours.'

'God! Can't you switch to a Qantas flight? I told you not to take an El Cheapo.'

'You did,' he admitted reluctantly. It had been the subject of heated words a few days ago when she found out he was on a cut-price ticket. 'You told me this whole self-financed trip to meet with the BBC was a big gamble and a pretty stupid idea.'

'I shouldn't have said that,' she replied after a prolonged pause. 'I just thought I'd call to wish you luck.'

'Thanks. I might need it.'

'Fingers crossed, darling. What's that babble I can hear in the background?'

'An announcement of another flight, taking off for somewhere else with a lucky load of happy smiling passengers.'

'My, we are stressed.'

'Pissed off is the word. The latest rumour is the flight could be cancelled, and we'll be shoved into a hotel for the night. I've run out of clean clothes and security says all luggage stays on the plane until we reach Paris.'

'Paris? So you're still determined on that mad pilgrimage to go looking for Grandfather Stephen?'

'Hardly looking for him. I've budgeted for time in France, that's all. I want to follow the places he mentions in his diary.'

'What's the point? After so many years, Patrick, what really is the point?'

He was silent for a moment. If you have to ask that question, Patrick thought, I don't think I can give you a coherent answer. He'd tried but failed to make her understand how deeply Stephen's diary with its cramped writing and poignant words had affected him – how it was like a voice that bridged two generations – but before he could even make another attempt to explain this there was a loud cheer as the flight indicator shuffled its lettering from DELAYED to BOARDING. He heard the perfect English tones of the Arabian hostess announce Flight 01 to Paris was now resuming, and to kindly switch off all computers, PlayStations and mobile phones. An instant queue formed, the relieved passengers quickly forgiving the airline at the prospect of reaching their destination today after all.

'Gotta go, Jo,' he said hastily. 'At long last it seems we're taking off. Talk to you in a day or two.'

'But what *is* the point?' she persisted.

'I tried to tell you once or twice. You weren't listening.'

'Okay, I'm listening now.'

In the transit lounge people were streaming past. The place was rapidly emptying. At the departure gate, ground staff were looking in his direction.

'Now I've got to go. I'm out of here.'

'Then send me a postcard from one of the war memorials – if you have the time,' she said abruptly.

'Don't be like that.' He changed the subject, not wanting to leave on an acerbic note. 'Good luck with the rest of the filming. You'll be finished shooting before I'm back.'

'Two more weeks. When will I see you?'

'Depends. I have to stick around to try and sew up this deal, even if it takes me a month.'

'Be positive, darling. Don't let the Brits push you around. And don't waste too much time in La Belle France.'

'A few days is all I can afford.'

'Well, whatever it is you think you're looking for, I hope you find it.'

It was cramped in economy. The man in front farted repeatedly, and what drifted back was virulent with garlic. The woman in the seat beside Patrick slept, while her child who had claimed the aisle had a head cold and a running nose. It was going to be a long last leg of the journey. He looked wistfully towards the sharp end as flight attendants carrying trays bustled through the curtains, and he glimpsed the luxury of business class and the distant opulence of first.

It had been a simple choice. Save money on the fare and be able to stay at a modest hotel in central London. Since this was a trip at his own expense, economy was vital, if not very comfortable. The delay in Bahrain had not helped, nor had the inopportune timing of Joanna's phone call.

He'd been edgy with her. It had been happening too frequently of late. There were tensions since their lives had been transformed by the acclaim that followed her award. Even before then the relationship had been a delicate balancing act; that was inevitable with her a major film director and he a working writer for television. In their industry these were two quite different levels of achievement. Now she'd moved up in the world to where the press speculated on the size of her salary, and if they ever thought of him it was probably as the house husband. This made things awkward, particularly when she wanted to transform their lives with her good fortune: a more up-market car, a prestigious apartment when she found the perfect one, as well as wanting to finance his trip, which they'd rowed about. He knew she'd rung to express regret for that spat, because it was their custom not to let rows fester. Like their other private rule: never go to sleep after a major quarrel – make love first. They'd had too many quarrels and tried to compensate with a great deal of love in the past six months.

A screen on the bulkhead was showing news from around the world, including highlights on the eve of the Olympic Games in Sydney. The opening ceremony was just two days away. There were impressive views of the Olympic venues; thousands of volunteers had enrolled and the city was *en fête* with anticipation. Joanna could not comprehend how he could bear to be out of the country for the Millennium Olympiad. Easily, he'd told her, and argued that she'd have had no real interest in the Games if she had not been shooting a movie that was using it as a background.

They'd met six years ago at a film premiere. Patrick had heard of Joanna Lugarno and her talent, had even seen her photographs, but was unprepared to find himself so instantly smitten. The previous year she'd been the star graduate from the Film and Television School's directors' course, and was considered to have it all: the talent as well as brains and beauty. Magazines competed for her presence in their pages; her slim figure, Italian good looks with exotic almond-shaped eyes and a sensuous mouth made many think back to the beauty of the young Sophia Loren.

The attraction had been mutual. The following day they met for dinner, and went back to his apartment where they spent an ecstatic weekend together, most of it in bed. On the Monday morning, hoping he could persuade her to move in, he was startled by the news she was leaving for Hollywood that week. Her American agent had insisted she must make the quantum leap; only by arriving there and becoming visible could she hope to succeed. The agent claimed this would lead to interviews with the right people, and he was certain that with her status, plus her more-than-useful looks, offers to direct a movie would be bound to follow.

It led to their first quarrel, Patrick remembered ironically. He'd tried to warn her Los Angeles – although he preferred to call it Toxic City – was a hard, tough place, and many of the fringe agents there were shysters. It was one thing to be invited with airfare paid and an offer on the table; quite another to arrive and expect things to happen. Some of his friends had done that and returned with nothing to show for it but busted bank accounts and disillusion.

Joanna had thanked him nicely for the warning, but said her Italian father hadn't listened to sound advice when he migrated to Australia in the 1960s, and he was now on the local council and owned half a street of houses in Leichhardt. At the youthful age of twenty-three, she felt caution was not an option. It had been a truly lovely weekend, and she admitted she hadn't told him until now because she did not want to spoil it. And if he was ever in LA, she hoped to return the hospitality by offering him bed and breakfast.

It was nine months before she had come home and admitted he was right: it had been awful, bleak; an ugly nightmare. She had spent most of the time alone, sitting in coffee shops reading the trades as no one there seemed to read anything else. A mobile phone was her companion. Like the phone in the apartment she'd rented, it rarely rang. Hollywood – she used the word like a malediction – was full of people she'd thought were friends, but few had bothered to call her. In the City of the Angels it was not considered a smart career move to be seen with someone who might be headed for failure.

Six weeks after she returned, they were married. They wanted a quiet ceremony, but her father the councillor had a few hundred close Italian friends who would feel insulted not to be invited, so it was a nuptial mass in the cathedral, then a wedding breakfast that was more like a pageant. Joanna was twenty-four, Patrick just three years older. Friends predicted a successful showbiz marriage: a rarity. Or, as his best man confided, it was bound to last because any man would be crazy to split with a chick who looked like her. And if he did, her dad might put the Mafia onto him.

If Patrick thought the LA experience would stall her career, he was mistaken. Her ambition after it seemed relentless, as though fuelled by that failure. She directed several television dramas, and her first feature film a year later was a production made on a shoe-string. The critics loved it. One called it 'a low-budget movie that makes all the high-budget films we're turning out look third rate. Joanna Lugarno is a big talent, very much in the style and mode of Jane Campion.'

When they talked of the future it was about work, sometimes Patrick's TV scripts, but more often her films; they put the idea of children on hold. Her widowed father was impatient for them to start a family. Joanna was his only child, and while proud of her accomplishments, he had a Latin longing for grandchildren and a large dynasty.

'When will you have *bambino*?' was Carlo Lugarno's constant question, and becoming impatient, he once reproached Patrick. 'You and she only want to make films, not babies!'

Joanna did not dispute this, saying she loved her dad, but had no intention of becoming an incubator in order to make him a patriarch. Later on, she promised, they'd have a child, but this was the best creative time of her life and she did not want to stop the clock, not yet anyway.

She directed three more films in the ensuing five years, all on location so they became used to separations. Time spent apart made them *amorosa,* she always said, and that was why it would be good to be together again. If there were to be quarrels, so what? Some lusty *amorosa* was the best way to solve everything.

Patrick left his hotel near the Quai Voltaire soon after dawn, while the roads out of Paris were free of traffic. By the time he passed Compeigne the sun was rising, lighting the farmlands and hillsides greened by recent rain. He detoured from the motorway and drove along quiet roads through the countryside. This sector of France once known as Picardy, the scene of so many ferocious battles, was now unmarked by war. Wheat and corn grew; cattle grazed in peaceful fields. At the next village that Patrick reached shops were opening, and people were leaving the bakery with fresh loaves of bread.

It felt unreal. The only photographs he had seen of this place, Villers-Bretonneux, were those of mutilated streets and bombed houses and, worst of all, a park where soldiers lay choking after a gas attack. Cruel pictures tarnished by time, kept in the back of the diary of a man he had never known: Stephen Conway, who had gone to war at the age of nineteen and never returned. Long ago, his father had told him that Stephen was apparently killed somewhere near this village. But like so many others interred in mass burials or blown to pieces, there was no grave.

A café was open. He ordered coffee and croissants at a table outside. As he waited a number of children entered a large building opposite. The proprietor brought his breakfast, and indicated the house as if he might be interested.

'*Salle Victoria*,' he said. '*Jeune elementaire l'ecole*.'

Patrick smiled his thanks, unsure why his attention had been directed to it, but divined from the age of the pupils that it was an infants' school. Moments later he heard a piano inside the building play an introductory bar, then followed by the massed voices of the children. He almost spilt his coffee. The tune was unmistakable, but he had never heard *Waltzing Matilda* sung with such animation. Their soaring young voices, the words cogent even if unfamiliar in French, gave the song a special eloquence.

'*Bravo, oui? Le Waltz Matilda*.' The owner returned to join Patrick, smiling as he nodded his head in time to the music. He was a rotund, amiable man, eager to share in Patrick's surprised enjoyment.

'Who on earth taught them to sing it?'

'Their papas, mamas. Parents, is that the English word?'

'Yes.'

'And the parents of the parents. Each parent teach their child, since the school was rebuilt after 1918.'

'And how often do the children sing it?' Patrick asked.

'Every day,' the café owner said. 'When I was there at school we sing to remember the Australians who save this town. Not only Villers-Bretonneux, they save Amiens, perhaps even Paris itself.'

'Did they really do that?' Patrick asked.

'More than that. Much more. After your coffee, you should go and see for yourself what it says on *le plaque*.'

He crossed the street where it was quiet now. He glimpsed attentive children through a classroom window where an elderly male teacher was busy writing sums on a blackboard. To Patrick it seemed his visit might be an intrusion, but the friendly café proprietor had been insistent. It was a school day, but he would be welcome. Australians always were. That was why his country's flag flew here on official days, and a painting of kangaroos was displayed on their civic building.

The plaque was framed by a garland of flowers. The inscription was kept brightly polished and from it Patrick learnt rebuilding the school had been a gift from children in Victoria who had raised the funds for it. There was a glowing tribute paid to the Australian soldiers who had given their lives in the heroic recapture of the town and were buried in local graves. The engraving ended with the words:

MAY THE MEMORY OF GREAT SACRIFICES IN A COMMON
CAUSE KEEP AUSTRALIA AND FRANCE TOGETHER IN BONDS
OF FRIENDSHIP AND MUTUAL ESTEEM.

Another teacher, middle-aged and sombrely dressed in a grey skirt and cardigan, stopped to watch him read it, then exchanged greetings. She guessed he was Australian by his interest in the plaque.

'Come and see the playground,' she invited with a friendly smile, and went with him to the rear of the school where there was an asphalt court with basketball hoops. Behind this area was a sign whose vivid lettering created in Patrick a sudden frisson of emotion. The sign was huge, in English, and it read: NEVER FORGET AUSTRALIA.

The teacher, conscious of his astonishment, told him that in the district there were streets named after his country. There was deep affection here for *Les Aussies*. Many tourists came to visit. Perhaps he was a tourist?

Of sorts, he replied, and explained that his grandfather had fought here in 1918.

'Then he was here, when the Australians recaptured the town!' she exclaimed.

'Yes. He kept a diary, and one of the last entries was about this place.'

'Did he . . .' the teacher hesitated, searching for the right word, 'survive?'

Patrick shook his head. 'He was killed soon after. Perhaps here. As far as we know.'

She looked puzzled. 'As far as you know?'

'It's so long ago in the past. And we can't find any records.'

'There will be some, somewhere.' She was a kindly woman and eager to help. 'Here in Villers-Bretonneux you should visit the Australian Memorial and the cemeteries. I'm sure you will find news of him.'

At the cemetery Patrick found an immaculate garden with trim lawns and perennial flowers. White headstones were set in neat formation, like the shades of young soldiers on an eternal parade. People of all ages walked among the graves, pausing to read names, to admire the garden and floral tributes. The place had the ambience of a lovingly created outdoor cathedral. Even the lawnmowers and the click of pruning shears seemed muted.

Patrick saw there were many nationalities buried there: the names, rank and army numbers with distinguishing national emblems on the headstones bore witness to this. But by far the majority of them carried no identification at all, just the same brief words: 'A Soldier Known To God'.

The repetitive phrase became an irritant; he felt the phrase deceptive. How could God know them? If He did, how could He have allowed them to die so young? But even as he thought this, other familiar words came unbidden to his mind:

They shall grow not old, as we that are left grow old,
Age shall not weary them, nor the years condemn.

He took out a sepia photograph of his grandfather, one his mother had found in a discarded family album. Stephen Conway was in uniform, a new recruit looking both shy and proud, a youth barely twenty who would never reach his twenty-fourth birthday. Which means he'll always be younger than me, Patrick thought. Perhaps it was possible in this peaceful place to feel the truth of that well-worn epitaph.

He climbed the stone steps of the memorial tower to gaze at the view. Fertile fields extended as far as he could see, and he knew from his guidebook that all of them had once been ravaged battle-grounds. There was an almost surreal feeling to his realisation that somewhere down there, perhaps in those very tranquil farmlands in front of him, his grandfather had fought to help regain the village, and according to the diary, had been ordered to remain with his unit to repel the fierce German counterattacks that followed. And if so, this was probably where he had died.

Patrick stood there for a long time thinking of this, thinking that if he was the least bit religious he would have managed a prayer. He took one last look at the view. It was so utterly serene, yet down there eighty-two years ago a ferocious artillery barrage had presaged a German assault to retake this village, and the Australian battalions, worn out and deserving a rest, had been called back to bolster the line. Somewhere in those frantic days Stephen's death had occurred. It seemed to fit. There was no exact date on either of the letters of sympathy that Granny Jane had received. But in mid-1918, which the guidebook stated was the period of a major counterattack, the diary had abruptly ended. Without even looking at it Patrick could clearly remember the last entry:

Exhausted. Each week is worst than the last. If Pozieres was hell, Passchendaele Ridge was worse, and this one numbs the mind. Now all our battles seem to merge into each other. Our battalion is in a bad way, down to about 200 men, and that's barely a quarter of what it should be. We're starting to feel the British Command are pushing us into scraps their own troops don't want. Soon there won't be an Australian Corps. There won't be enough of us left. And we're so damn tired.

This talk of what great fighters we are, what heroes, and how not even machine guns can stop us, is such rubbish. We're not heroes, and of course the bloody guns can stop us. Pozieres cost us badly, so many men, so many good mates. Even cost me my stripes back then . . . demoted to private because I upset a pompous English major who hates 'colonials'. It could have been worse. A lot worse. At least I managed to stay for those few stolen days with M.L. There was such a shambles after we took the town that I got away with it, and no one found out.

But I was mad to leave. I wish I'd stayed with her. That's what I should've done. Now all I can hope for is some rest, some peace and quiet away from this carnage, and if we get out of here one day soon we can all go home.

After he descended from the tower, Patrick spent several hours carefully reading the memorial walls. Stephen's name should be there, he knew that. On this shrine were supposedly inscribed all the names of the Australian soldiers killed in France whose bodies had not been recovered, and who had no known grave. According to the records, there were eleven thousand of them. But eventually he had to concede defeat. Stephen Conway was not listed among them.

A friendly tourist guide, an elderly Englishman with whom he had struck up a casual conversation, suggested he should try Belgium. Less than two hours drive away was the town of Ypres.

'Go to the Menin Gate,' he advised. 'It's the biggest memorial of all. There are names there, thousands of names. So many, and so young. It's a heartbreaker, that place.'

Chapter Nine

A gendarme's whistle shrilled, and his raised arm brought the evening traffic to a standstill. Crowds of tourists were gathered in expectation. Patrick could hear Australian accents among them, then a silence fell as a squad of uniformed buglers, white gloves holding their silver trumpets, played the haunting notes of 'The Last Post'. In the hush after the final chords came the familiar words of the ode to the fallen: 'At the going down of the sun and in the morning we will remember them.'

An old man cleared his throat and a young woman wearing jeans and a T-shirt found a tissue to discreetly dab her eyes. It was astonishing, Patrick thought, how the people of Ypres regularly observed this act of homage every day of the year. And rare that the tribute had been sustained for generations. The respectful quiet lingered until the policeman released the traffic, voices began to comment on the ritual, and the evening's progress to bars and restaurants resumed.

The simplicity of it moved Patrick. He stood alone when most of the crowd had gone, looking at the vast monument and its illuminated panels with what seemed like an endless list of names carved there – fifty-five thousand soldiers, all without a known grave – having learnt with incredulity that this space had proved insufficient to accommodate the names of all the missing dead. Those who built the great memorial had seriously misjudged the numbers, and another thirty-five thousand names had to be inscribed on another shrine at the nearby cemetery of Tyne Cot.

Earlier he had spent time carefully studying the names in both places but again found no mention of Stephen Conway. He was beginning to wonder how many more there were like his grandfather whose papers had gone astray; young soldiers unlisted, unburied and seemingly unknown, even to God.

The same woman who had dried her tears during the tribute was also still there, gazing at the floodlit ramparts of the Menin Gate. Patrick was about to leave, unsure whether to try the hotel restaurant or find a bar first and then a place to eat. He had just decided his hotel was the easier – it would mean an early night – when she produced a camera from her shoulder bag and approached him.

'Would you mind awfully?' She held it out. 'I'm afraid it's one of those new-fangled digitals that you just point and click.'

Patrick assured her it was no trouble. He took several photos of her and handed back the camera. She thanked him, turned as if to move away, then hesitated.

'If you're alone,' she said uncertainly, 'I mean, I don't suppose you were thinking of having a drink?'

'I was just contemplating it,' Patrick said.

'I was contemplating if I could ask such a question! But I don't fancy a bar on my own.'

She was English, home counties by her accent, he thought, and he placed her in her late twenties. She had auburn hair, green eyes and scattered freckles. An engaging smile replaced her initial diffidence.

'I'd say a drink sounds just the shot,' Patrick said in reply, smiling.

'Are you Australian?' she asked.

'Rumbled,' he said, 'every time I open my mouth. And you? London?'

'Fulham. But I grew up in Kingston. Surrey,' she added.

'Anywhere near the river?'

'Yes. Do you know it?'

'I used to. When I dropped out of uni in Oz, I spent a year working at the old Thames studios, on the lock at Teddington.'

'Heavens!' she exclaimed with surprise that animated her face. 'We were almost neighbours. Until I was eighteen I lived nearly opposite. Our house had a view of the studio – well, really a view of the car park, with all those posh cars.'

'Not my posh car,' Patrick said. 'A bashed-up Renault bought for a hundred quid. It broke down once a week.'

They exchanged names; hers was Claire Thomas, and they went to a nearby tavern filled with people who had also been to the Menin Gate. An assortment of nationalities, a melange of languages and accents were in chorus discussing the ceremony.

'It reminds me of a performance,' Claire said amid the hubbub. 'Interval at the National Theatre, with everyone analysing the play.' She sounded as if she was offended. 'But it's not a play, and they weren't actors. They were kids, some not old enough to vote, persuaded to go and die for King and Country. I found out a great-uncle of mine was only sixteen! Can you imagine?'

'What happened to him?'

'Invalided out before his eighteenth birthday, lungs affected by mustard gas. And apparently ill for the rest of his life, poor man. I just wanted to come and see this place, because he fought here at Ypres and Passchendaele. It was an awful battle, but of course they were all awful.'

Patrick explained his own quest. 'My grandfather died in the last year of the war but we can't find out where. My sister and I are on the case, but not getting very far.'

It was hot and noisy in the overcrowded bar. They took their drinks outside and discovered a courtyard where seats were improvised from old wine barrels. The summer night was humid, but the lack of decibels was a relief. They found it easy to talk as strangers often do, knowing they were unlikely to meet again.

Patrick spoke freely of his family: his mother coping with life on her own after forty years of marriage, his sister Sally in her new beachside apartment, and his wife the film director.

'Any children?' Claire asked, and regretted the question almost as soon as she spoke.

There was a slight pause before Patrick replied. When he did it was an oblique answer. 'My Italian father-in-law complains we only make films, not babies.'

Claire changed the subject. She asked about his sister and Patrick relaxed, telling her about Sally's view of rolling surf along the coastline that was so spectacular.

'Sounds wonderful. Do you love the beach?'

'I grew up on one. Christmas holidays could never be too hot or too long. Sal and I loved the water; we spent the summers in it like a pair of dolphins.'

'You sound fond of her.'

'Very. Just the two of us, only a year apart.'

'That's nice,' Claire said gently. 'I never had siblings. I was just a spoilt brat who spent a lonely childhood inventing companions like your sister. But I had a great mum who's still my best friend.'

When he smiled Claire felt she'd made a lucky choice with her camera at the memorial. With his untidy mop of blonde hair and good physique, she could readily imagine Patrick at home on a beach.

'Are you here for long?' she asked.

'Till the end of the week,' he replied. 'And you?'

'Leaving tomorrow. On the Eurostar from Lille.'

'The channel tunnel? I hear it's the way to travel,' Patrick said. 'No fog delays or engine troubles,' he added with feeling.

'So we seem to be ships that pass in the night, if I can mix my metaphors,' Claire said. 'In a few days you'll be home in Oz. Back to the Olympics.'

'No, I fly to London at the end of the week. I've got some meetings there.'

After a leisurely dinner they walked back to the *pension* where she was staying. They crossed the cobbled square. Both had enjoyed the accidental evening; neither wanted it to end.

'Did you know,' Claire said, 'that centuries ago this place was a thriving city-state? According to my Internet research.'

'Been Googling?' he asked.

'A fetish,' she admitted. 'Before I travel, I swot like mad on the net. I arrive stuffed with vast amounts of information and a strong feeling I've already been there. And please don't say I should save the cost of the fare, because friends are always telling me that.'

'But you have to check out Google's data in person. Besides, it's a way to meet new people.'

'Like Australians.' She laughed.

'Like Australians,' he agreed, 'who come from down-under and need to know these things. About Ypres for instance. Tell me what else the Internet said.'

'"Wipers", most soldiers called it because they couldn't cope with the pronunciation. It was the trading centre of Flanders, a prize for invaders, and always a battleground. Fought over by the French, the Spanish and Dutch. But in 1917, what the others couldn't do, the Germans did. Their guns destroyed the place. All the wonderful mediaeval architecture reduced to rubble.'

'But cleverly rebuilt.'

'Yes, the Europeans are good at reconstruction. With so many wars they've had enough practice.'

'I'm glad you ignored your friends and came here,' Patrick said. 'It not only brought me up to speed on "Wipers", but it would've otherwise been a lonely evening.'

They reached the *pension*. Claire hesitated, unsure whether to offer her hand or her cheek. Before she could decide Patrick asked how she would reach Lille station in the morning.

'A mini-bus is part of the package,' she told him.

'I want to see Lille,' he ventured. 'Could you give the mini-bus the flick and I'll drive you?'

'Sounds good to me.' She smiled and kissed him on the cheek before she went into the hotel.

The next morning he watched as the sleek train slid away from the station and it left him on the platform feeling lonely. In an hour and a half she'd be in London, with the arrival of the Eurostar at Waterloo Station. 'The French are upset about the name,' she confided while they waited, 'the defeat at Waterloo was not Napoleon's finest hour. Being met by the sign Waterloo as the train arrives puts them in a bit of a tizz. They consider it a classic example of *l'arrogance d'Anglaise*.'

Patrick would miss her appealing smile, the freckles and her flippancies.

He headed south from Lille, taking the motorway again to the Somme towns. Today was his fourth day, and he'd begun to realise the impossibility of the task he had set himself. There were no answers here. The huge memorials and the neat cemeteries had been a gift of love and compassion for the young dead; it was an irony that after the Great War families could not afford to visit them, for the price of a pilgrimage in those days to mourn their sons was beyond most people.

Now, eighty years on, there was a generational gap. Youth and middle-age both came to venerate family members that none had known. Grandfathers, great-grandfathers: they were young men whose faces were faded photographs in family albums. It was good their descendants came and laid flowers – it was even fair that a tourist industry had been established from it; in today's packaged travel that was predictable. Battlefield towns that had suffered attack now underwent a different invasion: hotels, restaurants, private homes offering B&B, as well as museums and tourist guides, were all making a living from the influx. He had no argument with that.

It was the massive lists of names that daunted him. He felt unable to comprehend the naivety of the thousands of eager boys and men who'd rushed to a European war so far from their homeland. *A great adventure*, his grandfather had written in the pages of his diary, and stated how anxious they were, training in the sands of Egypt, that they might miss the fun.

Whereas the British officer class of the time, Claire told him from her research, considered the war a kind of hunting party; live Huns to pursue instead of frightened foxes. It was characteristic of her, the way she could switch from mischievous banter to sombre reflection. She'd read about an English captain of the Royal Dragoons who had declared: 'I adore the war. It's like a great big picnic.' The captain's picnic had ended violently in the mud of Flanders a few months later.

By now, he thought, she would be through the channel tunnel, and in the Kent countryside. It had been a nice evening; he had a feeling it need not have ended, but perhaps it was as well. Despite their promises to meet and their exchange of details – he had her email address and a phone number in Fulham, she had the name of his hotel in Bayswater – Patrick was uncertain if there'd be time for meetings. Or if it would be prudent. Yet while thinking that, he wished he could've taken her to hear the schoolchildren sing *Waltzing Matilda* in Villers-Bretonneux. That rare moment was his abiding memory of the days so far. He would go there once again in the morning, have coffee in the café, and listen to the kids.

It was good to be returning south. The towns in Picardy were where Stephen Conway had served his war. Patrick wanted to revisit the museum on the river at Peronne and have a last meal at Tommy's, the friendly café with its collection of battle relics, where everyone on a tour seemed to gather.

While the Menin Gate had been superb, the bugle notes poignant in the clarity of the night, it was a staged ritual. Each evening the traffic stopped, tourists gathered, trumpeters played. Claire had shed tears – there I go, he thought, thinking of her again – but the tears, she'd said later over dinner, had been as much for the poet Siegfried Sassoon as for her sixteen-year-old relative. Sassoon, she explained, had hated the memorial. He felt it mocked the dead and wrote a bitter poem about it, of which she could only remember one corrosive line: 'Here was the world's worst wound.'

'Sassoon?' Patrick had been startled by the link. 'My grandfather wrote a verse of a Sassoon poem in his diary.'

'Bet you can't remember it,' she'd challenged.

'You lose. Surprise coming,' he'd said and quoted it:

> *I died in hell,*
> *They called it Passchendaele: my wound was slight*
> *And I was hobbling back; and then a shell*
> *Burst slick upon the duckboards; so I fell*
> *Into the bottomless mud, and lost the light.*

'Surprise indeed,' she'd said, and seemed glad they'd met.

Patrick went to the Internet café in the town of Albert. Email had accumulated over several days. One was from his mother, saying what a superb spectacle the Olympic opening ceremony had been. Sally had managed to get them tickets, such good seats, and she wished he'd been there with them. Now the Games were in full flow and she was staying home each night to watch. How was France, and had he found any places where Grandfather Stephen had been?

He replied saying he felt he'd trodden in Stephen's footsteps but the trail was elusive. He told her of the memorials and the children singing, and how northern France was a revelation – so welcoming to Australians. Next in his inbox was word from Sally, dated several days earlier.

Dear Bro, No news your end or I'd have heard. Meanwhile I've met someone. Don't freak out, he's not like that last limp dick in the rabbit warren. Charlie (he prefers 'Charles', but stuff that) has promised to teach me golf. Yes, golf! You read it here first. He plays off a handicap of two which is a bit of a worry, but says I have the right kind of body for a good swing, and doesn't think my tits will get in the way. So I'm off to borrow Dad's clubs which he left to you. I promise not to smash them. Or lose them. Much love, Moi! xxxx

There was a long email from Joanna to say she only had four days' filming to go, and she and the editor had put together a rough cut that looked terrific. As for France, she hoped his detour there wouldn't distract him from the main game at the BBC. He should remember he'd written a script that was different – a clever, original comedy – whereas searching for traces of his granddad, while it seemed a nice notion, was really a bit of a romantic wank.

So fingers firmly crossed for this one with the Beeb, darling, it could be important. Keep me up to date on progress. I'll look forward to seeing you in a few weeks. Amoroso, remember? Can't wait for that, and hope you feel the same.
Love, Joanna.

He was about to reply as his mobile rang. Everyone gazed at him reproachfully, particularly the severe madame behind the desk.

'Monsieur, please! It is printed in large letters. All mobiles should be switched off, or it may affect the satellite reception.'

'I'm sorry,' he said, and started towards the door.

'But Monsieur, you have not paid. Thirteen Euros.'

While Patrick fumbled for notes he realised this was close to thirty dollars, and could barely restrain the impulse to declare it highway-bloody-robbery. He hurried out before his message bank could intercept the call. It was Sally.

'I just finished reading your email.'

'Forget that, it's already out of date. I've got important news.'

'You and Charlie have eloped.'

'Fat chance!' she shrieked with laughter. 'Charlie's a dill! He's about to become a pharaoh, which, you might remember from when we were kids, means ancient history.'

'That was quick.'

'Hopeless. A fantastic golfer, brilliant tennis player and so far up himself he's almost out of sight. I can pick dickheads.'

'You said it.'

'You've said it often enough. Do you want the news or not?'

'Please.'

'I've found the letter! The letter we looked for, the one that came with Stephen's diary.'

'Sally! Where did you find it?'

'In Dad's golf bag! The one I borrowed. With a bunch of cards, souvenirs of the best rounds he ever played. Remember his level par at the Lakes? And the pro-am with Greg Norman? The cards were in the pocket of his golf bag and the letter was hidden with them.'

'Hidden? You mean intentionally?'

'*Hidden*,' Sally insisted. 'And I do mean intentionally. I'm sure of it. He didn't want us to find it. But being Dad, he couldn't bring himself to chuck it away, so he put it in a spot no one would look. Anyway, Pat, I think we're wrong. Way off beam. I don't believe our grandfather died in the war. In fact I'm bloody certain he didn't.'

'Oh, c'mon, be serious . . .'

'I'll fax you a copy. I'm sure he died about the time this was sent. More than forty years *after* the war ended.'

'But how is that possible?'

'I don't know.'

'What about those letters of condolence his battalion padre and the medical officer sent to his wife?'

'Well, wait until you read this one. Then tell me what you think.'

It was quiet in the hotel dining room. One battlefield tour group had left that day for Belgium; another was expected in the morning. Patrick found a table by the window and ordered a demi-carafe of Beaujolais and an omelette. While he sipped his wine, he again read the letter Sally had faxed him that afternoon. The notepaper had a printed Surrey address. The handwriting was firm and clear.

The Lodge
Shepherds Green
Leatherhead
Surrey
25th May, 1964

Dear Mr Conway,

I do hope I have found the right Richard Conway, for I went to Australia House in The Strand and they provided an address from the Sydney phone directory. I believe this is a diary that belonged to your father, and which he kept during the First World War. I don't think I should go into details, but I found it among his belongings, and felt that even after so long it should be returned to you. He was a good man, despite what may have been said, and I shall miss him.

Yours faithfully,
(Miss) Georgina Rickson

He called Sally.

'I think you're right.'

'You agree he survived the war?'

'Sure looks that way.'

'Never died in 1918? Despite the letters of condolence?'

'Seems not.'

'You know what I think?' Sally asked. 'He must've deserted.'

'I thought you'd say that, and hoped you wouldn't.'

'What other answer is there? A few months before the end of the war. After that last entry in his diary. I mean, how else could there be no grave, or any mention of his death or discharge? I wish I didn't think so, but I can't help it.'

'But if he deserted, that would surely be on record.'

'Would it? Don't forget what was said down in Canberra. We had those officials admitting papers do go astray. Patrick, he survived, that's for sure. And never came home to his wife and baby son. He just pissed off and abandoned them. What an absolute bastard!'

'Now, don't jump to conclusions.'

'It's not a conclusion, it's a simple bloody fact. He shot through on his family. On *our* family. His wife and our dad.'

'It is starting to look that way,' Patrick had to admit reluctantly.

'No wonder Granny Jane never wanted to talk about him.' Sally was unforgiving. 'Perhaps she knew. Obviously Dad must have realised from the letter, which I suppose we have to accept is why he hid it.'

Patrick told her that since reading the letter he'd changed his plans; there was nothing more to be achieved in France. He'd booked a British Airways flight and would leave for London late tomorrow. Once there he'd rent a car, drive to Leatherhead, and see if he could find Miss Rickson.

The coast of Normandy gave way to sluggish grey waves of the channel and the distant land haze of the English coast.

It had been a busy last day in France. In the morning he had fulfilled the promise to himself to drive early to Villers-Bretonneux again and have breakfast at the café in the Rue Victoria. After the children arrived, he listened to their liquid voices singing 'Waltzing Matilda', and experienced the same emotional response as the first time: surprise and pleasure that on this side of the world there still existed this daily ceremony in a village school that bore its unique badge of gratitude: NEVER FORGET AUSTRALIA. He wondered if some of the people back home – xenophobes who railed at asylum seekers and upset people like his mother, or just the majority of Australians who had never been here – would believe it.

After that there was just time to drive to Pozieres and use the remaining film in his camera. No matter what news he would bring home about Stephen Conway, he wanted a photo of the tribute at The Windmill. There, while traffic on the adjacent road sped past, he focused on the words:

THE RUIN OF THE POZIERES WINDMILL WHICH LIES HERE
WAS THE CENTRE OF THE STRUGGLE IN THIS PART OF THE
SOMME BATTLEFIELD IN JULY AND AUGUST 1916.
IT WAS CAPTURED ON AUGUST 4TH BY AUSTRALIAN TROOPS,
WHO FELL MORE THICKLY ON THIS RIDGE THAN ON ANY
OTHER FIELD OF WAR.

Heathrow was packed. Long queues of foreign nationals waited while Britons and citizens of the European Union walked through a special gate showing their distinctive passports. There was some grumbling about the delay and lack of immigration staff. Near him,

Patrick heard a Kiwi voice airing a complaint.

'How things change! We fought with Britain. Now we're bloody aliens, while the *Luftwaffe* strolls past. Welcome to London, Mein Herr. Did you come to see where your bombs landed?'

There was laughter around them.

'Be quiet,' a woman patrolling to keep charge of the queue snapped. 'Delays are unavoidable. Complaints don't help.'

'Extra staff might,' a well-groomed American woman said.

'Honey, take it easy,' her male companion advised. 'Don't you know it's afternoon tea time? We're in England, babe.'

The official gave them both a searing look, then strode off.

'Who the hell does she think she is?' someone asked.

'Hitler's daughter,' Patrick said, amid renewed laughter.

It took almost another hour before he wheeled his luggage past crowds waiting for friends and relatives at the customs exit. There was a long queue for taxis. I hate Heathrow, Patrick thought. I've always hated it, and the more terminals they build the worse it gets. Gatwick Airport was a paradise in comparison. Best option of all would have been the Eurostar to Waterloo, which made him think of Claire.

It was steamy hot, and there was a squall of rain as the traffic slowed near Chiswick on the M4. Patrick had been fortunate enough to hail a cruising mini-cab. The driver, a cheerful Pakistani, talked about the weather and its vagaries until discovering Patrick's nationality; after that it was non-stop Olympics for the rest of the journey.

'Such a spectacle, sir, such a wonderful opening ceremony. I am fortunate that I record it, and already my family have watched it several times. Superb. The parade of horsemen, all those children dancing, so much surprise and entertainment, then the great moment when your Catherine Freeman ran up the steps carrying the flame and lit the cauldron.' Patrick was able to contribute to the driver's enthusiasm by relating that his mother and sister had been in the stadium to see it.

The Clayborough Hotel in Bayswater was one he'd selected from the Internet, trying to find a tariff that wouldn't blow his slim budget while remembering that London had become one of the world's most expensive cities; the current exchange rate was an exorbitant three Aussie dollars to a pound sterling. The hotel was modest but convenient, close to the Lancaster Gate tube station and across the road from Hyde Park. He checked in, and to his surprise there was a small package waiting for him.

'It was left this morning, sir, awaiting your arrival.' The desk clerk had a practised welcoming smile. 'Splendid to have you with us, Mr Conway, and if you wish to dine we have an excellent chef. The dining room is open from seven-thirty each evening.'

Patrick followed a porter to the elevator, and was taken to a room on the third floor. Like the hotel itself, the room was modest. He had forgotten to acquire English coins for the expected tip, and the only option was his smallest currency: a five-pound note. A moment's mental arithmetic made him realise, to his alarm, that he had just tipped the man fifteen Australian dollars. The elderly porter was most appreciative. Patrick tried to look as if it was normal. Before leaving the porter said that while it was none of his business, he must warn against the dining room. He hoped Mr Conway would keep it confidential, but in his opinion the chef was highly overrated, and the prices there were outrageous. Mr Conway assured him it would remain off the record, and the porter added that the forecast for the next few days was for more of this warm Indian summer weather, and wished him a pleasant stay.

Patrick unpacked before he remembered the package left at the desk for him. It was wrapped in bookshop paper. He assumed it must be from the BBC, but inside was a slim volume of *War Poems* by Siegfried Sassoon. There was a note with it that read: *Welcome to London. Claire.*

Chapter Ten

Finding the market town of Leatherhead in Surrey was no problem. During the two years he lived in London Patrick had often attended plays at the local theatre there. After picking up his rented car it was familiar territory across Hammersmith Bridge to Roehampton and Robin Hood Gate, then down the Kingston bypass. There was no difficulty until he reached Shepherds Green. But finding the Lodge was a different matter.

The Green faced onto the river, an area affluent with pseudo-Tudor and Georgian houses. It was a lengthy cul-de-sac. He drove slowly to the end of it and back, hoping for someone to ask for help, but the homes seemed shuttered against the unusual September heat. The temperature was predicted to reach eighty Fahrenheit, and the surcharge for renting an airconditioned car already seemed worth it. While Patrick drove, he thought about Claire.

His first impulse had been to pick up the phone to thank her for the gift. Then other thoughts began to intrude. There had been no doubt in France of an attraction between them as the evening progressed. He'd made the excuse to drive her to Lille the next morning, and was acutely aware he'd been constantly thinking about her since then. Her ready smile, her sense of fun. The gift of this book, including as it did the very poem she'd spoken of, was an overture and required a response. As she was unaware he was in London a day earlier than expected, it gave him time to think about just how to respond.

Ahead of him Patrick saw a tall young woman intently watching him from imposing entry gates. As he pulled up and stepped from the car, she remained standing there. The house behind her was substantial. A watering system was soaking expansive lawns and flowerbeds, while two small children shrilled as they ran through the spray.

'Excuse me,' Patrick said, 'I'm looking for the Lodge.'

'You've been driving up and down here for some time,' the woman replied, 'and we're wondering why. I've never heard of the Lodge.'

'Isn't this Shepherds Green?'

'I'm sure you know it is. I should tell you I've asked my *au pair* to call the police unless you can explain what you're doing. All I need do is signal her.'

Patrick saw a blonde girl inside the house waiting at one of the bow windows.

'Please don't. I can show you my driving licence, or an Amex card, if that reassures you. Better still, I have the copy of a letter.' He fumbled for it in his shirt pocket. 'It's from a Miss Rickson, who lived there in 1964.'

'But that's nearly forty years ago. I wasn't even alive!'

'Nor was I,' Patrick said.

'Do I call them, Missus Meredith?' The *au pair* had opened the front door. She wore a sun top and very tight shorts. She was tanned, and judging by her looks was Scandinavian.

'No, I don't think it'll be necessary, Karen.'

'Swedish?' Patrick asked.

'Not even close,' Mrs Meredith said. 'Northern Italian.'

'Oh well.' He smiled. 'Miss Rickson's name was Georgina. English, without a doubt. She apparently was acquainted with my grandfather.'

'Which is why you're casing the neighbourhood? That seems too implausible *not* to be true.'

Patrick laughed. 'Do you think there's anyone around here old enough to remember 1964?'

'You'd best come in out of this heat,' Mrs Meredith said, relenting. 'I'll ask Karen. She knows everyone in Shepherds Green. She jogs each day in those very brief shorts. Some old codgers around here have taken to walking their dogs at the same time, wanting her to teach them Italian.'

Andrew Gardiner arrived twenty minutes later. A jovial man in his mid-eighties, he was tall and erect with a ruddy complexion and neatly brushed white hair. He shook hands firmly with Patrick while his eyes seemed to slide wistfully towards Karen's slender legs.

'Of course I remember the Lodge,' he said. 'It was a grand old place. Pulled down in –' he hesitated over the date, 'can't swear on the Bible, but I'd put my money on 1975.'

'The house was demolished?'

'Despite a hell of a row. Massive protests. All the save-the-planet people were here, and rent-a-crowd. Oh yes, we had 'em in those days. You young people don't know what a good protest is. Mind you, I was sorry to see it go. Bulldozers moved in, smashed the walls . . . only took a day or two. People living here at the time, we all felt upset about it. Great big house. Victorian, or Georgian. Blest if I know about architecture and all that. But a fine house. Huge grounds, several acres of lawn, stables and a tennis court.'

'Acres? Around here?' Mrs Meredith was surprised.

'End of the street,' Andrew Gardiner said. 'Where those eight new homes are now. Well, they were new in those days, after they chopped the land into pieces. Some developer chappie put up those houses instead, cheek by jowl. That's the way it is today. Cheek by jowl. End up like battery hens, I wouldn't be surprised. Disgraceful.'

'Mr Gardiner, did you know Georgina Rickson?'

'Of course I did. The Rickson girls. There were two of 'em.'

'Two?' Patrick repeated, surprised. 'One was called Georgina?'

'That's right. And the other . . . hang on a second . . .' They waited while the old man looked thoughtfully at Karen's thighs, as if he might find recollection there.

'Henrietta,' he said abruptly, 'that's it. Henry and George, we'd call 'em. Or George and Henry – alphabetical order, so to speak. Their mother used to get furious.'

'Why?' It was Mrs Meredith who asked.

'Because of the names. "They're girls," she'd say, "not chaps!"' He shook his head in wonderment. 'George and Henry, well I'm blest. Fancy someone asking about those two after all this time.'

'You know what happened to the Lodge,' Patrick said, 'but what happened to them?'

'It was pulled down. All those new houses . . . I told you.'

'No, I'm sorry. I meant what happened to the sisters?'

'George and Henry? One died.'

'Which one?'

Mr Gardiner paused, his face creased in thought. 'I can't remember. But one did, and after that, the other couldn't cope. Taxes, rates, cost of domestic help. All got too much for her, so she sold to that lout of a developer. Shame. Nice looking girls.'

'Do you know where the one who survived might be?'

'At a guess I'd say Golders Green or some other cemetery,' Mr Gardiner answered. 'Both were older than me, and I'm not buying any green bananas these days. If you want to see George or Henry, son, I think you've come along a bit too late.'

Patrick had a leisurely pub lunch in Leatherhead, then went to the council chambers. After a long delay, a clerk found time to see him. There was no Georgina Rickson listed as a householder or ratepayer at any address in the shire. Nor a Henrietta Rickson either, the clerk assured him, and would that be all as he was rather busy? With no trace of irony, Patrick thanked him for the use of his valuable time, and went out to his car.

The temperature had risen sharply. Patrick wondered what else he could do here. It occurred to him that if the house had been as splendid as Mr Gardiner described, and the agitation over its demise had created such protest, there should be a record of it. He asked for directions to the municipal library. There a helpful librarian apologised that they had a rather restricted local historical section, and at the moment all their computers were down. She would search for the name of the house and its owners; if he cared to phone tomorrow she would try to help. Or there was the Epsom library, she suggested, which had a more comprehensive archival unit. Patrick thanked her, drove to Epsom, but the library there had just shut. He had forgotten about British traditions like half-day closing.

Disappointed, he headed back towards London. After crossing Putney Bridge and reaching Fulham he realised this was close to the address Claire had given him. On an impulse he turned towards the river and into Ashburton Road where she lived. Her flat was on the second floor of a large terraced house, but there was no reply when he rang the bell. Below the security system were four mail-boxes. On one was the stencilled name C. Thomas.

He scribbled a brief note: *Called to say thanks for the book. Sorry I missed you, Patrick.* He put it in her box, and drove back to Paddington to return the car.

Late that afternoon the temperature reached the predicted eighty degrees Fahrenheit. In Patrick's hotel room the airconditioner was a window unit, both noisy and ineffective. He called reception to ask if something could be done about it, as it was decidedly not cooling. The same desk clerk said unfortunately the company who serviced their machines was busy because of the weather, and unable to come for several days. He could offer Patrick a far better room on a lower floor, larger and cooler with ducted air, but naturally more expensive. A matter of an additional fifty pounds a night, but for Mr Conway they could perhaps make one available at forty-five.

Patrick decided to remain where he was. He switched off the clattering window unit, and phoned the BBC.

'Tim Carruthers' office,' a female voice said, and when Patrick gave his name he was told Mr Carruthers was on leave at present.

'I have an appointment with him,' Patrick said, feeling some faint stirrings of alarm, 'on Monday.'

'What name?' the voice asked again.

'Patrick Conway.'

'Oh. Well, I doubt if Monday is possible. Will you hold?' He heard what seemed to be a muted conversation, before she spoke again. 'Mr Conway? I'm sorry, but Monday is out of the question.'

'Look, we exchanged emails on this. I've come from Australia on the assumption it was a firm date!'

'I realise that. The best I can do is a week on Tuesday.'

Eight extra days, he thought dismayed. Eight more bloody days than he'd anticipated in this dump of a hotel.

'Are you there, Mr Conway?'

'I'm here. Is there no possibility before then?'

'Unfortunately not. Will that be satisfactory? Are you available Tuesday week?'

'Yes,' Patrick said reluctantly, 'if Tim will be back by then.'

'Right. That's confirmed. I'll put you down for 10.30.'

'Thank you.' He hung up feeling disconcerted. It seemed an odd phone call. He'd expected at least to talk to Tim, whom he knew from working together on a drama series at Thames. It had felt strangely impersonal, like an exchange with a computerised voice.

Since he had extra days on his hands, his only consolation was more time to try and trace Georgina Rickson – if she was alive. There seemed no reason why not. The helpful Mr Gardiner was well and truly alive.

He picked up the book of Sassoon's poems and turned to the verse Claire had spoken about. A footnote said Sassoon had chosen to keep this work secret, and therefore the bitter poem was unknown until after his death. Entitled 'On Passing the Menin Gate', it was bitter indeed:

Who will remember, passing through this gate,
the unheroic dead who fed the guns?
Who shall absolve the foulness of their fate –
Those doomed, conscripted, unvictorious ones?

Crudely renewed, the salient holds its own,
Paid are its dim defenders by this pomp;
Paid, with a pile of peace-complacent stone,
The armies who endured that sullen swamp.

Here was the world's worst wound – and here with pride
'Their name liveth forever' the Gateway claims,
Was ever an immolation so belied
as these intolerably nameless names?
Well might the dead who struggled in the slime
Rise and deride this sepulchre of crime.

He sat pensive, long afterwards, hardly aware that most of the afternoon had gone. Traffic was heading out of London along Bayswater Road, and the girls who had been sunbaking in the park were wrapping on their skirts and preparing to depart. He kept hearing the poet's scornful words in his mind: *Well might the dead who struggled in the slime, Rise and deride this sepulchre of crime.*

Claire had not understated the anger. This was the writing of a man who had been there, had fought in muddy trenches, a poet with the poet's power to express what war was really like. Had his grandfather felt as angry as this?

There were entries in Stephen Conway's diary that suggested it. Patrick knew he must read it again, far more carefully this time, studying it for traces of fear or anger. He must search for what had motivated Stephen to desert – if that was what he had done. It now seemed difficult to believe anything else. And yet . . .

He went downstairs to the nearby delicatessen and bought a sandwich. Back in the hotel room he poured a beer from the mini-bar and began to read, skipping the early pages, the naïve thrill of Stephen's first ocean voyage from Australia, the tedium of training in Egypt, even much of Gallipoli.

Patrick flicked to the later pages. To the Somme again, but this time it was after the terrible winter of 1917. It was there the tone of the entries changed. That was where Stephen Conway had become a different person.

Chapter Eleven

I sometimes look back through what I have written here, and no longer care if it offends the military or breaks any of their arcane laws. What I put down in these pages may be seditious: the truth is often considered subversive. If anyone ever reads this it is of no consequence what they think of the opinions I express. The diary has become a release from the sheer misery of these dreadful past months, that have been like Pozieres all over again, only far worse because I'm a year older and nothing has changed. Nothing will change. No one is winning, and it seems to us as if no one can win.

At the end of this year I will be twenty-two, and if I had been smart and not listened to inflammatory rhetoric or the fever of military bands, I would be graduating soon and have letters after my name that would enable me to be a solicitor. A bachelor of the law: a dreary life I always thought then, but how desirable it seems now. I would make wills, do conveyancing, perhaps even appear in court on behalf of people in debt, or defend petty thieves.

Instead, I'm here. Amid this fucking madness. In the dark of this stinking trench the artillery barrage sounds thunderous, and the candle is worn down. Soon the dugout will be pitch dark. There is just time to finish these few new pages. To say what's in my mind.

I now believe that these bastards are all insane. I don't mean the poor bastards on the other side of the wire, the ones we have to fight – I mean the thick-skinned bastards on our side, the ones who command us: the wheyfaced, great-coated men who sit in a safe chateau far behind the lines and plot what's to happen next. Cold old men, playing their deadly games of chess with our lives.

All through the freezing winter we were here on the Somme, at times fighting to hold places that looked exactly like ones we thought we'd fought in last year. All winter it was confusion; none of us sure any longer what land we'd won or lost, because the villages with different names all looked the same. Just rubble and mud. No trees, no buildings, rarely if ever any people. Just shitty little places that Haig and his generals gave orders for us to capture. And when that was done, without time to stop to bury our dead, further orders would come instructing us to advance to the next objective. Or else retreat, because a mistake had been made, wrong commands issued, wrong orders given.

That often happens, wrong orders. What we call an 'own goal' – when our guns fix on a target and blast the hell out of a place but it's us instead of the Huns trying to hide in there, us poor devils trying not to be blown to bits from our artillery because it seems like a bad way to die. Wrong orders, wrong alignment, wrong linearity – the maths and measurements all fucked up. There's been an awful lot of that.

We live in this kind of turmoil, in such chaos that I can no longer believe anything I'm told. I know weeks ago, on the 25th of April, it was my son's second birthday. I believe that, because my wife wrote and told me. She said her mother made a birthday cake, and my mother brought candles, and Richard was such a clever boy because he blew out both candles at his very first go. She writes me letters like that, Jane does; prudent and guarded, as if nothing else is happening at home: no national referendum about a vote for conscription being defeated, no talk of how everyone goes surfing at weekends or else watches the footy. I think she's trying to be kind.

But I do clearly remember Richard's second birthday because I spent it in the field hospital behind the line at Bullecourt, hardly a day's stroll down the road from Pozieres – and does anyone know whether that bloody place is still ours or theirs, because I certainly don't. I was brought in sick with trench fever, weak as a kitten and shaking like a leaf, plagued with headaches, leg pains and riddled with lice that bred in the trenches and were now breeding under my skin. The rash was all over my body, and a nurse, one of the young English volunteers they call 'the Roses of No-Man's-Land' told me in confidence I'd most likely be invalided back to Blighty.

My heart sang at the thought of this wonderful news. A few weeks in hospital, I envisaged, and with luck a slight relapse, only a very slight one, but just bad enough to keep me there until August and the end of summer. By then, perhaps the war might be over! August, that's the anniversary of the third year of fighting, and surely neither side can go on much longer. Both of us must soon run out of bullets to fire and enemy troops to kill.

I believed my Rose; she looked so sweet and serious, and for two days I dwelt in the luxury of this probability, imagining hospitals with nice nurses in clean starched uniforms, lawns to walk on, chairs to sit in where patients could rest or read. It's been two years since I have been able to properly read a book. I had no particular preferred place where this hospital would be, just as long as it was across the channel. London, I felt would be suitable. Or even better, somewhere in the countryside – a view of farmlands, sheep grazing, elms and spreading oaks . . . the quiet, peaceful English country landscape to me would be akin to heaven.

But when the doctor came around – a young captain who looked barely old enough to be a first-year medical student – he maintained I was a malingerer. It was not a serious case at all, he told everyone in the ward within hearing, there were far worse cases than this. Men were limping back to their units with a lot more wrong with them than a rash. They weren't trying to pull up stumps and declare their innings closed!

What fucking innings?

I wanted to ask him if he'd ever played a game of cricket in front of a mob of taunting Turks, not knowing if the next shot would be a late cut through the slips or a bullet in the guts.

'Invalided to Blighty?' he snorted dismissively, 'who put that absurd idea into your head?' The same nurse accompanying this oaf on his rounds was about to speak, but I got in first.

'Nobody put it into my head. It's common knowledge that trench fever is caused by lice, and our trenches are full of them. Lots of cases have been sent back for treatment and convalescence.'

'Convalescence, eh?' The doctor seized on this like a greedy dog with a bone. 'So that's the objective. Not on my watch, Private Conway. Definitely not while I'm on roster. You're a shirker, using this mild complaint as an excuse to dodge duty.'

'Sir –' My Rose did her best to interrupt, upset at his cavalier attitude.

'Just a minute, Nurse,' he snapped. 'Can't you see I'm talking to the patient?' When the poor girl subsided, cowed by this school bully, he glared at me. 'It's a very simple matter, Conway. Simple! A thorough wash in disinfectant is all the treatment you require.'

So that was my present on the day my son blew out his candles on the other side of the world. I was doused in a concentrated dose to kill the lice, and it bloody nearly killed me. The stink of the muck burnt my throat and made me spew. After this the baby-face quack discharged me as fit and I was told to return to the trenches.

Are they the same trenches, I asked him, where lots more lice are lurking ready to breed again, to swarm all over me like blowflies at a picnic? Will they take up their customary positions in my hair, on my balls and up my arse?

Don't use such crude language in front of the nurse, he replied.

Don't worry about the nurse, I said. She's seen up my arse and she knows it's not a pretty sight.

He looked at me as if I was beneath contempt, and went off on his rounds. The Rose sneaked an approving grin at me, then had to follow him while he set forth to stuff up some other poor bugger's dreams.

The guns keep firing. At least tonight the shells are not landing on us. Tonight some genius has worked out the lineage or the range. We can sit in the trench and celebrate that we're safe from our own gunners. But the candle has flickered out and in the pitch dark there are other problems that trouble me. It is no longer possible to accept this is a good war, or a fair war, or even a necessary war; it is clear that back there on National Recruitment Day we were conned and deceived by the flags and the cheering crowds. Crowds and streamers, I can still see it in my mind, us so young and keen – and worried we'd be too late to fight, Christ help us. They are all dead now, the blokes in our platoon who sailed with me down Port Phillip Bay. A whole group of good mates gone, and none to replace them. After Bluey died I deliberately did not seek to make new friends, because losing them is too painful. I have lots of close friends scattered all over hillsides or buried in the mud, and it becomes unbearable to think about.

Some nights I manage to sleep, but I never welcome it because there are dreams. Uncomfortable images – I don't like to call them nightmares – more like delusions. Such as turning to answer a tap on the shoulder and finding Jeff Gilmore, who was buried on Gallipoli, lighting a cigarette and grinning at me, asking where have I been lately and insisting we go and join a game of two-up. We win a fortune until the Turks come and break up the game, shouting that gambling is a sin and take all our money. They say they'll use it to build a mosque for Allah.

Other nights I'm in London with Double-Trouble, and everywhere we go women come rushing up to him and put their arms around him. They're all his wives, and he has a marriage certificate for each one of them. I ask him how he can have all these documents, and he says he prints his own. We take a bus with a lady bus driver, and she says we don't have to pay the fare because it turns out she's one of his wives too. 'See you at home, darling,' shouts Double as we get off at Piccadilly, and he tells her to drive carefully.

Often at night I think I'm up on the Monaro, the snow country, shearing alongside Bluey. Once I dreamt we had a contest to see who could shear the most sheep, and to my surprise I won it. I know bloody well he let me win. He laughed and told the whole shed that I was now the gun shearer, but that was typical Bluey Watson, so big-hearted, brave and likable. He haunts my thoughts.

I had another dream about Bluey. We were in London on leave, and we met Major Carmody, the Pommy officer who put me on a charge and lost me my stripes. Still the same shiny Sam Browne and spotless uniform, with his crowns of rank gleaming on his epaulets.

Excuse me, Bluey said, blocking his way, would you by any chance be Major James Carmody, of military headquarters?

I most assuredly am. Salute when you speak to me, soldier, he said with the same arrogant look, as if we were a bad smell somewhere beneath his nose and his neat little clipped moustache.

I want to ask an important question, Blue told him, then we'll salute. You're real good at slapping blokes on charges, aren't you?

When they deserve to be, the major said, glaring at me.

What if they just think something, Major? Can anyone be put on a charge just for *thinking*?

Of course not, he retorted. You can *think* whatever you like.

Well, in that case, Carmody old man, Bluey said, *I think you're a real arsehole and a fucking bastard.*

We each gave him a two-fingered salute and strolled off. That was one of the good dreams. The last time I saw Bluey he told me he was about to join up again, so he could get back to England, find his girl and marry her. I promised to be his best man.

There are other nights with very different delusions: more intimate ones. These take place in beds that have clean sheets and fleecy wool blankets where I'm making love, sometimes at the French farmhouse with Marie-Louise, other times at the Carrington Hotel in the bridal suite with Jane. Even more confusing is when I wake from these encounters palpitating, and more often than not I'm gazing into the soft grey eyes of Elizabeth Marsden. It's strange how well I can remember Elizabeth from a few hours spent talking in a teashop, and from a hasty kiss on my cheek. Even stranger that no matter how hard I try, I cannot recall the name of the place where she lives, although I feel certain she told me.

It's this memory of Elizabeth that sometimes makes me feel guilty and disloyal to Jane. Which is peculiar, because nothing really happened between me and Elizabeth, and absolutely everything happened between Marie-Louise and me. If I think of M.L. in bed naked, the heat we generated, how we could hardly bear to stop even when our love-making left us completely exhausted, it was the most erotic experience of my life. It arouses me just to think of her wild cries and the way her body trembled against mine. But at the end I did walk away from Marie-Louise – and now I remember her less and less with each passing month. Which is something I cannot seem to do with Elizabeth, who is so often in my mind.

Too often, perhaps. Is that it? Is the real unfaithfulness, the act of unforgivable adultery, is it in the mind? Perhaps that's why I feel so disloyal. But after all, memories are all we have here to keep us sane. I can so easily remember Elizabeth – our parting on Kings Cross Station – whereas there was no real farewell for Jane and me. No waving goodbye, no tears, no last hug or last streamer from the ship to bind us; instead there was just disappointment and the extinguished hope of a few days together before embarkation. Then nothing. Except three years of letters.

I know – it's hardly fair that Jane's careful letters have to compete with the unruly thoughts in my mind. I sometimes complain, but I know it'd be unbearable without them. They arrive in batches, ten or more at a time after months by sea. One of my simple pleasures is assembling them in the correct order, even though they nearly always say the same things: telling me how our son is growing up so fast, and how much they and my parents all miss me.

Once, back in the days when we first came to England, to the camp at Salisbury, I used to find this repetitive, now I draw a sort of comfort from the similitude. Even if it is on the other side of the world, it is consoling to realise that in the thoughts of these few special people I am remembered and loved.

Yesterday, August the 4th, was the third anniversary of the war. Nobody lit candles. All week there were constant rumours there might be a truce, like on Christmas Day in 1914 – when both sides met in no-man's-land, exchanged a few handshakes, buried their dead, even played a game of football that Germany won 3–2, before they went back to killing each other. But they say that could only have happened in the first few months when the war was fought along more chivalrous lines, before the hatred corroded us.

There was no truce this day despite the rumours. Instead there was mayhem, some treachery and bloody carnage. All because a German general issued an infamous battle order forbidding his troops to ever retreat. Some mad militaristic Prussian declaring it was better to die than surrender, and if the enemy wanted to advance it must be over heaps of German corpses. It seems that Haig or one of his acolytes decided this was a fair invitation and they'd take the Hun at his word.

The rumours were spread deliberately by our own side. Word was leaked to the Germans that both armies should discuss a day's cease-fire, even perhaps a few days', and the thought was planted it could possibly be the prelude to something more permanent. Clever and persuasive. Everyone was tired; three years was time enough. We believed it – because we badly wanted to – and so it seems did they. It brought some of their senior officers to the front-line to cautiously find out more.

For months past a division of British Royal Engineers had been tunnelling deep under their lines. Now with an urgent need to complete the tunnel, some of us were compelled to work with them. Day and night we dug below no-man's-land, crawling and chipping our way for hundred of yards like coal miners. Rails were laid, small coal trucks used to excavate the tons of earth. After us came the sappers rigging explosives and laying cables directly beneath the German line of trenches. At noon on the anniversary there was a curt exchange of messages.

The Germans demanded to know if this rumour of a possible cease-fire was a false alarm, or some kind of trick.

The British indignantly denied this and asked if senior officers were there with whom they could seriously discuss the matter?

The German reply was terse. A field marshal and his staff were available, hoping their journey to the front had not been wasted.

Not wasted at all, was the answer, and the signal passed down the line to engineer headquarters. The explosives went off with a deafening roar. The earth trembled and shook - we could feel our own trenches shudder as if they might collapse and bury us. The sky was filled with a choking miasma of dust and debris, after which there was silence. A long appalled silence. We were supposed to fix bayonets and charge, but there was no one left alive for us to kill.

Just a single letter from Jane this month, which means it's likely a ship with the rest of our mail has been sunk. Whenever there is a gap in letters from home it's almost certain a ship, either naval or merchantman, has been torpedoed by a U-boat. There has been news for months that the German subs are causing serious food shortages in Britain, and the grapevine says this is why the Huns keep fighting in France, even if they lose thousands of men and don't gain a yard for weeks. They feel certain they can win as soon as they starve Britain into submission. I don't know if it's true but it might be; there has to be some reason for this insanity to continue like it does without prospect of an end.

I went looking for a dry spot to sit down and read the letter, away from the water that swirled in the trench and smelt like piss. Well, why wouldn't it, since half of it is piss? Nobody goes outside for a leak when you could get blown to bits like poor old Double, or get a bullet, an unlucky one right in the family jewels.

The letter was a surprise: longer than usual, and very different:

My dearest,

I've had a serious falling out with my mother, and because my father felt bound to support her, I've had a falling out with him too. Which I feel bad about, because I love my dad. I love Mum, too, only not all that much, not just at the moment. But never mind that for now.

I've been sitting here tonight, thinking of us, remembering all kinds of things. Do you remember the train – that moment when I was so ready for you to make love to me? Remember the sour faces of the old couple opposite? Do you think they were ever young and wild for each other like I was for you?

I keep wishing we'd done it in the train. It would've been exciting. Something to look back on in years to come. Do you think, when you come home, we could park Richard for the night and take another train, book a sleeper and fuck – I know girls are not supposed to use that word, but that's what I want to do with you – fuck each other to the rhythm of the wheels and be absolutely alone in a locked compartment where nobody can interrupt? I've never described the feelings I had when we did it the first time in bed – how it was arousing but slightly painful, but I didn't mind as you were so pleased and exhilarated. I did just slightly wonder what all the fuss was about. But then the second time . . . Oh, darling, the second time! And every time afterwards in our marvellous but horribly short honeymoon it was so thrilling – pure heaven – and even thinking about it now and writing this makes me feel excited and full of longing for you.

I wish I'd written like this before, but the row with Mum today seemed to provoke it. I confess, my darling, I've dreaded writing letters to you for the past two years, because there appeared nothing new or interesting or the least bit important that I could say. All those questions you asked – about the morale at home, about people going to the races and the football, even about those soldiers rioting – I found them so difficult to answer that it was easier for me to ignore them.

Why were they difficult? Because we were constantly being told that soldiers' wives and families should be careful not to air subjects that might upset them. Everyone kept saying this. My parents, Father Geraghty, all our friends – they said it was unfair and unkind to cause any of our lads so far from home the slightest concern. It was best to stick to uncomplicated domestic matters.

So I did. Dull and trivial things that would not upset you; things like the weather, local gossip, or my mother taking care of Richard while I found a job as a kindergarten teacher. And of course our son's first words and first steps – although that wasn't the least bit dull or trivial to me, and I know it wouldn't be to you, if only you were here to share it.

What I really wanted to say, and will say now, is that I hate the wretched war. I hated the way it created such excitement, as if fighting was all that mattered. I hated the cheering, and the crowds. I even thought I hated you for a time, because I had this stupid idea that you felt sailing off to war was better than settling down to married life. That you preferred it to me. I hated reading stories in the newspapers about some of our boys living with, or even bigamously marrying English girls. That made me afraid. You were a long way from home, you were young and handsome: why wouldn't I feel scared?

And I was completely terrified at the sight of anyone delivering a telegram. I still am. There've been four in our street already.

Darling, perhaps I've said too much, but these are things in my heart and I must say them. If I don't share them with you I will tear myself apart, and I've been doing that for too long. Nearly three years – perhaps it will be three by the time you read this, and today I made a decision about my life. I need to tell you about today, and it seemed like a good time to tell you all the rest.

It's been getting more and more difficult at home. When Mum first suggested I live here with the baby it seemed the ideal solution. She would look after Richard during the day so I could finish my studies and take a job as a teacher. After all, trying to survive on the army's matrimonial allotment and whatever you could send me would mean a rather lonely existence in a cheap room and a bit of a struggle. Whereas you know our family home has plenty of rooms and a garden, as well as my loving parents who were so keen to look after their first grandchild.

And it was a perfect arrangement while Richard spent his days in a basinet or a playpen. But then he learnt to walk, and Mum began to find it difficult. He was forever climbing out of his cot, and when he was a few months older began trying to climb the fence or open the gate. She was often angry, reprimanding him, and her attitude was having an effect on him and making him resentful and cheeky. It's awful, but they've begun not to like each other. He's a lively child – a bit too lively for my mother. Today it seemed to come to a head and we had a blazing row.

I was late home from school, and Mum was in one of her moods again. She complained he's been disobedient and naughty, swinging on the front gate waiting for my return, and asking her the time every few minutes. Eventually he ran out into the street to start looking for me, and Mum had to roam the district asking neighbours had they seen him, and getting very agitated because there seems to be so many more cars on the roads now, and she was scared he'd be run over.

I understand her worry, he was a very naughty boy, but when I came home she blamed me – said I was a rotten mother, and you and I had been rash to marry so soon, that we were irresponsible and stupid to have a child when you couldn't be here to help with his upbringing. I tried to calm her down – made her a cup of tea and told her the reason I was late was because the headmistress had asked me to remain for a chat, and that I had some good news. News that I'd hoped for: I've been promoted to take on the second form, which means slightly longer hours and an extra two shillings a week.

I was thrilled, but my mother said it was out of the question. In fact, for weeks she had been intending to tell me I had to give up the job and take care of Richard like a proper mother should. We could stay on in the house and pay no rent, but Richard had now become a problem she could no longer manage, and I was to tell the headmistress that not only must I decline the new promotion, but I would be leaving the school and my job altogether at the end of the month.

We started shouting at each other; I can hardly believe the things we said. I think I told her she was a selfish bitch, that my dad would soon be home from work and he'd agree with me. I do remember she laughed and said if I thought I was still 'Daddy's girl' I had a shock coming, because he was greatly concerned she was being treated as an unpaid nanny or nurse, and if it came to a question of who he supported, they had decided last night that inviting me to live there had been a bad mistake. I'm afraid I cried, then I saw this small face gazing at the pair of us and felt ashamed that we – his mother and grandmother – were behaving like a pair of fishwives.

I told Mum I was sorry, but much as I loved my own child the job made life endurable. It occupied my mind and prevented me from brooding over the way fate and this wretched war had seemed to play such a mean trick on us. I said I'd take Richard to the park where I let him play on the swing until it was almost dark, then I walked around to see your parents. They were expecting me. They knew.

They asked me to come and live with them. Your mother sat me down and said she would love to look after Richard all day so that I can go on working. She seemed to read my thoughts when she said I need work to properly occupy myself until you come home. Because that is the truly important thing in our life, my dearest, our future and our child. Your mother seems to understand what mine can't; that teaching helps me to stay calm and able to believe this frightful war will soon be over and you'll come home safe and sound. I have to say that I love her, and it makes me understand why I've loved you all my life.

Finally, my darling, I'm trying to think of what else there is to tell you. I'm sitting here with pen poised over the inkwell. The truth is all this pen will allow me to write. So, this is my truth.

I'm twenty-one years old, and I've been privileged to know what love is like, but only for those few beautiful days and then deprived of it ever since. I often wake in the night and need you, dearest. Need your flesh in mine. If this isn't over soon, God alone knows what will become of us.

I sat reading the letter over again, and I felt the prickle of tears in my eyes. I was still in an emotional state when a group of young British squaddies came into the empty dugout. I wished them to hell, but they were a bunch of newly arrived recruits who proceeded to take over the place. Then the youngest of them, who looked as if he should still be at prep school, let out a yell and pointed in horror to where a human arm and a leg projected out from the wall. On the skeletal arm a helmet was hanging; on the leg a gas mask and cape were draped.

What the fuck are those? he shouted.

I asked him what did he think they were, and told him it was obvious: one was a coat rack, the other was a hat stand.

Jesus Christ, another boy said, those are real arms and legs. *They were actual people!*

I agreed that they were. And told them all these were good blokes in their time. Now, I explained, they were doing their best to be helpful as coat racks and hat stands.

The first recruit voiced the perception that everyone here was fucking mad. He said this while still staring at the embedded limbs jutting from the clay wall.

I confirmed his opinion that we are – fucking mad and no two ways about it. Mad because we were volunteers here by choice, whereas they were dragged here as conscripts. Which means we were simpletons who came to the slaughter without even being forced. Were there ever such fools in the history of war?

But I explained we have rules in these trenches among the

foolish and the mad. For instance, I told them, this leg and the arm they'd picked out are mine: my pegs to hang up my coat, my hat, my water bottle, whatever I like. The leg, I pointed out, is especially useful, you can even sling a rifle on it. It was a good sturdy limb, that one. Dependable. It would not break like some legs do after a few months.

Shit, he's off his bleeding trolley, a third recruit muttered, starting to look really scared as he gazed at me.

Just explaining the rules, I told him and said not to worry, there were plenty of bones to go around. The walls were full of them. I suggested they take a good close look; they would see all these trenches are almost entirely made of clay and pieces of old soldiers.

I left them gazing fearfully at the walls, the awful realisation in their faces that what I'd said was true. Miles of trenches made of femurs, fibulas and bits of vertebrae. Long ago I had undergone the same gruesome induction, but back in those days I would've spared them this cruelty. Trouble is, I could not forgive their intrusion on my grief, and I've spent far too much time living with these grisly remains of the dead to be either sparing or rational.

I found a corner of another dugout knowing they would not follow me to encounter more of my insanity. Isolated and in peace, I read Jane's letter again and this time wept until my tears were exhausted. It was something to treasure, too precious to risk losing. The only safeguard was to transcribe it into my diary. And now that's done. My fingers are cramped, but I've written it down, every word until the concluding words of her postscript. *By the time you receive this I will actually be living with your family, in your old room.*

In my room, in my bed, I thought, and felt the warmth of love engulf me, and with it a desperate yearning to be there with her.

Chapter Twelve

It was after nine when Patrick finished reading. He felt tired, but it was far too early for sleep and there was a great deal on his mind. He sat and watched the glow of light that softened the London streets. To him, the words in his grandfather's diary did not sound like the feelings of a man who would run away. Or was he prejudiced? In the mad and ugly world Stephen Conway and Siegfried Sassoon had lived in and written about, who could tell?

He felt deeply drawn to this man whose life and death he was trying to trace. Striking parallels to Patrick himself had emerged from this new and more extensive reading. Stephen had shed law school halfway through the first year because of war, perhaps because the times dictated a young man must enlist for his country; more probably in the end, because of his yearning for 'adventure'. Patrick had lasted two years at university, then his desire to be a writer had been strong enough to make him abandon law for a new and precarious career. One had made the choice in war, one in peace, but each time he read his grandfather's words he felt a deep affinity, a correlation he had never known before with anyone. Certainly not with his own father, who was the link that bound them, and who had bitterly opposed Patrick's change of profession. A family rift between them had only been averted by his mother, who had been his sole supporter.

He felt at a loss wondering what to do with the remainder of his first day in London. There were old friends in his address book, but after the hours spent with the diary that had touched him anew with its pain and disillusion, he was in no mood for casual company. Besides, it was getting late to contact people, almost nine-thirty. He had missed dinner but had no appetite.

The room felt hot and claustrophobic. The Clayborough did not live up to its glossy promise on the Internet. Patrick kept reminding himself that the tariff was reasonable for London, and at worst it was only a brief stay. Even briefer if things did not go well at the BBC meeting now delayed until Tuesday week.

He put the diary and Sassoon's book away, and contemplated a walk towards Queensway where there would be a pub, but instead decided to call his sister and give her an update on his search for the Lodge. Her voicemail told him Sally was unavailable, but to please leave a message.

'Some interesting news of Miss Rickson, but no real progress yet. I'll call you tomorrow,' he said, and after hanging up found himself wondering if it would be too late to phone Claire – or if it would be sensible. A visit plus a call on the very day of his arrival? Well . . . perhaps he could just ring to apologise for missing her, and tell her how impressed he was with the poem about the Menin Gate. On the other hand, he thought, looking at the time, perhaps not. It would be too patently transparent for words.

The Clayborough provided what they called 'guest amenities': an electric kettle, a cellophane-wrapped biscuit and the choice of a supermarket teabag or a sachet of instant coffee. He boiled the jug while trying to choose between tea and coffee, switched on the television in time for the late news, and turned them both off again as his mobile phone played a few discordant bars of *Eine Kleine Nachtmusik*.

'Mozart speaking,' he said.

There was a startled 'Oh!' and a gurgle of laughter.

'Sally?'

'Not Sally,' a voice said, and he knew it instantly.

'Claire?'

'Yes, it's me.'

'I was just thinking about you!'

'Really?'

'Are you at home?' Patrick asked.

'No, I'm downstairs.'

'Downstairs where?'

'Downstairs at your hotel,' Claire said.

It was long after midnight. They lay naked with blankets discarded, even the lone sheet that was draped across them damp with sweat. The air in the room was oppressive. The window unit rattled with noisy futility, unable to cope with the rare September heat. Outside on Bayswater Road the traffic was sparse, with only the occasional sound of a diesel engine as a taxi prowled by.

The high temperature still suffused the city, whose brick and concrete buildings held it like an oven. On nights like this Patrick missed the breeze; there was no relief here like an Australian southerly buster to cool the air. Londoners loved their occasional hot spells; Patrick had always disliked them. When he had worked here his English friends had told him not to be ridiculous. How could he hate the heat, when he came from a sunburnt country? He'd tried to explain how such extremes at home quite often ended in a thunderstorm, followed by milder days and soft breezes. He sighed at the nostalgic thought. Even a trace of the softest breeze would be welcome now.

'You awake?' Claire reached out an exploratory hand to establish this, and murmured pleasurably as his arms drew her close. He kissed her, then ran his tongue down her forehead to the ridge of her nose, where he told her that the nicest of her freckles were to be found.

A deep feeling of affection enveloped her. In the dark their bodies moved in renewed desire. This time it was not the urgent coupling of her arrival; this was gentler, longer-lasting and infinitely more erotic. They reached orgasm together in a surge of joy, and she lay awake for a long time afterwards, feeling a happiness that she knew could not possibly last.

Claire had been working late. On arriving home she'd found his note and was elated he had called to see her like this, but dismayed at missing him. She'd tried to decide what to do and thought of phoning. But if he was out and she had to leave a message, then what? Then, she'd have to hope he'd call back, but if he didn't . . . if he didn't that would seem to be the end of it.

She'd showered and taken a taxi, hardly stopping to think he might be visiting friends, or more intimately engaged. By the time she reached the hotel, this and other disturbing thoughts had occurred to her with such force that she'd felt the onset of panic. It was something Claire had never done before. Not come on to someone as strongly as this. Impulsive, she thought. Crazy, she told herself, even if she had been attracted to him in Belgium, perhaps more than just attracted, she admitted, especially that moment in the crowded restaurant, when he'd grinned and softly quoted Sassoon's lines to her from his grandfather's diary.

The whole evening had been so easy and companionable after the lonely few days she'd spent in Ypres that she'd even wondered if they might end up in his hotel, thinking it would only be a one-night stand and they'd never meet again – until the moment when he said he'd be coming to London. All the way home in the train she'd thought about this, aware how much she wanted to see him again, while at the same time trying to talk herself out of it because it would be unwise: he was married, and the worst time of her life had been a tumultuous and eventually ill-fated love affair with a married man. So what was she doing now, like a silly schoolgirl outside his hotel?

'S'cuse me, darling.' The taxi driver had turned on the cab lights and switched off his meter. 'This is it. The Clayborough. Bayswater Road.'

'Yes,' she said, 'thank you,' but remained frozen, feeling she'd embarked on a foolish adventure. She realised the cabbie had turned around to study her.

'Are we getting out, luv? Or do you want to move into the cab as a permanent tenant?'

'I'm sorry,' she said.

'S'alright,' he answered. 'If we're unsure of things and revising our plans for the evening, I could as easy run you home, if that's where you'd rather go.'

He was a kindly man, Claire thought, who knew she was on the edge of a personal precipice. He'd wished her all the best, hoped things would work out when she'd paid the fare and gone into the hotel. And now . . . in the dark while Patrick slept with his head against her breasts, she felt very glad she had not responded to his offer and fled straight back to Fulham.

In the morning Patrick told her of the letter Sally had found, and his frustrating trip to Leatherhead. He was unsure what he'd do today but he supposed Claire had to work. If not, perhaps they could spend the day together. See a movie, maybe have lunch at a pub somewhere on the river? Claire replied that she wished they could, but there was a conference set up at the accountancy firm that she worked for in Knightsbridge.

While he was in the bathroom she rang the head of her department saying she had a problem. Her mother had been taken ill. She must find someone to look after her mum's house and pets, plus get her into hospital. After that she called her mother to tell her she was sick, just in case someone checked. She'd cancelled a rather important meeting; her boss was not well pleased.

'What have I got, darling?' her mother asked.

'Pneumonia. It was spur of the moment, Mum, but I really need today. If you know what I mean.'

'Oh, I do. Frank, I imagine, has surfaced again. How is he?'

'Still in New York. Still wants us to try again, but I'm not sure.'

'I see. Different chap, new chapter.' Her mother seemed pleased with her *bon mot*. 'Would I like him?'

'I'd say so,' Claire said, 'in fact I can guarantee it.'

'Which means you're serious.'

'Which means I like him. I don't know what happens from here on, but I feel desperate to spend today with him.'

'You're serious,' her mother said.

In the shower Patrick was having a conversation with himself while experiencing contradictory emotions. Guilt was at variance with happiness. He'd had just one affair since marriage, a transitory and unsatisfactory encounter at a Writers' Guild weekend. Joanna had had a fleeting relationship with a producer in the third year of their marriage. Each had confessed their lapse and put it behind them. Belonging to an industry where many people had liaisons because of long periods spent apart on film locations, they had decided sex with each other was better than with anyone else.

But last night . . . while he tried to reproach himself for weakening . . . last night had been a revelation. Tender and deliciously different. Just thinking of the joy they shared started to stir him. It was probably as well they could not spend the day together – although he had to admit in the privacy of the shower that he wished to God they could.

When Claire broke the news that she was free after all, it seemed the only way to begin the day was by making love again. After which they slept for another hour, and woke to the sound of Mozart on the mobile. Patrick sleepily fumbled for it, assuming it would be Sally.

'Mozart. Is that you Beethoven?'

'I beg your pardon,' a woman's voice replied. 'I must have the wrong number.'

'No, I'm sorry,' Patrick said, 'I thought it was my sister.'

'This is Mrs Meredith. You gave me this number when we met yesterday. I hope I didn't wake you.'

'No,' Patrick assured her. 'I've been up for ages. Even had a jog around Hyde Park.'

Claire smiled at him from her pillow.

'Karen's also been out for her jog,' Mrs Meredith told him, 'which is why I'm telephoning. She met old Mr Gardiner. He has asked if I could ring – he wants to see you. I think he's remembered something.'

Andrew Gardiner arrived looking bright and alert. He'd had a hair trim and wore a blazer, as if this was an occasion. He seemed to be disappointed Karen was missing. Mrs Meredith explained she'd taken the children to Chessington Zoo.

'Good zoo that,' Mr Gardiner said, telling them it was near Ashtead Woods, where he used to ride horses as a boy. Mrs Meredith passed around a tray of cold drinks for everyone, as he changed the subject.

'Two things,' he said suddenly. 'Woke up and remembered last night. George and Henry . . . one of those girls was in the war.'

'Which war?' Patrick felt a quickening of interest.

'The first war, of course. One of 'em was a nurse; she went to France as a sort of volunteer, a what'd-you-call-it.'

'VAD?' Claire suggested.

'That's it, young lady. People used to call 'em the Roses of No-Man's-Land. There was a song about them in the music halls,' Mr Gardiner said. 'My dad had the sheet music when I was a nipper. 'Course the war was over, so nobody sang it any more, but sometimes he'd play it on the piano. He was out there, you see. Lost a leg. Said he would've died if it weren't for them. Great girls, he always told me. Brave angels. My dear old mother got sick of hearing about 'em.'

'And which sister,' Patrick asked carefully, afraid they would lose him amid this nostalgic recollection, 'went to the war?'

'George, I'd say. Could've been Henry, but I'm fairly sure it was George. I'd put me money on her.'

'That's what I hoped,' Patrick said.

'Now what else did I want to tell you?' He frowned. 'Don't say I've forgotten . . .' They waited in varying degrees of suspense and some embarrassment. 'Ah!' he exclaimed, with an air of triumph. 'Of course! The protests about the Lodge's demolition. Remember that hullabaloo I spoke about? There were reporters. It was in the newspapers. Not London papers . . . but it was in the local rag, so you might check their files.' He stood up and shook hands with Patrick. 'Anyway, best of luck. I hope it helps, but not sure if it can. I'd say she's long gone.'

'It's a start, sir. Thank you for taking this trouble.'

'Not at all. Good to flex the old memory. Nice to know it's still in working order!' He gave Claire a warm smile. 'Jolly pleased to meet you, my dear.'

'And you,' she replied.

He turned to Mrs Meredith, as if something else had just occurred to him. 'What if I nip down to Chessington Zoo in the car later on, Mrs M. Be hot for that gal with the kiddies. I could bring them home for you. Buy 'em all an ice, if it's not against the rules.'

'You are kind, Mr Gardiner,' Mrs Meredith said.

Afterwards Andrew Gardiner walked briskly along the Green to his own house. Patrick offered him a lift, but he insisted the walk was good for him. Claire waved as they drove past. He flicked her a smart salute.

'Must have been a right dasher in his day,' she said.

'He doesn't believe his day's over yet. Mid-eighties and still on the prowl. There's hope for all of us in later years.'

'Rather a sweetie. I'm surprised widows aren't queuing up!'

'I think,' Patrick said, 'his preference is for lusty young blondes in very tight shorts.'

'Well, the best of luck to him.' Claire laughed. 'I'm sure he won't die wondering.'

The Leatherhead Advertiser in Church Street was unhelpful. Their office manager said it would be rather complicated. Yes, they had back copies stored, but nothing on microfilm or computer from that long ago. Patrick could make an application in writing, but there would be a substantial charge for the search, which could take several weeks.

They walked to the library. No luck, the librarian explained.

'I did phone Epsom on your behalf, but they have nothing that relates. Not without a computer search, and our whole system is down still. It's apparently a virus. Causing absolute havoc for all the linked libraries in Surrey.' As she saw them out she had a suggestion. 'There's the local history society in the next street, though. It could be worth a try.'

The district historical society occupied rather picturesque premises called Hampton Cottage. STRICTLY MEMBERS ONLY said a notice outside. Patrick looked at it ruefully.

'She might've told us.'

'She was in a flap over her computer virus. I wish I'd had a chance to help her solve it.'

'Could you have done that?' Patrick asked.

'Well, it's my job.'

Patrick looked surprised. 'I thought you worked for a firm of accountants?'

'I do. A multinational with offices all over Britain and Europe. I run their computer network.'

'Seriously? You're a nerd?'

'You see what you've got yourself into – if you'll forgive the expression!'

He laughed. 'I certainly didn't know nerds could look like you.' He turned to the MEMBERS ONLY sign again. 'And I was silly enough to think history was for everyone. Why don't I go in and ask if I can join?'

'In England, joining anything takes about a week to process, then you wait for a letter of invitation by second-class mail.'

'Bugger.'

'Would you let me handle this?'

'How?'

'Just stay here,' she said, and went inside. She returned a few minutes later and beckoned him.

The interior of Hampton Cottage was cool; its size belied the quaint outside appearance. There were high ceilings and shelves filled with books and folios. Walls were covered with photographs of the town in times past: there was an impression of breweries, tanning factories and a timber yard on the banks of the River Mole.

'This is Mr Goldsworthy, director of the society,' Claire said, introducing him. Patrick shook hands with an amiable-looking man in his forties. Mr Goldsworthy had thinning hair and wore horn-rimmed glasses. 'I explained you're here to do a film with the BBC, and I'm your production assistant, factotum, gofer and what-not. And you want to recreate a house that existed here thirty years ago.'

'Absolutely right,' Patrick agreed, trying to participate in this charade she'd concocted. Not just a pretty face, he thought, and turned to the director. 'I had hoped to find the original, and shoot the scenes here in Leatherhead. But designers can do just about anything these days with computer imaging. Did Claire mention the place?'

'No, she said you'd explain.'

Patrick decided something akin to the truth was best.

'It's what we call a docudrama, Mr Goldsworthy. Based on a real event, with moments of dramatic licence. My own grandfather was a part of the story, as it happens. During World War One he apparently met a nurse serving in France. A Miss Rickson –'

'Rickson,' Goldsworthy interrupted him, 'if you mean the family who owned the Rickson Brickyard, you must be talking about the Lodge in Shepherds Green.'

'Yes, that's right.'

'One of the finest old homes in this part of Surrey. Quite dreadful, the way it went. Modernising, people tried to call it.'

'Vandalising,' Claire remarked. Goldsworthy nodded agreement.

'I don't suppose you'd have any details –' Patrick started to say, and the director smiled.

'If you'd like to begin with a photograph of the house, it's there on the wall behind you.'

They drove home leisurely by what Claire called the nostalgia route. First the Thames-side road at Kingston Lock where she had once lived, followed by a detour past the studios at Teddington where Patrick had worked. Then to Ham Gate and Richmond Park, where herds of deer still roamed and a memorial marked the palace where Cardinal Wolsey had lived and Elizabeth I had died. After a beer in Richmond itself, a jewel of a town but congested with traffic, they walked to its classic theatre which they had both attended, though in different years; the familiarity of these places bonding them, like the day had.

Mr Goldsworthy had been a find, obliging and eager to help. After showing them the photo of the Lodge that occupied pride of place on the society's wall – a classic Georgian manor house, photographed in its prime with a collage of miniatures that illustrated huge sweeping lawns, tennis court and stables – he had returned with a thick folio of very different pictures. These were an unframed assortment: some of them glossy prints, others aerial shots and photographs cut from newspapers that recorded the demolition.

'Terrible,' Goldsworthy said, and they agreed. It appeared as if a bomb had dismantled the slate roof and everything below it. There were other devastating images, not all of it mechanical destruction. Neglect over years had left its forlorn imprint. On the tennis court weeds grew wild, and the perimeter netting sagged with rust. There were the remains of a stable block that had once been home to sturdy shire horses; its walls crumbled and lost to rot or termites.

Patrick studied the demolition pictures again. In several of them was a glimpse of an elderly woman standing in the grounds, who seemed to be watching the wrecking crew. Grey hair, erect; a handsome woman, he felt, but which of the sisters it might have been he had no way of telling.

'Do you think there'd be any details about the occupants?' he'd asked, and Mr Goldsworthy felt sure there would be. He made a note of Patrick's hotel number, promising to search. They left with the director's assurance he'd be in touch. A few days at most.

'A paper trail,' he remarked, 'I enjoy that sort of thing. And I look forward to seeing the end result. But I gather the making of films is rather like the mills of God – it grinds exceeding slow.'

'I'm afraid it does,' Patrick agreed, feeling guilty about the deception after receiving such cooperation. If this produced a positive result, he might have to explain his real quest and apologise to Mr Goldsworthy.

They went home by Fulham and stopped at Claire's flat for her to collect some clothes. It occupied half the upper floor. Patrick liked the way she had furnished it sparsely but with style. Only her spare room that she'd turned into a study was a clutter: filled with computers and their components, it was clearly a workshop. Half her salary, she told him, went on new technology. The other half took care of the mortgage, but it was better than paying London's exorbitant rents, or moving to the country and spending hours in train travel.

'Besides, it has a view of the Thames,' she told him with her radiant smile. All Patrick could see were chimneypots on the roofs opposite. 'Not from this room. In the loo, on tiptoe, at high tide, you can see the river. At low tide all you see is mud flats. In the world of real-estate speak it's called "occasional water glimpses".' She laughed. 'This flat cost more than the one downstairs, but I'm told my asset is appreciating. One day if I move out and live in a tent, I could be almost rich.'

Claire packed sufficient clothes for a week. By then, she said, he would be busy with the BBC and, after all, they both knew this was transient; she had an ex-boyfriend who hoped they could revive their relationship if he returned from New York, and more importantly, Patrick had a wife in Australia. A week – and if no one knew there'd be no harm done. Some lovely private memories, and then it would be over.

Chapter Thirteen

After the weekend, to no one's real surprise, the weather changed. Thick clouds brought a drop in temperature, and some relief from the heat, although the forecaster on the BBC mourned the end of such a superb Indian summer. Too good to last, he declared with routine pessimism. Occasional showers and cool winds were now the promise, and viewers were advised not to leave home without a brolly. The British preoccupation with their climate never changes, Patrick thought.

They had spent a wonderful two days together, but this morning Claire was due at work. She selected a smart linen skirt and a matching shirt, and did a model's pirouette for his inspection.

Patrick said if she kept twirling like that, he'd try to persuade her to stay, and leave the rest to her imagination.

'My imagination,' she replied, 'is already working overtime. Which is why I'm out of here.'

'One more twirl,' Patrick suggested.

She told him to cool it and fled. Soon afterwards Patrick had a call from Mr Goldsworthy. The files relating to the family had proved to be worth a look.

'One or two items,' he said in his dry and courteous way, 'if you could spare the time, Mr Conway, I feel sure you'd be interested.'

Patrick spent most of the day at the Leatherhead Historical Society, in a quiet room Mr Goldsworthy had arranged for him, reading through the folder of cuttings about Georgina Rickson and her forebears. It was a bulky, informative file. He learnt that the Ricksons had become one of the wealthiest families in Surrey, an affluence that derived from an event in the eighteenth century when a young man, a carter, chanced upon the village of Leatherhead. His horse had broken down, forcing him to take lodgings for a few nights. His landlady was a buxom widow, and the young man found her responsive to his advances. He sold his cart and stayed with her, marrying and establishing a small back-street brickyard.

During his lifetime it remained a modest business; it was to be his children and grandchildren who reaped the benefit. In the industrial surge of the nineteenth century the tiny firm became a prosperous enterprise as London spread southward across the Thames into burgeoning suburbs. Bricks were essential for this expansion. The middle classes were in search of a better lifestyle, demanding fresh air and green fields in which to raise their families. They could not find this in the clustered terraces of Chelsea, nor afford the spacious luxury of Hampstead. So they came south, where Albert Rickson, after inheriting the firm and marrying a young woman from Hampshire with a good dowry and wide hips for child-bearing, set about creating his own dynasty.

By the early years of the twentieth century, at the age of forty, Rickson was an influential and patriarchal figure. He and his wife had five healthy children: three boys sent to Cranley College near

Guildford (a good, no-nonsense school he called it, dismissing Eton and Harrow as overrated snob factories) and two younger daughters, the girls having a private education and being nurtured in the graces of gentility. He was the owner of the district's finest house, with twelve acres of river land. He was admired and widely known. The prime minister Lloyd George came to visit, creating a minor scandal by bringing one of his mistresses, and he asked Albert Rickson to stand for parliament.

Rickson declined. His aptitude for business told him there was far more benefit being elected to the local council, where he became a leading figure and, in due course, the mayor. He had no desire to be a backbencher at Westminster, or to spend valuable time in London away from his work and his family. He took great pride in his sons, bringing them into the business as soon as they left school. 'Bricks,' he was quoted as saying, 'are the backbone of Britain. My lads are best working at their trade, not reading up at university. Let others study the books. We'll build the future.'

He had big plans for expansion, and vigilant ones for the preservation of his family wealth. Lawyers structured his estate so that all three sons would each inherit a section of his empire; he had no liking for the 'eldest takes all' philosophy of the upper classes. As for his daughters, they'd be suitably provided for, and would doubtless marry well.

Less than ten years later this utopian dream was in ruins and the family had been devastated. All three sons, who'd promptly answered the call to the colours – as Rickson so proudly declared in 1914 amid the first flush of patriotic fervour – were dead.

Bertie, the first born, was killed by a sniper at Ypres; the second son died of wounds received in the battle of the Somme, and the youngest, after a year in the trenches then invalided out with an extreme case of shell shock, was hit and killed by a bus while drunk and trying to cross Piccadilly.

Patrick was hardly aware of the day passing, engrossed in these bleak fragments of tragedy from long-ago newspapers. The two daughters were rarely mentioned. There was a tiny paragraph taken from the *Surrey Gazette* that Miss Rickson, eldest daughter of the Mayor and Mrs Rickson, who had suffered grievous family losses as their readers would know, had joined the Voluntary Aid Detachment and was shortly to leave for service in France. It gave no first name, nor did it say if the eldest daughter was Georgina or Henrietta. Patrick could find no mention in the same newspaper of her return when the war ended.

One thing was clear from the press reports: Albert Rickson had never recovered from these crushing blows. He had resigned from the local council after a speech reported as 'unusual', in which he declared the wild and irresponsible recruiting campaign – the ferocious demand for men not to be shirkers, and the strident call for enlistment – had led half the country's best young men to untimely deaths. It was a scandalous waste, akin to murder, and he blamed the government. He blamed Lloyd George.

On another occasion, termed 'an unruly public incident', he made an angry speech in the main street of the town and blamed others also. He was scathing about Lord Kitchener, angry at the erratic campaigns of Winston Churchill and scornful of the tactics of Sir Douglas Haig. As for the vigilante mobs of women indiscriminately handing out white feathers, he asserted that they were deranged, and not fit to look at themselves in their own mirrors.

Rickson sold the brickworks, and after that rarely left the grounds of his home. He died a still-wealthy recluse in 1925, and apart from a formal death notice, Patrick could find no community tributes – not even an obituary. It seemed strange he could have been so utterly forgotten after his retreat from public life. Patrick felt sure it was the angry tirade, the 'unusual' speeches that had made him a pariah for the rest of his life, and even pursued him to the grave.

His wife's death came ten years later, and according to a notation made beside this by Mr Goldsworthy, records showed the two daughters had jointly inherited the Rickson wealth and the Lodge. The same handwriting added a footnote regarding another branch of the family: Albert Rickson had one sibling, a younger brother who had moved away from Leatherhead after the war. Apparently neither brother nor their families had ever been close.

The research had been painstakingly gathered at considerable trouble, and Patrick went to offer his thanks.

'Glad to have been of help,' Goldsworthy said. 'Got quite absorbed myself. Awfully sad the way things happen to families.'

'Especially *this* family.' Patrick was still stunned by the extent of their tragedy. 'I'd say Rickson died of a broken heart.'

'I'd agree. There must have been a great many broken hearts at that time, Mr Conway. All those fine young men dead, the best part of a generation, and a lot of widows as a result. So many young women with no one to wed, and no choice but to remain spinsters or maiden aunts.'

'Which is my next job, I guess. Find out if either sister married . . . and any other details I can.'

'I hope you don't mind but I took the liberty of telephoning the General Registry Office,' the older man said. 'Amazing how the mention of your BBC venture gets such a quick result,' he added slyly. 'I usually have to wait days for an answer to enquiries like this. But here it is, a fax came through just half an hour ago.'

He took it from his pocket and handed it to Patrick, who read the birth certificates of both sisters and the death certificate of one, and could not help showing his disappointment.

'Not what you were hoping for?'

'Not quite. This says that Henrietta Rickson was the older sister, by six years. So it looks like she's the one who went to France as a volunteer nurse.'

'In view of the gap in ages, she has to be.'

'But according to these records she died in 1956.'

'Is that a problem?'

'It's a puzzle, Mr Goldsworthy. Our family was sent a letter eight years after that. From Georgina Rickson. I assumed she was the nurse and that's how they'd met. An elderly neighbour who knew both sisters thought so too.'

'The neighbour's mistaken. Look at her birth date. Georgina had only just turned sixteen when the war ended. The VAD were strict – they would never have accepted a girl that age.'

'No possibility?'

'None. But I did notice there's no date of death on this. Which has to suggest that Georgina is still alive.'

Patrick stared at him. 'Is that likely?'

'Very likely, I'd say. Or it would have been listed. They're most meticulous about any personal detail, particularly that one.'

'She'd be a hundred!'

'Not quite.' Goldsworthy chuckled. 'After all, the Queen Mother's a good example of longevity. Perhaps your Miss Rickson is of the same calibre.'

'It'd be impossible to find her.'

'Difficult, I imagine. Not necessarily impossible.'

'How?'

'The estate agent, Tom Rutledge, who handled the sale of the Lodge is still in business. He has an office in Church Street.'

'Do you know him?'

'I bought my house from him. We meet occasionally and have a pint together. Shall I give him a call?'

They met an hour later. Patrick said no one was to put his hand in his pocket; this was his shout. He'd have a light beer as he was driving, but how about a couple of large scotches for his guests?

'A pint's my tipple,' Tom Rutledge said. He was a robust man with alert blue eyes and neatly cropped grey hair. 'Here's the only address I had for Miss Rickson after the estate was sold.' Patrick took it, with a nod of thanks. 'Mind you, I haven't heard from her in years, so I can't say where she might be now. She was very upset about the demolition. So was I. We had no idea the buyer would go to the council, and that they'd allow that development.'

'I'd say money changed hands,' Mr Goldsworthy offered.

'Very likely,' the agent agreed. 'Nothing we could do to stop it, but at least Georgina did get a good price for the property.' He turned to Patrick. 'I hear you're working on some story about the family, for a film?'

The barman came with their drinks, which gave Patrick time to carefully consider his answer.

'I'm hoping so. But like property sales, Tom, we never know about films until the cheque is in.'

'Too true,' Rutledge said.

'And I don't mean in the mail . . . I mean firmly in the bank.'

'Even truer!' Rutledge chuckled, and downed the rest of his pint. Patrick bought them each another round.

'Also,' Patrick added, 'it depends if I can find Miss Rickson.'

'If she is alive, her niece would know.'

'Niece?'

'Her only living relative. That address I gave you. It's the niece's house in Esher. Georgina went to live there.'

Helen West was a thin woman in her fifties, with hair that had been dyed blonde too often and was now a nondescript beige colour with black roots. She was far from welcoming, and reluctant to even talk about her aunt. Her house was outside the town, from where they could hear the drone of traffic on the bypass to Portsmouth.

'Who are you, and what do you want with Aunt George?'

Patrick introduced himself and Claire who'd accompanied him, but Mrs West appeared to have no intention of inviting them across the threshold. It was a two-storey house with mock-Tudor beams, much of it covered by concrete stucco. Patrick tried to conceal his instinctive dislike of the house and its owner.

'Miss Rickson was a friend of my grandfather,' he said, 'and the agent who sold her family home kindly gave me this address.'

'Did he indeed?' Mrs West replied coldly. 'That's like his cheek. He had no right to do so.'

'Is there a problem?'

'Yes, I think there is,' she said. 'The whereabouts of my Aunt George is none of Rutledge's business. He got his commission when the Lodge went to the highest bidder, and that's twenty-five years ago. He did quite nicely out of us, and we've not had even a Christmas card from him since.'

'Did you want one?' Claire asked politely.

'Who are you?'

'Mr Conway's assistant. He's researching a film about the Rickson family, hoping to make it as a drama for the BBC.'

Her unblinking gaze moved from Claire to Patrick, a new air of calculation now apparent.

'I'm a Rickson,' she said, 'or I was before marriage. I don't think you could do anything like that unless you get some sort of signed agreement from the family.'

'That's the usual procedure. Obviously I wouldn't attempt it without consent,' Patrick responded, 'but nor would I bother to continue unless I can find Georgina Rickson.'

'Well, she's not here,' the woman replied abruptly. 'Mr Rutledge was correct. She did live here, but she's no longer with me.'

'Did she die?' he asked.

'No, she just got old and became difficult. Like some people do in their dotage.'

Then she's alive, Patrick realised. He tried to contain his elation and to remain conciliatory in the face of this belligerence, but was finding it difficult. 'May I know where she is?'

'It'll do you no good.'

'Why is that, Mrs West?'

'Because if you want to talk about the family, she can hardly be expected to discuss what she can't remember.'

'You mean she has Alzheimer's?'

'I believe they prefer the term dementia. It's supposed to sound less threatening. Besides, if you're talking about permission and so forth, what's the point of seeing her? She can't sign anything. I'm her only living relative and the heir to her estate. So I suggest you don't bother poor old George with things she won't understand . . . just discuss it with me.'

'I think we'll leave it,' Patrick decided his only recourse was to bluff. 'I have other projects, and this is clearly a waste of time.'

'Hang on a minute!' Mrs West was not prepared for this. Despite her uncompromising attitude, she wanted to find out what was involved. 'Your lady friend just said it's for the BBC –'

'My *assistant*, actually, and she said we're in the research stage. Which means an early stage. If I don't meet with the only remaining member of the family, we move on and abandon this project.'

'I'm the only remaining member of the family!'

'I mean the *direct* family. Those who lived at the Lodge.'

'And if she's gaga, lying there like some old fossil?'

'You clearly don't like her very much, do you?' Patrick's tone was terse. For the first time Mrs West appeared to recognise that she might have exceeded the bounds of civility.

'You'd better come in, if you want,' she said reluctantly, 'it looks like it's going to pour down with rain any minute.'

Patrick was about to refuse. Only a faint pressure of Claire's hand on his arm made him change his mind. They went into a front room occupied by a floral lounge suite. Artificial leadlight windows felt the first splatters of rain as Mrs West suggested they sit down.

'Don't like her, is that what you said? It's not a question of *like*. You mentioned the Lodge. The famous Lodge. Do you know we were never invited there? Our side of the family, I mean - we never existed as far as they were concerned. Like chalk and cheese, the Ricksons. My father always said his brother Albert couldn't give tuppence for us. Same with his daughters. Pair of old spinsters, they had that great big house, just them alone after the parents died. Never invited me to stay. Their only niece, their only living relative in the world, but they had no interest in me. Not until she was old and stuck there on her own, unable to cope and needing help. Then

I tried to overlook the snubs of the past and took her in. And what did it get me?'

She continued before either could reply. 'I'll tell you what. It got me a difficult old woman who spent her time complaining – about the size of this house, the size of her room, the pokey garden. She was used to better things, and made it obvious. It cost me my husband, who packed his things and went off. Couldn't stand another minute of the old bat, he said, but he didn't tell me he was leaving with his secretary, and they'd been having it off since she came to work for him. Truth to tell, I didn't mind it, seeing the back of him. I was only forty – I could've had a bit of a life. But there was eighty-year-old Auntie George . . . who was likely to barge in if I brought anyone home, and who was starting to forget if she'd been to the loo or not. What do you think that did for my hopes of a new life?'

'Not a lot, I imagine,' Claire said with some sympathy.

'And then there was the lawyer.'

'Whose lawyer?' Patrick asked.

'Hers. Peacock & Marsh, in Epsom. Albert Rickson had them in his day, and the solicitors who run it now still handle the estate. He left a will that imposed strict conditions on his daughters, so they told me. I went to see them, to say I'd sell this house and buy a bigger place that she'd like better, if I could have an advance on my inheritance. One of them said a clause in the will would not allow my drawing on the legacy. A protective clause he called it.'

The rain had increased to a downpour. Dark clouds outside the window made the living room gloomy. Mrs West switched on a lamp beside her chair, raising her voice over the sound of the storm. Her lips were compressed, her mouth like a trap.

'Protective clause! I found that insulting. I said I was the one who needed protection. I told him she forgets to dress, forgets to bathe, she stinks and I can't stand it any more. He tried to lay down the law, saying the will only allowed money to be spent on her welfare. So I said I'd had a basinful, and for her welfare *and mine*, I was putting her in an old people's home. At least he couldn't object to *that*.' She stared at Patrick with a glare of outright hostility. 'Blame me if you like, but how could anyone your age understand?'

'I'm not blaming you,' Patrick said, 'I'm just asking to see her, and wondering why you won't allow it.'

'You'd be wasting your time, I already told you that.'

'But it's *my* time, Mrs West. So if you could tell me where . . . I could organise it.'

'It's not that simple. I'll have to make arrangements.'

'I don't want to put you to any trouble.'

'There's no other way. They require proper notice of a visit. I had great difficulty finding a suitable place. They were either full up or far too costly. Nothing's easy, nowadays.'

'Then may I phone you tomorrow?' Patrick was carefully patient now that she seemed to be consenting to his request.

'As long as it's in the morning,' she replied, rising to indicate it was time for them to leave. 'I play bridge of an afternoon. Mind you, I never get decent cards, never have any luck, but I play just the same. I mean, at my age, in view of the hand life's dealt me, what else is there?'

'No wonder the husband shot through,' Patrick said later, driving back to town. 'Talk about belligerent, she was like a bulldog. I felt any minute she'd start to bark.'

'Don't be awful,' Claire said.

'I thought I was fairly restrained, considering.'

'You were. But I daresay Georgina Rickson did hate that house, after the kind of place she'd spent her life in. So perhaps she was difficult.'

'She had money,' Patrick said. 'The family estate, and the sale of the Lodge. I can't imagine why she didn't find somewhere better to live.'

'On her own,' Claire reminded him, 'growing old and alone after her sister died, she turned to the only family she had. And I suspect at first, with prospects of that inheritance in mind, her niece made her welcome.'

'Oh, friendly bomb, descend on Slough', the poet John Betjeman once wrote, and Patrick, as he left the M4 motorway and headed into Slough's gaunt industrial area, understood what had prompted this caustic line. It had not been a good journey. He had followed Mrs West's explicit directions to the nursing home, which proceeded to get him lost, and finally he had to pull into a pub near Windsor to ask the way.

'Englefield Green?' the publican said. 'Blimey, you did get a bum steer. About ten miles back at the interchange; if you'd taken the M25 you'd be there by now. Probably been there ten minutes ago.'

Patrick bought a beer and thanked him. 'After Englefield Green, I have to find a place called Clarendon Palace Gardens.'

'Dunno that; it sounds posh,' the publican replied. 'I'll draw you a map to Englefield. From there you're on your own.'

Following the sketch, it was soon clear how thoroughly Helen West had misled him. Patrick wondered if he was becoming paranoid about the woman, for he suspected it was deliberate. It had taken her two days to get a decision on his visit. She claimed the nursing home was discussing the matter, unsure if her aunt was well enough to see strangers.

Patrick did not voice his disbelief. He did not know the name of the home and with no means of finding out, she controlled the situation. She'd added if they did agree to his visit, he must go alone and not take his friend. The implication was intentionally provocative, but he managed to keep his temper.

Then that morning, she rang to say he had an appointment for today. He must be there by eleven. It was already nine-thirty, and he had to listen to her directions which had added half an hour to his journey. It was clear he would be noticeably late, and felt certain that was what she intended.

He drove around the perimeter of Windsor Great Park, then along a winding road that led to Englefield Green, a bleak region of mainly council flats. Graffiti abounded. Children kicked a football in the street. One shouted at him to get his sodding motor off their pitch. After passing through another village, Patrick took a minor road that led him to the retirement home.

Clarendon Palace Gardens was a name that had been carefully selected to impress. The publican had thought it sounded posh. Doubtless it looked good on brochures and letterhead, but the reality on first sight was shockingly different. Patrick was stunned and revolted. He couldn't think of a more inappropriate name. It was no palace and there was not a garden in sight. The grounds were filled with archaic breezeblock buildings; they might once have been army huts, for they conveyed the impression of a wartime barracks. Nothing could have prepared him for this; he felt disgust that elderly citizens had paid to live out the remaining years of their lives in this awful place.

In the shabby front hall of what had been the original house was a row of plastic chairs for visitors. A desk contained a sign: ADMINISTRATOR. A middle-aged woman in a shapeless cardigan sat engrossed in writing out what seemed to be a roster. Patrick waited patiently for her to acknowledge him.

'Miss Georgina Rickson,' he said, when she finally put aside her task. She asked his name, frowned and consulted a schedule, telling him he was late.

'Not too late, I hope,' Patrick responded.

'The appointment was for eleven. I made that quite clear to Mrs West, the niece. We have strict meal times which are followed by rest periods. That's compulsory, on doctors orders. I'm sorry, Mr Conway, but I did tell her that.'

'She forgot to tell *me*.' Patrick explained that he'd unluckily got lost. He did hope they could stretch a point on this occasion, as he'd come from Australia to see her.

'All that way?' She seemed surprised, and less severe. She said Miss Rickson's niece lived half an hour away at Esher, but hadn't been to see her for ages. Literally for years. In fact, the staff were talking about it recently – all the time she'd been here, poor Georgie had only two visits from Mrs West, who had brought a bunch of wilted flowers on each occasion.

'They beg for a place in here, because our charges are so low,' she said, 'then they hardly ever bother to turn up afterwards. Not on birthdays, not even at Christmas. Some of these old people are just simply abandoned and left to rot. It's a real disgrace.'

She called an assistant to take her place at the desk, saying she'd show Patrick the way. Miss Rickson was in Block 24. To Patrick it sounded more like *Stalag* 24. As they went past the rows of make-shift buildings that served as the wards, his designation of the place as a prison camp seemed even less fanciful.

They entered a long bungalow accommodating forty people. The walls inside were unlined; what appeared to be a coat of kalsomine painted on the breezeblock was the only attempt at decoration, and although it was a warm day outside the building was chilly. It felt surreal. In rows of beds far too close together were elderly men and women, with almost no privacy between them. Two nurses sat chatting at the end of the ward. The pervasive smell of Dettol was unmistakable.

'It's the best we can do,' the administrator confessed, aware of Patrick's look of disbelief. 'We don't profess to be up-market, despite the rather fancy name the owners gave it. There are a great many places like this around the country, for those in low-income groups. People who simply can't afford anything else.'

'But she's a wealthy woman!'

'Miss Rickson? No, I'm sorry, that's not correct. We were told there's hardly any money.'

'Then you were told a lie,' Patrick declared. He didn't even know this elderly woman, but felt an impotent rage at the unworthy way she had been treated. 'I assure you, she can certainly afford something better than this *Gulag*! I apologise for that expression, but it's quite wrong for her to be here. She's entitled to better. She's been robbed of the last part of her life, and that's more than a disgrace, it's an outrage.'

'That may be so, Mr Conway, but are you a relative?'

'No,' he had to admit.

'Then I don't think there's anything you can do. She's very old now, in her late nineties, and remembers nothing of her life. But if, as you say, she's been robbed of the last part of it, that's very sad.'

'More than sad. It's illegal and grossly unfair.'

'Perhaps it is. However there's no possible way you or I can alter it. That's entirely the business of her next of kin.'

'I know, but –'

'But nothing, Mr Conway. I've bent the rules to allow this visit, so please don't make a fuss. It won't help.' She pointed to the rows of somnolent figures. 'You'll find her in bed eighteen,' she said, and abruptly left him.

Patrick saw the beds were numbered. He walked slowly down the ward – he had to think of it as a ward, although it was truly more like a cell block – and stood at the foot of bed eighteen. One of the nurses stopped chatting as she caught his eye. She seemed surprised, and came towards him.

'Miss Rickson?' he asked.

She nodded, pointing at the dozing figure beneath a blanket. 'That's the one. George, they call her,' the nurse confided. 'She was one of the famous Roses of No-Mans-Land in Flanders. Not much like a rose now, poor old thing.'

Patrick didn't try to correct her. He went and sat beside the bed. She seemed to be asleep: she could as easily be dead. Her face was leathered by age, yet it looked strangely peaceful.

'Georgina,' he said softly, 'can you hear me? I've come a long way to see you.'

There was no response. Then the old eyes blinked opened. They stayed on him, unfocused and confused, until at last there came an instant of clarity and surprise, with the dawning of what seemed like recognition.

'Stephen!' she whispered, and before he could deny this, she reached out a hand to hold his. Hers was tiny and wrinkled, with liver-brown age spots and fingers bent out of shape by arthritis. 'My dear, dear Stephen. You don't look even a day older.'

Chapter Fourteen

When Patrick left Clarendon Palace Gardens he found it difficult to drive, he was so disturbed. The priority, he knew, must be to somehow get Georgina out of there, but how to accomplish that with Mrs West as next of kin was beyond his comprehension. How anyone could treat an elderly relative in such a way appalled him.

It had been a strange few hours. The staff were sympathetic. The nurse who overheard her mistake him for Stephen said it was the first time poor old George had spoken for weeks.

'Just when you think they're really gone,' she said, 'no mind or memory left, something like this happens. So who was Stephen?'

'My grandfather,' Patrick explained. 'He was with the Australian army in France in the 1914 war.'

The nurse seized on this. 'Then they must've met when she was one of the Roses of No-Man's-Land!' she decided, and once again he did not correct her. As it seemed to be Georgina's only mark of distinction in this place, why deprive her of it?

'Perhaps they did,' he replied.

'Do you think there was a romance?' she asked.

Patrick said he had no idea. The nurse clearly liked the idea of a romance, saying he could stay as long as he liked, never mind the rules. Meanwhile she'd tell Mrs Greenfield, the administrator, about what had happened. They all had a soft spot for Georgie, she said, partly because they felt she had been unfairly abandoned by her family, but mostly because she had once been a Rose.

When she had hurried off Patrick remained by the bedside, but Georgina's eyes had closed again. After that brief moment of lucidity she had drifted back into her private state of oblivion. He kept a gentle hold of the frail hands while he continued to talk to her, but there was no response to either his voice or touch.

Mrs Greenfield arrived, clearly well informed. She said Kitty, the nurse, had been thrilled. 'It seems that your grandfather and George were lovers.'

'Kitty the nurse has jumped to her own conclusions,' Patrick replied. 'They certainly knew each other at some stage in their lives, but I don't know if it was in the biblical sense.'

'But you can't be sure?' Mrs Greenfield smiled. It made her seem younger, Patrick thought, and he returned a smile.

'No. But I suppose it'll become local folklore, at least among the nurses. The Rose and the Aussie soldier.'

'You wouldn't mind, would you?'

'Not in the least,' Patrick said. 'I just wish she'd been able to say a little more, but there's been nothing since. Not a word, not even a physical response.'

'Sometimes it's like that. A moment or two, after weeks or even years. Some tiny trigger brings back a trace of memory. Do you think you resemble your grandfather?'

'I've never thought so. But I've only seen one photo of him. He was about twenty at the time, and his digger's hat covered half his face. I'm not sure how he looked when he was my age.'

'Did she know him then – I mean after the war?'

'Yes,' Patrick replied, aware of the other's eyes on his face, and her interest in his answer. 'I think she did.'

'I might be able to find you some photographs. George had a few when the niece brought her here. I seem to remember she came with little else: some clothes, hardly any possessions.'

'How long ago was that, Mrs Greenfield? How many years has Miss Rickson been in this place?'

There was a pause. The other appeared uneasy. 'I'd have to look it up,' she replied, but Patrick sensed this was a prevarication.

'How long?' he repeated quietly, and this time her eyes did not evade his gaze.

'Soon after I started here. Fifteen years ago.' She paused, sighing. 'Had we known the truth, I'm sure we wouldn't have accepted her. And doubtless you feel she'd have been better off.'

'I'd like to talk to you about that. Do you think it'd be possible to have her moved? I don't mean to be offensive, but –'

'You're not being offensive. But I think it'd be difficult. You'd have Mrs West to contend with, and the problem of finding a new home at short notice.' She shrugged and added, 'I just work here, so there's no self-interest. We'd easily fill the bed, but that's not the point. Think about it. Do you imagine she'll know the least difference? Will she feel any better?'

I know *I* will, Patrick thought, and felt she read his mind. 'Think carefully, please, Mr Conway, before you broach it with the niece. We could discuss it more fully, if you'd like to come back to see Georgina again?'

'Tomorrow,' Patrick said, 'with your permission.'

'Tomorrow would be fine,' the administrator confirmed. 'I'll ask the girls to check her locker. The photos should be there.'

Patrick thanked her. Before leaving he bent and touched his lips to Georgina's shrunken cheek. 'I'll be back tomorrow,' he whispered, but there was no response. No sign that she heard or felt anything.

To Patrick's surprise, Claire supported Mrs Greenfield's opinion. That night after she returned from work they walked through Hyde Park to the restaurant on the Serpentine. Below them on the lake families in rowing boats were making the most of the twilight. Claire and Patrick watched from a table on the terrace, where they ordered drinks while she listened to his denunciation of the place.

Not only was it a disgraceful dump that should never have been registered for aged care, but the administrator had confessed the owners kept her on a really tight budget, and they, Mrs Greenfield had reluctantly admitted, were a group of Harley Street specialists.

'Rich bloody doctors!' he exclaimed angrily, 'what do you think of that?'

'I think it's deplorable,' Claire said.

'That's too kind a word. It's fucking outrageous!' Patrick gave it emphasis by thumping his fist on the table. An adjacent couple looked across as if speculating on what was happening. A waiter brought their drinks as though nothing had occurred.

Claire waited until he had gone. 'It is outrageous,' she agreed, 'but if you make a fuss, Mrs Greenfield probably gets the sack and it sounds like the place might be worse without her. As far as moving a patient in that condition, I think she's right. Poor Georgina won't have the faintest idea she's in a better home. She may even feel unsettled.'

'So I shouldn't do anything?' Patrick hadn't expected this.

'I'm sure you want to,' Claire answered, 'but apart from anything else, Helen West is bound to kick up an almighty stink.'

'Mrs West,' he retorted, 'might get a very nasty shock.'

'Patrick, she's a relative. What standing do you have?'

'None. But how would Miss Rickson's lawyers feel, I wonder?'

'Her lawyers?'

'Peacock & Marsh, in Epsom. The firm who handles the Rickson estate. What happens if I blow the whistle, and tell them of the conditions their client has been living in for fifteen years? Filthy, revolting, third-rate, third-world conditions. All to save money so Mrs West gets a bigger payday from the inheritance. The tabloids would kill for that kind of story.'

Claire stared at him. 'They would,' she granted.

'So what does a respectable old firm of solicitors do about it, confronted by that? Don't they have some duty of care?'

'You've been thinking about this ever since you left there.'

'Look, I don't blame the staff. I blame Helen West, and a mob of bloated Harley Street quacks. The thought that a bunch of doctors own that shit heap is disgusting.'

'Patrick, I know you're angry –'

'Bloody oath I am!' he said heatedly, almost banging the table again, until he caught a glint of amusement in her eye, sensed the interest of neighbouring diners and restrained himself. 'Truly, I've never felt like this,' he continued more quietly, 'Georgina Rickson may be ninety-seven or -eight, very frail and unable to remember her life, but she has some rights. She shouldn't be in a place that looks like a derelict army camp. That woman in Esher . . . the nasty, greedy bitch . . . I'm sorry, Claire, if I'm making us the floor show, but yes, I've never felt this angry about anything.'

'Don't be sorry for that,' she said and took his hands, ignoring another waiter alongside them, his pad and pencil poised hopefully for their order.

'I'll come back,' the waiter said, but they barely heard him.

'Don't be sorry,' Claire repeated and kept holding Patrick's hands while gazing at him. She wished she'd been there today. She wanted to share his anger, this deep concern at the way an old lady he'd never met before had been treated. She could think of many people who'd walk away, uncaring. But not this man.

It happens to me across restaurants tables, she thought: if the dinner table in Belgium had begun something, what the hell was happening here tonight? It's too soon to feel like this, she tried to tell herself, but knew exactly how she felt.

'I wish you'd been with me today,' Patrick said, echoing her thoughts. 'Tomorrow, if I can't get her out of there, at least I'm going to somehow try to improve the way she's treated.'

'How, Patrick?'

'I don't know yet. If all else fails, maybe try the lawyer blackmail. Use Peacock & Marsh as a bargaining chip. Anything, just to get her a clean, decent bed – and a bit of personal space.'

I'm in love with you, Claire wanted to say, but knew she couldn't. Instead she asked, 'Can I come with you tomorrow?'

'What about work? Can you spin your boss another story?'

'I'll think of something,' she promised with a smile. 'I'm good at that. And I want to meet Georgina.'

. . . And spend every minute of each day together with you in the short time we have left, she could have added, but did not say this either.

They stayed late, drank a second bottle of wine and walked back arm in arm and slightly unsteadily across the park to the hotel. The desk clerk gave them the key with his practised smile and a sly look that undressed Claire. The lift grumbled its way upstairs. There was a message on the mobile from Joanna.

'I'll have a shower,' Claire quickly said, and left him alone.

'Hello, darling!' Joanna's voice sound excited. 'We wrapped last night. Great fabulous piss-up party, and everyone's mad about the movie. We'll have a rough-cut edited and ready to show the studio nabobs in a week.

'Now, *big* news. I've found us *the* apartment. Don't complain you hate moving until you get a load of this place. Tomorrow expect an email with photos. You'll love it, and you can either sell Neutral Bay or keep it and use it as your office. My accountant says hanging on to it might make sense, because he's sure property will go gang-busters after the Olympics.

'Nothing much else, sweetie. Oh yes, I've definitely decided to trade in the car for something a bit more up-market. Send you a photo of that tomorrow too. Hope you're all geared up to take on the BBC. I'm feeling a bit lively tonight, spring is in the air, you know the feeling. Pity you're not here. Just keep thinking *amorosa*, darling, but save it strictly for me. Love you. Call me when you see the pics of the fabulous joint we just *have* to live in.'

They made good time along the motorway, and this time left it at the M25 interchange. Although Patrick had prepared Claire for the nursing home to some extent, he was aware of her shock as they drove into the grim institution that made such a mockery of the name Clarendon Palace Gardens.

In the hall they were met by Mrs Greenfield where Claire seemed to pass scrutiny. It was that sort of day, Patrick thought, something to do with the more clement weather. A real September day: vivid blue skies with wisps of white cloud drifting overhead. There was even an improvement in Block 24. The bed linen had been changed, and a screen placed around Georgina's bed. She had been bathed and her hair washed. She wore a fresh nightgown, brightly patterned instead of yesterday's drab calico.

'She woke this morning and asked if Stephen was here,' Kitty the nurse told them. 'It's brilliant!' she confided to Claire. 'Not a peep since last Christmas, and today she spoke about somewhere called the Lodge. Even said she might go home there soon.'

'It was pulled down years ago,' Claire explained, and Kitty shrugged and said well, it was still progress – of a sort. They all knew it was a bit optimistic to expect miracles at this stage.

She brought an extra chair for Claire, and they sat either side of the bed. The day that had begun so well became one of gradual frustration. Patrick talked softly, he stroked her frail hands, but she remained unresponsive. Her eyes, when they opened, studied him blankly as if he was some puzzling stranger. At times they moved to Claire with a look of equal bafflement. After an hour of this they began to wonder if they were frightening her.

Mrs Greenfield came to ask how they were getting on.

'Not too well,' Patrick said.

'I might be upsetting her,' Claire added quietly, 'I feel she keeps wondering who I am.'

'I think she's just tired out,' the administrator replied. 'She was so alert for a moment this morning. We all got excited, and what with the bath and having her hair washed . . . perhaps we overdid it. Why not get some fresh air, and let her sleep a while?'

They went outside with her. She asked if Patrick had any further thoughts about trying to move Georgina.

'I talked it over with Miss Thomas, but she doesn't think it's a good idea. She agrees with you it'd be too stressful.'

Mrs Greenfield nodded with renewed approval at Claire. 'If she was younger, in a less advanced stage, it might be worthwhile. But I suspect a row with Mrs West might be the only outcome.'

'Nobody wants that,' Patrick said. 'But can I talk to you about shifting her to a small ward? Something more private. Is that possible, without us bothering Mrs West?'

The administrator said it would be possible. A single cubicle was more expensive, but she felt it could be arranged without additional payment. The least they could do for someone who had nursed the wounded in France, and lived through an entire century.

'And I haven't forgotten the photographs,' she added. 'I'll have the nurses check her locker when they've finished lunch rounds. If you're wishing to leave, I could post them.'

'I thought we'd have a snack at the village pub,' Patrick told her, 'and after that, if you don't mind, try another visit. Just a few moments, in case she remembers.'

They drove through narrow lanes fringed by hedgerows, and found a small pub opposite a village green. There were tables in the shade of a big oak tree. Sitting there, Claire watched as Patrick carried out their pints of lager, reflecting on how much her life had changed in little more than a week. Almost too rapidly, she thought, but after all, lives can alter in a few moments, or a single glance . . . If not, then what on earth would songwriters do for romantic lyrics? 'Enchanted evenings' . . . 'My heart stood still' . . . all that sort of stuff.

'You're smiling,' Patrick said. 'Secret thoughts?'

'Song lyrics.' She smiled again. 'Silly thoughts,' and touched her glass against his in the way they'd done since the first evening after the Menin Gate. She had something she wanted to broach, and right now seemed as good a time as any.

'Patrick, any idea how long before you go home?'

'Depends on the meeting next week. Maybe ten days. Or less, if things go pear-shaped.'

Such a short time, she thought, but she kept her smile in place. 'Are they paying for your hotel, or are you?'

'They won't pay a cent till everything's settled. I cover all expenses and my hotel. Which is why it's such a crappy place!'

'It is a bit,' she agreed, 'and not especially cheap.'

'Nothing is in this city. But I can claim it against tax. Or pay myself back from the budget if I get the show on the road.' He smiled at her. 'It's a risk any dumb TV writer who gets ideas above his station and wants to be a film producer has to take.'

'I have an idea – nothing to do with tax deductions. Why not check out of that flophouse and stay at my place?'

'Because –' he paused, realising it would be a big step and might presage a big commitment. He took a sip of beer to delay replying.

'Because you don't want to be tied down?'

'You didn't mention tying down. Is that included?'

'Shut up,' she said. 'Be serious. It's such a brief time, and I'd like us to spend it together. No desk clerks, no sly looks from the cleaners, just us. Fulham's a fun place. We could stroll down to the World's End and have a jar. Do you know the pub at the World's End?'

'One of my favourite watering holes when I lived here.'

'So . . . will you come and stay with me?'

'Claire, I'd like to. I'd really like it very much.'

'Thank you,' she said softly, 'you've just made my day.'

He felt a strange warmth at this, a rush of such affection that it took him by surprise. He reached for her hand and held it to his lips. A boy running past at the time stopped to gaze at this.

'I've seen 'em do that stuff on the telly,' he called out. 'Is she your fancy woman?'

'On your bike, sport,' Patrick retorted, and as the boy ran to tell a group of his friends Claire laughed happily and they touched glasses again.

They shared a ploughman's lunch. When the boy and his friends left, waving to them and making extravagant hand-kissing gestures they cheerfully waved back then lingered over coffee. There was no rush. The sky was clear, even the wisps of cloud had vanished as they drove back to the nursing home.

An ambulance was parked at the entrance to the main house. Kitty, the young nurse, was in tears. Paramedics came past with a body on a stretcher. Kitty told them that George had passed away; it must have been only a few minutes after they had driven off. It was very peaceful; she had shut her eyes and died so quietly that for a long while no one even noticed.

Mrs Greenfield was genuinely upset. She told them she found it so difficult, these sudden deaths. Although you were surrounded by people so old and infirm that death was expected, when it came it was always sad, often devastating. Most particularly Georgina, who had been a woman of some station in life, wrongly abandoned here, with only two perfunctory visits by her niece in fifteen years until Patrick's arrival. It was doubly sad, because they had prepared a nice cubicle room, clean sheets and a more comfortable bed. And it seemed desperately unfair she should die just when fragments of returning memory might have given, if not a new lease of life, then at least a few precious moments of recollection.

She spoke for the nurses, she told them. It was more than the end of one life. A piece of the past had gone today. Their Rose of No-Man's-Land was now dead, and they all felt the loss. Those young women, Mrs Greenfield said, were so brave, quite unique. From a country that didn't even allow its women the vote at that time, leaving their middle-class and sheltered lives, they had gone willingly to France as volunteers. They went to care for the wounded and the dying; they lived in tents and were often in the front-line under shell-fire. Some were killed, most came home damaged by the frightful experience. They were a special kind of young woman: very gallant, and she had been greatly privileged to know even one of them.

After this moving eulogy, Patrick had no wish to disillusion her that the older sister had been the Rose and Georgina herself still a schoolgirl at the time. So he remained silent, while Mrs Greenfield produced a cardboard box of photos the nurses had retrieved. There were a number of Rickson family snaps, including the two sisters as young children which revealed the six-year age gap.

There was also one of Stephen. Identified by his name on the back, written in the same distinct hand as Georgina's letter, it instantly dispelled any possibility he had been killed in the war. Patrick studied it, captivated. His grandfather wore civilian clothes and stood in front of a Ford car that belonged to an era at least fifteen years after hostilities had ended. He seemed to be in his late thirties when it was taken, and he did look a little like Patrick, Mrs Greenfield commented. Claire agreed. A very slight resemblance, but probably enough to startle Georgina into memory.

There was something else, the administrator said, that she felt sure had belonged to Patrick's grandfather, and therefore was no business of Mrs West, who was arriving shortly. She'd like to dispose of it before the niece could interfere, and she handed Patrick a thick notebook. He opened pages, staring at the handwriting that had become so familiar to him.

'What little I read,' she said, 'made me feel it must be his.'

'It is,' Patrick replied softly. 'I know his writing. I have a diary he kept for most of the war. It stopped in mid-1918 when the family thought he'd been killed.' He hesitated, realising she must be speculating. 'It was a mistake. They were wrong. He simply never came home for his own good reasons. And perhaps one of the reasons was Georgina.'

'Or perhaps the reason's in there,' Mrs Greenfield answered quietly. When they looked at her in surprise she appeared unsure whether to continue. 'It seems to be about what happened to him. I think probably after the time he stopped writing in his diary.'

'Is there something wrong?' Patrick asked.

'Look, I only read a page or two, so I'd rather not comment. But I read enough to know it is very personal, and should be given to you and to no one else. To be honest, Mr Conway, if you weren't here to take possession, I would almost certainly have burnt it.'

They drove back to London, leaving the nursing home with a promise from Mrs Greenfield to let them know the date of the funeral. The day that had begun with such expectation had turned to sad disappointment, although to be sad for Georgina, Patrick felt, was to ignore the reality that her proper life had ended a long time ago.

'It's still sad,' Claire said. 'It would've been wonderful if she'd known you were there. Stephen's grandson, after all these years, helping to take care of her.'

'It would've been special,' he agreed. 'But as Kitty the nurse said, a bit optimistic to expect miracles.'

Yet it had been a sort of miracle in its own way, he thought, just finding her. If only it had happened sooner. There were so many things Georgina might have been able to tell him, that now he'd never know.

Claire asked to be dropped at her flat, after which Patrick went to return the car and check out of the Clayborough. The desk clerk declared it unusually short notice but, swayed by a twenty-pound gratuity, professed himself happy to pass on the phone number if there should be callers. He trusted the hotel would have the pleasure of his company again, and with sly complicity hoped Mr Conway's friend had enjoyed her stay.

In a taxi on the way back to Fulham, Patrick checked his mobile. One message, the display informed him, and there were no real surprises when he saw the caller's ID. Joanna sounded a trifle terse.

'Well, what do you think of the place? Didn't my email with the attachment arrive? Darling, I wish you wouldn't switch off your phone. It's a bit of a one-way street trying to keep in touch. All I get these days is your bloody message bank.'

He was about to return her call when he remembered the time difference; it would be after midnight in Australia. Instead, while the cab was gridlocked in traffic, he opened the laptop to view his mail.

The attachment was full of photographs. There was a shot across the harbour to the Opera House, looking so close that he thought it must be taken on a telephoto lens. There were views of the city, which seemed right on the doorstep, and one taken at night where the blaze of lights looked like New York. The slide show was arranged like a tourist brochure of the harbour: ferries crossing from Circular

Quay, racing skiffs like a fleet of white sails, plus a close view of a freighter passing alongside, then a great passenger liner, and all of them – unless the camera lied – just outside the windows of what seemed to be a penthouse apartment.

'Holy shit,' Patrick muttered, and minimised the pictures while he scanned her email.

It's real, Joanna had written, and it can be ours. Right on the very waterfront at Kirribilli! A pair of duplex apartments converted into one lovely spacious penthouse, with a view to die for, and a roof garden with trellised vines and fruit trees . . .

'Christ Almighty,' Patrick said, and wrote her a quick reply to be sent later, saying it looked fabulous – like something in one of those glossy magazines worth millions – but there was no way in the wide world they could even begin to afford it.

While he unpacked, Claire found a plastic cover to protect Stephen's notebook. It was in a precarious state, with many pages loose and the binding unravelling, while the writing in pencil was sometimes badly smudged and difficult to read. It was large for a notebook, more like a bulky accounting journal, and Stephen had filled it entirely, writing on both sides of each page. Sometimes this was neat and careful like in the diary, but Patrick also found sections where his grandfather's writing became an unruly scrawl.

'Tomorrow,' Patrick said, 'while you're at work, I'll start to read through this.'

'Tomorrow,' Claire answered, 'I'll help you'. She told him she'd spoken to her firm, had asked for and been given leave.

'Just until you go home. I don't want to waste what precious days we have left.'

'Have they agreed?'

'Yes, provided I'm on stand-by, in case they need me for any emergencies.'

'Very understanding firm,' Patrick replied.

'They have to be.' She laughed. 'It was me who set up the computer system. I made it so complicated, that I'm the only one who can fix it. So they have to treat me nicely!'

In the late afternoon they went for a stroll to Kings Road, then drinks in the pub at the World's End. When they returned to her flat laden with shopping Patrick presented options: a Chinese meal at Choy's, Italian at Luigi's, or French at Antoine's, all of which she refused. Dinner tonight, she told him, was at Chateau Claire's; scallops flambeau followed by poached perch, asparagus and sautéed potatoes.

The meal was delicious, the evening an intimate *tête-à-tête*. Claire looked dazzling in a strapless dress, her auburn hair let loose and falling to her shoulders, Vivaldi's *Four Seasons* playing softly on the sound system, and twin candles lighting an old dining table she'd bought at a street market and restored.

Afterwards they went out to her balcony with the remainder of their wine, to an almost full moon that seemed to be hanging above the chimneypots of the building opposite. Patrick felt happy; he tried to think when he'd last experienced such a feeling of contentment. Much later he realised he'd forgotten all about Joanna's email, and turned on his laptop to send the prepared reply. He hoped it would be the last he'd hear of the magical harbourside apartment that was way beyond their means.

The next day, as they began to decipher the dilapidated pages, they realised how different it was to the diary. If there was anger in Sassoon's poem, there seemed a deeper anger in Stephen Conway's notebook. He was only nineteen years old when he abandoned a law degree to volunteer for the army, and he did not have Sassoon's phenomenal way with words. But he had endured experiences that changed him beyond all expectation, ordeals that Patrick found it difficult to imagine, and reading it he frequently found himself in tears, although whether they were tears of grief or rage he could not be sure. They were certainly tears for a man who had endured experiences beyond today's capacity to envisage.

Patrick made notes and sometimes read aloud to Claire while she did her best to repair detached sections of the book. She also scanned faded pages in the computer to improve their image.

As they progressed, the notebook began to make certain things clear. It was written more than two years since he had reluctantly left the arms of Marie-Louise after the recapture of Pozieres. In those years, apart from when the battalion was spelled behind the lines and twice given leave in England – only a brief respite each time – he had not really been away from the sound of battle.

He had certainly not died in 1918 as they had been led to believe. He had simply been mentally and physically exhausted; his ears were shattered from bombardments, his mind numbed by the frequency of killing with bayonet thrusts into other men's bodies. He could see the shock of death on the frightened faces that appeared so like his own; he witnessed the killing of these enemies long into the dark of the night, and often dared not sleep in case they were there waiting for him in his dreams.

Some of this information Patrick had gathered from the last pages of the original diary. There he had recognised the increasing signs of despair and exhaustion in his grandfather. But he soon found the notebook was quite different. It was apparent his entire world had altered, and like Stephen himself, it had begun to disintegrate.

In the summer of the fourth year the war entered a new and alarming phase. That was when Germany advanced with massive ferocity, retaking all the ground they had lost in the past. They had daunting new weapons like flamethrowers, heavier guns like the 'Big Berthas' and far superior tanks. The vaunted British tanks had not been a success: they lumbered forward on caterpillar tracks like Jurassic monsters, their ultimate speed just a mile an hour. Troops, able to march faster than this, stared at these apparitions in despair; their officers had promised the invention would free them from trench combat and its horrors. In London the machines were lampooned in vaudeville, with chorus girls performing a satiric and bawdy dance called 'The Tanko'.

By the summer the Germans were poised to cross the Somme and drive on Paris. Giant guns were shelling Parisian suburbs. Australian divisions were assigned the task of attacking them. In the notebook Patrick discovered the reason for the enduring affection he had encountered in the town of Villers-Bretonneux, the frequent memorials and the schoolchildren's song.

For when the morning mist rose from the river, the AIF divisions cut their way through the Somme valley to this village. They surged into the German lines like they had at Pozieres; this time driven by a desperate desire to end the carnage and go home, and this savage longing for their own shores was an incentive that made them unstoppable.

Stephen Conway was among them, but after that day nothing for him was ever the same.

Chapter Fifteen

I don't know how I got here. I'm trying to remember. They say I was shoved on board an ambulance ship and brought across the channel and unloaded at a pier in Southampton. Then all of us were put into carriages drawn by four horses that galloped along a cobbled road and down the hill at such a speed that a few patients died on the way; they simply croaked from the fright of the journey or the vibration. That's how you come to this place, either half alive or stone dead.

It's called Netley. A place of screams. No, not dreams - there are no dreams here, only nightmares as black as the pits of hell. It's like a prison. It lies on a spit of land called Spike Island in Southampton Water, with iron gates guarded by sentries. Behind these gates is where I am now, in what is known as the 'nuthouse', or the place where the dregs are sent, or the fucking 'coward's castle' - that's another name for it - but its official title is the Royal Victoria Military Hospital.

It is named for the old Queen who ordered it to be built, against the express wishes, it is said, of Nurse Nightingale. But the Queen prevailed, as royalty always does. I mean, why bother being royal if you can't get your own way? Especially against poor old Flo Nightingale who, when all's said and done, was just a lady with a lamp.

This gargantuan building, this asylum filled with us, the war's new victims, is actually part of a town. The strangest kind of town. It contains its own railway station, post office, stables, kitchens, shops, bakery and even a library. It has as many people as an ordinary town: cooks, gardeners, bakers, blacksmiths, artisans of all kinds, as well as nurses and doctors. The hospital is vast, like a grand hotel. They tell us every day how fine and grand it is, and how lucky we are to be here. Lucky, as the devil might say, as he beckons you in the direction of his fiery hearth. Here they constantly boast it is the world's biggest hospital: us poor buggers who endure it know it is by far the world's worst.

It is a bizarre place. Grotesque. It even produces its own photo postcards, and does a steady business in happy smiling pictures of soldiers in uniform. And other smiling pictures of soldiers without legs or arms, but with little captions that say: 'Are we downhearted? No . . . never at Netley!'

Visitors can be photographed on the hospital's pier, or the spacious lawns; a patient can even have a personal picture taken with the surgeon who amputated his limb, the doctor cheerful and full of gruesome medical jokes as he poses by his butcher shop; or, as he prefers to call it, his operating table.

I have no visitors, and thus no need for smiling photos to present to them. No surgeon, either, for they say I had no injury: no bullet wounds, no shrapnel, no signs of damage that anyone can see. Therefore I am branded a coward, a malingerer – that word again, the one the schoolboy doctor called me – too scared to remain in France and fight the foe. They do not seem to hear me when I speak, when I say I have been in France and Gallipoli before that, fighting the foe for more than three years. The foe becomes so awfully familiar to me, at the end of a bloodstained bayonet, or lying in the mud with sightless dead eyes, that I no longer know if he is a foe or just a poor wretch of a comrade who happens to be on the other side. I begin to feel he could even be a friend, and by saying this I am committed here – for to declare the enemy a friend is either serious insanity or a heresy close to treason.

We are not altogether insane, just slightly so. Like the big dour Scottish quack who diagnoses me, and writes on his chart: 'A wee bit dangerous'. This is the place where they bring the 'dangerous', where they take away our uniforms and dress us in hospital blue and strip us of our identity, for in here we are all dangerous, unsafe cases with numbers now instead of names.

Netley is considered an ornament, like a majestic palace. It is a shrine to caring for the wounded; ever since Crimea, the Sudan and the Boer War it has commanded royal patronage. It is today a place where the ambulance ships bring the broken bodies back. I hesitate to even mention the broken minds. But they come too, to D Block, where the lights remain on all night, and nurses patrol in case some poor victim of gas or shell or the inability to cope with endless fear flings back his blanket and goes raving bloody mad.

We are suffering from what they call 'shell shock'. It is a new term and many doctors do not believe in it; but as we are in a state of temporary insanity we can be given experimental remedies and subjected to new and frightening therapies. Electric treatment that sends us into awful paroxysms, drugs that numb the mind, hypnotism that is meant to persuade the deranged that going back to filthy muddy trenches and bursting shells will give us renewed stature and improve our chances in future life.

Like a prison, I said. A strange sort of prison, for behind the palatial facade are rows of wooden huts where we live crowded together, and rail lines where a real train brings carriages with more victims, more wounded bodies and injured minds. D Block is the domain of the nursing sister who my neighbour in Bed 10 calls Attila the Hun.

'What do you mean, Attila the Hun?' I ask him, when he first calls her this. 'Attila was a bloke.'

'So?' Bed 10 says. 'Ever had a close look and seen her neat little moustache? I reckon she must shave twice a week.'

Her real name, I find out, is Penelope Parker-Browne, and her father is an earl with an estate that takes up half of Monmouthshire. Bed 10 says that she was brought up like a boy because the earl has no male heir, and is upset his estate will go to his brother's son. So he took it out on his child for being female, and thus losing the heritage. Whatever the reason, it's made her a repulsive creature, a cruel bully. Even if it explains her anger and the way she ill-treats us, the Honourable Sister Penelope is feared and hated by all the patients in D Block.

Whereas most of us are in love with Sister Henrietta, who is plump and caring, with flaxen hair and the warmest smile that makes us all want to hug her. Not in any sexual way – because Henry, as everyone calls her, is not at all sexual. Perhaps to some, but not to me. Perhaps Bed 10 fancies her because often after she has been on her rounds, I hear his bed springs start to squeak as he beats his meat beneath the blankets. He might think of Henry while he does it. Whereas to me she's like a sister or a favourite cousin. She helps me write letters to Jane when my hand shakes too much to hold a pen, after I have had the electric treatment. Or when they put the terminals on my spine to discover if I am truly shell shocked, because after this treatment I tremble for hours and cannot walk unaided.

Henry thinks it is cruel, the things they do to us. Not that she ever says so, but I can see it upsets her. There are times when I'd like to tell her about Marie-Louise, and the few days we had together after Pozieres. But I can't; she helps me write to Jane, and anyway, 'M.L.' is a lifetime ago. Another life, when I was twenty-one. A lifetime before that was Jane and our few days of honeymoon, where we stood admiring the Three Sisters, and heard our voices echo along the valley. But when I work it out carefully it's only been four years, and back home there's a son I've never seen whose name is Richard. At least I think it's Richard. Sometimes memory lets me down. At times it's hard to remember people's names, and there are days when I even forget where I lived with my parents when I was growing up. It's like a different existence that seems indistinct and far away.

Letters from Jane don't seem to reach me here. Maybe the ships with our mail are still being sunk, or else they think that letters from home might be bad for us. I really miss her letters. I really miss Jane, and the small boy who is our son. Even if it is hard to miss someone you have never met.

Whenever I tell Henry I'm a father, she smiles and says I'll be looking forward to going home some day soon, and I can teach him to play cricket and football. I'm not sure if she really believes I'm a father.

They don't seem to have many records, or know much about me – except that I'm a 'wee bit dangerous'. I can't help them, because I don't know much about myself, not really. I only know I had friends who are mostly dead, and there were whiz-bangs that never stopped and made it really difficult to remember things. But at night, after Sister Henry talks in that kind and gentle way, I sleep soundly, thinking of home, of being a dad to a small figure holding a bat or a football.

I often try to think of Jane and what she looks like now, but the only photograph I had was lost, along with all my papers. I had it when I dived into the mud, trying to escape the bombs that were going off inside my head. That memory is clear and horrible. They pulled me out, but couldn't find my belongings. Everyone seemed to be shouting and looking at me as if I was trying to lose the war, and they said they didn't give a bugger about my stupid photo. That was why I tried to dive back in the mud again to find it, before they tied me up. I've still got the marks of the rope on my body where I fought for hours trying to get free. Till the ambulance came. At first I thought it was a hearse. Same thing, really. They call them meat wagons, those motor vans that collect the dead.

There was a lot of trouble about losing my papers in the mud. Nobody cared about my photograph of Jane, but without any papers you're a misfit. You give your name, and they don't believe you. Tell them where you've fought, and they say you're lying. I'm like someone who doesn't belong in this world or anywhere, not without my papers.

Tonight I have to stop writing. Attila is on the prowl. She suspects me of something, but she doesn't know I keep this book and a pencil underneath the mattress. If she found out she'd destroy it. Especially if she reads what's said in here about her. One night I was stupid enough to tell her that I had a son, aged three. And that he was born on the day we landed at Gallipoli. I was very pleased with myself for remembering that, but she looked scornful.

'Really?' She had a sarcastic way of speaking, while gazing down what I suppose was an aristocratic nose, that made everyone feel she didn't believe a word of anything she was told. 'How do we know you were at Gallipoli?' she said.

I tried to tell her I was. Even if they didn't have my papers. That I really had a son. And I was going home to teach him how to play cricket and football. She pretended not to hear, then brought me a tablet, one of the knockout ones, and stood there making me take it, saying I was hallucinating and going off my rocker.

But if any of us go off our rockers, it would only be because of the names she calls us. Terrible names. Weasels, cowards and lily-livered scum; when she gets wound up she's liable to say anything. We're told we're in a funk; we're spineless, craven creatures who all deserve white feathers. Or a bullet at dawn, that's what she really has in mind. She'd like to be the marksman who fires the gun. She would, she's said so.

It would not be at all quick, she tells us. One in the balls to start with – only she calls it the groin – then one into a knee, followed by a hip and a shoulder, before she decides to take pity and puts one through the heart. She's a good shot, she boasts, from killing deer and pheasant with her daddy, the earl. She never says these things when there are doctors around, or any witnesses to hear the filth she spouts. And it is filth. Her eyes seem to flash and her face goes the colour of brick. At times like that I start to wonder if Attila herself might be the one who's going off her rocker.

A week's gone by, I think. No letter from Jane. One from my mother, though, who said she goes to church each morning to pray for me. She hopes we have proper beds and enough food, and expresses the wish that I'm being given plenty of leave so that I have a chance to explore England. I don't really know how to reply to my dear, sweet mum. She seems to be imagining a different kind of war to the one we've been in.

Nothing's happened at Netley. A few people died, a few arrived as mad as the rest of us. But there is *something* going on here; all week there've been rumours – strange rumours going around this place. People getting together, whispering, nodding, asking each other: Have you heard the news? Do you believe it can be true?

'You mean the war's over?' some poor dill asked, and we told him to keep taking the tablets and get off himself, the war's not over, this war's going to last for-bloody-ever, like wars used to in the olden days. Hadn't he ever heard of the Hundred Years War? This one will be the Two Hundred Years War. No, the rumour is about Attila! And already, this morning, it's more than a rumour.

I was right about her! She *is* off her rocker!

Last night she was taken away. Bed 10 told me when I came back from having treatment. He was jumping about like a jack-in-the-box, laughing in celebration, as if he was going genuinely crazy.

'Attila the Hun's gone!' he shouted excitedly. 'They took her off in a straitjacket. She threw acid over some poor sod, just because he wet himself. So we're finally free of the old bitch, free of her at last!'

I sleep much better after hearing this. I dream about being back at university. It was a good dream, but then all the uni students turned into Turks. They invited me to come home with them, back to their beautiful home called Gallipoli, and the next thing I'm on a steep hillside where the hundreds of dugouts look like deep mine shafts. Only now they're telling me to watch out because they're going to start shooting at me and bury me down deep where not even Jane can find me.

They're good shots, those Turks. Fatal to stick your head above the parapet. Put up one of our periscope mirrors, and they smash it to pieces. So we know what'd happen to our heads if we were silly enough to raise them for a squiz at the view. Anyway, who the hell wants to see the view? What is there to see? Just the wounded on stretchers being taken down to hospital ships, or the dead being buried in bulk. God's Acre, they used to call that burial ground, before it became too big and had to be renamed God's Square Mile. I can remember things like that, but I'm still not sure if my son's name is Richard or something else. I seem to remember it was going to be Emily, but that can't be right!

Sometimes on Gallipoli, the enemy trenches were so close that we could hear them talk or sing. Great singing voices, the Turks. One of our mates could play the violin, and some nights when he played a sonata all went quiet in their trenches, and after he finished we'd hear calls of '*Bravo!*', even shouts of '*Encore, encore!*' and the sound of their applause. Sometimes he would oblige them and play again. They like music. I don't think we hated the Turks. We just had to kill them, or else they'd kill us. Kill? I tried to tell my Scottish doctor that must be the worst four-letter word in our language. The most savage and uncivilised. He just shook his head and looked at me as if I was stupid.

I don't know what the Turkish word for kill is. All we could hear when they attacked was, 'Allah, Allah!'

'We'll Allah you, you bastards,' we'd shout back.

We called them bastards so often that one we captured asks if Bastard is one of our gods? My mate Bluey tells him: Yeah, 'course it is. He explains that Bastard is a special god. The Big God in charge of all the others, that's the Bastard.

Bluey Watson, shearer from Walgett, rough as guts, best bloke to have with you in a pub fight or holed up in a dugout. Flattened

Double-Trouble after our first leave in London, then cried his eyes out when Double got blown to bits. Was the first time I knew a tough shearer from the bush could cry. Tried to pretend he wasn't crying, that some grit got in his eyes. A dim corporal, thick as two planks called him a poofter because of it, and three of us had to hang on to Bluey while the dill ran for his life. Dear old Blue. Got a flesh wound at Pozieres, and they reckon he's dead! How can anyone die from a stupid bloody flesh wound?

'Gangrene?' I asked the doctors, and they told me to get to buggery out of there. Said they were too busy to answer silly questions. I should've gone back to the farmhouse, back to Marie-Louise and stayed there with her. Stayed warm and cosy in bed, where there was someone to love me. Let the fucking politicians fight the fucking war. The old men who send the young men to be killed are always big on rhetoric and aggression. Never seen a shot fired in their lives, but they like to make wars. It's good for their prestige, making wars and being photographed with soldiers.

Yes, I should've stayed with her. Yesterday I told the Scottish quack that's what I should've done. He just listened and wrote some words down on paper. It's a new sort of treatment. I suppose it's better than the last one: where they used to give me so many shocks with the electric voltage that I felt like a light bulb. Sometimes my legs would shake so much after it that I couldn't control them, I'd try to walk and just fall over. Helpless, like a young baby trying to take a first step, or an old bloke trying to take his last. Bed 10 reminds me that Attila used to watch and laugh at this, but we don't think she's laughing now.

The new sort of treatment is talk. We sit and talk to the doctor, tell him anything we want to, and he listens, writes things down, asks questions. It's called the 'talking cure', but the Scottish quack says there's also another name. Something therapy. Invented by some quack in Vienna. We just go on talking until we've got nothing left to say, then we go back to the ward and next day we talk some more. I told the Scottish quack all about Marie-Louise. He wrote that down. Then asked me questions about if I'd enjoyed it, and was she nice, so I told him it was none of his bloody business.

'Of course it's my business,' he said. 'It's part of the treatment. We have to know how you behave, both in and out of bed.' He kept on and on, so to shut him up I said she was a wonderful fuck, the best ever, and he wrote all that down too. Today he asks me when I last had leave. Ages ago, before Christmas, but I can't remember which month. November, I think, and tell him it was cold. Perishing, the English call it. He asks me what I did on leave.

What did I do? What the hell can anyone do in a place where they're a total stranger, with only a few lousy days? Not much. Not much at all. I saw odd things. Like little English children being carefully taught to hate the enemy. A picture of a baby holding a bayonet, so it looked like he was defending his nice mummy from the ferocious Hun. In the shops, in children's picture books, I saw a poem about a house that went like this:

This is the house that Jack built.
And . . .
This is the bomb that fell on the house that Jack built.
And . . .
This is the Hun that dropped the bomb, that fell on the house that Jack built.
And this . . .?
This is the gun that killed the Hun, who dropped the bomb that fell on the house that Jack built.

I asked the Scottish quack what he thinks of teaching little kids such things, but he doesn't answer at first. Just stares at me. Strokes his thick Scottish beard. 'I'm the one who asks the questions,' he says at last. 'What else did you do on leave?'

What else? I wanted to go to some village near Cambridge and talk to Elizabeth Marsden, but I can't remember the name of the place where she lives. I can remember telling her all about my family – about great-grandfather Jeremy Conway, and Matthew and Daniel who were currency lads when Sydney was a convict town, but the name of her village is lost in a faraway afternoon, when we sat and talked in the teashop and walked to Kings Cross where she kissed me goodbye. I remember that kiss, her soft warm lips on my cheek. I often think of Elizabeth. I suppose it is because I don't have a photograph, although I can remember what she looks like. But not where she lives.

It was only a few hours, and you can't really fall in love with someone in a few hours – at least I don't believe you can, yet I keep thinking of her and wishing I'd met her sooner, not at the end of my leave. So why can't I remember the name of the place? If I could, then I'd be able to find her again, I tell the Scots quack, and that way I could find out if I really did fall in love with her.

He writes it all down. Pages of it, hour after bloody hour. God only knows what he'll do with it. I began to run out of things to tell him. I thought I'd have to make some up. I remembered one thing – meeting a woman who works in the Woolwich Arsenal where they make the munitions. There's thousands of girls and women of all ages who work there. The one I met was quite old, at least forty. She told me that some of the workers get ill – TNT poisoning – and lots of them, even the young girls, die from it, did he know that? He makes some sort of murmur, clears his throat, and doesn't bother to write this down.

What else? he wants to know. I tell him I stayed in a hostel. Two shillings a night. Looked out the window at people in the streets walking past. Then one day I went to a picture show and saw a film with Mary Pickford.

What else? Not much else.

Oh yes. Something else. I got into a row because I didn't properly salute an English officer. In Piccadilly, it was, near the Circus. Going on leave we were all given these warnings. All the officers, especially the British, have been complaining Australian soldiers won't salute them. Orders came that we were getting a bad name, and any soldier caught not saluting would be reported, have their pay docked and their leave cancelled at once. Trouble is, we're not good at saluting. We're not conscripts, we're all volunteers who decided to go and fight for our country, which makes us feel we're as good as any other bloke! So why should we salute some joker with a few pips on his shoulder who probably works in an orderly room or an army Q store? Most of us reckon the only salute they deserve is a two-fingered one, or else the famous Outback Aussie salute, which is waving your hands to get rid of flies while you curse the flaming little buggers and tell 'em to piss off and buzz in someone else's nose and mouth.

Still, I wanted my six days without any trouble. God knows I'd earned it – it'd been nearly a year since the last leave. The trouble with six days, you hardly get to know the place or find your way around before it's back to the train and off to the bloody trenches. We never get a proper chance to meet people, which is why so many blokes spend their leave with the prostitutes. What else is leave for? most of them reckon. It's too hard to make friends with anyone in six days, so that leaves the scrubbers or the amateur ones – the town bikes – who see a slouch hat and they're like bees around a honey pot.

But no tarts for me, I decide, and I'll do my best to salute. What's more, I keep to it. Until this dag in a shiny new uniform comes the raw prawn and says I didn't salute him with *proper respect.* That really got my goat. He was only a young lieutenant, but he reminded me of the Pommy major who cost me my stripes, so I remember the old joke and ask this galah who the hell he thinks he is. Is he General Birdwood? In that case, he should shove his feathers up his arse and fly away like any other bird would. His face goes sort of purple, his eyes bulge, and he starts to shout for a military policeman.

'Stand to attention!' he bellows at me, while we can hear the whistle of military police from not far away.

'Stand to attention be buggered!' I yelled, and took off down this street called the Haymarket like a rabbit with a greyhound on his tail.

The Scottish quack chuckles and writes it down. Then he asks if I had any 'relations' while I was there. I pretend I don't know what he means, and say, I've got no relations here. Only got relations back in Australia.

'Lassies, I'm talking about,' he says. 'They say London streets are full of whores.' But it comes out of his mouth sounding more like 'hooers'. I say it might be full of hooers, but it's also full of the clap, and I'm a married man who'll be going home to his wife when you people have finished your war. He gives me a bit of a sharp look and then decides to write this down too.

When we're not busy with the talking cure, we're made to go to classes, where we're taught other things to help us. We're taught how to sew and do basket-weaving. They say these are good and useful pursuits which will calm us down and help prepare us to go back to the front-line. They don't like it a bit when some of the patients say it'll come in handy later on if we get our legs shot off, or if we cough out our guts from the mustard gas. It'll be real useful when we're sent back home in a sling or a wheelchair, because we can make baskets or sew for a living. I tell this to the laird doctor who frowns and pretends he hasn't heard it, and doesn't bother to write it down.

At the end of our next session, he breaks some very bad news: the news that I'm cured. Fit and well, he says. In good enough shape to return to the war.

'I don't feel in good shape,' I tell him, 'and I'm bloody certain I don't want to return to the war. Let someone else fight the rotten bastards. You go and do it, mate,' I say to him. 'Get off your arse and see what it's like over there.'

'Conway, you've got two choices,' he says, not a bit friendly now. 'You either go back to France and do your duty, or else you face a court-martial and then a firing squad for desertion.'

'Great choices,' I reply. 'What a fucking nice bastard you turned out to be. You great fat slob of a Scots git! You lump of stinking haggis! Now shove me on a charge for insubordination, and I'll get at least three months in the clink for insulting an officer.'

But he just smiles: he knows what I'm trying, and says he wouldn't dream of charging me. It'd be unfair. And besides, he says: in his opinion I'm not fit or well enough to spend any time in a bad place like gaol.

Chapter Sixteen

It was midnight. Patrick had not realised it was so late, caught up in another day of the notebook and its disturbing memories that seemed to make his grandfather so painfully alive to him. Claire was asleep as he slid carefully into bed, managing not to wake her.

Tomorrow, at last, was his appointment with Tim Carruthers of BBC Films. A preliminary skirmish to get reacquainted while they discussed the script, mulled over casting and Carruthers presented notes on his screenplay. It was all tactics, a game he knew well. If he agreed on the cast they proposed, they might give way on script demands. Extra editorial notes were sometimes included for that reason, inserted as a bargaining chip. Tactics and compromise, he thought. It was not necessarily the best way to produce a good film. But to raise the finance there was always some kind of compromise required.

There had been no recent word from Joanna. Nothing since his reply about the waterfront apartment which had created a flurry of emails between them. The first from her the next morning read:

Received your vote of no-confidence, so I hope you approve of this *purchase. I traded in our boring sedan for something a little bit more interesting. See attached digital snap of the latest me – in company with the new occupant of our parking space.*

He had opened the attachment and there was his wife, dressed in a bikini for the photo, posed provocatively behind the wheel of a brand new convertible Porsche, looking gorgeous and smugly aware of it. Under the picture was printed: *Come home and drive me soon.*

Amusement had prompted his return message:

I don't know what was wrong with the boring old sedan, but I must say I've never seen a better-looking Porsche and driver.

Which had brought a quick response:

Thank you, kind sir. Paid for out of my own account, so don't lie awake worrying. In fact, don't lie awake at all. Sleep soundly and return home soon, with battery charged and in top gear. Signed, the Porsche driver.

He needed sleep, but Joanna's frivolity gave way to images of his grandfather, and the enormity of a doctor sending a sick man back to the trenches. Somewhere he remembered reading that because of the casualties and lack of recruits, returning unfit soldiers had been common practice. Clearly that also included the shell shocked and mentally disturbed.

He slept at last, and dreamt. He was in Piccadilly, being confronted by a furious officer who was ordering him to salute. He tried to explain he was a writer and film-maker, not a soldier, but the officer said not to be ridiculous. He must salute, and smartly, or he'd be reported, and unless he apologised profusely he would be dispatched back to the war and the front-line immediately.

Patrick told him he should take a look behind him, because he had a bouquet of feathers stuck up his arse. Then, while the officer reacted to this, Patrick turned and ran down the length of the Haymarket and across St James's Park, a platoon of military police pursuing him at breakneck filmic speed, like a bunch of zany Keystone Kops. As he reached Buckingham Palace and they were about to overtake him, he woke up. To his surprise Claire was curled tightly in his arms, and he seemed to be firmly erect and excited.

'I had a peculiar dream,' he said.

'Feels like it,' she murmured, smiling.

'Not that kind of dream.'

'You want to go back to sleep?'

'Absolutely not!' Patrick replied.

Near dawn he woke again. Claire was sleeping blissfully. Gazing at her lying so quietly beside him she seemed soft and vulnerable, and he had a strong recollection of the way Stephen had described Marie-Louise. With it came a moment of realisation that this must end. They no longer talked about it but both knew that soon – much too soon – he'd be going home to Joanna, her Porsche, and the rest of his life.

The BBC television centre is a curious circular building, a short walk from Shepherds Bush, a dishevelled section of London where Spike Milligan began his career in an office above a fruit shop, writing scripts for *The Goon Show*. Patrick knew the office and the fruit shop were long gone, but the comedy Milligan invented was alive and making each new generation laugh as they discovered it.

At security he was given a pass to pin on his lapel and sent to the fifth floor. There a secretary was waiting to conduct him, although not to the person he had expected to meet.

'Slight change of plan, Mr Conway,' she explained. 'You'll be meeting Charlotte Redmond. She's the new head of co-productions for BBC Films.'

'Not Tim Carruthers?' Patrick said, startled.

'Mr Carruthers is no longer with us.'

'But I spoke to his secretary last week. It was you, wasn't it? Weren't you his secretary?'

'Until they fired him. Now I'm Lottie's secretary.'

There was no time to discuss it further as she showed him into an office suite. Charlotte Redmond was on the telephone; she nodded and kept talking while pointing him to a chair and miming the secretary to bring coffee. She was young, he noticed, suntanned with sleekly brushed black hair and impeccably groomed; she wore a tailored skirt and a blazer that looked smart and, he imagined, expensive.

The call seemed to take an inordinately long time, to the point of discourtesy, Patrick thought, and if designed to make him feel uncomfortable it was having that effect. On first impressions he had a feeling that he and the immaculate Miss Redmond might not become the best of friends.

Finally, she hung up and gave him a fleeting smile which stopped short of apology.

'Sorry about that. Rather important,' she remarked, and Patrick managed a polite nod. From what he had heard it seemed a trivial chat. He tried to avoid the feeling it was a technique she used to assert herself.

'You're Patrick, I'm Charlotte. Lottie to intimates, but I prefer it to be Charlotte at this stage.'

'I gather that Tim Carruthers has walked the plank?'

'Spectacularly,' she said, with a lift of an eyebrow that suggested most people must surely know this.

'What happened?'

'He had one of his increasingly long liquid lunches, came back and insulted almost everybody. You knew Tim, no doubt?'

'Only slightly. We worked together at Thames Television, but that was eight years ago. And we exchanged letters on this project, of course.'

'Ah, yes.' She opened a folder on her desk and he could see his script with notes attached, as well as ominous coloured markers. A great many notes and markers, it seemed to him.

'I thought it only fair we should meet at this stage, Patrick, so I can explain the situation to you.'

'Is there a situation, Charlotte?' he asked carefully.

'There's a change at the top of this department, so obviously it creates a domino effect. I need time to find out which of Tim's projects I wish to run with. The others will be cut.' She smiled as if conscious that he was fidgeting. 'No need to look apprehensive, Patrick.' It was a brittle smile that seemed to relish her new status: the large desk, the title so recently acquired, and the power which included authority over him and other petitioners. 'I've made no selections yet. But I will be soon.'

'Have you read the script?' he asked.

'I understand your circumstances, Patrick.'

'My circumstances?' It was disconcerting she had not bothered to answer the question.

'Coming all this way from down-under . . . no doubt there are return flights and other obligations . . .' She did not wait for an answer. 'So my position is this. I'll be deciding within the next fortnight. That's if you haven't made plans to leave before then?'

'No particular plans,' he replied, trying to remain unruffled.

'Good. I've already formed certain opinions, but I want to consider them more carefully. And when I have, we'll have another meeting. Is that satisfactory with you?'

'Within two weeks?' He knew it was pointless to argue. It was clear from the way she sat back in her chair with confidence that there would be no other option.

'Splendid.' Charlotte shut his folder and put it on a pile of others as the secretary returned. She brought a small coffee tray, on which there was only one cup. He saw this with disbelief; it appeared she'd known it would be a short meeting, or else the corporation's cost-cutting had extended to rationing coffee by not serving visitors.

Patrick rose and thanked Charlotte for her time. He left the building in White City and began to walk towards Shepherds Bush. He felt some vigorous exercise might mitigate his anger. In the end he walked right across West London, all the way back to Claire's flat in Fulham.

New to the brutalities of the film and television business, Claire was indignant for him. 'What a bitch. What a frightful cow!'

'Power play. Flexing her executive muscles.'

'She sounds an utter shit.'

If Claire was incensed, Patrick now felt more detached. The walk via familiar parts of Kensington and the North End Road markets where he'd bought their dinner had proved therapeutic. It was late afternoon, but the sun was still warm. They were having a drink on the balcony, Claire in a cotton shirt and little else except a pair of bikini pants she had changed into after work. A boy riding a bike on the street below looked up and whistled with a cheeky optimism.

'What's with him?' she said. 'I've got knickers on.'

'Only just.'

'Tell me more about Miss Charmless. Was she attractive?'

'What does that have to do with it?'

'Just checking,' Claire said. 'It would be consoling to hear she has buck teeth and a serious squint.'

'No consolation on that score. I'd even say she's handsome.'

'Handsome, eh?' Claire laughed. 'Handsome is not always a great compliment to women.'

'In that case, she's definitely handsome.'

'What a pity your friend Tim got pissed and committed professional suicide so successfully.'

'It is. In fact it's a bit of a bugger.'

She studied him. 'You're as worried as hell, aren't you?'

'Uneasy. Not one of the great meetings.'

'No. The lack of coffee seems particularly alarming. As well as being unbelievably discourteous.'

'There were other ominous signs. I'm afraid she's going to muck me about, and it may not have a happy ending. I don't think I could afford her delaying tactics if I wasn't staying here with you.'

'Where else do you want to stay?'

'Nowhere else. But you might be stuck with me longer than we anticipated.'

'I can put up with that,' Claire replied softly, trying not to show her gratitude for this unexpected reprieve.

They were finishing breakfast the following day when the telephone rang. Claire went into the bedroom to answer it. Patrick heard her as she picked up the phone and gave her name. 'Claire Thomas.'

There was a pause, then came her reply in which he detected a note of surprise, before she returned looking discomforted.

'It's your sister,' Claire said and handed it to him. She began to clear the dishes while he answered.

'Sally?'

'Sorry about this,' Sally said.

'Lucky you found me here. I've just arrived this minute for a script conference.'

'A conference?' He could tell there was no point in pursuing this; her disbelief was palpable. 'Come off it, ducky. I called the hotel because you keep switching off your mobile. And the guy at the Clayborough said you moved last week to this number.'

In the rush to leave the Clayborough, he realised, he'd given Claire's number instead of his own.

'Ah, well –' he began, but she interrupted.

'Never mind, Patrick. None of my business. I just called to see if Joanna had been in touch.'

'We've exchanged a few emails. Why?'

'No particular reason. I just thought she might've been.'

'But why, Sal?'

'Look, it really isn't my concern, but on the other hand –' she hesitated, which he thought was unlike Sally.

'On the other hand, what?'

'Oh shit, I wish I hadn't rung now. Look . . . I bumped into Carlo last night at a party. Carlo, as in your father-in-law.'

'I do know who you mean. How is he?'

'To put it bluntly . . . No, forget it. Tell me about this notebook that belonged to Stephen –'

'Sally, *please*!' he insisted. 'To put it bluntly, what?'

'To put it bluntly,' she said reluctantly, 'he was over the moon. I got the strongest possible impression from what he said that Joanna is pregnant.'

'*What?*'

'Well, how does this sound to you? In his lovely Italian way he said, "I tell them they only make films, not babies, but I'm wrong!" That's what he said.'

'Jesus Christ.' Patrick was stunned.

Claire heard this reaction. It sounded like the kind of call that needed privacy, rather than having her in such proximity. She went into her workroom and closed the door.

'Is that all he said?' Patrick asked. 'Nothing else?'

'He was with friends. No time for anything else. Look, I might be completely wrong, but it's been his mantra ever since you got married. However, if Jo hasn't called you, perhaps I am wrong. Or she's saving it as a surprise. Or darling Carlo has got it arse-up, or else I have.'

'Carlo's not given to stuffing things up,' Patrick said.

'Then it must be me. Pat, can we please forget this call and do nothing till you and Joanna talk? In other words, ducky, you did not hear this from me. Okay?'

'Okay,' Patrick agreed reluctantly, 'but you've sure opened up a can of worms here, Sally.'

A light wind made intricate patterns on the ocean as Katherine sat on the balcony and waited for Sally to finish her phone call. She could see the distant promontory of Long Reef where freighters lay offshore at anchor, held in an aquatic queue because of a customs strike. There was a transcendental hue across the sea from the rays of the setting sun, making it look like the glow of a Stretton painting, she thought. No wonder her daughter had mortgaged herself to the hilt for this. She could hear the rise and fall of her voice as she talked to Patrick, and was quietly glad that after the squalls of childhood her children had become friends.

Sally came out with the last of the white wine, planting a kiss on her mother's forehead.

'He sends his love,' she said, and poured the remainder of the bottle into their glasses.

'And . . . ?' Katherine prompted, expectantly.

'There's some kind of delay at the BBC, but I've a lot to tell you about Grandpa Stephen. It's just remarkable how Patrick managed to trace Georgina Rickson —'

'Sally, what about the reason for your call?'

'He's heard nothing from Joanna.' She had already decided not to tell her mother about Claire. 'Perhaps I made a silly mistake, Mum, about Carlo Lugarno.'

'You seemed so certain.'

'All that Italian charm. A noisy party, Carlo waving his hands about. I may have got things a bit muddled. I think we should wait for Joanna to say something - because, after all, it's her baby, if there *is* one on the way.'

'Hers and Patrick's,' Katherine pointed out, disappointed at not having confirmation she was to be a grandmother.

Claire was preoccupied all day. It had come as a shock, the call from Patrick's sister, like a sharp reminder: a caution that these days of happiness were evanescent and he had another life. Disturbingly, Patrick had been rather vague about what was discussed; rather *more* than vague, she thought; perhaps equivocal was the word. Just a chat, he'd said, dismissing it. What Claire had heard before absenting herself did not sound like 'just a chat'. There were other elements that troubled her. She knew his was a close family and could not help wondering if they were now speculating about her on the other side of the world. It made her feel uneasy and insecure.

Claire had always had the capacity to be totally honest with herself. She knew the affair was of her making; she'd been lonely and instantly attracted to him in Belgium. Then the book of poems which was an unsubtle way of ensuring they met again. It was to be a casual interlude, a week or two of shared liking and lust; that's what had been intended. Liking and lust – she couldn't help a smile at the alliteration – but love had not really been on the menu. Claire had been deeply in love only once before, and that, although she hated to remember it, had been a harrowing disaster.

Patrick had immediately tried to ring Joanna at home, where the phone rang until he heard his own voice requesting him to leave a name and number. For a time he tried to concentrate on more of Stephen's notebook, and found it impossible. Now with Claire spending a few hours on a promised visit to her mother, he tried to reach Joanna again. She was not at the apartment. Her mobile was switched off; he felt it pointless to leave another message, but did so anyway.

'Jo, it's me again. I need to talk – where the hell are you?'

Earlier he had left messages with her production office at Fox Studios, who confirmed they'd finished shooting last week. Great wrap party, the first assistant told him, and his wife had been there looking a million bucks, but he hadn't seen her since then. Probably editing, he suggested, and added they had a beaut movie that might win her another gong at the next awards.

Patrick had already rung Harvey the film editor, expecting Joanna to be working with him, but that had proved fruitless. Harvey relayed the news that Joanna had said she'd be busy, and asked him to work on the edit alone until she got back.

'Back from where?' he'd asked.

'Dunno, Pat. Tough shoot; she was tired. Some of the guys said she'd taken a few days' relax at the beach.'

Which beach, he wondered, but Harvey said he didn't think she'd gone to a beach. He was almost sure she was on a lightning visit to America; recently she'd taken a lot of calls from LA about a movie there that was in serious trouble with its director. Harvey thought they wanted to delay the movie and have her take over.

'What movie?' Patrick asked.

'Mate, if you don't know, I sure as hell don't,' he was told. 'But there were these frequent conference calls she took in private. She had a screenplay she spent a lot of time reading, but kept the title of it to herself. Secretive kind of lady when she wants to be, your missus.'

Patrick thought he and his missus would doubtless be the subject of speculation in the editing suite at Fox tomorrow. He debated whether to ring his father-in-law, and decided not to. He'd left enough messages for Joanna to get back to him wherever she was, which she would assuredly do.

There was a light shower of rain, but despite it Patrick went for a jog down to the river and along the towpath towards Battersea Bridge. The misty rain seemed to match his mood. Sally's chance discovery of his whereabouts, apart from the other hares she had set in motion, felt like an intrusion on the idyllic week since moving to Fulham. He was aware how much the call had disturbed Claire, and was angry at his mistake in leaving her phone number in case of emergency. Particularly as the BBC would never have bothered trying to reach him. Charlotte Redmond, from the tenor of their meeting, would have felt only relief at being unable to find him.

The rain became heavier, and he turned back before reaching the bridge. It was slippery on the towpath and he felt it safer to walk. While he trudged through the increasing rain, thinking what a stupid idea a jog was on a day like this, he reflected on the situation he was in. After six years of her father's hopes and hints, it now seemed as if Joanna had changed her views on parenthood, and he was about to become a dad. Sally clearly thought so.

Despite upheavals of late, he and Jo had enjoyed a passionate relationship. They were on the Sydney list, prominent at show-biz events like premieres and awards functions. Their lives revolved around the profession they both worked in, so Joanna would be concerned if there was a hiccup with the BBC. She'd understand the stress he was under – months of work wasted, as well as a financial loss: tension he was trying to conceal from Claire. He and Jo had known such defeats and disappointments before. Pressure, tough times, even shared failures had bonded them.

But perhaps that was the extent of what they could share. He doubted if Jo would understand other things he was sharing so readily with Claire, like the mystery of his grandfather's extended life, or tracking down Georgina Rickson, who had caught a glimpse of her past and held his hand like a lover. Even the fascination of the notebook, because he knew that buried somewhere in it was the answer to what had really happened to Stephen Conway. Joanna would profess interest, but unless there was a film to be derived from it, that interest would be brief and limited.

Two very different women and one terminally confused man, he thought ruefully after shedding his soaked clothes, showering and sitting down to read more of Stephen's notebook. It needed to be handled with great care, for its age was a handicap; despite Claire's best ministrations the glue that held the pages was breaking each time it was touched. It was difficult in other ways; there were no dates accompanying the entries, unlike the diary that had always given an indication of place and time. The diary had contained a sense of order.

This was completely different. In these pages were sudden comments after Stephen left the hospital, and Patrick had to read very carefully to work out when and where the events had occurred. Some were wildly irrational. One was a surprise that instantly caught his attention.

After Netley I was offered leave, seven lousy days, but who did I know in England, and where would I go? Would I sit in Hyde Park watching the rowers on the Serpentine, or go to St James's and count the ducks on the ponds? Do I wear uniform, and get pestered by the prostitutes? Or go around London in civvies, and have some mad-eyed woman rush up and hand me a white feather, while ordering me to go off and kill someone for her?

No thanks.

I wanted to tell them to shove their leave, but then I remembered. All of a sudden it came so clear in my mind. Elizabeth Marsden – it was like yesterday, with us sitting in that Lyons Corner House, that cosy teashop, and her saying she lived in a village near Cambridge that was called Grantchester.

Chapter Seventeen

A week of leave, they said; it was always a week, a whole seven days offered before anyone was sent back to France. What they meant was a last chance to live a bit, meet a woman, make love, or just catch a glimpse of life before going back to whatever was going to happen over there in hell. I said no, hating the thought of being lonely in London again. Then, half an hour later, I came back to the office and said yes.

'Make up your mind, laddie,' the Scottish doctor demanded, after this indecision was reported to him.

'I've made it up,' I told him, but didn't explain why. He'd be the last person that I'd tell, how all of a sudden I had remembered the name of the town.

So yes, I said to him, I'll have my seven days. And I'll go to Grantchester near Cambridge, and see Elizabeth Marsden. Only I didn't say that to him or anyone else, because this was personal, my private life, perhaps my private love. Or was it just an afternoon with a nice girl who talked to me kindly, so kindly that I can't seem able to forget her? Going to Grantchester, I thought, perhaps I can find out the truth of how I felt at last.

They gave me back my uniform and a leave pass. Because I'd mucked them around they got their own back, delaying me until the daily launch across the water to Southampton had gone, so the only way to get to the town and the main line train station was to walk to the terminus. A mere six miles, the Scottish quack said, for a fit bloke like you just a stroll in the park. Halfway there I got a lift on the undertaker's wagon from the hospital that was taking some poor sods to be buried, and I sat in the back with the cardboard coffins all the way into the station.

The express to London got me there in the late afternoon, into the terminus at Victoria where it was crowded because a troop train had just arrived and another was about to leave. Men were being welcomed home: shabby and exhausted-looking blokes were hugged and met with joyful kisses; others, mostly young recruits on the platform opposite, were being farewelled with hugs and tears. There were ambulances too, and nurses; there was a line of blind soldiers being led, and stretcher-bearers carrying the wounded who could not walk.

On the concourse a young woman took my arm and said she had a room around the corner, and did I want to stay the night? She liked Anzacs, she told me, and didn't do this for a living – just to distribute a bit of kindness, a bit of warmth and love. I don't know why, but the use of the word 'distribute' seemed to single her out as someone telling the truth. Anyway, I thought she seemed sincere and thanked her, but said I was on my way to meet a young lady I hadn't seen for nearly two and a half years. She gave me a kiss on the cheek and wished me luck.

I found a room for the night: four beds in an attic, two drunken sailors and an old man for company. It was a relief to get out of there, and by dawn I was walking through Bloomsbury and High

Holborn on the way to Kings Cross station. Empty streets in the early morning, bringing back vivid memories of my first leave and the way I'd explored London. I bought a ticket and went to the very same platform where I'd said farewell to Elizabeth. I remembered it so well, even remembered how the fast trains left at fifteen minutes past the hour, and found the timetable had not changed.

'Nothing ever changes round here,' a cheerful station guard said. 'No changes on this line, matey, since they first invented the steam engine.' I recalled the cranky guard who yelled at me when I was trying to get Elizabeth's address, but this one was friendly, so that was a change for the better. He asked me about the war; was it as bad over there as people said? The things he'd heard, they surely couldn't be true, could they? Not wanting to talk about it, I told him about Elizabeth instead. He wished me luck and we shook hands before I boarded the train.

It was not quite ten in the morning when we arrived at Cambridge. I would've liked to visit the university, but I wanted to see Elizabeth first. It occurred to me that after we'd met, we could go there together. Tour Trinity College and its famous quadrangles. Imagine walking where Byron, Isaac Newton and Tennyson all studied in years gone by . . . And after that we could even hire a punt for the afternoon and enjoy a row on the Cam, like I'm sure Byron did.

I found a bus that went to most of the local villages including Grantchester. People on the bus seemed welcoming. The driver said it was a nice little spot, and when I got off there he also wished me luck. Some of the passengers waved. All these good wishes from strangers were like a favourable omen. It felt wonderful to be among such friendly people, and in such a pleasant village.

How to describe a place like Grantchester? Small cottages, some of them quaint, all old; tiny gardens alive with flowers; a sense of absolute peace that felt as if it belonged to another time. Very few shops, only a chemist, a draper's, an ironmonger's and a food store that sold magazines and postage stamps. A corner shop, they call it, with timber beams that looked at least a century old, and a thatched roof. I went in there to ask directions.

A woman serving behind the counter was slicing bacon and weighing it while talking with a customer. I stood waiting near the door until they had finished, and became conscious they had noticed my uniform and the slouch hat. The customer paid for her groceries and started to leave, so I opened the door for her.

'Thank you,' she said, and that was when I couldn't help staring at her. She had the same fair hair and grey eyes, a slim nice-looking woman in her forties, with a face that was at once recognisable to me. It felt like a sort of miracle, but after all, it was a tiny village. She started gazing curiously at me while I kept holding the door open. It seemed like a long time that I waited for her to speak.

'You're Australian,' she said finally, and even though the voice was similar, she seemed uncertain. 'We rarely see that uniform here.' She shook her head. 'Almost never. But surely . . . you couldn't possibly be . . . it's too unlikely.' She shook her head again and walked past me. I shut the door and followed her outside.

'Elizabeth Marsden,' I told her. 'That's who I came to see. You look so exactly like her.'

She gazed at me again, so silent that I began to wonder if she would answer. Then she finally nodded. 'So you must be Stephen. But I thought . . . I was told you were a sergeant.'

'I was in those days.'

'But not now?'

'No.' I thought it was a subject for later discussion when we were better acquainted, and apologised for my sudden appearance. 'I'm afraid I don't know the number of your telephone, or I would've rung up to see if it was convenient.'

'We don't have a telephone,' she answered.

I started to realise she was different to her daughter. Despite the similar appearance she was not the same – not a bit the same – quite difficult to talk to, in fact, and without any trace of Elizabeth's vivacious smile and warm manner.

'I've been in hospital,' I said, trying to start a conversation.

'Were you wounded?' she asked.

'In here,' I replied, and touched my head, a clear mistake for it made her look worried. 'It's really nothing,' I quickly tried to assure her. 'In fact they say I'm so well they're sending me back to France, but I have a few days' leave. And although it's more than two years since I last saw Elizabeth, I've often thought of her. I'm the one who made her miss her train that day. Several trains in fact,' I admitted with a smile.

'Yes, she told us,' her mother answered in a flat, toneless voice. She no longer sounded the least bit like Elizabeth, and I began to wonder what was the matter with her. All this time we were still standing just outside the shop. An elderly man approached and went inside after a nod to Mrs Marsden and a curious glance at me. When he'd gone I asked her if I could carry her basket for her.

'We live past the church, along this street,' she replied after a pause, handing me the basket with some reluctance. She added that I might as well walk home with her. There were things to talk about, she said.

But she didn't do any talking. I felt impelled to fill the void between us. I praised the lovely village she lived in, told her how much I liked the old houses with slate roofs or thatch. I said the thatch seemed best to me, because it was not something we ever see back in Australia. We walked past a large Victorian house – it was the manse – then a sturdy Anglican church with its tall spire dominating the village and the fields around it. The sign on it said it was erected in 1790, and I told her how strange this antiquity was for me and that there were no real buildings in Australia back then, except perhaps the governor's cottage. Governor Phillip, I explained, who brought out the First Fleet and several boatloads of convicts. They had nothing to live in but mud huts, or sometimes bark and wattle shelters called humpies, while the army had tents.

She listened constantly, but made no reply, so I felt I had to keep talking.

'It's so beautifully peaceful here, Mrs Marden, so English. I saw countryside like this in Hampshire, when we first came here after being evacuated from Gallipoli. But it was winter then. On the train yesterday the same fields were growing crops, and they were full of activity. Farmers cutting hay, cattle and sheep grazing. It's a lovely part of the world . . . I don't know how to describe it exactly . . . serene, perhaps. I like the hedges, so orderly the way they divide up the farmland. I like the symmetry of them. I admire the whole English country so much, I feel so content here that I might not want to go home again.'

Her silence made me talk too much, I knew that, but all she did was nod and shrug. Then suddenly she stopped and asked me what hospital I'd been in.

Netley, I told her, and when she admitted she'd never heard of it, I started to explain. I told her about the Scottish quack, and how I'd been given electrical shocks, but when she looked alarmed I explained the way the treatment had been changed to the so-called talking cure. Away from Netley all this seemed impossible. In the quiet of this Cambridgeshire village everything I told her about

Queen Victoria's grand hospital sounded utterly bizarre.

I began to wonder if my telling her all this was unwise, but I felt reassured and able to talk this way because she looked so like Elizabeth. Or at least the outward resemblance gave me confidence. Her lack of response I took for shyness, I suppose, but it did occur to me that until then she had not actually mentioned Elizabeth's name.

'How is Elizabeth?' I asked. After all, this was my purpose here.

She made no attempt to answer. But she stopped walking and I knew we'd reached their house. I admired it, said it was beautiful, which it was. There was thick Virginia creeper all around the oak front door, and window boxes full of colour. It looked like the kind of English house I had seen in magazines when I was a child.

But even while admiring it I realised Mrs Marsden had not replied. That was when I began to feel sure that she didn't like me. She seemed to flinch each time our gazes met, as if she were afraid. I thought I must be mistaken – after all, she had nothing to fear from me. I hadn't come here to make trouble. I'd just come to see her daughter again.

'Is Elizabeth home?' I asked, now determined to put an end to this. 'I've come all this way, so may I please see her?'

She just stood there staring at me. 'Elizabeth is dead', she finally said.

I took a sudden step backwards, stumbled and almost fell. I shook my head in disbelief. It was some mistake or a dreadful joke. It made me angry, because it had to be a lie. I wanted to shout at her, 'Elizabeth is young, my own age, and she's beautiful; I have been secretly in love with her since we met, and it is not possible she is dead!' I started to say some of these things at this cold woman, then the front door to the house opened.

'She's dead!' I heard his voice before I saw the man standing there. A tired, middle-aged man who looked like a schoolteacher. It was then I recalled her telling me her father *was* a teacher. In the same moment that the man came to take his wife's arm, she removed the basket of groceries from my grasp. They moved towards the house in an oddly defensive manner that looked as if they would stand guard there against me trying to enter.

'But how?' I asked him numbly. *How could she be dead?*', I felt like screaming at him.

'Your fault!' His voice was like ice.

'That's not fair.' It was the mother who had found her voice. 'You ought not to say that; he's not himself. He's been ill.'

'It was his fault,' her husband persisted, staring into my face. Perhaps he could see that I didn't understand how it could be my fault, because he continued. 'All your fancy talk about your convicts and currency lads. All that illusion. Put strange ideas in her head, you did. She was a quiet girl, settled in her ways - she had a chap. Simon. He was a nice boy, exempted from conscription because he was studying to be a dentist. After the day she met you, she couldn't be bothered with him; could hardly be bothered with any of us. We were ordinary: not from a far off place on the other side of the world. We weren't over there in France, fighting for King and Empire.' Stephen felt the man was about to cry. 'Our daughter, our lovely gentle Lizzie, gave Simon a white feather. She told him her Aussie friend was in France defending us, while he was spending the war learning to fill teeth.'

'Stop it, Jamie!' Mrs Marsden begged him, while I stood mute as though stricken.

'No, I'm sorry, but I won't stop it.' He gazed at me as if puzzled by what he saw. 'Perhaps it wasn't entirely your fault. Perhaps our girl was a silly child, and invented some kind of romantic nonsense. But Simon took it badly. Gave up his studies, enlisted and went to the war. For six months he was in the trenches, then we heard he was coming home on leave. I think Elizabeth felt guilty: any rate, she dressed up to meet him. Looked a real treat, she did. A pretty girl – I'm sure you remember she was pretty.'

I nodded. It was all I could do. His voice became quiet; there was a feeling of exhaustion as if he could hardly bear to relive this.

'She took the bus to Cambridge, to the railway station. But after she left we had an urgent message from the village shop. There'd been a telephone call. He wasn't coming home after all. Not Simon. A German plane flew over the docks at Calais where troops were about to embark, and machine-gunned them. We were here at home knowing he'd been killed, and there was Elizabeth with her feelings of guilt and remorse, waiting for him at the Cambridge railway station.'

'Christ,' I whispered it, but her father heard me.

'I've given up Christ,' he said. 'I've no time for religion, not since my Lizzie got so quiet, then one day went down to the river and chucked herself in. I know it's unfair to say it's your fault, but if you two had never met I think she'd be alive and married to a dentist. There might even be grandchildren, which we'll never have now, as she was our only child.'

He took the basket from his distressed wife, who went inside without another word. Elizabeth's father remained for a moment looking at me, then shook his head as if all the answers were beyond him. He followed his wife into the house, shut the door and slid home the bolt.

I stood there paralysed, wanting desperately to try to convey my sorrow, but the house was closed, and their locked door would never be open to me. I can't remember how long I stayed, but it seemed ages before I could find the strength to move away. Eventually I managed the walk back through the peaceful village to wait at the bus stop. The cheerful bus driver asked if I'd found my girl, but I couldn't reply. I expect my face gave him his answer, because I was crying. I could never cry for my mates, but I cried for Elizabeth.

The next day I was back at Netley.

Chapter Eighteen

Claire was unexpectedly at work, summoned to a problem with the Knightsbridge accountancy firm's computers. Since there was still no reply from Joanna, despite his persistent calls, nor any word from Charlotte Redmond, Patrick tried not to think of his personal problems. Instead he was focused completely on the crumbling notebook. Trying to decipher pages that were almost incoherent, he felt such a deep kinship and involvement in his grandfather's life that his own concerns became inconsequential. The entry after the visit to Grantchester was filled with so much bewildered torment that Patrick could feel the anguish.

I told them I don't want any more leave. Not for me. One day was enough. One terrible day in the village of Grantchester. I wish to God I hadn't remembered the name. But that's cowardly, wishing I didn't know what happened. Poor Elizabeth. Her parents hate me. They think I caused her to die, caused both her and Simon's deaths. All I did was like her! Was it wrong to like her? To talk and laugh? Two hours in a teashop, that's really all it was. I feel as though I've committed a dreadful crime, but the only thing I did was ask her to have a cup of tea.

So I'm back at Netley. I don't want the other few days of my leave. I can't bear the idea. I'd see a Lyons Corner House and feel sick with guilt. I'd walk to Leicester Square and stand where we met, and wonder why I keep on living. What else could I do for the rest of my leave? Be stuck in a hostel for days, not knowing anybody, sit and watch people walk by, see motor buses drive past, feel miserable and alone among the millions of people?

The loneliest place in the world is a big city when you don't know a single person in it. So I said no thanks to that, and they sent me back to France. The last glimpse I had of the hospital was of this awful great edifice that looked the size of about six English seaside hotels stuck together; the last person I saw was the Scottish quack, standing at the gate watching me leave, the big bearded bastard in his kilt, sending me back to hell. When he raised a hand in farewell, I turned away. I had no wish to bid any sort of farewell to him.

Patrick tried to imagine it, the vast hospital where the wounded were brought by the shipload; the bodily wounded to be healed if possible, while the mentally wounded endured strange and often cruel treatment by doctors who seemed to believe they were shirkers.

His grandfather had hated Netley, but from his notebook one thing was abundantly clear. Totally unfit to fight, he had been sent back into the cauldron that was the battlefield along the Somme. Whatever had finally happened to Stephen had occurred in those last stages of the war, long after he was thought to be dead, somewhere in France during the last months of 1918.

That night after dinner, Claire read the account of the day in Grantchester and wept. Patrick had deciphered more unstable pages, where at times the writing was very uneven now; patches of neat lettering degenerating into a wild scrawl.

'Poor Stephen,' Claire said softly, wiping her eyes. 'As if he didn't have enough awfulness to cope with. And poor Elizabeth and her family. God, that war seems so cruel.'

'This is a bit different,' Patrick remarked casually, indicating another page he'd bookmarked for her. 'There's something here I'd really like you to read.'

'Will I need Kleenex?'

'Not for this one,' he replied, and leant down to kiss the tears on her face. Then he sat beside her while she read.

Hell is the same place, the Somme again, but now I'm with a motley bunch of infantry, none of whom I know. No acquaintances or friends here. I had hoped I might see Sassoon again – his name was Siegfried Sassoon, an English lieutenant who wrote poems, one of which I'd read months ago and written a part of it in my diary. A poem about that fearful place they called Passchendaele.

Claire turned and looked at him. 'When did you find this bit?'

'This afternoon. Surprising?'

'Amazing.'

'Keep reading.'

I met Sassoon at Netley, because he came there on leave to visit Wilfred Owen, another English poet I'd got to know. They were both in a hospital up in Edinburgh, because Wilfred had shell shock. Sassoon was sent there after he won the military cross for bravery. He was so brave he was called 'Mad Jack'. But Mad Jack started to hate the war. He wrote a letter to his colonel, with a copy to the editor of The London Times, *saying he was opposed to the fighting: that it was immoral, a crime against youth; an infamous war waged and plotted by old men, politicians and arms manufacturers, and he would have no further part of it. They didn't know what to do with him – he was too famous to imprison or shoot – so they sent him to the nuthouse called Craiglockhart in Scotland.*

He still refused to fight, so then they gave him the persuasion treatment, persuaded him it was setting a bad example and was even cowardly to skulk in hospital while others fought for him. They worked hard on him, appealed to his sense of honour, his patriotic pride, so he eventually went back. And on leave he came to Netley to see his friend Owen, and Wilfred was a friend of mine by then. He sometimes read me his poems, and when Sassoon came to visit, he introduced us.

I said I knew his brother, Hamo, at Gallipoli. His younger brother, killed there in 1915. Siegfried said it had destroyed his mother, who has séances to make contact with him, and keeps his room at home exactly as he left it, with clean sheets every week and fresh flowers each day. He asked me if his brother was brave.

'Too bloody brave,' I said. 'Brave and crazy, like you.'

'Like us all,' Sassoon replied. 'Especially the crazy part. But I hope he didn't let the side down.'

It was such an English thing to say. A decent thing. So anxious for his brother's good name. I bled for his grief and promised him that his brother certainly did not let the side down. He might've been a poet too, I said, because he talked of it, but never had the time to find out.

I hope Siegfried has survived. Wilfred Owen said he was the war's greatest poet, and Siegfried said that was rubbish – Wilfred was brilliant, remarkable. They each read me a poem, and I told them they were both *brilliant, both remarkable. Siegfried's poem was dedicated to Hamo. Called 'To My Brother', it was bitter and very sad.*

I'd like to see him again, but it's so different back in France. Even at a place like Netley, although they had officers' wards and officers' quarters, we could still be mates. But back here, he's now a company commander, I heard, and I'm a private. Officers and men in our army can be mates; in their army that isn't possible. But for a few days there, we truly were real friends. And I suppose if I could write like them, I'd write a poem about that bearded Scottish bastard, the last time I saw him. Something like this:

> *Dwarfing the sentries at the gate, making sure*
> *I went safely back to death and war.*

If I'm lucky enough to meet Sassoon again, I'll ask him to knock it into better shape for me.

To Claire it was astonishing. On the page in front of her was an extraordinary link between her favourite poet and her lover's grandparent. Siegfried Sassoon had become a very special part of their lives. And he had been, she thought, ever since Patrick quoted from his poetry the night of their first meeting.

That day, after leaving him, she had gone home in the train from Lille, under the channel and then through the orchards and the hop fields of the Kent countryside, thinking of how he had looked as he spoke the few lines. She was unable to forget that moment. By the time the Eurostar reached Waterloo – another memory of Patrick, their shared laughter about the terminal's impact on French sensibilities – she already knew she must see him again. And Sassoon's volume of verse had brought them to this moment in their lives. It was uncanny that in this battered notebook retrieved after so long, they should encounter him yet again.

The book was dangerously close to coming apart now, and Patrick was concerned to preserve it. Claire did some further repairs with binding and glue. As long as they saved the pages, she said, even if the notebook fell to pieces as they tried to read it, she could do a proper restoration job after they'd finished deciphering all the contents.

'And talking of jobs,' she said, being carefully offhand, 'I've fixed the computer system and told them I'm still on leave. They weren't especially happy, but I insisted. Besides, I want to go to Georgina's funeral with you.'

'I'd like you to. How long does your leave last?'

'For as long as you want,' Claire said, then added quietly, 'until the time comes when you go home.'

Patrick put his arms around her, and realised he didn't want to think about going anywhere. He just wanted today and tomorrow, and the days that lay ahead with Claire. But there was Joanna whom he couldn't seem to contact. And there was her news, if true. So this was only a gift of time suspended, and then what? Eventually, inevitably, he would go home to whatever lay in store there. A child? A marriage to repair?

All the while he kept thinking of his grandfather, who had never gone home. And during the days that followed he continued to search through the notebook for the reason why.

Chapter Nineteen

The first I knew about it was when I heard this English voice shouting the news. Something about the French. About them being revolting. I thought it was the usual Pommy whinge against the frogs, because for two armies on the same side who were described as allies, nobody could ever call them friends.

Then another voice yelled out, calling the first voice a stupid booger, and correcting him. Saying the French might be revolting, but that wasn't the point. They were *in revolt*. On strike.

We couldn't believe it. French troops had mutinied! When we heard, it seemed as if the war must soon be over, perhaps a matter of days. If one side wouldn't fight, how could the war continue? And they were definitely refusing to fight; that was the news that came along the line. They were all telling their commanders they weren't going into the trenches; not only that, they were not going to shoot anyone – they'd had more than enough. Two million of their comrades dead so far, and another hundred thousand just killed in a campaign that didn't gain them a yard of ground, devised by their young bastard of a field commander, General Nevelle. Arrogant, they said he was, and ambitious to become a field marshal, no matter how many infantry lives it cost.

For days we thought this had to be just a weird and wonderful whisper on the grapevine, but within forty-eight hours we learnt it was actually true. The French soldiers were bleating like sheep whenever they were given an order, to demonstrate their feelings of being lambs led to the slaughter. That's how the mutiny had started, with the bleating. And after that we heard whole battalions were in revolt, no longer bothering to bleat, just determined not to fight no matter what the cost. The British brass hats in our sector were in a state of disbelief and absolute rage.

'The fucking bastards!' I heard one officer shout – it sounded quite funny because he had this very plummy accent, terribly upper-class to us misfits from all over the place, Poms and Aussies stuck in together, with some N Zedders, a few Boers and other odds and sods. A mixture of Empire troops, we were called, as motley a lot as you'd ever see, but not as motley, according to Colonel Plummy-Accent, as the unspeakable revolting French. It was supposed to be kept a strict secret, and there he was effing and blinding about the treacherous frogs at the top of his voice. 'Deceitful, underhand two-faced shits! We're here helping to defend their country, and the bastards decide not to fight!' he bellowed. His words swept through our lines in a matter of hours. How the entire population of Flanders and Picardy didn't know, as well as all of Paris, was beyond us.

But apparently they didn't. Somehow the French High Command managed to keep it quiet. They hurriedly arranged a conciliation meeting at which the hated General Nevelle would address the troops. But the moment he stood up they started a chorus of abuse and catcalling so nothing he said could be heard, and after that they grabbed their rifles and started firing shots in the air.

We had a dispatch rider, a young English bloke named Dave, who knew all the gossip. We didn't need a rumour mill in our sector, we had Dave.

'So what happened when they started shooting?' I asked.

'The general legged it,' Dave said. 'Almost pissed himself . . . and went for his life. What's that word you blokes use?'

'Shot through?'

'That's it. He shot through like a turkey at Christmas time.'

It was Dave who kept us up to date with what came next.

Somehow the troops and the High Command came to terms. The troops were made to realise that if the public got to hear of the mutiny, there'd be country-wide panic. The Germans would simply walk into Paris. So the troops agreed to go back into the trenches, but only to defend their country, not to attack the enemy.

Dave brought us details of what happened then. And what happened was just unbelievable; horrible.

'These old French generals,' he told us, 'once they got them back in order, they weren't going to put up with any more of their shit. So what's been going on in their army in the past few weeks is something called decimation.'

What the hell is that? we all wanted to know.

'Decimation,' he said, his usually cheery face looking sombre, 'is picking out every tenth soldier in the battalions involved, taking them out and shooting them. No questions, no trial - just outside, matey, stand against that wall and - pow! One more dead. They've killed a few thousand poor buggers like that already.'

We soon found out this was true. What's more, the units they were concentrating on were mostly black North African troops - Algerians and other conscripts from the French colonies. One in every ten! God knows what our own High Command thought of it. According to some, Haig forbade any mention of it in his cosy chateau headquarters. Which sounds right to me – the old field marshal refusing to even think about it. He's got so many deaths on his conscience, what's a few thousand more? Especially as they're frogs. I keep wondering if Siegfried Sassoon has heard about it, and what kind of poem it might stir him to write. Or is Siegfried as exhausted and disillusioned as the rest of us? Too beaten with the futility of it to feel anger or outrage, just waiting for the bloody thing to end so we can go home and try our best to forget we were ever foolish enough to be here.

It's late September now. If there were trees still standing they would be turning to colours of gold and red and amber, those tints of autumn that can look so beautiful, especially to us from the southern hemisphere where the seasonal decline and regeneration is less visible. But of course there are no trees any more. I haven't seen a living tree, not a green leaf or flower growing since they sent me back here from Netley nuthouse. I think it was three weeks ago, but it seems longer.

In the confusion that exists now, they didn't seem to know what to do with me, so I was put in with this mixed battalion of Empire troops. A mob from 'the dominions' they call us; none of us know each other, and nobody feels as if they belong here. Especially me. I asked if I could be put back with an Anzac brigade, and a British lieutenant said that was out of the question at the moment. He told me that because of the heavy losses at Villers-Bretonneux, some of the Anzac units had been converted.

'What do you mean "converted"?' I asked him.

'Amalgamated and reorganised,' he said. 'Not enough men left, so some have been disbanded. We don't know your old division, but it was probably one of those, which means you have to go with this Empire group till things get sorted out. And don't ask me when that'll be, because nobody has the faintest idea.'

He was a reasonable sort of bloke, and in hindsight I wish I'd told him that if I was to die, I'd rather be with my own and not among a mob of strangers. But a fat lot of use it would've been. He'd have probably stopped being reasonable, told me to shut up, to do what I was told and await further orders. But the truth is we are all strangers, and in the eyes of these young untried recruits I am an old unwelcome guest, an ageing Anzac soon to be twenty-four years old. I am shell shocked, cynical, very likely mad, and not the least bit like these boys from school.

This place where we've huddled in a sprawling network of trenches is near St Quentin, and somewhere not very far away must be the cow shed where I fell asleep, and woke up to find my Angel of Mons. I wonder what's happened to her, and whether her fiancé or her father returned there. I hope so. I keep remembering my last sight of her, a lonely girl in a ragged dress waving to me until we could no longer see each other. And until I could no longer see the tears on her face.

I almost went back, almost didn't leave there at all; she said I could wear the fiancé's clothes and work on the farm with her, and no one in my army would know I hadn't been killed at Pozieres. I tried to tell her there was Jane, waiting for me at home. She tried to tell me that when her fiancé came back we could stop loving each other and I could go home to Jane. There were a few hours, perhaps a day or two, when I thought it possible. But in the end I knew I couldn't stay. If good things happened in this world I could see her again, maybe; find out she's safe and happy, married to her bloke, and then I could go home to Jane and my son. But good things don't happen like that. I even wonder sometimes if the farmhouse still exists. Or did some stray shell misfire and demolish the place – and her with it?

We've been stuck here in these trenches for over forty-eight hours. Eardrums shattered by our own guns firing at the Huns, followed by the sound of our aircraft overhead. New recruits are told this is a bombing raid to help soften up the enemy. What they aren't told is that this is bullshit, the usual deceit for the mugs in the trenches handed out by the brass in their safe havens far from here. For instance, this morning when planes of the Royal Air Force flew over us they were not bombers but reconnaissance aircraft sent to view the result, and soon afterwards our artillery resumed firing. Which means all the shells and salvoes fired for two days and nights did not hit their targets; there are still blockhouses intact with machine guns waiting for us, like the machine gunners at Pozieres that scythed down Bluey and so many other mates.

No, not Bluey. Hang on, he died of a flesh wound. Those callous doctors, God I remember them, all right. Told me to clear off when I tried to ask how somebody could be allowed to carelessly die like that. I remember the one who shouted he didn't give a fuck about the dead, he was too busy trying to save the living.

Well, none of them are living now. None of our platoon who left Melbourne in a flurry of streamers and such young dreams of glory and adventure. None left except me, and a corporal who lost his leg from frostbite the time it snowed at Gallipoli. Lucky old Bob Hargreaves. Still has one leg and two arms, and alive somewhere back in Australia. Tate and Dan Ridley were lost at Ypres. Others at

Bullecourt. There are so many whose names I struggle to recall, so many forgotten. A platoon is three ranks of men – I can see them standing on parade in my mind, all gone except for one-legged Bob and me. Poor silly Duggie Chandler – Double-Trouble – boasting of his women and the four fiancées waiting to marry him. If they existed at all, which Bluey and I doubted. It wasn't many kilometres from here that Double went out of the trench for a pee and a breath of clean fresh air. Sometimes I can still see the explosion when the shell burst and, worst of all, the moment afterwards when nothing was left, not an arm or a leg or anything . . .

'What's up, digger? Eee, y' look a bit down in the mouth, matey.'

He was a young Pommy, a skinny kid with buck teeth and a voice like a cross-cut saw, one of the new recruits, staring at me because I'd started thinking what a lousy end it was to a joker who'd always been a bit of fun and given us plenty of laughs. If my eyes were a bit moist, it was none of his business.

'What's up, chummy? Look like yer was waterin' the cheeks. Havin' a bit of a blub, eh?'

'I'm all right.' I didn't feel all right, but I didn't need this kid to be intruding.

'Yer don't look all right to me, yer look shit-scared. Like you need a white flag to wave.'

'Just sod off!' I told him, but he didn't seem able to take a hint.

'You're windy, yer bleedin' are! Plain as day. I thought the ruddy Anzacs were supposed to all be such heroes.'

'Shut up, you stupid turd!'

But he wouldn't shut up. 'Eee, lads,' he called out, 'get a fooking look at this! We got a bleedin' Anzac here with the wind right up his Khyber Pass!'

I don't know what I would've done next to get rid of him. But that was when an English corporal came and told the boy to clear out. He sent him to the far end of the trench. We could hear him as he went, still saying that one of their new reinforcements, a fooking Anzac of all people, was green around the gills and havin' bleedin' kittens. The corporal yelled at him and shrugged at me with what seemed like sympathy.

'Stupid lad. He'll learn.'

'By the time they learn, it's often a bit late.'

'New reinforcement, he called you. As if you were fresh out from Blighty.'

'Wish it was true, Corp. Wouldn't mind being brand new and innocent, like some of them.'

'Name's Ted,' the corporal said.

'Stephen.'

'Been in a few horrible places have you, Stephen?'

'Too many. I was thinking of the mates I lost at Pozieres, down the road from here, when that kid saw tears in my eyes.'

'I'll sort him out. Sit and take it quiet for a while. Be a couple more hours, by the sound of it.'

'That'll mean the middle of the day, Ted. It'll be bloody murder.'

'Got no choice, day or night. If the officers start blowing their whistles, we have to go. Or the trench police shoot us from behind.'

'Trench police?' It was a new one to me. I was puzzled by the term.

'Maybe you Aussies never had 'em.'

'I don't think we did. Are they coppers?'

'Sort of. They often come as recruits, so we got no idea who they are till their revolvers come out before we go over. If someone cracks or holds back, they kill him. So he can't panic the rest.'

'God Almighty.' No, I certainly didn't remember us ever having friendly persuasion like that behind us.

'They're all conscripts now, see. They didn't want to come here. That stupid kid, he's more scared than you or me.'

He was in his twenties, the corporal, a compact build and rather keen face. On edge like all of us, but making a better fist than most.

'What exactly are we doing?' I asked him. 'Does anyone know the purpose of this attack?'

'Not really. But it seems the brass need them trenches the Huns are in, to mount a big push. The attack should've been at dawn, but the guns got the wrong targets.'

'Nothing changes, Ted, does it?'

'Not much, mate.'

'So many mistakes. Bullecourt, our own guns got quite a few of us there. Thirty tanks we had in support, twenty-five of them broke down, and our bloody guns were behind, shelling the shit out of us. Nothing ever bloody changes.'

'Relax, Stephen. I know it's impossible to sleep, but try to rest a bit. We'll get a tot of rum before we go.'

A tot of rum, I thought. Dutch courage. I tried to rest. The guns were silent after a time, and I began to feel my stomach knot with expectation. Then more aircraft flew over, and soon afterwards artillery fire resumed again. The whole morning went by, and we were told to line up with our mess kit. A watery stew was served, but who the hell had any appetite? I threw mine into the oozing mud, and saw the sludge stir as rats fought over it below the filthy surface.

For two more hours our composite battalion of rejects and recruits sat obediently waiting. While I could vividly recollect the nightmare of hand-to-hand combat, I'd almost forgotten the sheer tedium of the trenches. Hours, sometimes days, of waiting. No chance to relax because of nerves that were so on edge, yet we were supposed to sleep in these waiting periods of daylight. The nights were reserved for work, digging latrines, guard duty, as well as laying down more duckboards and repairing the damaged dugouts.

The next predicted two hours passed. My mind seemed to be a turmoil. Maybe another hour, someone said, and that was when I knew I couldn't wait any longer, or fight any more. There were steps set up for us to climb when the signal to attack came. I stood up, climbed them and I was out of the trench. It was so quick and casual that hardly anyone was aware of it until the rifle fire started from the German trenches on the far side of the wire. I heard a shout; it was the same young Tommy.

'It's that dopey fookin' Anzac!' he yelled.

I just stood there for a moment, oblivious to him and everything else. I must've been silhouetted against the sky, somehow not hit by the shots from the enemy rifles, while rejecting the shouts from my own platoon to get back in the trench and take cover.

I ignored everything, told the whole world to go straight to hell and walked away from both sides. I'd come to the conclusion the French had been right; this war was no longer worth another single life, and I was going home to my wife and child. Even if I had to walk all the way.

Chapter Twenty

It was late at night but Claire and Patrick continued to read. Lying in bed, their minds were focused on the events of that extraordinary day eighty-two years ago, when a young man's life changed forever. Miraculously spared by the enemy fire, Stephen Conway walked away from the conflict and tried to explain why. Perhaps it *was* the example of the French mutineers, or the savage reprisal that followed. Perhaps the angry poems of Sassoon or Wilfred Owen, volunteer officers now bitterly against the war. But more likely it was too many bloodstained metres, too many lives squandered for so little gain, and most of all too much time spent in the awful state of rage that he knew lay ahead, a state he and his mates had always labelled the slaughterhouse.

Claire and Patrick read these attempts in which Stephen tried to clarify his feelings, the fumbled sentences, the misspelt words scratched out, the raw pain exposed in the scribbled pages. There was a veracity that kept them reading, although they felt nauseated.

The slaughterhouse is what we call it . . . that's the hard bit, the worst part . . . the hand-to-hand combat where we fight and the sound you hear is grunting. We grunt like pigs. It's a wild sort of madness that lasts a long time after . . . a long time . . . hunting out the enemy after we reach their trenches . . . hunting and killing the bastards. No prisoners taken . . . not yet . . . not a chance of that, not till the blood starts to cool down, till the mind gets a bit calmer. It always takes an hour or two to be sane again . . . then we stop knifing them in the guts with bayonets or shooting them in cold blood while they're helpless. We stop enjoying it, and the slaughterhouse is over for another day. When we cool down we can bear to escort them as prisoners to a lockup, knowing they'll be safe to see out the war in there. Hating them for being able to survive, when we're not sure if we will. It's sick, horrible . . . but that's how we are, we're like animals till the slaughterhouse ends.

It's what we were taught . . . they trained us to be murderers . . . taught us on dummies, on wheat sacks stuffed with straw back home at training camp . . . if you didn't scream and yell as you shoved the bloody broom handle – pretending it was a bayonet – into the dummy's straw gut, you got leave docked, or made to peel spuds in the cookhouse, or else empty the putrid stinking dunny cans. We fought first with broom handles – when we got real bayonets we were in shit if the dummies weren't ripped apart. That's how they taught us. You learn it, then you find you're killing people . . . the dummies have become flesh that screams and blood that spurts . . . you can't stop because you've been taught too well.

How can you turn it off, that frenzy, when a whistle blows? But that's what they expect, the bastards who trained us. You're supposed to stop, the game's over lads, shake hands. Another game real soon. Perhaps tomorrow . . . more murder tomorrow.

'Jesus Christ,' Claire said shakily, 'no wonder Mrs Greenfield at the home thought of burning this.'

They continued reading. They felt close to the truth, the reason Stephen Conway had never returned home. The explanation was here somewhere in the last tortured, unstable pages.

It was that ferocious aftermath of battle, Stephen's notebook insisted, the dreadful hour of triumph when they stabbed and shot and murdered the enemy so indiscriminately that caused it. The killing was what he could no longer bear, and the thought that it would happen again and again. For during that period of time it seemed they were not human, not amendable to reason; afterwards, when a sort of sanity returned, there was always a sense of horror and shame.

Whatever the cause, he had to get away.

Four years was more than enough. Nobody, four years ago, had expected to be here this long. If they had there would have been no volunteers, no brass bands or recruiting rallies that enrolled the thousands of lads who were afraid *not* to join – afraid of being called cowards and singled out to be humiliated by being given white feathers.

If any of them had had the least idea what it would be like, most would've braved the jeers and feathers and never left home.

Surely he had done enough. Done what they called 'his bit'.

More than his bit.

What about those people back home on the beaches; blokes his age playing cricket and football; what about the crowds at race meetings? What kind of fair go was it, if he was not allowed to go home and join them?

He described walking along the road that led towards the town of Peronne, and looking for a field hospital where he intended to report he was ill and needing treatment. He had no real idea of his whereabouts. It was a British command area; General Monash's Australian headquarters was miles away, too far to walk for his feet were blistered and he was already limping badly.

Thus what happened from then on could not have been foreseen. Without those blisters he could have marched into more friendly terrain, or so it seemed to Patrick reading this more than eighty years later.

Stephen Conway was stopped and questioned by two British military policemen. As a result of his confused answers and his futile attempt to run away, they drew their pistols and tried to shoot him. The bullets missed, but his confusion grew into muddled panic. He had come along this road, trying to seek sanctuary from the war, but it seemed he had brought the war with him.

Falling to the ground, a quivering wreck, he was caught; his arms were twisted as the police forced his hands into shackles they locked behind his back, then he was frogmarched to a detention barracks and accused of being absent from his post, disobeying orders and resisting arrest. He was incoherent and angry, hence unwisely abusive, which brought a savage beating by the military police, after which he was shoved into a cell and held there for further interrogation.

That night, after more questions - hours of questions - after being provoked into yelling back at them by the throbbing in his head and the explosions inside his mind, after sobbing and telling them to all get fucked, that he would never fight again, he was formally charged with desertion in the face of enemy fire and arraigned to face a court-martial as soon as possible.

Nobody thought to advise him he could have a legal representative. His mind was so addled by years of bombardment while living in mud, it did not occur to him that being a law student he could even attempt to defend himself.

His feelings were scrawled in wild sentences, but precisely *when* they had been written was unknown. It had to be after the trial, Patrick felt, but how long afterwards? Until they knew the totality of what exactly had happened, it was impossible to tell.

Sometimes he and Claire had to reassemble the scrambled words, to assume some events from a phrase or two as they tried to construct the happenings of so long ago. The court-martial, for instance, seemed to have been delayed while the British authorities discussed the protocol. A question had been raised: should Private Conway be tried by his own senior officers of the Australian force? Not if that could be prevented, seemed to be the answer.

For they knew that because of political differences at home, Australian military courts did not enforce the death penalty. Hence Allied Command was determined to deal with the problem of Private Conway itself. One British colonel in particular was most insistent. He pointed out many Canadians had been tried for serious crimes by High Command court-martial, and these soldiers had been executed without protest from their government. In his opinion, the Australians were not a separate force at all but British Empire troops, and the accused had been serving in a unit that was under British command. It therefore established a clear precedent for the matter to be dealt with by them, and it should occur without delay. This war must be won, he declaimed; if soldiers could escape the penalty for desertion, thousands would run away! Morale would suffer, the war could be lost. In the colonel's opinion this was no routine case, it was a matter of crucial concern.

It was Claire who realised the colonel's identity, by delving back a few years into Stephen's diary.

'Carmody,' she said. 'Major Carmody! Remember him?'

Patrick realised she was right. This relentless colonel was the former Major Carmody, who declared the accused was a known troublemaker, a sergeant reduced to the ranks for insubordination. He announced he could personally testify to that crime. The Australian was also a shirker, hiding from the war at Netley Hospital, which his fellow officers would agree was a well known bolthole for malingers and cowards.

His fellow officers declined to air their opinions on that, but they did concur on the jurisdiction. They favoured the notion they should try the case. After all, if Canadians had been court-martialled by the British military when circumstances warranted, why not Australians? Both countries were dominions, both under the supreme command of Field Marshal Haig. Why should special privileges be granted to any Australian criminals? If they were able to escape the ultimate penalty, then what was India, South Africa, New Zealand and the rest of the Empire going to say?

The Colonel's rhetoric prevailed. It was agreed Private Conway would face a court-martial of British officers.

Chapter Twenty-one

The cemetery was at Surbiton, which today seemed directly below the flight path to Heathrow. The minister, an Anglican priest engaged for the occasion, had a fragile voice that was frequently drowned by aircraft as he read the service and asked His Father in Heaven to take Georgina Rickson into His Kingdom. Apart from knowing her name, Patrick wondered if he had the slightest idea who on earth he was assigning into the care of his deity.

The sermon sounded thoroughly pedestrian – like a job, which it doubtless was. Patrick guessed the reverend probably did a dozen a day, using the same format with different names, and earning a fair stipend, although his bounty from this one might disappoint him, unless he'd negotiated his fee in advance with Mrs West. He reflected she must be delighted at the turn of events. She had her hands on the inheritance at last, and . . .

A nudge from Claire disturbed his thoughts. He realised everyone else was rising for a brief final prayer and the service was over.

It took place in the smallest chapel. Expecting no one to be present except the niece, Patrick and Claire were agreeably surprised to find over twenty people. Pleased, too, for the group included

Mr Goldsworthy from the Leatherhead Historical Society and the estate agent Tom Rutledge, as well as Mrs Greenfield and Kitty the nurse. A man in a formal dark suit introduced himself as Georgina's solicitor from Peacock & Marsh.

'Fine woman,' he said, 'I hoped she'd see out her hundred, and get a royal telegram.'

'That would've been nice,' Claire replied with a diplomatic smile, and steered Patrick away before he could make a comment. She knew his republican sentiments on condescending telegrams from the palace that were most likely dispatched by royalty's junior clerks. Patrick realised he was being manipulated, and rather enjoyed the feeling. Just to prove it he openly took her hand; she smiled at this and interlocked her fingers with his, a warm, intimate gesture which he found even more enjoyable. They went to greet Mr Goldsworthy and the agent.

'I suppose this is the end of your search,' Goldsworthy said, and appeared not the least surprised to see their clasped hands.

Patrick told them of finding Georgina in the nursing home, but made no mention of conditions there. They spoke to Mrs Greenfield and Kitty while Helen West ignored them. She was in conference with the solicitor, then left in a chauffeured limousine. They were not the only ones feeling she was already spending the inheritance.

'Patrick, look!' Claire pointed to an elderly figure, only now leaving the chapel. He was accompanied by a smartly dressed young woman.

'Good Lord, it's Andrew Gardiner.'

'It certainly is. Who's the girl?'

'Karen, the *au pair*.' Patrick said. 'I didn't recognise her for a moment with her clothes on.'

Andrew Gardiner said he'd have a pinkers. Bit of a risk, a drink like that in a local pub, but it was an old naval habit. He began to tell the barman the required amounts of gin and angostura bitters, but the barman replied he'd worked in a shore base, and Sir was not to worry. When it came, Karen sniffed and declared it smelt nice, wondering if she should have one.

'Better not, my duckie,' Mr Gardiner said, 'not if you want to drive us back afterwards.'

My duckie, Patrick thought, my goodness! He tried to avoid Claire's gaze. The old codger was doing rather well for himself.

'He's teaching me, so I get my English licence,' Karen said. 'He's a very kind and patient man.'

She settled for a lemon drink, and Claire and Patrick ordered lagers. They expressed their pleasure at seeing Andrew Gardiner again.

'I read about the funeral in the local paper,' he told them. 'At my age it's the first thing you read. Just to see who's fallen off the twig. Felt I ought to show up. Dear old George, she was always kind to me. And young duckie here wanted to practice driving, so we put on our best bibs and tucker and came along.'

'Best bibs and tucker means good clothes,' Karen confided with great earnestness to Claire, 'whereas tucker on its own means food. And bib on its own means the little towel for babies when they spill. Very confusing sometimes, the English language.'

'It is,' Claire agreed. 'And how's your driving?'

'Good. Only one red light today.'

'You only got stopped by one?'

'No,' Mr Gardiner said, 'she only went *through* one. Better than yesterday. Lucky my old ticker's up to it. Fit as a fiddle, lately.'

'That's another English mystery,' Karen said. 'How can a fiddle be fit? A fiddle is a musical instrument . . . I know because Mr Andrew often says there's many a good tune played on an old fiddle.'

Patrick tried not to choke on his beer. He looked at Mr Gardiner, who winked at him and raised his pink gin.

'To Georgina,' he said, and they all echoed it and drank a toast. 'I thought that minister was a dead bore,' he observed. 'Hadn't a clue about her. The niece should've given him a bit of background, then he could've said less about God and more about George. How she was a nurse, and all that –'

'But Andrew . . .' Patrick felt it time to be less formal if he was going to disagree, 'I don't think she really *was* a nurse.'

'Of course she was, old boy. Definitely a nurse.'

'Oh, well . . .' He felt Claire's hand take hold of his below the table. It was asking a lot of an old man's memory.

'But . . . she wasn't a Rose,' Andrew Gardiner added, and they both turned to gaze at him while he took a sip of his gin, aware he had their interest. 'Too young for that. Henrietta was older – *she* was the Rose. I got that wrong the last time we met. *Tempus fugit*, or as they say these days, a "senior's moment".'

'I see . . .' Patrick started to say, but the other was in full flow.

'I started thinking about it, and the old brain box was in better shape this time. I can even remember the song, but don't make a run for the door; I won't sing it. Just try to rattle off the words.'

They leant forward to listen as he recited:

There's a Rose that grows in No-Man's-Land,
And it's wonderful to see.
Tho' it's sprayed with tears,
It will live for years, in my garden of memory.
It's the one red rose the soldier knows,

It's the work of the Master's Hand;
In the war's great curse, stands the Red Cross Nurse,
She's the Rose of No-Man's-Land.

'Bravo!' Claire cried, and they all applauded his recollection.

'Terrible load of old twaddle, but my dad loved singing it. He'd open the piano and bash the keys – long after the war when everyone else had forgotten it. My poor mother hated that song.'

'So they were both nurses?' Patrick prompted him back to the Rickson sisters.

'They were, but at different times, old lad. Henry during the war, so I was told. Serving over in France for a while, then back in Blighty at a rum sort of place called Netley.'

'She was at Netley?' Claire was now as intent and absorbed as Patrick. It was as though the words in the notebook were coming to life in this unlikely locale, a corner table in a nearly empty pub in Surbiton.

'Absolutely. Heard of Netley, have you?' Andrew asked. 'Never saw it myself, but it was supposed to be the biggest hospital in the world.'

'Yes,' Patrick replied. 'They sent the shell-shock cases there.'

'That's so. Hadn't a clue how to treat 'em properly, from all accounts. Poor devils. Dreadful war. All wars are dreadful, but that was the worst because it never should've happened. Morally wrong, all about territory and national pride.'

After the drinks they walked out to the car park. Karen went to sit at the wheel of the car, an elderly but well-preserved Rover; rather like its owner, Patrick felt, as they made their farewells.

Andrew said he was glad he'd come, and was extremely pleased he'd met them both again. He hoped it was not out of order to wish the pair of them good luck. And on another matter entirely, he was going to leave strict instructions that on no account should he have that parson at his funeral.

'How about a woman celebrant?' Claire suggested, and Andrew's eyes sparkled at the idea.

'I'll tell my daughter,' he promised. 'I want a nice-looking one. As pretty as you!' He asked if she'd mind, but he'd like to kiss her goodbye. After a chaste kiss on the cheek and a firm handshake with Patrick, he got in the car beside Karen.

Patrick and Claire linked arms and watched as she started the engine.

'As pretty as me,' Claire repeated, 'what a charmer!'

'They don't make them like that any more,' Patrick assured her. It was all he had time to say, as Karen accidentally pumped the accelerator and the Rover shot out of the car park into the road. There was a screech of brakes. A furious male driver who stopped only inches from them honked his horn angrily while bellowing abuse. From her seat in the Rover Karen gave him a sweet smile, blew him a kiss and drove sedately off.

There was still no news of a meeting at the BBC and, even more surprisingly, no reply to any of the messages Patrick had left for Joanna. By now the staff at Fox studios would be speculating on the state of their relationship after his frequent calls and emails. It was a puzzle, and since she remained so determinedly out of touch – for that was how it appeared to him – there seemed nothing else he could do but make direct contact with his father-in-law Carlo Lugarno.

But after some consideration he rejected this. For despite their outward rapport, he had always been aware that Carlo viewed his daughter's marriage with some negativity; having clawed his own way from indigent refugee to wealth and influence, he'd had elaborate plans for his only child. Few men could match his expectations, certainly not one from the arcane world of showbusiness. Carlo had worn his disappointment with good grace, but Patrick knew his father-in-law secretly wished she had married a leading lawyer or a blue-chip industrialist, almost anyone but a 'journeyman writer' – particularly one foolish enough to toss away a legal career.

Also, Carlo's impatience at their failure to produce children, and the accusatory comment of them making films, not babies, had been levelled at Patrick, not at his adored Joanna. He'd never believe she was averse to providing him with grandchildren, so the lack of progeny after five years would not be blamed on her. There was little point in seeking Carlo's help; it was a matter of waiting until Joanna chose to make contact. However, it was now over a week, and while in their times apart there had been longer periods than this without communication, his sister's phone call made this one strangely perplexing.

Meanwhile the weather in London continued to be kind, and the days were full and tranquil. Patrick and Claire sometimes ate at a favourite restaurant on the river. Each morning they went for a jog on the Thames towpath, and later strolled along Kings Road to buy prawns at the fishmonger's, followed by a beer at the World's End where they began to meet friends. Their simple domestic routine in the time since he had moved to Fulham felt euphoric, like a stolen honeymoon.

Patrick woke at two the following morning and found himself alone in bed. A spill of light came from the study where Claire was engrossed. She had been following links on web sites, she told him as he appeared, and sounded excited.

'It's all here, Patrick, just like Stephen said! The French mutiny, those poor devils they executed. All true! I haven't found more names yet – but if I keep tracking we'll find something.'

Her excitement was infectious. She wore a short towelling robe, and with her long bare legs, her face devoid of any makeup and her auburn hair tied back, she looked like a lovely vivacious schoolgirl. He sat beside her, feeling a rush of happiness, the same feeling that had taken him by such surprise at the village pub the day she had asked him to come and stay with her.

It felt like love, but it seemed premature and reckless to say so.

'You've got mail,' Claire told him the following afternoon, for Patrick's laptop was now networked to her computer. Patrick saw a list of senders in his inbox, but there was nothing from Joanna. The only personal letter was from Sally.

'God Almighty,' he said, reacting to her news.

'What's wrong?'

'My wife's been in hospital. Not at home, she was taken ill in Los Angeles. She's on her way home now.'

'What happened?'

'I don't know. I've been leaving messages for the past week. This explains why they weren't answered.'

Claire was certain he was being evasive, just as he had been after the surprise phone call. But why, she wondered, and felt her heart plummet. The acute disappointment made her reply abruptly.

'Then you'll want to go home. Better call the airline. Check if there are seats.'

'Let me think about it, Claire.'

'But you must go home. Surely your wife will expect you to?'

'The email's from Sally.'

'Even so . . .' Desperately wanting him not to go, Claire found herself almost insisting that he should. 'If she's been ill . . .'

'I'll wait until later, till breakfast time in Australia, and talk to my sister first.'

'At least you can make a tentative booking in case, and cancel if necessary. I'll take your shirts down to the laundrette.'

'Getting me ready for take-off?'

'It seems silly not to be prepared.' She put his washing and some of her own into a bag. 'Won't be long. Here's the phone book. The airline should still be open, if you ring soon.'

'Not trying to get rid of me, are you?'

'Don't be so fucking stupid,' she said, and went out while he was reflecting on what sort of an answer that merited.

When Patrick heard the street door below slam shut he read Sally's letter again. Her emails were often verbose, but this one was different. Brief and to the point.

Knew you were worried, plus Mum bugging me about news on the preggers/grand-parentage aspect, so rang Carlo. He's in shock. She flew to Los Angeles for some film meeting, and was ill there. He thinks it was a miscarriage, 'cos she's no longer pregnant, but I have to say I'm not quite sure what I think, Pat. She's back tomorrow. Felt you should know, luv S.

Patrick knew what the letter was hinting. Why hadn't Jo let him know? Why, suddenly, was he hearing this news via his sister and father-in-law? And how did he feel about *not* being a dad?

Disappointment or relief? Sally was clearly intimating an abortion. Sal sometimes jumped to hasty conclusions about her sister-in-law, but if this by any chance happened to be true, then why hadn't he been consulted?

Claire sat watching the clothes and soapy water swirl in the window of the machine, wishing she hadn't snapped at Patrick like that, and wondering why she hadn't brought a book or newspaper to read. Probably because she'd never sat waiting like this before; she always left her washing with Mrs Rhani, the obliging Pakistani, who dried and folded it for a small extra charge. But today she'd said she would wait, and now realised that watching clothes being washed, rinsed and spun-dried was akin to watching grass grow, and about as exciting.

So why was she doing it? Because she didn't want to go back to the flat just yet. After an exit line like that, she couldn't think of the right one for an entry. And Patrick needed space, time to think. She knew it wasn't his fault; it was just rotten luck that on one of the best days in her life, a day when she had felt happiest, this news had to spoil it.

Ever since the funeral, being greeted by people they'd previously met together, especially dear old Andrew Gardiner, she'd felt the comfort of knowing they were regarded as a couple, an item. Even Mr Goldsworthy, to whom she'd told the story about being Patrick's PA, seemed to accept that the relationship had moved on. It was a good feeling. It had been a long time since she had been seen as a partner with anyone, a real item. Nearly four years, which at her age of twenty-eight was a very long time indeed.

There'd been attachments, a few lovers, but no actual love.

Frank, the most recent and now far away in New York, had never been a real contender. Not since Donald had stormed his way into her life – and out again after two years of love and pain: two years of exquisite joy followed by the reality of deceit and humiliation – had she allowed anyone to occupy a place so deep in her affections again.

Not until she'd gone to the Menin Gate.

And if the day of the funeral had been heart-warming, today was even better. It had been an ordinary and yet extraordinary day, full of simple things: jogging, breakfast, shopping together, a stop at the pub, and she was not sure if Patrick felt it, but to her it was as if this could be the pattern of a life. She'd made herself forget that he was married, that he already had a life, and was soon going back to another country and another woman. She had been idiotically happy until a sign on her computer told her he had mail. As an expert who made her living in the IT world, she profoundly wished the bloody things had never been invented. Although that was a stupid thought; bad news could always be sent by phone or fax machine. She was being childishly aggrieved.

Claire felt she could no longer bear to watch Patrick's shirts and pants tumbling in the soap suds. 'I'll be back,' she told Mrs Rhani, and leaving the laundrette she walked down to the towpath.

The tide was out, and on the mudflats gulls fossicked and noisily squabbled for the scraps that pleasure boats had dropped. She felt it sad the way people treated the river. She could see old tyres that had been dumped, and a rusted pushbike lay almost buried in the mud. Other debris lay waiting for the next attempted clean-up. Old father Thames, the song said, but Donald had always claimed the river should be feminine: she was a grand old lady. If that was so, today her mascara had run and left her looking like a tired old tart.

She hadn't thought of Donald in a long time. Had resolutely not wanted to, although after a gap of four years it was less an ache than a distant and distasteful memory. He had been her first boss in a large communications company; she'd been selected, from a veritable army of applicants, to work in an elite group that set up computer systems. At first she believed that she'd been chosen on merit; later, much later, he told her he had seen her legs first, then looked at her other credentials, the ones on paper. Donald had had enough wicked charm to get away with that sort of remark, and by then they were lovers.

He had a flat on the river at Canary Wharf, expensive and new. There was an ex-wife in Oxfordshire and two young daughters. It was at his former family home he spent most weekends; his wife was content to move out of the house to join her new partner at Chiswick, while he had his time with the children. Revolving doors, he called it, a civilised way for him to have part custody of the kids without uprooting them from their environment. Even now she flushed at the thought of how gullible she'd been for the time they lived together.

Two blissful years, until one day she came home to Canary Wharf to find a group of people crowded into their apartment. Standing at the door in surprise, a striking blonde woman greeted her with the remark that she must be Claire.

She agreed she was indeed Claire, but who were they? Was Donald here, and what was going on?

'This is Claire.' The blonde woman introduced her to the mixed group, all very smart casual, who seemed to be enjoying her drinks while they sprawled in her chairs. Hers and Donald's - of whom there was not a sign.

As she looked around for him the blonde said, 'Claire warms the bed for Donald . . . Mondays to Fridays. And in case you haven't already twigged, Claire darling, I'm Patricia, his wife.'

Everyone seemed to think it a tremendous joke.

'Ex-wife . . .' was all Claire could think to say, feeling angry at the invasion and bewildered by what was happening.

'Quite definitely not ex, sweetie,' Patricia replied. 'Never have been ex, and don't intend to be.'

'I'm sorry,' Claire said, 'but I'm a bit confused.'

'I'm not at all surprised!' Patricia smiled, and her smart friends laughed again. Brayed, Claire thought; that was more the sound, instantly hating them for the sly way they found her discomfort so amusing. She tried not to show her anger, deciding she must remain unruffled and confront the situation.

'Where is Donald?' she asked firmly, but was hardly prepared for the answer.

'In Paris, I gather, with our mutual rival. The latest one.'

'We hear her name's Mirabelle – like the restaurant,' one of the friends said with a snigger.

'Well, we know what Donald's like. If it's crumpet, the name doesn't matter,' drawled a slim effete young man. 'Or, let's face it, the age or the colour. Horny bugger. Shags for England!'

'I don't expect you've met Mirabelle,' Patricia said. 'She's the new one he took to Bournemouth last week.'

'Bawdy Bournemouth,' another friend cooed, and they all seemed to think that hilarious.

'He was at a convention there,' Claire said, beginning to feel quite desperate at the witless banter of these upper-class twits and their expensively dressed Sloane-Ranger women.

'If you believe that, Claire, then you're too young and far too innocent for a conniving sod like my husband. Where do you think he is this weekend? Come on, poppet. Where did he say he'd be?'

'At . . . at home. Your home. With the children.'

'What children? We haven't got children.'

'He has photographs of them! He showed them to me. Their names are —'

'There are no fucking names, dear, because there are no fucking kids.'

'Gillian,' Claire said helplessly, 'and . . . and Lucille.'

Even the smart friends began to quieten at this moment of such complete humiliation. Patricia shrugged. Her smile was now a trifle more sympathetic, less hyped by malice.

'The photos are of a cousin's children. In fact their names *are* Gillian and Lucille. But they're not ours. Your predecessor took only six months to tumble to it. Your tenure has been . . . what, eighteen months? A little longer?'

'Two years,' Claire stammered.

'Did it never occur to you . . . no, I can see it obviously didn't. And no one at the office ever said anything?'

'Nobody there knows about us.'

'Oh, I'm sure they do. But good jobs are hard to find, and Donald *is* the boss. Or at least I am, since I own the company, but he likes to pretend it's his firm. There's a woman there in projects . . . her name is Josie, I believe . . . he spends occasional weekends with her. Those times when I say I don't want him coming home to me.'

Claire remembered wanting to angrily reject this, to say it was a lie; Josie was a friend, her *best friend* in the firm, but she couldn't frame the words. She vividly recalled the sudden rush of nausea and running to the bathroom, where she attempted to be sick quietly, but the bile choked her and she vomited again and again, no longer caring who heard. When she looked in the glass she was a dishevelled mess. She tried to clean her face, mop the tears, wondering how she could go back and face them. But when she did summon the courage to leave the bathroom, only Patricia was still there waiting.

'They've gone to the bar downstairs. You were the spectre at the feast, I'm afraid . . . or whatever that saying is. Rather spoilt the party. Might've been better if I'd warned you; on the other hand, why do I need permission to come to my own apartment? It *is* mine. And not only this one – I own the whole damn building.'

'And you own Donald,' Claire had replied bitterly. 'Is that it? You keep him as a trophy, like your father probably kept heads of the animals he shot, mounted on his walls for people to admire.'

'I say, that's a rather bitchy fun thought. My grandpa, actually. He was the one who left me all the loot. Cut dear old Daddy out of the will, so Daddy and I haven't spoken since.'

She collected a scarf she had left on a chair, and slipped it around her neck. Claire knew instinctively it was an Armani.

'A trophy? I must remember to tell Donald the next time we're in bed. It'll amuse him. A very valuable trophy whom I indulge with the professed ownership of a firm – together with this apartment and girls like you.'

'Not any longer, not me. But if you care so little for him, why do you cling on to him?'

'I thought you were brighter than that. After all, you said he's a trophy. Impeccable family lineage. We'll be the Duke and Duchess some day, if two elderly relatives manage to die. In the meantime we prefer other people in bed. Except when he comes home for a family fuck on our occasional weekends . . . with our phantom kids.'

Claire could recall every awful moment. The relief when Patricia had gone, crossing the wharf below to the bar where her friends were waiting. She flushed even now at how she'd hastily stepped out of sight as they'd laughed and looked up at the window, how within an hour she'd packed her clothes, plus a lithograph of the river that she'd bought, left her key on the table and locked the door behind her.

She had never returned to the firm. Just sent him a formal note of resignation, and had been surprised to receive – at her mother's house, where she'd taken sanctuary – a fulsome reference.

Claire shivered, and realised it had grown cold. The sun had now vanished behind clouds and the wind was rising; the best of the day had gone. She felt a mood of deep dejection. In a few hours it would be time for Patrick to make his overseas phone call. To his sister, or perhaps his wife. The obviously talented and so beautiful Joanna, whose picture he carried in his wallet. She'd glimpsed it once when he was buying wine, and knew it could never be an even contest. Not her measured against Joanna Lugarno.

She told herself not to be a fool; these were stupid, resentful thoughts. Whoever he chose to ring, the result would be the same. Tomorrow he would be gone. Good sense had warned her not to fall so completely in love with a married man again, but good sense had nothing whatever to do with her feelings since that night at the restaurant on the Serpentine. She knew it had been recklessly impetuous and that she had only herself to blame.

Claire made her way back to the warmth of the laundrette. She shut the door before she saw him sitting there, in one of the chairs opposite the machines. He merely nodded a hello as she blinked and took the vacant seat beside him.

'Patrick.'

'Mrs Rhani said you'd be back soon.'

'What are you doing?'

'Watching our smalls being tumbled. Like waiting for a kettle to boil, or watching grass grow.'

'Oh God,' she said, feeling such an outbreak of joy at seeing him that it caused an actual pain in her chest. 'What's happened?'

'I rang Sally.'

'But it must be . . . what time . . . some dreadful hour there?'

'Five in the morning. Woke her up, but she's given me a few sleepless nights in her time. I had to confirm what she said in her email. Claire, there's something I've been keeping from you, because I didn't know if it was really true or not. But it isn't, so I can tell you.'

'Patrick darling,' she said fondly, 'you're not making sense.'

'I know I'm not. Well, put it this way. There was a rumour in our family that Jo was pregnant. But she apparently isn't.'

'Oh.' She tried to think of what to say, but he was continuing.

'That's what I've been hiding for over a week. Trying to reach her to find out the truth.'

'You're disappointed?'

'No,' he said firmly. 'Jo never wanted kids . . . so I think I'm relieved. And it means you don't have to try to get me on a plane, especially as I don't want to go.'

She slipped her hand into his, and leant against him. She saw Mrs Rhani glance at this, then continue the chore of folding clothes. A small child came and gazed at them; the mother called her away, told her to mind her manners and not to stare at people.

'You didn't even *try* to book a flight?' Claire wanted her moment of happiness confirmed.

'Didn't even look up the phone number,' Patrick replied. 'So we can collect the laundry tomorrow if you like. On our way to do our daily shop in Chelsea, and have a cleansing ale at our pub.'

They walked home, arms linked, their steps in joyful unison.

'Where were you?' he asked.

'Down at the river.'

'The tide's out. I saw it from your loo.'

'I know. It looks horrible.'

'It did, even from the loo. Down there it must've been absolutely gruesome. Probably matched your mood.'

'Stop it.' She smiled.

'What?'

'Reading my mind.'

'I'm very fond of your mind.'

'I'm mad about yours,' she answered, 'and the rest of you.'

He put his arms around her and kissed her. A well-dressed man walking two small fluffy dogs on a lead was asking them to please be good boys and do their business. The dogs came and sniffed at the legs of the couple clinging so closely together. Their owner tugged on their leads, trying to steer them away.

'Henry . . . George . . . stop that!'

In the midst of their passionate kiss, Patrick and Claire drew apart and looked at each other in amazement. 'Well, blow me down! I'll be a monkey's uncle!' Patrick exclaimed.

'Henry . . . George . . . Come here, boys . . . at once, please!' Their owner was desperately anxious to leave the spot.

'We knew some sisters named Henry and George,' Claire tried to tell him, in an attempt to excuse their laughter.

The man looked startled at being spoken to, as though it was an unwarranted intrusion. He jerked on the dogs' leads, and all three scuttled away. Patrick and Claire stood watching their retreat, and were home and in bed ten rapturous minutes later.

In the early hours of the morning, when a sudden storm woke them, they sat by the window and watched the lightning transform the black sky somewhere over south London. They tried to speak about the future. Claire found it like walking on eggshells. Patrick said the future was always too complicated to predict, so it was best that they tried to concentrate on the present.

'And my present feelings are quite simple. I don't want to lose you, my love,' he said.

The next morning he woke to find her curled up in his arms, her bright green eyes wide open and studying him from only inches away.

'God, it's early.' He tried to focus on his watch in the pre-dawn gloom.

'The sun will be up in an hour or two,' Claire said. 'Shall we leap out of bed and go for a healthy jog, or stay here and keep each other warm?'

'Let's stay.'

They stayed. And afterwards, happily satiated and on the verge of sleep, he heard Claire murmur.

'Am I really your love?' she asked.

'Yes,' Patrick said.

'Your fancy woman?'

'That too.'

She smiled and snuggled in closer.

Two days later there was finally an email from Joanna.

Darling,

Home at last after an adventurous time, during which I got food poisoning and spent two days in the Cedars Hospital. Home to find lots of messages from you. You must have wondered, but the truth is I had an urgent call to go to LA, and wanted to resolve things there so I could surprise you with my fantastic news. I flew the sharp end, all expenses paid, a suite at the Beverley Wilshire, and I've signed to do a big-budget movie. Details can wait until we meet, but I start pre-production in a month, so hurry home soonest – as they say on the coast.

By the way, I bought the Kirribilli apartment you said we couldn't afford. I just couldn't face letting someone else live there and have that stupendous view, and it'll make a wonderful pad when we come back to Oz from America between movies. Don't worry about the price, darling. That's all taken care of. I would have rung you from California with all this news, but fancy getting food poisoning at a dinner in my honour! At least the studio paid for a private hospital suite – as well they might.

About you, what news of the BBC? If they don't play ball, tell them to shove it. There's plenty of work in LA, and an agent who wants to meet you. Call me to prove you're not cross at me for being secretive, but you know how I feel about Hollywood and its pitfalls. They owed me big-time for the icy reception six years ago, and I wanted to do this solo. I can't tell you how great it feels, I'm walking on air.

Much love, and eagerly waiting here to show you how much,
Jo xxx

PS. There was a strange rumour that I was pregnant. Your mother sent a sweet note saying she was sorry I lost the baby, but I rang her and explained there wasn't one. I think it was my dad who started the false alarm, a case of wishful thinking. Let's face it, we may love our nearest and dearest, but sometimes families are hell!

That night, when it was morning in Australia, Patrick rang her. He said he was thrilled to hear her news, and listened to her enthusiastic account of the visit and details of the proposed movie. It was being rewritten, and she was receiving new pages daily. After they dealt with the acquisition of the new apartment, and how she'd organised a special deposit so she could move in immediately, she asked about progress with the BBC. Patrick admitted there was no word from Charlotte Redmond.

In reply to Joanna's suggestion he pack and come home, that they didn't need the hassle, Patrick dissembled. Despite the fact that he was sure the assertive Ms Redmond would have her own slate of productions and would not welcome leftovers from her disgraced predecessor, he said a meeting was imminent. Truthfully, each day he expected his screenplay to be returned with a note of rejection. He was so sure of this happening that he had started not to care. There were more important things in his life just now: one was the continuing search for what had finally happened to his grandfather, and the other was Claire.

They hung up after mutual assurances they'd see each other soon. As Joanna did not raise the subject of her postscript in the email, he made no mention of the pregnancy that may or may not have been a delusion.

Patrick and Claire's Indian summer lingered through October as the leaves began to fall. As if time was against them, they spent more hours trying to decipher Stephen's court-martial account and its aftermath in the increasingly brittle pages of the notebook. It was more difficult now, the sentences disjointed and unstable, his once neat writing erratic, and the vital final pages badly smudged and faded.

Chapter Twenty-two

I don't know where it was held, this trial, or as the army likes to call it, court-martial – a phrase that has a more ominous sound. I was brought there in chains from the cell, leg irons and handcuffs, with armed guards around me as if I was truly dangerous. It wasn't like a courtroom at all, not a bit like the ones I saw when I was a law student, those times when we were taken to the criminal courts at Darlinghurst, in the process of being taught the noble trade of administering justice. This was just a room, a large office, a long, safe distance behind the lines. I know it was not within miles of the front, because there was no thud of artillery firing, no explosions or the fierce chatter of machine guns; it was so peaceful that there might have been birds singing, except there are no birds here any more.

Not one in the sky, no birdsong to be heard or martins to be seen building nests, for when walls are smashed by bombardments and lie as rubble on the ground there are no nesting places for even the busiest of builders. The swallows and starlings, the wrens and rooks and finches, even the eagles who might have soared arrogantly high above it all must have fled Europe – escaped from France and their mud-filled trenches when the guns began to fire four years ago – and flown south along their migratory escape routes to warm undisturbed Africa and beyond. And perhaps in pursuit went the predatory cuckoo, intent on seizing one of their new nests when they settle in their peaceful destination. I wonder if they will ever come back?

I thought about this while trying to avoid looking at the four judges. All of them British. Four officers sitting at a table, caps placed in front of them, four rigid and frosty faces staring at me. Immaculately uniformed, all with polished leather Sam Browne belts and straps, their shoulders bearing the gleaming icons of rank, each officer with cropped military hair and hostile eyes. The colonel in charge, the president of the court, seemed particularly antagonistic.

Colonel Carmody was the name the prosecutor called him, and I had a strange confusion in my mind. Had I met him before, or did all his kind look alike? Apart from me and the guards and my four judges there was hardly anyone else there – no defence counsel, only the prosecuting major and a man, an army captain, who was called 'the prisoner's friend'. A rather odd name, for he was no friend of mine; we were total strangers. As for what he was meant to do, that still puzzles me, for he did absolutely nothing, except to smile at me occasionally, generally when the court-martial was being told that I was a disgrace, a coward and a deserter in the face of the enemy.

Even though this all happened nearly a week ago, I can still see his smile. Aimless. Rather vacant and hopeless. I wasn't sure if he didn't care, or was just there to make up some kind of quorum. If he was the prisoner's friend, I think he should have been on my side, but I soon realised there would be no help from that direction.

When the court proceedings began, the prosecutor took only a few minutes to state this case against me.

'The accused soldier left his post at a critical moment. He ignored orders to stay in the trenches and ran away from the impending attack in the most craven manner –'

'I didn't run,' I called out, 'I walked.'

'The prisoner will be silent!' the president of the court snapped, and he said if I could not be quiet I would be removed, then tried and sentenced *in absentia*. He told the prosecutor to continue.

'. . . ran away in the most craven manner,' the major repeated. 'What's more, as an experienced soldier and a member of the Australian and New Zealand forces, the so-called Anzacs, he was setting an appalling example to many new young recruits from Britain and our dominion nations. It was one of the most blatant cases of cowardice that one can imagine. After fleeing from the scene of battle . . .'

I wanted to protest again that I didn't flee – but saw the president watching and waiting for this. Instead I shook my head to rebut the accusation. The 'friend' gave one of his vacuous smiles, the court president reprimanded me for making derogatory gestures that were in contempt, and the major continued his prosecution.

'After fleeing from the scene of battle, he was seen by two military policemen. He was ordered to stop, but tried to attack them . . .'

I waved my arms and shook my head in objection at these lies, and this time the president ordered my wrists to be handcuffed behind my back so I would be prevented from doing this. I kept thinking that his face was somehow familiar, but from where I just couldn't recollect. I knew one thing for certain; it was not a friendly face. It was becoming very clear that I had no friends at all in that courtroom.

'The military policemen displayed great courage in resisting the attack. The accused then started to run away. They pursued him and in due course after a chase they captured him . . .'

All untrue! I wanted to shout. I was limping because my feet had blisters and I was trying to find a field hospital. How could two military policemen display great courage when I didn't even try to attack them? Two of them with pistols, me without a weapon.

Why don't they tell the truth here? I wanted to demand. Why don't I have someone to defend me, instead of that captain who keeps smiling as if everything is going just the way it should? Why aren't I allowed to speak? I ran away from those MPs because they tried to shoot me! I fell down, they gave me a working-over and shackled me, and later on they bashed me like a pair of vicious thugs.

'That completes the case, Colonel President,' the prosecutor said. 'The evidence is conclusive.'

'Indeed it is,' the colonel asserted. 'I also feel obliged to inform my fellow judges that this prisoner has a long history of insubordination and poor behaviour. He was once an NCO, a sergeant, reduced to the ranks for disobedience and wilful defiance of an order by a senior officer. He managed to get himself sent to Netley Hospital, which has an unfortunate history of sheltering certain shirkers. The prisoner is, in my opinion, the worst type of soldier. Abusive, rebellious, and finally showing his yellow streak – his utter cowardice – by this desertion of his comrades. The ultimate crime – abandonment of his military duty in the face of the enemy. I suggest there can be only one verdict, and I ask my fellow officers to give me their decision.'

I heard all this as though in a daze, feeling as if he might be speaking about someone else. Surely this wasn't me! I was the bloke who left university to volunteer, the nineteen-year-old who was only scared of one thing – that he might miss the war, the big adventure. One of the original mob who fought at Gallipoli, and then for two years in France. I had a platoon full of mates who could testify that I'm not a coward, but of course they can't be here. They're all dead, and even if any were still alive I doubt if this court would wish to hear them.

I saw the officers conferring. It seemed to take less than a minute. Then they all turned and stared at me while the colonel cleared his throat.

'The verdict is unanimous,' he announced. 'And there is only one punishment for this crime. You are sentenced to execution by firing squad. You will be taken from here to the prison, and kept there until the sentence is carried out.'

The president and the three officers rose, bowed, and left the room. The prosecuting major collected his papers and followed them. None of them even looked at me until the captain, 'my friend', gave a shrug and a smile as if to say he'd done his best.

Then the guards took me by the arms and tried to make me march, even though my legs were in irons. When I fell over I nearly brought them down with me. They kicked me before they forced me to get up, and said I was a piece of fucking garbage, better off dead, and that'd be taken care of in the next few days.

I couldn't complain to the court, because the court had adjourned and left me to the mercy of these mongrels.

It's been a week. We're in a cell block, us garbage who are condemned to death. There are others besides me. Ten of us when I came here, all British except for one Indian and a New Zealander.

One went yesterday, another two this morning. We could hear the boots march in unison past our cells, the sound of command that called the firing squad to attention, a cry of despair from one lad, God knows which one, the shouted order to fire, then a volley of shots and distant voices. I suppose they were checking if the poor devils were dead. Once there was the sound of a pistol shot. If they're not sure, they say it is kind to put a bullet through the brain, just in case. Kind! What fucking tripe! My cousin in the bush used to say the same when they were culling sheep or cattle.

The first day I got my kitbag returned to me; not much in it except some dirty clothes and my notebook.

'You won't want no clean clothes,' one of the guards said, ''cos you won't have no time to change into 'em. And as for this book, I dunno about this. What's in it?'

'Just a sort of diary,' I told him, trying not to appear too anxious. 'Nothing special.'

I was scared he was going to impound it, probably tear it up or burn it to show his power, but to my surprise he shrugged and said I could keep it. Might occupy my time until it was my turn. Which could be any time, tomorrow or the next day.

But it hasn't been tomorrow or the next day. One week so far. I spend much of the time writing, trying to remember things to put down, hoping the stub of this pencil will last as long as I do.

Don't worry, it'll be soon, the guards keep telling me. Tomorrow or the next day is like a refrain. They love to scare you, to watch your eyes when they say this, hoping to see the fear.

Meanwhile others die. It's been going on every day, the culling and the killing. Can't do too many each day, for the army says it must be done at dawn. I wonder why it must be dawn? Is that a good time to cull and kill? Do they get the rest of the day off, the soldiers who make up the firing squad? And is it true only one or two have real bullets up the spout, the rest have blanks, so nobody knows who did the killing? I find I spend time occupying myself with these strange questions, which have come to seem quite important.

Another week. Nine of the men who were in here – all found guilty because I don't think anyone before these courts is ever found innocent – are now dead. Their crimes ranged from desertion to some pathetic cases. A young lad being absent from the front-line for two days because he was cut off and had lost his way and his memory – he was shot. So was another bloke for hitting an officer. Killed for that. Then there's one poor bastard of a Tommy who was shot for refusing to wear his cap. I thought it had to be a rotten sort of joke, but it seems it is true. He was charged with disobeying a lawful command, given personally by his senior officer. Akin to mutiny, they called it. He pleaded guilty, the silly bugger, but only because he was persuaded it was the best thing to do to get the trial over and done with. He never dreamt they'd shoot him. Nineteen years old, he was. Shot because he 'antagonised' an officer. Are they all raving mad, or just mad with power? What kind of army is it that'd shoot a young kid for such a trifling offence, and what sort of a cold awful bastard is the general who signed the deed of execution?

For a while I've been alone in the death cells. Then two others came here – one a Canadian, the other Scottish. The Scot was hard to understand with his thick brogue when he did decide to talk, which wasn't often; most of the time he was singing and laughing and chatting to himself. Crazy as a loon. Hardly aware he was in here, or what would happen to him. Kept singing 'Loch Lomond' and Gaelic things, mournful as a dark wet Sunday. Singing his poor head off when they took him out, still singing till the shots stopped him in the last chorus of 'Auld Lang Syne'. They let him get almost to the end . . . 'should auld acquaintance be forgot' . . . then they killed him. But not quite!

God, the sounds he made before the pistol shot reminded me so much of Wilfred's poem, the one he read to me at Netley. Sassoon said forget Shakespeare, read Owen. I can still remember Wilfred's young and angry face as he spoke the words written after a friend died from a gas attack. Sweet Jesus, it was so vivid and so bloody savage.

> *If in some smothering dreams you too could pace*
> *Behind the wagon that we flung him in,*
> *And watch the white eyes writhing in his face,*
> *His hanging face, like a devil's sick of sin;*
> *If you could hear, at every jolt, the blood*
> *Come gargling from the froth-corrupted lungs,*
> *Obscene as cancer, bitter as the cud*
> *Of vile, incurable sores on innocent tongues, –*
> *My friend, you would not tell with such high zest*
> *To children ardent for some desperate glory,*
> *The old Lie: Dulce et decorum est*
> *Pro patria mori.*
> [It is sweet and right to die for your country.]

The Canadian didn't believe they could execute him. Said he was a dominion soldier, not British, and they didn't have the right. Told me his government would have a whole heap to say; they wouldn't stand for it. I didn't like to tell him about the Indian or the New Zealander who'd gone out the door. Or that I'd heard of other Canadians being executed. The Canadian army isn't even told - or so the guards say. It'll be the same with me. Nobody will bother to get on a soapbox about a cowardly deserter . . . which is what that colonel at the trial called me. I keep on feeling I've met him before, but I can't remember when or where.

The Canadian did give me some other news. He said there was a great big new push at a place called Le Hamel, and the Aussies were right in it. That they were pleased, because the whole five AIF divisions - it seems we're down to only five divisions now because of the losses - are grouped as a single army under the command of General Monash. An Australian in command at long last. Thank Christ - and good on him!

No more bloody dreadful old Haig with his horrible plans of containment. The Canuck said Monash had a new plan - to bring up supplies by tanks, so the troops would not be burdened down. Make a nice change that, I said - we always had to carry too much stuff. Made us like packhorses or mules. It slowed us up, but how would High Command know such a thing, that mob sitting on their fat bums in their comfortable armchairs at headquarters, moving us about like pieces on a chessboard. They'd never have bothered to even think of it. But Monash would, I said.

This Canadian seems to know a hell of a lot. Maybe he's a spy, I tell him, and we both laugh. Just a deserter, he says. Then he tells me he even joined up with a bunch of deserters of different nationalities who live rough in the empty sand hills out near Dunkirk, on the coast. I've never heard of this before, but he swears it's true. A whole mob of them - there's even some Germans who skipped from their side. They've got guns, plenty of food, and after a few attempts to round them up, nobody bothers any more. They're like a sort of gang who come into the towns after dark and steal all the supplies they need. But he started to feel bad about it, and like a dill came back, gave himself up and confessed, and they found him guilty after a ten-minute trial.

'You got ten minutes?' I said. 'You must be important. Mine felt more like five.'

The Canadian says Monash has a brand-new plan to recapture Villers-Bretonneux, and to use the Australian Flying Corps to bomb Le Hamel and the valley behind it. I'd really like to be there with them. I wish they'd let me out of here so I could die there among Australians, with my own kind.

He went on talking about these battles that were taking place, and I didn't know half the names. But I did remember Villers-Bretonneux.

'I was there,' I said.

'Where?'

'Villers-Bretonneux. We captured it.'

'When?'

'Months ago . . . Sometime this year. I can't remember when, but I was there.'

'Well, maybe you did,' the Canadian replied as if he didn't believe me, 'but if you did then someone else fucked up – because your guy Monash has to go there and try to capture it back again.'

It was nice to talk to someone instead of having to listen to Scottish ballads all the time, but they took him the next day. He fought the guards – they didn't like it, so they gave him a belting, knocked him down and kicked him, then had to tie him up. It was when he was all trussed like a turkey that he started to cry. He said his family would never live down the disgrace, they'd have to move from the town they'd lived in all their lives. It wasn't fair, he kept shouting – which it certainly wasn't, but a guard hit him in the guts with a rifle butt, and when they dragged him out he was vomiting and crying so much he couldn't speak. And a few minutes later came the command and the shooting, and then I was the only one left in the execution block.

I don't know how much time has gone by. Could be weeks. It feels like it. I know the sun rises and it sets, but on days when there's no sunshine it's like night in here, so I lose track of the exact number of passing days. I know one thing, the guards are annoyed that I'm still alive. They don't like having to be made to look after one person, and every single morning they do a threatening march towards my cell, like a culling-killing squad about to eliminate the next one. They make it sound as if they are coming for me. They like to tell me that since I'm the only one left, I must be next. They go into the details about how the others died. They enjoy telling me about it: that some screamed, some prayed, some cried or shit their pants. These guards are sadistic bastards – they like to see that I'm afraid. But the strange thing is I'm not sure I am. All my real friends are long dead, all the poor buggers caged in these cells with me are gone – I no longer know how I really feel about living, or if I even care.

Except for never being able to go back to Jane. I care about that, but she feels a lifetime away and I don't even have a photo to remind me how she looked. I don't know my feelings about the boy – I still think his name was Richard, though I'm not certain – I can't tell how I feel because I've never seen him. I don't know what he looks like. I do know he's three years old, born the day we landed at Gallipoli in 1915, so that makes him three, but the baby photos are all I had, and they were lost. I desperately want to go home and see him. I want to pick him up and hug him. It's not right to be the proud father of a three-year-old son and never be able to hug him.

Today I had visitors. The cell door was pushed open and a guard brought in two men. Two officers in Australian uniform, which was a surprise. One had an insignia and a cross that showed he was a padre. The other was a medical officer.

'Do you remember me, Private Conway?' the padre asked.

'No, sir, I don't think so,' I replied.

He told me he was Chaplain Packard of the First Division, and then I knew the name. He was in Gallipoli and at Pozieres. Buried plenty of mates of mine. I could even remind him of his nickname.

'Pack Up Your Troubles Packard? Was that you?'

'That was me, son,' he said with a grin. 'I doubt if you ever came to my church parades, but I was sure you'd know the cheeky song they used to sing about me.'

I remembered, I told him, and sang it:

Pack up your troubles, for its old Packard,
Drumming up a church parade,
Don't let him bury yer in God's Square Mile,
Just duck boys, that's the style . . .

The other officer was a major. He watched this while trying not to show impatience. When I'd finished he briskly shook hands with me.

'I'm Major Cornwall, Stephen. Tim Cornwall, M.O. of the First. We're here because the news is pretty bloody bad. They're saying that you'll be executed tomorrow.'

'Shit,' I said. From him it had more veracity than the predictions and taunts of the guards.

'Shit indeed,' he replied. 'A very shitty business altogether.'

'I came to say a prayer for your soul, my boy,' the chaplain said, but the medical officer told him to hold off the Bible bash until he could explain things properly to me.

'It's a scandal, Steve, a bloody disgrace. I managed to get your medical records from Netley, but the court refused to reopen the case and allow them to be admitted. No one seems to give a stuff about cases of shell shock. They prefer to call it cowardice, but clearly it's not. It's a mental disturbance, an illness like influenza or TB. A decent court would've at least attempted to understand the medical implications, but that was not a decent court. We tried to do our best for you, which I'm afraid was not good enough.'

'Now we'll say a prayer together,' the chaplain tried again.

But Major Cornwall - Tim, as he told me to call him - did not seem as anxious about prayer as the padre. He said there was more to discuss, and that was why they were *really* here.

Tim said the sentence would be carried out in private: it was how the British did these things, they never gave out the names. So he and the padre were going to write the usual letter home - the one called the bereavement letter - with all the same stuff about dying bravely, and say to Jane that I'd been reported missing, believed killed in action. That would not necessarily mean a lie - well, not a *big* one, he said, looking firmly at the padre - and in time it would come to be accepted by my family at home that I'd died in battle.

They said it was all they could do, and had never previously done it for anyone. But I was one of the few remaining originals, and they both thought I'd had a truly rotten deal. The trial had been a complete farce, they'd heard. I was undefended, and it had only lasted a few minutes.

'You were well and truly fitted up by a pompous and vindictive British officer,' Tim said. 'We think the bloody man's a disgrace, and if the war wasn't in such a state with confusion everywhere, he'd never have got away with it.'

'I keep feeling as if I know him,' I said, and they both went a bit quiet. It was about then, perhaps because of the expressions on their faces, that I remembered him. 'He used to be a major, is that right?' I asked.

When Tim confirmed it with a grim nod it all came back to me. Major Carmody, the one in the trenches at Pozieres, when I told the joke about old Birdwood. I remembered how he'd brought the charge after I had to leave Marie-Louise, the same day that I'd found out Blue was dead, and everything seemed like such a rotten hopeless waste. We'd won Pozieres, but lost thousands of decent blokes like Bluey Watson, and here was this overdressed, gutless wonder telling lies, saying I'd threatened him and I was unfit to be a sergeant . . . The same joker, sitting with a smile on his face while he presided at my trial, pretending to be unbiased.

'That's the bugger,' Tim said. 'The truth is, if you'd been in full possession of your faculties, your own legal knowledge would've made you realise it was improper for him to preside. Not that anyone would've cared in a kangaroo court like that.'

'We've tried to point some of this out,' the padre explained, 'but the trial's over, the verdict's confirmed, and no one will listen.'

'And,' I said to them both, 'I did walk away from the line.'

'After three years and God knows how many bombardments

and bayonet charges, as well as living with rats and lice, it's a bloody miracle you could walk at all. But the chaplain's right. Nobody is prepared to listen, let alone consider an appeal.'

'So Tim and I talked about it,' the padre continued, 'and we decided to both send a routine letter as if you were still serving with the battalion. We won't put the exact date on them, so nobody will be able to check the details. We just wanted to come here and tell you that, so you'd at least know it'll be better for Jane. This way she'll never know the truth.'

I was hardly able to thank them, I was so close to tears over what they were doing for me.

'Now,' the padre said, 'may we please say a short prayer?'

'I'd be grateful if you would, Captain Packard,' I said, and knelt on the floor. They both knelt alongside me.

'Dear Lord,' the chaplain said quietly, 'I would like to commend my comrade and brother Stephen Conway, aged twenty-three, who joined our army at nineteen to help protect his country. If it were not for this war he would have remained a student, and perhaps by now have qualified in his chosen profession. Guide and protect his wife and son, and cast your blessing on this man who has done no wrong, but has been wrongfully treated. May the grace of Your Light, and the Fellowship of the Holy Spirit be with him evermore. Amen.'

'Amen,' I said, my face now awash with tears. When I managed to dry my eyes and compose myself, we shook hands and they left. The warmth of their visit, how they had tried to help and what they proposed to do, has remained with me the whole day long. But it is evening now, and I think I am finally afraid – because if it is the last day of my life, I will never encounter such kindness as that again.

Tomorrow, or tomorrow. I hope I'll be brave. At least the pencil has lasted as long as I have. I can throw the stub away now.

Chapter Twenty-three

That was where the notebook ended. The few remaining pages were blank. To anyone without their prior knowledge it would seem certain Stephen Conway had been executed the day after that final entry. But the photograph Patrick and Claire had seen was clearly taken years later and Georgina's letter sent with his diary was their confirmation he had survived. How he had done so was beyond their comprehension.

'She sent the diary to my father. Why didn't she send this as well?' Patrick wondered.

'Protecting him, surely.' Claire felt convinced of it. 'In those days, I think people would've been shocked to know a soldier in their family had been sentenced to death. Even if it was unjust. The diary finished in May, before he went to Netley. All this in the notebook – the hospital, the trial and death cell – everything in here would've shattered your father, and especially your grandmother. I feel sure Georgina knew that.'

Yes, Patrick thought, attitudes had changed so much with the years. People were now understanding about what was once labelled 'malingering' and 'cowardice' by the rigid military mind. These days it was known there were invisible wounds. There was a new medical vocabulary, with conditions like post-traumatic stress syndrome.

'And for that reason,' Claire continued, 'she took this with her to the old people's home and kept it safely hidden in her locker, until she got sick and no longer remembered she even had it. Perhaps she would have burnt it, if she'd had the chance.'

'I'm glad she didn't,' Patrick said. 'It's very painful, but to me there's nothing in it that's shaming or disgraceful, except for the court-martial itself. My grandfather wrote the truth – he certainly wasn't off his head and hallucinating, because there really were those letters from his unit padre and medical officer. I've seen them. My father kept them with his papers.'

'That awful trial!' Claire said. 'Can you imagine a colonel who'd brought a charge against him being allowed to preside? What a travesty of justice!'

She poured them each a glass of wine and they sat on the balcony where the last rays of the sun were reflecting off the windows opposite. It was almost the end of another day, and as they touched glasses Claire wondered how many more they had left. It was also the end of their search, for there seemed nowhere else to go from here.

It left Patrick with mixed emotions – satisfaction that from the chance discovery of the diary he had reached so deeply into his grandfather's life. But that was the only achievement. There was anger at the brutal way he'd been treated, and disappointment they'd never know what had saved him from execution. Nor would they ever find out details of his life afterwards. So many questions left unanswered; the frustration lay in realising they would always remain so.

'Tomorrow I'll try to repair the notebook some more, so you can take it home for Sally,' Claire said.

The subject of when he would go home had begun to occupy

both their minds, but Patrick was not anxious to talk of it. 'Maybe I'll post it,' he replied. 'Sal will freak out when she reads how men with shell shock were treated. They were running out of troops. Doctors were told to get their patients out of bed and back to the war. That was the real disgrace. It's obvious he should never have been diagnosed fit to be sent to France again.'

'But there must be something more,' Claire said. 'I don't know how we'll find it, but there must be an explanation of how he survived.'

'Nobody's alive to tell us. And even if Georgina had lived, she wouldn't have remembered.'

But Claire was adamant. 'Think about it. He was in a death cell, everyone was shot except him. Not just British troops. The Canadian, an Indian, a New Zealander, but not Stephen. Why not? Why was he the only one spared?'

'It couldn't have been a change of heart by the court-martial. Or an illegality, like undue prejudice.'

'Not in those days. But *something* happened,' she persisted. 'He survived. How? And why?'

There seemed no answer to it.

The following day when Patrick came home with groceries from the supermarket and an armful of flowers, Claire called excitedly to him from the study.

'Patrick?'

'No, it's the milkman, bringing flowers.'

'Nice milkman. Gorgeous flowers.' She put them in the sink, kissed him fondly and took his hand. 'Now quick, look at this.' She led him into the study. Patrick sat and stared at the screen, where a web site was illuminated.

SHOT AT DAWN, the site was named. Above it was a graphic of uniformed men tying a soldier to a post prior to his execution.

'It's a campaign to gain pardons for soldiers executed in the First World War!' Claire explained. 'Shot At Dawn. The acronym is SAD.'

'For once the acronym seems completely apt,' Patrick said.

'The people who run this crusade have probed hundreds of military executions. They call Marshal Haig "the butcher", because he signed death warrants for men who were sick, drunk, or even just insubordinate. He said executions set an example: they kept the men in order. He had a pair of British soldiers shot two days before the armistice – to set an example.'

'God Almighty!'

'Another one: absent for five hours with dysentery. Accused of desertion and executed. Unbelievable cases. Your grandfather didn't exaggerate about those men in the death cell.'

'But how did Stephen escape? We still can't find that out.'

'I think we can. Read this.' She clicked on another file. A heading appeared: A REPORT ON VIEWS HELD OF THE AUSTRALIAN POSITION.

'It's a government file,' Claire told him, 'released under the Freedom of Information Act. The people who run the SAD crusade published it as support material. They're hammering the British government to get retrospective pardons, and in the process they've turned over a few rocks. This is one that interests us.'

Patrick began to read it as the printer released more pages. An indifferent researcher himself, he was startled at the expert way she had found this data. More than that, as he read the file with growing astonishment, he realised here was an explanation he had never imagined. Perhaps, at last, the answer to their questions. It seemed to explain how Stephen Conway had escaped a bullet at dawn, and even to reveal what had happened to him during the final days of the war, and afterwards when the guns fell silent.

First there was an article that was suppressed by politicians of the day to preserve the illusion of Empire solidarity. But such solidarity, in fact, was far removed from the truth. Ever since the first Anzacs had landed at Gallipoli, a massive row had begun between Britain and her former colony. It was predicated on the entrenched determination by the Australian government that none of their troops would ever face a firing squad.

The rationale for this was based on a simple fact: these men were volunteers, enlisting to fight in a war that, while it concerned the Empire, was not Australia's own conflict. A proposal to introduce conscription had twice been put to a national referendum, and twice defeated by the people. As a result the army consisted only of voluntary recruits, unlike British and other allied forces. Discipline and punishment were covered by the Commonwealth Defence Act. And Section 98 of that Act was a model of clarity:

> *Those who volunteer to serve outside the country cannot face capital punishment, except for mutiny, treachery, or desertion in the face of enemy fire. However, no sentence of death can be carried out unless it is confirmed by the order of the Australian Governor-General.*

This sentence buried in the Act meant vice-regal power had total dominance over all domestic or foreign military decrees. The Governor-General, despite his high-sounding status, was a political appointee, a figurehead counselled by the prime minister and his cabinet. He did what he was told. And the cabinet had no intention of allowing volunteers to be shot – which would not only discourage future enlistment, but also ensure their party lost the next election.

It meant that while a number of Australian soldiers had been condemned to death, in every case the sentence had been commuted. It was totally political. The government had twice been given a clear message by the electorate that conscription would not be tolerated, and they knew military executions were unacceptable. These had become vastly unpopular since the trial and execution of Lieutenants Harry 'Breaker' Morant and Peter Hancock in the Boer War.

Australians were also starting to feel their country was too far away from this European conflict, and although there had been great support and enthusiasm for it in 1914 – now, after four years of casualty lists, that fervour had faded.

'So the government stopped the execution!' Patrick said.

'It wasn't altruism,' Claire replied. 'Just the usual self-interest. Politicians trying to save their own skins. And by sheer chance, saving a life or two.'

'But this is all surmise, isn't it? We can only assume . . . or is there something else?'

'There is *definitely* something else,' Claire said as she clicked and the screen was lit with a new background graphic depicting a slouch hat with the familiar badge of the rising sun. Patrick stared at the wording of the title.

'Is this Stephen?'

'Read it. See what you think.'

He sat in front of the computer and began to read. It was a report entitled THE CASE OF THE UNNAMED SOLDIER.

The strange case of an unnamed and unknown soldier in France during September 1918 accused of desertion in the face of enemy fire has been kept classified for almost eighty years until now. It was disclosed on the file that he was an infantryman who had joined up in the first weeks of the war, had served with distinction in Gallipoli where he had been promoted to sergeant, and following this spent over two years, much of it again as a private soldier, serving on the Somme.

The British court-martial insisted in this case – as he was temporarily attached to a British unit at the time of the offence – that no immunity could exist. This, at last, was to be the exception to a rule that had irritated the High Command throughout the war.

Speedily sent to trial and found guilty, his execution was scheduled, but then deferred because of immediate protests of illegality. The Australian Consul-General in London was adamant. They alone must rule on this matter. A ferocious argument, never made public at the time, then broke out between the two countries. Field Marshal Sir Douglas Haig, who had already signed the execution paper, passionately put his own army's point of view. How could the AIF continue this insistence on being treated differently from the British and all other Empire troops, while they were in the same field of battle, fighting the same enemy in the same war?

The British cabinet vehemently pointed out that as long as two years ago, the Honourable Secretary for the Colonies had requested the Commonwealth agree to their soldiers being placed under the British Army Act.

Australia's prompt reply to this acid reminder asked: Did London not yet realise they were no longer a colony? Had they heard of Federation, or did they still think the country was a prison settlement, run by expatriate old governors put out to pasture and following the dictates of their masters in England?

The increasingly furious High Command would have none of it. The execution of this unnamed soldier, they argued, was a positive step to prevent men fleeing from battle and escaping punishment by claiming they were suffering from 'nerves'. It was important that, having been properly and fairly tried and sentenced to death, the sentence must be carried out. If this were not to happen, court-martials would become a farce.

In the heated exchange that followed, the Australian government held firm. The AIF was a volunteer army, and as the men in it had chosen to go to the aid of the Empire and to face death, they could not be forced to also face the unreasonable penalty of death while on a duty which they had willingly and cheerfully elected to serve.

London was not impressed. 'We wish to know why you are being unreasonable in this absurd and continuing fiasco!' Whitehall bellowed.

'My God,' Patrick said, 'you mean all this was going on while Stephen was held in prison, believing every day would be his last?'

'It certainly was,' Claire answered. 'Keep reading.' She sat close beside him, as they watched the screen and the details that unfolded.

An agreement had to be reached: this was jeopardising relations between friendly countries. His Majesty King George V was asked by Sir Douglas Haig and the British prime minister to intervene. The King considered the matter; he consulted his close advisers, who felt it had awkward political implications, and could best be solved by politicians acting in good faith and with a measure of plain commonsense.

Prime Minister Lloyd George felt the King's reply put the onus on the Australian government. Commonsense was the requirement, and until now his stubborn counterpart in the southern hemisphere had shown little sign of it. In the interests of sensible conciliation, it was suggested the government in Australia relent. Relations were being endangered by a positive storm in a tea cup. After all, it was only one man.

Australia refused. It was certainly not *only one man, they replied, it was also their future as a government. The so-called unnamed soldier could be punished by a term of imprisonment, but he could not be executed.*

And while they had previously been pressed to agree that names of deserters could be published in the newspapers along with details of their prison sentences, many editors had felt this a harsh and unfair burden placed on the innocent families. Some had even refused to publish. Because of the history of shell shock in this case and other disturbing elements relating to the court-martial proceedings, Australian cabinet opinion was that the interests of justice would be best served if the name of the soldier concerned was not made public.

In a fury at this equivocation, Whitehall ordered the court-martial in the case to reconvene. Colonel Carmody was instructed to return from Paris where he had spent much of the war as a special liaison officer, and told to immediately put his mind to meditating on a valid new sentence that could stand scrutiny – one that these awkward antipodeans would accept.

The court deliberated. Within an hour they handed down a new verdict, and the accused was sent for. He appeared before them chained, for in the words of the President of the Court, he was considered to be extremely dangerous.

The sentence was commuted to ten years' imprisonment with hard labour. He would receive a dishonourable discharge, although his name would be suppressed from publication. However, he would be removed to a prison in England, and there he would serve the full ten-year term, without any remission whatsoever.

'So they got him in the end.' Patrick sounded defeated as they walked along the towpath to their newly adopted Italian restaurant that evening. He had a distinct sense of anticlimax. After the excitement of their discoveries they'd reached the finishing line, but there was no tape to mark it. Just a blank wall.

'At least they didn't kill him,' Claire replied. 'We don't even know if he served the full ten-year term.'

'It looks like it.'

'Not necessarily. The report stopped right there. I've searched, and it's not mentioned anywhere else.'

'Poor bloody Stephen. He truly became the unnamed and unknown soldier.'

Claire sensed his mood and tried to be optimistic. 'There are cases of others who were sentenced like him, then released after the armistice,' she assured him. 'I don't know if we can find out whether it happened to him, but I'd like to try.'

'You've done heaps already. It would've been impossible to get this far without you,' Patrick said, and took her hand.

They walked towards the lights of the restaurant. Beppi, the owner, was standing outside. He had come to know them, and often sat with them after dinner to share a liqueur on the house.

'*Buona sera!*' he called to them.

'*Buona sera!*' they replied.

'Tonight,' Beppi said, 'we have a nice chianti with your names on it, beautifully chilled and waiting for you.'

'Tonight, Beppi,' Patrick said, 'I think we need a bottle of French bubbly. We have an anniversary.'

Claire turned to look at him with pleased surprise.

'Tonight,' Patrick told the restaurateur, 'is exactly one month since we met at the Menin Gate.'

Her Majesty's Prison Service in High Holborn is a bustling, modernised department. There, a civil servant with whom Patrick had an appointment, made it abundantly clear their records were concerned with present-day prisons, which they preferred to call 'correction centres', and they were not in the business of answering questions about detainees of so long ago. After more than eighty years, he said, it was hardly likely they'd have the details being requested in this application under the Freedom of Information Act.

The civil servant had thick bushy eyebrows that he raised while studying the application form without enthusiasm.

'Stephen Conway? Army deserter?'

'Unjustly accused,' Patrick pointed out.

That was neither here nor there, he was told. 'If it was an army matter, Sir, you've come to the wrong place.'

'I think he was sent to a prison, perhaps Dartmoor. A few other Australian soldiers were sent there about that time.'

'Have you been in touch with Dartmoor?'

'They said they have no facilities for this kind of enquiry, and referred me here.'

'If he was sent to a civilian establishment, do you know how many hundred correction centres we have in the United Kingdom, not to mention the many that have changed names or no longer exist?'

'I'm aware it's a big ask.'

Raised eyebrows told him indeed it was a big ask. He typed the name Stephen Conway on a computer and Patrick waited hopefully.

'This is all I can do, you realise?'

'I know,' Patrick said. 'I appreciate your time.'

When the response came the civil servant appeared to be vindicated by the result.

'I'm sorry. I'm afraid no record exists in the files.'

'Or else it's been deleted.'

'I really can't imagine why. It's most unlikely that records were preserved, except on high-profile prisoners.' He gave a wintry smile. 'We have extensive detail on Irishman Sir Roger Casement, for instance, hanged for high treason. Nothing on Stephen Conway, an Australian soldier who managed to escape the same fate.'

'His trial was the subject of a row between your country and mine. I thought there might be some trace, because of that.'

'It seems not. Perhaps you're right, and for political reasons the name has been expunged. He may've been important after all.'

'He was to me. An unknown, unnamed soldier, and a most unlucky one.'

The civil servant seemed more sympathetic. 'But after so long, Mr Conway, what is there to find out?'

'The date of his release. I was told many soldiers in jail were freed after the armistice. I wondered if my grandfather was given a similar reprieve.'

'If not, he'd have served until 1928. But I'm afraid we'll never know that.'

Patrick went back to Fulham, feeling defeated by the passage of the years, and the obfuscation that seemed to put the final chapter of Stephen's life beyond his reach.

Claire had spent the morning researching details of Netley's bizarre hospital from the Internet, but time made that equally difficult. There were no lists of patients or staff, apart from a passing mention that the war poet Wilfred Owen had once been treated there. She printed the available photographs, and they were startled at the immensity of the place.

'My God, what a monster!'

'Isn't it? There's the pier, the stables, bakery, post office – even the railway station.' Claire pinned some of the photos to a cork-board alongside her desk and pointed to the places in turn. 'Here's the officer's mess: very Italianate and suitably grand. That's where Sassoon and Wilfred Owen must've dined. And this building over here, you can tell what this is, can't you? The asylum ward in D Block, taken at night with all those lights blazing.'

Patrick gazed at it, unable to prevent thoughts of the pain and anger that had been experienced there. It conjured up a too-vivid image of his twenty-three-year-old grandfather facing the relent-less probing of the Scots doctor; enduring the experimental electric shocks; and returning here in despair after learning of Elizabeth Marsden's death. He'd come back to this place because there was nowhere else to go, Patrick realised, and felt a deep sadness that no one would ever know the real fate of Stephen Conway. To his wife and child and other family of that time he would've been a man who had literally vanished as surely as if he'd been swallowed up in Flanders mud. Not even he and Claire would ever find the truth about the rest of his grandfather's life.

'Patrick . . .'

'Sorry, I was miles away.'

'And years away, I'd venture. Is this where you were?' She handed him a scenic photo she had just enlarged. It was a wide-angled view of the hospital taken from offshore. He studied it and nodded.

'That's where. It looks just the way he described it. What was it he wrote?'

'"This haughty and gargantuan building . . . the size of six English seaside hotels",' she reminded him.

'He was deadset right about that. On the water's edge, with so many acres of ornamental gardens. More like a maharajah's palace than a hospital.'

'Makes him seem quite close,' Claire said, 'doesn't it?'

'Netley dome,' the guide announced as the tour boat approached across Southampton water. 'A fine example of Victorian architecture was preserved when Netley Hospital, the largest infirmary in the world, was partly destroyed by fire and then demolished in the 1960s. What you see was originally the chapel and centrepiece of the hospital, built after the Crimean War by Queen Victoria, who planned it in collaboration with Florence Nightingale.'

On board among a group of tourists, Claire smiled at Patrick. According to their Internet research, the outspoken Nurse Nightingale had disliked the place intensely, declaring the corridors were far too long, the wards too small, that too much money had been spent on appearance instead of patient comfort, and the country had been landed with a stupid mistake - and an expensive mistake at that.

In Claire's view this was why the nurse had never been made a Dame of the British Empire, nor received any official honour while Victoria lived to resent such comments.

'Miss Nightingale,' the guide continued, 'personally selected the site, approved the architecture, and gave it her blessing.'

'So there,' Patrick whispered, and Claire stifled a giggle, tucked her arm in his, and watched the land approach.

They went to the dome, now a museum. Inside were images of the past on ancient spools of film. They showed glimpses of the wounded brought by troop ships, then transferred by lighter to the pier, and taken to the hospital by horse-driven carriage down a steep cobbled road - the speed of the ancient sprocket film making it seem like a dangerous headlong gallop – while a modern soundtrack explained that some unfortunate patients had died from this experience before actually reaching the wards.

'It's like hearing it straight from Stephen,' Claire whispered.

They spent several hours there, studying photographs and the original postcards his grandfather had found so grotesque. They left feeling it was an interlude that achieved nothing other than satisfying their curiosity. The search was at an end. It was doubly disappointing, for they had come so much further than Patrick had expected, but tantalisingly not far enough.

They drove along the winding coast road to East Sussex and the Cinque Port town of Rye, spending the night at the historic Mermaid Inn. The next day, returning to London via Romney Marsh and the back roads of the Kent countryside, Patrick's mobile rang. It was Charlotte Redmond's office, her secretary saying that Ms Redmond would like to see him at White City next Tuesday if it suited, at ten in the morning.

Chapter Twenty-four

Charlotte Redmond was on the phone again, gesturing a casual wave of recognition at Patrick, and making the same signal for coffee to her secretary. It's a bloody charade, he thought as he sat waiting, then realised anger would be pointless. What would happen if he stood up and walked out? Nothing much, except she'd put his screenplay through the shredder.

Before he could progress this thought she terminated her call. 'Well, Patrick.'

'Charlotte,' he acknowledged her. There was a moment before she responded.

'Ah yes, your project.'

She looked at a folder in front of her, as though recollecting why he was there. She's a poseur, he thought, full of shit. Anger might be pointless, but it was extremely difficult to avoid it with someone like this. He realised she was removing the script from the folder and sliding it across the desk to him.

'I'm sorry to disappoint you, Patrick. This may have been Tim's sort of film, but I have to be honest and say it's not mine.'

'In other words, you hate it,' Patrick said, 'so I have to ask, did it really take so long to decide that?'

'Of course I don't *hate* it,' Charlotte replied. 'I think it has charm, but it's not what I'm after. An 1820 bank robbery in Sydney Town, and some lucky convicts who turn into prosperous English gents. To me it's *The Lavender Hill Mob*, with kangaroos and kookaburras. Perhaps that's why Carruthers was fired; not that he was stoned and insulted everyone, but that he could never pick winners.'

'A bit traumatic, Charlotte, to hear you denigrate the idea, and then label me a loser,' he said, stung by her remarks.

'I didn't mean to suggest that. I'm trying to say, however terrific your film may turn out to be some day – with another company, of course – it's definitely not my sort of movie.'

'I see.'

'No, I doubt if you do.'

'Well, it hardly matters now, does it? You've done the demolition job. You could've told me this at our first meeting.'

'I was trying to be fair, and give it another reading.'

'It obviously didn't improve on closer acquaintance.'

'Look,' she said more forcefully, 'I'm here because they want to change the culture of this place. Change the old-boy network, and the dated concept that Aunty BBC is the only game in town. It's a hell of a long time since those halcyon days, but the melody lingers around here as if this was still 1960, instead of a new century. I'm on a performance-linked contract to get this department right, or out I go. My whole thrust is to make movies that get into the cinemas. Put them on TV later, when the juice has been squeezed out. Like the film on the life of Queen Victoria . . . *Mrs Brown*, with Judi Dench and Billy Connolly. Made heaps on the big screen then still topped the ratings on free to air.'

'I saw it,' Patrick said. 'Went right off in the last reel. As if they didn't know how exactly to end it.'

She stared at him. Having made her defining statement, Charlotte was clearly impatient to see him leave.

'So what are you going to do, now that we don't want your script and the project?' she asked coldly.

'Go home,' Patrick retorted, all of a sudden not caring a fried shrimp in hell what she thought. 'Go home and get to work on a new screenplay. One that's become very important to me.'

'And what might that be?'

Her condescending tone infuriated him. 'Nothing you'd be the least bit interested in.'

'How do you know that?'

'Because it's a love story.'

'I like love stories.'

'This one you wouldn't. It's set in the First World War.'

'I have nothing against love stories in a war-time setting. I mean, look at the success of *The English Patient*. Does it have a title, this screenplay you're going to write?'

'It might have. At least a working title.'

'Is it secret, or am I permitted to know?'

'*Some Disputed Barricade*,' Patrick said.

'Really.' She allowed a long pause. 'And do you think this is a title that has resonance?'

'Absolutely. Just as much as *The English Patient*.'

'You didn't like it?' She sounded incredulous.

'Who cares if I did or not?' he replied. 'Or if you like my title – or not – since you're not involved. It's based on lines by a poet killed in that war. "I have a rendezvous with death, at some disputed barricade".'

'His name was Alan Seeger,' she said, surprising him. 'Not as prominent as Wilfred Owen or Sassoon, but a war poet.'

Fifteen love to you, he thought, determined to show no sign of being impressed. 'I may change it, call it *The Menin Gate*. Because that's where they met.'

'Who met?'

'A soldier and an English girl. She's a volunteer nurse. They were called the Roses of No-Man's-Land. She's a Rose.'

'I see.'

'From a sheltered, middle-class background. Her father's a vicar, she's a virgin. The Roses were a special sort of young woman, they went as unpaid volunteers to France, slept in tents, put up with the rain and the slush, helped treat wounded men under fire, risked their lives.'

'Sounds like a good part for a top young actress.'

'A great part. Up to her knees in mud and blood, she's bossed around by the matron and sisters, groped by the doctors and has half of the half-dead patients falling in love with her.'

'What age is she?'

'Early twenties. I've called her Georgina.'

'You seem to have done a lot of work on this story.'

'How do you think I filled in time,' Patrick said, 'while I sat around waiting for this meeting? Naturally I've registered it with all the writers' guilds. British, Australian, America East and West.'

'Very protective.'

'I can't pitch it unless I protect it.'

'Are you pitching it now?'

'Of course not. It isn't your sort of film.'

'How do you know?'

'It couldn't be. I don't *want* it to be.'

'Why?'

'Because working with someone who treats me with disdain is not my idea of enjoyment . . . and I like to enjoy my work.'

'Disdain?' she repeated, gazing at him, startled. 'What disdain?'

The secretary came back with one cup of coffee, and looked most surprised to see him still there. She put the cup in front of Charlotte, who summoned her own look of surprise.

'Didn't you bring a coffee for Patrick?'

'I'm sorry, but –'

'No thanks,' Patrick said to them both, 'definitely none for me. Can't stand coffee, and I'm leaving in a moment.'

The secretary went out with a shrug and a puzzled frown. Charlotte barely waited for the door to shut behind her.

'What disdain?'

'Don't let it bother you, Charlotte. Keeping people waiting with long phone calls about bugger-all is probably not true disdain. Just fucking bad manners.' He rose to leave. 'Anyway, that's it.'

'What do you mean, that's it?'

'You asked what I'm doing. I told you what I'm doing. I'm going to write and produce this.'

'You haven't mentioned the soldier. What about him?'

'Australian. Stephen. Joined up as a boy, and is now twenty-four but looks forty after the horrors he's seen.'

'Much horror?'

'War's full of horror. If it's real and not John Wayne crap.'

'I suppose he's heroic?' Her tone suggested it would be *de rigueur*, and no doubt a cliché.

'On the contrary,' Patrick replied. 'He *is* a hero, because he's shit scared all the time and does his utmost not to show it. She's the only one who can see it. She saves him from going crazy.'

'How?

'Lots of ways. Boosts his self-esteem. Fights with a Scottish doctor who tries to pronounce him fit and send him back to France.'

'To be honest, I'm beginning to like the sound of it.'

'I've already been honest. I don't think we could get on.'

'If it's to be made in France, you'll need a European partner.'

'Who says I'll make it in France?'

'Isn't it set there?'

'So what? That was France, 1916. Today along the Somme it's like a picture postcard: green fields, rebuilt towns. Trenches full of mud and shit can be filmed anywhere. Dead trees belong to the art department. Dugouts and blockhouses are best contained in a studio.'

'What if I said I might be prepared to offer you a deal? Better than the one Tim was offering for your convict caper.'

'Forget it. I won't be messed around on this one, Charlotte.'

'What makes you think I'll mess you around?'

'Almost everything about you makes me think it.'

She stared at him, taken aback by the bluntness. 'Are you trying to be deliberately offensive?'

'I'm trying to be honest. From the moment you kept me waiting, waffling on with gossip while you assessed me and put me in my place, my antennae said you're a pushy, ambitious lady. Well, fine. You pushed, and got to sit in that seat. But this story is special and my own project. I do it my way, or not at all. And certainly not with you, not unless it's completely on my terms.'

'You're a bit pushy yourself, Patrick. And pretty bloody personal, too. I could tell you to piss off.'

'Of course you could. I've already suggested it. In fact I'll make it easy by pissing off now.'

'Did it ever occur to you,' she said, 'that you have to be a bit pushy these days, or you get shat on from a great height?'

'I have been,' Patrick replied, 'often.'

'So have I. Which is why I'm careful not to make any mistakes now I'm behind this desk. Because I intend to stay here. The way to do that is come up with something refreshing, which your story suggests it might be. So can we at least talk more about it?'

'What's there to talk about, Charlotte?'

'Plenty. For a start, you could try calling me Lottie.'

Patrick decided to walk back to Fulham after he left the BBC, this time in a far different mood to the last occasion. He wanted to digest the events of the day. It was almost dark and he tried to phone Claire, but like earlier attempts her mobile was switched off and the landline was on answer mode. He was impatient to tell her. What a great turn-up, he thought, what an irony! You wouldn't bloody read about it in a bloody month of Sundays. He laughed, and a couple walking past gave him a curious glance.

Out of sheer anger at the contemptuous treatment meted out, he had improvised a phantom screenplay. Until that moment he'd never contemplated using Stephen's story as the basis for anything other than a report to his sister. It was a private matter. But he was determined to leave Charlotte's office with some dignity intact, and as the words began to flow, so the images started to build in his mind. Taking the elements of truth and marrying them to fiction, it rapidly developed into the love story of a shell-shocked 'deserter' and a young English Rose.

By the time he finished fashioning his outline, it had actually begun to excite him. And to excite her. Astonishingly, Charlotte

Redmond – Lottie, as she kept reminding him to call her – was impressed. She put through a call to someone she referred to as 'God' or 'Him Upstairs', telling him she had managed to find a rather unique war story, and was he available to take a meeting on it? She had then buzzed her secretary and told her to cancel all other appointments.

After which they went upstairs to see God.

He was a small man in a large and lavish office. They crossed what felt like an acre of lush carpet to where he sat at his desk on a raised podium. His eyes were sharply alert as he studied them from his contrived height advantage. His face was deeply tanned, his head elliptical and smoothly bald. Charlotte, who seemed over-awed with respect, introduced him as the Controller of Worldwide Productions, Ainsley Kegan-Potter. Mr Kegan-Potter was dressed in a lightweight wool suit that had surely come from an expensive tailor. It was ruined by a garish bow tie.

He listened in careful silence while Charlotte explained how she had discovered Patrick and his screenplay, which was a love story set in World War I between an Australian deserter and an English nurse. Patrick also listened carefully. It began to seem during this recitation as if a great deal of the credit was entirely due to Charlotte's brilliance and her flair for picking winners. Her ability to seize the day, and grasp the right story when it came along. But, as she said with coy modesty to the Controller, that was why they had given her the job.

'Could be promising,' the Controller said when she finished. He had a resoundingly deep voice for such a small man. 'It has nuances of *The English Patient* meets *Private Ryan*, but its not a replica of either, which bodes well. Do we have a title?'

'*The Menin Gate*,' Charlotte said promptly.

'No,' Patrick corrected her, '*Some Disputed Barricade.*'

'I like that.' God had smiled for the first time, displaying a set of well-capped teeth. '"I have a rendezvous with death at some disputed barricade",' he quoted while Charlotte frowned at Patrick.

'Exactly, Sir.'

He found it odd calling people 'Sir', but did so because the name Ainsley was a bit of a mouthful, and Mr Kegan-Potter was a hurdle his mouth could not handle, not without laughing. The Controller seemed pleased by the deference, and smiled again.

'Well, let's get down to the sharp end. Are we locked in? Do we have a deal memo?'

'Not yet.' Patrick was a split second ahead of Charlotte this time, quite determined she would not steer the meeting any longer. It was time to be heard. Clearly Charlotte had the same thoughts.

'It's downstairs ready for both our signatures,' she declared briskly, the lie accompanied by her eyes widening with contrived candour, 'now that you've given me the green light.'

'Before any signing takes place,' Patrick countered, 'there are important details Ms Redmond and I have to sort out.'

Charlotte began to seethe. The Controller seemed unperturbed.

'That's her department. Arguments over money, any minor details like that, Lottie's the one you talk to.'

'I'll be glad to talk with her,' Patrick told him, 'but these are not minor details. There's the matter of control. She knows I have certain strong ideas about creative control, and that I've also had other offers on this project.'

For the first time, God seemed disconcerted. 'Other offers? What offers? No one mentioned anything about others in the game. Is my time being wasted, Charlotte?'

'Certainly not, Ainsley,' she said, desperately trying to maintain a smile, 'Patrick is rather possessive about his story. But you can depend on me, we'll reach agreement.'

'I do hope so.' He studied her carefully for a long moment, then turned his gaze on Patrick. 'Don't forget, this is the BBC, old son. You don't turn us down lightly.'

'Not lightly, Sir, I assure you.'

'Not at all, if you want to be welcome here again.'

'I hear what you're saying.'

'Good. People usually do.'

'But in the long run,' Patrick said, 'I ought to make it clear – that entirely depends on whether I can work with Ms Redmond.'

'Everyone can work with Lottie. She's a pussy-cat.'

Patrick walked along North End Road relishing the memory. He could hardly wait to tell Claire what had happened. *Tell Claire*, he realised. Not Joanna, who'd feel he took a reckless risk, and might point out he could easily have alienated the Controller. No, he'd tell Claire – who would think it an absolute hoot – how Ainsley Kegan-Potter became so adamant that the BBC should secure the rights and not lose out to a crass commercial enterprise. And how Charlotte – Patrick enjoyed thinking of her as Lottie the pussy-cat – was made aware he would not look kindly on the failure of negotiations.

Back in her office the bargaining was brief. God wanted a deal signed and sealed that day; Lottie was eager his will should be done. So eager that she'd given him almost everything he'd asked for, which included a measure of creative control. There was only one remaining point of contention: since there was no script as yet, something on paper was required. A comprehensive treatment would be necessary.

Patrick confessed that he hated writing treatments. He felt they took all the energy and surprise out of the screenplay. But on this point Lottie was inflexible.

'I sympathise, Patrick,' she said, 'but I simply must have one. You know I can't go ahead without it.'

'When do you want it?'

'Today.' Patrick sighed. She smiled. 'When I get it, then we sign the contract, and you're on board.'

He was found an office and given the choice of dictating to a stenographer or a recorder. Choosing the latter he found, despite his reluctance, that the story flowed almost of its own accord. From time to time the secretary appeared to change tapes for him; when typed, the pages were sent to Charlotte.

Patrick, in sporting parlance, was suddenly 'in the zone'. Unused to dictation he was surprised how readily scenes were outlined and new ideas kept occurring to strengthen the narrative. His mind raced with an eagerness he'd never known. Thoughts came with a rush; he had been virtually living it each day, and the way he told it had the fluency of truth and the passion he'd found in Stephen's own words.

The Rose in his pages took on the twin personas of Claire and Georgina Rickson. Bluey and others in the original platoon, as well as Elizabeth Marsden, Marie-Louise, Colonel Carmody, the Scottish doctor and the poets at Netley were there in detail, but always the focus of the story was Stephen. His impulsive marriage and rush to enlist, his gradual deterioration as the war took possession of his mind, his hurried iniquitous trial, and the battle over his fate that led to a decade of hard labour in prison.

Not knowing the end of the real story, Patrick deliberately made his climax of the film ambiguous. He included a postscript stating there were two possible endings: one bitter and sad, the other an almost happy ending. His note said the conclusion would evolve from the writing, and the characters would in the end decide it – for this is what good characters did. When he handed over the last tape for typing, Patrick felt invigorated despite the hours he'd been working; it had developed with such congruity that he could hardly wait to begin writing the screenplay.

Lottie had no concern with the bilateral endings. She thought it was a clever tease that would intrigue everyone, and a super way of leaving his options open. The whole treatment, she enthused, was absolutely super. In fact this was one of her favourite words, as he rapidly learnt. God would *definitely* find it super. What's more, in her opinion Patrick himself was super, the way he'd worked at such a pace and come up with such a fine document. Absolutely super.

Quite dishy in fact, she'd said, eyeing him.

Patrick had given a quick glance at his watch.

Lottie agreed it was late, the afternoon had fled by, and the building was starting to empty. Any time now her secretary would be going home, so they deserved a drink, she and Patrick. She wanted to apologise for the rocky start they'd had. She'd behaved badly, and now she'd like to behave badly again – but this time in a way he might enjoy. A couple of drinks for starters from the bar behind her big television screen.

Patrick looked at his watch again, more obviously this time.

There's no rush, Lottie assured him. She was sure he'd noticed her office had a comfortable settee. It would be her first time on the settee. They could lock the door and cement their new relationship in the nicest possible way . . .

'There's a problem,' Patrick said.

'We've solved all the other problems,' Lottie replied, 'now it's play time.'

'Lottie, I'm truly flattered, but there's someone else.'

'Your rather famous wife?' She dismissed this with a grin. 'She's twelve thousand miles away. That seems like a safe distance.'

'There's someone far closer than that, with whom I'm very much in love.'

Lottie stared at him. For a moment Patrick thought that having voiced this truth at last, he had probably managed to shoot himself in the foot. Then she threw back her head and laughed.

'You bastard!' she said. 'What a pity. I thought a shag would be the perfect way to get this show on the road.'

It was dark when Patrick turned into Ashburton Road. Claire was waiting on the lighted balcony. She waved and called down to him.

'I thought you'd got lost, or kidnapped.'

'Nothing so simple. I had a meeting with God.'

'Where did that happen?'

'Top floor of the BBC. About as close to heaven as he can get.' He ran upstairs and kissed her, eager to dazzle her with his triumph. 'Big news, my love. I've been trying to call you.'

'I was out, all day,' she said. 'I've got some news too, darling.'

'About what?'

'About Stephen – about what happened to him after the trial. I've found out.'

Chapter Twenty-five

The idea had been growing in her mind for some time, she said, and today was the last chance to discover if what she'd been contemplating would work. She did not say how bleak it had felt in her flat, or how dejected she was after Patrick left for his appointment. His half-packed suitcase was a relentless reminder that he would be gone the next day. Whatever happened at the BBC, win or lose with his film project, they had decided this. He had to go home; continuing to delay it was becoming stressful, but having agreed, Claire feared the future. He had a whole life on the other side of the world, an existence that included a lovely wife and a close-knit family. How could all that be relinquished for a few transient weeks of love, no matter how intense? Surely when he arrived back home and had time to reflect . . . she tried not to think about it. It would be a relief to get out of the flat and the realisation of how empty it would feel tomorrow.

She had taken the underground to Waterloo, then a train to Esher. There were no taxis when she arrived at the station, so she walked to the house. Outside was a sign, FOR SALE BY AUCTION, and the porch was littered with packing cases. When Claire rang the bell it was promptly answered. Helen West wore jeans, and her hair had been styled and cut. She looked years younger.

'Mrs West. Do you remember me?'

'Should I? If you're here about the house, see the agent.' She was about to shut the door, but Claire managed to forestall her.

'Claire Thomas. I came to see you with Patrick Conway.'

'Oh, yes . . . I remember now. His lady friend, the one he called his assistant.'

'May I talk to you?' As the other hesitated, Claire added, 'I'm here on his behalf.'

'I can't imagine why. I'm busy packing up, as you can see. What could you or he want to talk about with me?'

'If you let me come in for a moment, I'll tell you.'

Helen West hesitated. Her eyes assessed Claire. She seemed both cautious and curious. In the end curiosity won.

'Come in, then. *Briefly*,' she added pointedly, and was at first dismissive when Claire asked where she was moving, but then could not resist the opportunity to air her new good fortune.

'If you must know, I'm getting out of this dreary dump and away from dreary neighbours I can't stand. I'm buying a brand-new villa at Chelsea Reach with a smashing view of the river.'

'That's nice.'

'Oh, it's better than nice. I'm moving into it with a brand-new boyfriend.'

'Good for you,' Claire said, trying to establish some rapport, and knowing it was going to be unlikely.

'Very good for me,' Helen West replied with relish. 'Marvellous the difference a few quid makes. My husband, the silly bugger, wanted to come back, to be reconciled, and I told him he'd blown it, dumping me for his bit of fluff. I said he's old and past it.' She smiled at the memory of this marital revenge. 'When he started to beg, to plead he still loved me, I told him about Larry, who's ten years younger than me, and got a dick like a policeman's truncheon. I don't know or care what your future is, Ms Thomas, but I'm all set to make up for about thirty lousy years.'

'I'm sure Georgina would want you to enjoy every penny of what she left you, Mrs West.'

There was a cold silence at this. Claire realised she had been mistaken about the woman looking younger. She was Patrick's same old Mrs Bulldog, but with an expensive haircut and designer clothes.

'What the hell business is that of yours? I'm her only relative, so I'm entitled to whatever's mine. Now you tell me what brought you here, then clear out because I'm busy.'

'I believe you can help me,' Claire said. 'When she was living here with you, I'm sure Georgina told you of her life at the Lodge?'

'Told me? She never stopped.'

'Probably talked about Stephen.'

'Forever. I got an earful of bloody "Stephen" night and day. What's he to you or your Australian friend?'

'Stephen Conway. He was Patrick's grandfather.'

'Was he now?' she said. 'I never knew his second name, she only ever said Stephen. Well, fancy that! So there was no film about the Ricksons; no BBC. Just a cheap way to check on the family tree.'

'You really could help me, Mrs West, if you wanted to.'

'How?'

'Very simply. Tell me about Stephen and your Aunt Georgina. The things she must have told you, over and over.'

'Sorry,' Helen West said. 'Even if I had time, there's no reason why I'd do that.'

'Instead, you're off to the good life, at Chelsea Reach?'

'Absolutely right, Ms Thomas.'

'If I don't stop you, Mrs West.'

Helen West gazed blankly at her. 'If you . . . *what*?'

'If I don't consult your lawyers.'

'Are you crazy? Consult them? You don't even know them.'

'Peacock & Marsh, in Epsom High Street. They should be warned of what's ahead.'

'What are you talking about?'

'I'm going to make them aware of the way you treated your Aunt Georgina,' Claire said calmly. 'Putting her in that disgusting old people's home, because it was cheap. How you lied to the board and said she was impoverished, so you could save money and get a bigger share of her estate.'

'You wouldn't dare! That's defamation.'

'Patrick wants me to approach the *News of the World*. A bunch of Harley Street doctors owning a third-rate nursing home, unfit to be registered. The *News* would love a story like that. And they're well used to defamation cases . . . it boosts their circulation.'

'Now you wait a minute –'

'I should tell you Mrs Greenfield is prepared to give evidence. Your lawyers will be in the frame, confronted by the failure of their duty of care, and they'll blame you. When you move to Chelsea your new neighbours will know you from the newspaper photos and lurid headlines.' Claire collected her handbag, and glanced at her watch. 'So I'm off to Epsom, to Peacock & Marsh. The young man we met at the funeral, Mr Langton. I have an appointment with him in an hour.'

She started to make her exit with a display of confidence, while worrying her bluff was being called. She had the front door half open as Helen West ran to push it shut.

'Wait. Why would you do something like this?'

'Because Patrick Conway asked me to. Because he's angry at the way you treated Georgina.'

'He has nothing to do with Georgina!'

'His grandfather did,' Claire said. 'Patrick is furious about what happened to her in the last years of her life, and all because of your greed.'

'You can't do this,' Mrs West insisted. 'I took her in. Tried to help. Now I'm starting a new life of my own. It just isn't fair!'

'Was what *you* did fair?'

'But she didn't know! She was past it.'

'Not when you first put her there. The nurses told me she used to weep at nights. Sob her heart out. She felt lost and bewildered, abandoned in a strange place like that. In the end it became full dementia. And *you* did that, Mrs West.'

Helen West had clearly never thought of it in those terms. She made one last vain attempt to bluster her way out of it.

'I'll ring Langton. Tell him he's not to see you.'

'It doesn't matter if he sees me or not. The *News of the World* will see me. Mr Langton and his fine old firm will be on the front page with you – the woman who dumped her elderly aunt into a cesspit and now lives on her money. Use your imagination, Mrs West.'

'Ms Thomas . . . Claire, that's your name, isn't it? Stop it, please. What do I have to do . . . to make you stop this?'

'I'm not sure I can stop it now,' Claire retorted bluntly. 'Or if I want to. Fifteen years, and you visited her only twice! People are going to hate you. You'll be vilified – just think what talkback radio will say . . .'

'Please . . . whatever you want. But don't do this to me.'

'I told you what I want. Everything you remember about Georgina and Stephen. Help me and you'll never see me again.'

Helen West stared at her with disbelief. She seemed confused, unable to accept it could be so simple. Claire had a strange feeling the woman was on the verge of tears.

'But it was so long ago, and I never listened properly. I can't recall half the things she said.'

'You must surely be able to recall enough to help me,' Claire said, becoming anxious.

'Honestly, I can't remember much. I just wasn't interested. And as for the book, I threw that out.'.

'What book?' The other looked at her blankly. 'Mrs West, *what book?*'

'It was in the back of a cupboard all these years. I found it when I was clearing the house. It was just rubbish . . . I never knew it was there till last week.'

Oh God, Claire thought, her heart beginning to race. Don't tell me I've come this close and . . . She realised with dismay what the other was saying.

'It was just some stuff she wrote . . . about him, but I didn't bother to read it. I put it out with the rest of the junk to be burnt.'

Claire handed Patrick a package. Inside was a plain exercise book, like a school primer, its pages filled with neat writing. And on the front in printed capitals, like a schoolgirl's caption of ownership, it read GEORGINA RICKSON, THE LODGE, LEATHERHEAD.

Patrick held it like a gift, and looked at Claire in wonder.

'Mrs West hired a man to help clear up,' she told him. 'If he hadn't been late for work today, this would've been a heap of ash.'

Part Three

Georgina

Chapter Twenty-six

These are events I learnt of long after they had happened. Stephen did not want to write any of it himself; he said he had exposed so much of his secret thoughts and feelings in his diary and the notebook in the past, and he could no longer face reliving some of the painful moments that had occurred since then. So I decided to try and record it, for time can erase recollection, and I don't ever want to forget how it was.

When the court-martial was ordered to reconvene and they reluctantly commuted Stephen's death sentence to ten years' hard labour, he was held in an army gaol until he could be transported back to England. This was in the first week of November, 1918. Five days later he was removed in a truck to the port of Calais and escorted on board a troopship. He was guarded by two military policemen, as well as once again being handcuffed and having his legs chained. Crossing the French dock, manhandled by his guards, he could feel the scrutiny of eyes from hundreds of British soldiers on the deck of the ship.

'Must be a murderer!' someone shouted.

Neither of his guards disputed this.

'Well, I bet he ain't on his way to Buck Palace for a bleedin' Victoria Cross!' another soldier yelled, raising a laugh.

'A lousy rotten fucking deserter,' someone else guessed, and the senior guard, a lance corporal, raised a hand and gave an obvious thumbs up in confirmation of this.

The crowd on deck began to boo him. It was the first time Stephen had ever encountered this kind of open hostility, and the shock of it brought him to a sudden halt. The abrupt stop annoyed the guards who jostled him so that the leg irons cut against his flesh and forced him to continue shuffling forward. Pushed up the gangway amid an angry chorus of jeers and hateful abuse, he was taken to a secure cabin deep inside the vessel, and locked in there for many hours until all embarkation was completed.

Late that day fog in the channel delayed the ship's departure, and it was not until the following afternoon that they arrived in Portsmouth. During all this time Stephen had not been given food or drink, and in his prison cabin there was no slop pail or lavatory. His guards remained on an upper deck and out of hearing until the ship berthed, then berated him as a filthy bastard because he had soiled himself and stank of urine.

They gave him a bucket of cold water and ordered him to get clean, telling him he'd better not try to escape, and reinforced this by checking the chambers of their pistols and aiming them at him.

How can I escape with leg irons? he asked them.

We've got our orders, they told him. You're a dangerous deserter who made threats to kill the colonel at your court-martial. They say you reckoned he was corrupt; a lousy stinking Pommy officer who was unfair and prejudiced. So you're going into a deep dark hole for a long time, mate. Real deep, real dark.

Unable to remember if he had actually made this threat against Carmody, he stayed silent, except to ask if they could undo the handcuffs. It was impossible otherwise to wash himself. The guards roared with laughter at this.

'You think we're stupid?' the lance corporal replied, and turned to the other guard. 'He does, this bloody Aussie thinks we're thick as two planks. Imagine taking off his handcuffs! The bastard would throw a punch, try to kick us in the balls, and be off like a racing pigeon.'

'You know what we could do, don't you?' the other said. 'We could shoot him. Save everyone a hell of a lot of trouble. Save the country the expense of having to feed him for the next ten years.'

'You mean in cold blood? That'd be bloody daft, that would.'

'No, we could take off his cuffs and the chains, then shoot him. Say he made a dash for it.'

Stephen numbly listened to them, hardly caring what happened. He'd endured weeks of threats like this and had become impervious to them. Sometimes he wondered if that would be the best way. A quick death and be finished with it. But in the end they grew tired of their games and threw the bucket of cold water over him. He was dripping wet and still shivering by the time the rest of the troops had disembarked, when he was taken off and marched to a cell in the Portsmouth naval base.

The following day an armoured van arrived to transport him to the military prison in Yorkshire. As Stephen was taken out of the building he heard the sound of distant bells ringing in the town and the noise of a cheering crowd. It was like a sudden window of memory from the past, the day they'd landed here in Portsmouth:

their first glimpse of England, their big surprise as crowds gathered on the wharves to cheer them – he and Bluey, and all the rest of his dead mates, including Double-Trouble, who had sneaked away to go to bed with two very friendly girls. The memory was so clear and poignant that it made him want to weep.

'What's the noise about?' he asked, and one of the escorts told him it was real good news, but he was afraid it was not good news for him. Not for a filthy deserter who'd up and done a runner. The guard took malicious pleasure in explaining it was the eleventh of November, and at eleven o'clock that morning an armistice had begun. At long last it seemed the war was over.

'Tough luck for you,' the other escort commented. 'We can all go home, but not you, mate. You're off to an army nick up north. A bastard of a place. They'll really sort you out. Be lucky to survive ten years' hard where you're going.'

Across the world in Australia, so Stephen was to learn later, the bells and cheering had been wildly premature. The startling news of a cease-fire had swept the country on Friday the ninth of November, and riotous celebrations had begun. Embarrassment and confusion had followed this false alarm. Finally on Monday the eleventh, after a sober Sunday when churches were filled and people prayed that it would soon be true, there was confirmation and the revelry commenced all over again.

But the cheering crowds were not joined by Jane Conway and her small son, nor by Stephen's parents. His mother and father, Edna and Stan, with whom Jane and Richard still lived, were distraught at the news their son had died so close to the cessation of hostilities. Barely a week earlier the two compassionate letters with news of his death had reached Jane, and while there had been not yet been an official war office telegram, the kindly messages from his battalion padre and the medical officer substantiated what they had been fearing for some time. It seemed to explain the lack of response for the past few months to Jane's constant letters, and never for a moment did she doubt the veracity of the information the officers had sent. In her grief she was almost thankful the unbearable telegram had gone astray.

Some weeks later the families, her parents and Stephen's, invited his many friends from school and university to a special mass at the local church, where the priest made prolonged mention of his life and service to the nation. Father Geraghty was in fine form; he reminded the congregation that Stephen had been one of the first to join up, had fought in the Anzac landing and in France, and was a hero who had given his life in a noble cause.

Jane's attempt to deal with her loss was bolstered by the words of the priest's sermon. Gradually she began to come to terms with the sorrow of her bereavement, she cried less at night, resolved to return to her job as a teacher, and decided that on April the twenty-fifth - the day they were already designating as Anzac Day and also her son's birthday - she would take Richard to the ceremony to be held at one of the newly-built memorials to the fallen. If she had to bring her son up alone, at least she wanted him to grow up in the knowledge that his father was a hero.

Bridgeway Detention Centre was set on an isolated and windswept moor in a remote part of Yorkshire, a harsh military prison, and from his first day there Stephen was regarded as a recalcitrant and high-risk prisoner. There was no likelihood of anything else after the damaging report on him by Colonel James Carmody, the president of his court-martial, in which it stated the accused soldier had a history of unruly behaviour and had made violent threats against him and other officers at the trial. This lie was to plague him for the next ten years, for the content of the court transcript precluded any chance of amnesty.

On arrival he was placed in a secure cell in virtual isolation. There was a cursory medical examination done by a local GP who was seconded to the prison – during which there was no mention of the words 'shell shock' – and his time at Netley was dismissed in the same way the court had disparaged it, as an escape from duty among the pack of malingerers and outright cowards who did their best to hide there.

When Stephen tried to tell the doctor his lungs sometimes troubled him because he had experienced attacks of mustard gas, he was first accused of lying because the masks would have been quite adequate protection. After all, they were army issue and the army was not given to supplying faulty equipment. There were two other possible explanations, the doctor told him. Perhaps he'd worn the gas mask incorrectly, or else there were instances of soldiers deliberately not wearing them at all – in the hope they would be discharged as unfit.

'You've never seen a man spewing and dying after a gas attack,' Stephen replied to this, seething at the doctor's bland uncaring attitude, 'or you'd have more bloody sense than to suggest such a thing.' In his anger he tried to quote his friend Wilfred's poem, but was distressed that he could only remember a few words. 'If you could hear the blood gargling from froth-corrupted lungs . . .' he attempted to tell the doctor, who turned and shouted for an orderly and demanded this crazy prisoner be taken away.

The doctor made a complaint to Major Norton, the military police commander of the prison, and the result was seven more days in solitary. It was another mark on his record, which was becoming increasingly full of them, giving him a reputation as a serial offender against authority. By the first Christmas, only six weeks after his arrival, Stephen Conway was already a target. In the work gangs that left the cells before the winter sun had risen, he was the one given the most laborious jobs. When they returned after the sun had set his limbs ached, and he often suffered from blinding headaches, but he soon learnt a protest was pointless for there was no compassion there.

Stephen had arrived at Bridgeway with almost nothing. His only prized possession was his notebook. He spent the rare rest periods reading it over and over again, occasionally adding to notes he'd made, reliving his nightmares. He preserved it fiercely, for somehow it symbolised a link with all the friends he had lost.

Eventually this obsessive devotion to a book aroused the curiosity of the other prisoners, and one night an ex-gunner who shared his cell got hold of it and started reading some of the most personal extracts aloud to those in the vicinity. Stephen asked for it back as calmly as he could. When the other refused he tried to physically retrieve it. The gunner then threatened to rip it to pieces, and was loudly encouraged to do this by those in the adjoining cells.

'Tear the bloody thing up!' they shouted. 'Give us some pages, so we can all have a read – then we'll wipe our arses on it.'

That was when Stephen went berserk. He had been stripped of everything else; now his only belonging was to be destroyed at the whim of a mindless mob. Rage gave him strength as he hit the gunner, then kneed him in the groin, and when the man doubled up Stephen took full advantage and went on hitting him. Guards were called and he was restrained, while the barely conscious gunner was taken to the infirmary. It meant another parade before Major Norton and a far longer spell this time in solitary confinement, but by now Stephen did not fear this. He had begun to prefer seclusion and his own company. When he came out the other prisoners accorded him a grudging respect, and they left him and his secretive and precious book alone.

The remoteness of the prison meant there were very few visitors, and the rules permitted inmates only one letter each month. Neither rule had ever bothered Stephen, for he was aware there could be no visitors for him, nor any letters either. He knew by now the sympathy messages from the padre and the medical officer would have long since arrived home, and he would now be regarded as dead. It was a strange feeling, and something he would have to face in the future, on a far distant day when he would be free and at liberty to go back to Australia. But that was still more than nine years away, and at the age of twenty-five it seemed like an eternity.

Then, one day after work, when the prisoners had been gathered for a mail call, his name was read out. He thought it was a mistake and took no notice until it was called again, shouted loudly this time, and with utter disbelief he took the letter – readdressed from the Australian Army headquarters in Britain – and recognised the familiar writing on the envelope as Jane's.

When it came, the shock was all the greater for Jane because she had no warning. She was alone in the house, Stephen's parents were out; it was also a half day at school, and she was busily occupied correcting homework. The dining-room table was covered with exercise books containing essays that had engaged her all the morning. When the bell rang and she answered it to find an army officer at the door asking if he could come in and speak to her, she felt sure it was to do with the missing telegram.

The officer, who introduced himself as Staff Captain Clarkson from headquarters at Victoria Barracks, appeared confused when she mentioned this. What telegram did she mean?

Jane thought it a strange question. She explained that she had never received an official army telegram reporting her husband's death. Hearing this Captain Clarkson looked perturbed and cleared his throat. He asked her courteously if there was somewhere they could talk in private.

Jane readily agreed. She showed him into the empty dining room and tidied away the school books. While busily doing so she explained that her son had been taken to the park by his granny, her mother-in-law, and that her father-in-law was at work. She wondered why she told him this, but the way he stood there, refusing her offer to sit down and constantly clearing his throat made her feel that he was apprehensive for some reason, and this unease communicated itself to her.

She asked if he would like a cup of tea, and again he politely declined. She began to feel irritated with his civility; something about the way he looked so apologetic alarmed her.

'This is a most delicate matter,' he finally said, the dry cough he tried to suppress clearly a nervous habit. 'I've been asked to come here today by headquarters to explain certain things to you. As you know, since Christmas the troopships have gradually been bringing our soldiers home. The last group should be back from overseas this month. We discussed the matter and felt you should be informed your husband will not be among them.'

'But I know that,' Jane replied, puzzled.

'Oh, then you've heard?' He seemed surprised and somewhat relieved. 'That makes it easier for me. My job is, first of all, to tell you the army promises to be discreet on this matter. We have a number of reservations about the way his case was conducted at the court-martial, so his discharge will not be made public, although of course by law it has to be a dishonourable one.'

'I beg your pardon –' she started to say, but he was intent on continuing and did not seem to be aware of her shock.

'We believe that releasing the matter would be grossly unfair to you, and cause unnecessary suffering to all your family. However, as a matter of conscience, you should know he's still alive.'

Jane looked at him in utter perplexity. 'What on earth are you talking about?' she asked. 'My husband was killed in action!' There was a silence that seemed interminable and unsettled her. 'Court-martial? Dishonourable discharge? That's impossible, there's been a terrible mistake!'

'Mrs Conway –'

Her temper rising because it seemed like a nightmare, she began to rail at him. 'Stephen died fighting in France. He was one of the very first volunteers, the first month of hostilities, and he died for people like you, who probably never even went overseas. I'm sure you spent your entire war in a chair at Victoria Barracks! How dare you! This is outrageous. I can show you letters that will prove this is a lie!'

Without even waiting for his answer she ran to her bedroom, snatched the two letters from a drawer and brought them to him. He read them with a frown before returning them to her.

'Mrs Conway.' He shook his head. 'I'm awfully sorry, but I can prove those letters are untrue. Your husband is alive and has been imprisoned for desertion.'

Captain Clarkson was clearly rattled by the situation. He told Jane he'd been sent because the army felt great sympathy; what her husband had done in the face of enemy fire was no fault of hers. The decision to send him here to explain this had been done with good intentions, but he wished they had known the circumstances and particularly the existence of those letters, for perhaps they would have followed a different course.

The letters – from a minister of all people, and a medical officer who should've known better – were doubtless well meant but had caused her an awful situation, with so many people believing Stephen had been killed in action; even her young son had been led to accept this. It posed a real problem, Clarkson pointed out.

Jane asked him if he would please go. She needed to be alone.

The staff captain said he quite understood. She had much to think about. Some day, after he'd served his ten-year sentence, or perhaps earlier if there was an amnesty, her husband would expect to come home. Mrs Conway would doubtless want to address her mind to what might happen then.

I was an impressionable sixteen-year-old by the end of the war, and deeply envious of my sister Henrietta, a volunteer nurse, and one of the so-called Roses of No-Man's-Land. They were so romanticised in the newspapers and on the music hall stages that I sometimes felt as if she was a combination of heroine and an angel of mercy.

I suppose it was a lasting perception, because in 1922, four years after the war ended, I enlisted in what was then known as Queen Alexandra's Imperial Military Nursing Service. My home at the Lodge had become an unhappy and depressing place; my three brothers dead, two in the trenches of France, and one in a London traffic accident. I left there with relief. There was no opposition from either of my parents, for the family was in total disarray ever since our loss. Only Henrietta tried to dissuade me, saying the war was over and there was no future or indeed any fun in an army nursing career. Although we were still friends at this time, we quarrelled about this. It was not our first disagreement, nor would it be our last.

After elementary training in a military hospital at Aldershot, I was sent as a junior nurse to Netley. The place was still full of casualties from the war, serious cases, many of whom would never fully recover. It was not the romantic job that I'd envisioned. It was tedious routine, and after twelve months of doing nothing more stimulating than scrubbing floors, washing dishes and emptying bedpans, I was forced to reluctantly agree that Henry had been right. I wanted to give up and go home.

But that, I learnt with a shock, was not an option. In my haste to join the service I'd enlisted for the minimum period of nine years. I soon learned it was as binding as an army enrolment. I applied for early release on compassionate grounds that my father was ill and needed a nurse's care. The hospital considered the case, agreed my father was indeed ill, but was being well cared for by his elder daughter, a former VAD who had served both at home and abroad during the war. The verdict was that with Henrietta's experience she would be more able to cope with the situation. My application was denied. Perhaps unfairly, I never quite forgave my sister. I suppose it would explain the rancour between us later.

So I endured five more years of drudgery, and at the age of twenty-six, facing at least another three years until I could leave this servitude, I felt that I had wasted my life.

Stephen served his full sentence in the harsh Yorkshire military prison, the only inmate who received no amnesty. In the ten years behind bars his health deteriorated; no attempt had been made to treat the result of his shell shock, and his lungs had become weakened by the excessive hours of hard labour and severe winters, as well as the after-effects of the poison gas. He was thirty-four but looked closer to fifty.

On discharge from Bridgeway, detainees were given a mandatory medical examination. A new doctor conducted this; he had only been at the prison a matter of weeks and did not know Stephen. He was a more sensitive man than his predecessor, and concerned about the condition of his patient. After a series of tests he declared Stephen was unfit to return to civilian life. He was emotionally unstable from damage suffered in France; it was likely he could harm himself, or even be a possible danger to others.

The tyrannical Major Norton, still commander of the prison, was not prepared to accept the medical officer's report. Conway was a difficult detainee he wished to get rid of, and as quickly as possible.

'You'll have to rethink this,' he told the doctor, who replied it was not only professionally out of order to change his diagnosis, but quite impossible. Copies of his report had been sent to provost and army headquarters. In his opinion, he had stated bluntly, it was the fault of the system and this prison. The man had been badly neglected, ill-treated and needed proper care and attention.

The matter was passed up the chain of command for consideration. The army was in a quandary, for they could not legitimately keep Stephen Conway in prison any longer, but nor did they want the responsibility of releasing him into the community after this troubling medical report. They took advice on the legality of what seemed the simple and logical solution. Eminent counsel agreed the problem could lawfully be sent back to its place of origin. An application was made to the Home Office for his immediate deportation to Australia. Stephen was paraded in the commander's office to be told of this intention.

'No,' he said, becoming distressed at the suggestion, 'you can't do that, and I won't agree to go.'

'That's where you belong,' Norton told him, 'and it's where you'll be going as soon as possible. If you make it necessary, you'll be taken to the first available ship under escort. Like the bloody convicts were taken on board in irons at the start of your country.'

Stephen lost his temper. He shouted angrily that nothing would make him ever go back to Australia. He no longer belonged there. That part of his life was over. His agitation became so violent that the guards wanted him restrained and Major Norton had no real solution except to propose another spell in solitary. It was pointed out to him by the same doctor that this could be unwise, because technically Stephen Conway was now a free man.

'Well, you opened this fucking can of worms,' the major snapped, 'so what are we to do with the bloody man?'

'Let's start by treating him like a human being,' the doctor suggested. 'I don't think that's a privilege he's enjoyed for a long time.'

The next day the doctor and Stephen went for a long walk on the moor together. It was with extreme reluctance that the prisoner was allowed out of the main gate, but risking further displeasure from authority the doctor argued that they could not have the kind of amicable conversation required within the walls that held only grim memories for him.

It was on the walk that the doctor encouraged Stephen to talk, and during this he spoke about the places he'd been during the four years of the war, among them Netley. The doctor asked if Stephen could face going back there. If not, there might be a successful move to repatriate him, however unfairly and even against his wishes. Stephen asked for time to think about it, and decided if it was a choice between that or deportation, the hospital in Southampton Water was at least a recognisable refuge.

So he came back to Netley by his own concurrence. He arrived there with an old kitbag, pitifully few possessions in it, but among them was the notebook, still preserved and treasured as though it were a talisman. He no longer wrote in it but read it sometimes, as if to recall his life.

The first time we met I was on my hands and knees, scrubbing out the men's shower block. Stephen walked across my wet floor, unaware his boots were dirty and left a trail of muddy imprints. I sat back on my haunches, annoyed at his thoughtlessness, and hurled my scrubbing brush at him. It hit his shoulder, and I shouted my candid opinion of him.

'Mind where you put your filthy feet, you stupid clod!'

To be honest, I was about to follow this with more abuse when he turned and stared at me, instantly sat down, unmindful of the wet floor, and burst into tears.

'Oh, come on,' I said, 'it was only a scrubbing brush. It didn't hurt you that much.'

This seemed to provoke a fresh outburst of tears. He began to sob uncontrollably, his hands held to his face as his body rocked back and forth in what seemed like an awful paroxysm of grief.

'Please don't cry,' I begged, now distressed, but it went unheeded. I stood up, wondering what to do. Should I go for a doctor, or call one of the ward sisters? Not being able to decide the best course of action, I moved across and sat on the wet floor beside him. Uncertain how to cope, I reached for one of his hands and held it.

'Get a cold bum sitting in the sopping wet like this,' I murmured, feeling it was probably the wrong thing to say at such an awkward time. 'Do you want to move somewhere else, where it's dry?'

He took his other hand from his tearful face and shook his head.

'Might end up with a chill, or a dose of piles.'

I waited for him to say something, but he just looked at me. At least he had stopped crying. I took off my nurse's cap and used it to mop his tears. 'What's your name?'

'Stephen,' he said, after a long pause.

'I don't think I've seen you around the hospital before. Have you been here long, Stephen?'

'A few weeks.'

'What do you think of it?'

'Better than it used to be.'

'Not your first visit?'

'No,' was all he said, and asked my name. When I told him he repeated it softly. 'Georgina.'

'It's a mouthful, so people often call me George.'

'Georgina, that suits you best. I'd never call you George.'

'That's good,' I said, 'because I don't like it either. Are you English, Stephen?'

'No.'

'Where are you from?'

He did not answer, his eyes beginning to fill with tears again.

'Don't, Stephen. Please don't cry. I won't ask if it upsets you.'

'Australia,' he said, 'but I can't ever go back there.'

'Why not?'

'She asked me not to.'

'Who did?'

'Jane. My wife. She said it would be . . . embarrassing.' He wiped his eyes with his sleeve, and struggled to continue. 'It would embarrass my son. So I can't ever see him. He's thirteen now; I've never seen him and I never will. He was only five years old when she wrote the letter . . .'

He took a few crumpled pages from his pocket and gave them to me. Reading it, I thought it the saddest letter. It explained how the two sympathy notes had made Jane believe her husband had been killed in action, then some months afterwards the shock visit of the army officer had revealed the truth. And how she didn't know whether to write, and having decided she must, didn't know where to send her letter, but could only address it to him at army headquarters and hope it would somehow reach him. And yet, because of the things she had to say, she also dreaded the day it might arrive.

I have agonised, it said, for so many weeks now.

Awful sleepless nights, losing my concentration when I try to teach the children in class, wrestling with the problem which seems to have no answer. For myself, selfishly I desperately want you home, but this news places me in a terrible predicament.

People can be vicious and cruel. Surely you can imagine the hurtful things that would be said. After all, we had a church service, where Father Geraghty eulogised you. All because of the two men who wrote to me. I'm sure they were trying to be kind and helpful, but their kindness means that your return some day can only cause anguish and misery to all your family. I fear what will happen when people learn the truth, as they assuredly will.

It would be humiliating for your parents who have been so good to me, and would be made to feel disgraced. I hate the thought of them being hurt. People would not take it kindly that they were misled, and I expect in the end they would blame me. I can put up with that, but I fear it would be especially hard for Richard to accept. He believes you died in battle and he venerates you as a hero. So do all your friends, as well as your parents, and after thinking about it deeply I've decided it's best not to tell your dad and mother, nor mine. Perhaps one day when Richard is older I might be able to explain it to him, but at present I feel it best not to do that.

My dearest – for you still are my dearest and there will never be anyone else – no matter how many years they make you spend in prison, you have every right to come home afterwards. No one can prevent you from doing that. But I ask you to think of the harm it could do. Think of your father and mother. Think of your son. And if you still have any feeling of love for me, you must see how it would completely destroy our entire family.

For this reason, I can only beg you with all my heart to stay away.

I didn't know what to say. Because of that, I carefully smoothed and folded the pages, then gave the letter back to him. It allowed me a moment to think of what reply I could make without hurting him.

'Poor Jane. It can't have been an easy letter for her to write.'

He looked at me, nodding agreement. It seemed as if it had helped. 'I've always wanted to write back and say I'd do as she asked,' he said softly. 'But I wrote her five letters and tore them all up.'

'It might've eased her mind.'

'Or made things worse,' Stephen replied. 'An overseas letter with an English stamp, and the address in my handwriting. My parents would've recognised it at once.'

I asked him questions about Jane, and Stephen seemed willing to answer. He spoke of their growing up together, and made me smile as he explained their first engagement at the age of eight, and told of their rushed marriage when they were both nineteen. He mentioned Echo Point and how he remembered the sound of their voices resonating past the Three Sisters and down the Megalong Valley.

While we talked his voice became calmer and more relaxed. He even smiled now and then. Time passed. The floor had begun to dry around us, but where we sat was still wet and uncomfortable. I suggested it was time to get up and a change of clothes might be a good idea, but before we could act on this the door to the shower block was abruptly pushed open and a piercing voice demanded to know precisely what we thought we were doing.

'Matron!'

I started to rise, forcing Stephen to his feet, for I was still clasping his hand. The matron kept gazing at this until our hands parted.

'Would you care to explain, Nurse Rickson? Sitting on the floor, your work unfinished, holding hands with a patient! I can hardly wait to hear your explanation.' Her quieter voice next was, if anything, more threatening. 'My room, I think, in ten minutes. That might just give you time to change out of your wet undergarments.'

'Yes, Matron. May I just say that Mr Conway was distressed –'

'Mr Conway seems to have made a rapid recovery,' Matron replied acidly. 'He might also wish to change his clothes, and after that I'll ask the medical superintendent to explain to him the rules about liaisons in the shower block with nurses. Ten minutes, Miss, to change your knickers and tell me what on earth possessed you.'

The matron's name was Isabel Hardy, and some of our nurses claimed that her family had descended from Flag-Captain Thomas Hardy – he of the famous 'Kiss me, Hardy' request from Horatio Nelson when the great British admiral lay dying.

'Juvenile rubbish. A stupid myth,' the matron had always declared when hearing of this ancestral elaboration, but the older nurses told me that the legend pleased her.

Matron Hardy was a tall, rather angular woman in her late forties. She had a lustrous head of brown hair that was gathered into a bun, and wore a *pince-nez* to effect sternness when required. She was wearing it as she sat behind her desk severely regarding me with disfavour.

'How old are you, child?' was her first question.

'Matron, I'm not a child,' was my reply. I could see it irritated her intensely.

'Then you're a fool. A child sits in a puddle of water – but only a fool sits in it with a man.'

I was twenty-six years old. I had reached that age having had brief crushes on boys in Leatherhead where I was brought up, including a close shave with a good-looking and cheeky stablehand who almost deflowered me in a haystack. There had been a few mild flirtations with patients at the hospital, but the truth is I had never known a real love affair. I fell in love with Stephen straightaway, virtually as we sat together on the wet floor of the shower block, and Matron finding us there, threatening disciplinary measures for such aberrant behaviour, only seemed to intensify my feelings.

Did I feel sorry for him, and fall in love out of sympathy? No, it was instinctive and immediate: I just wanted to hold him and care for him, and felt angry at the harsh way life had treated him. The emotional scars were deep, but I believed kindness and care could soothe them, even if I could not heal his wounds entirely.

And Stephen, because it had been so long since he had experienced warmth and affection from anyone, responded. It's not vanity or blind love when I say that his condition soon began to improve and his memory started to return. I began to realise that amid the bedlam of the psychiatric ward he felt calm and under control whenever I was there, and because I cherished him, I tried to make sure I was as close to him as the job allowed. I managed to get myself transferred to his ward. Whenever I was off duty, we spent all our time together.

Stephen talked; he had been silent for so long in his awful prison years that he talked with animation: he told me of his childhood, his school days, his year as a law student; he talked of everything except the trenches and the war. We walked along the paths and across the spacious lawns of Netley, our hands linked at first and fingers entwined, which was a lovely feeling, but even better was after that when we had our arms around each other.

We didn't care who saw us, but soon it became noticeable and then quite conspicuous, and before long the nurses had a subject for busy table talk at mealtimes. Even the patients began to spread gossip about us. So many rumours! I suppose there was nothing much else to enliven their daily routine. The staff dining room was by far the worst, and I was conscious of a lot of animated chatter that seemed to stop whenever I entered. I didn't really care what anyone said. People declared they'd seen us kissing down by the pier. Other tittle-tattle insisted that far worse was going on in the gazebo.

The matron sent for me again.

This time she removed her *pince-nez* and told me to sit in one of the comfortable chairs by her window. She sat in the other. She looked far kinder without the spectacles, but concerned. She asked me for the truth, and I told her. I said that we *did* kiss down by the pier, but it was untrue about what was supposed to have happened in the gazebo.

She believed me, but warned me it was a foolish relationship: Stephen was a disgraced soldier, psychologically damaged, although perhaps not his fault - he had, after all, spent four years at war, much of it in the front-line - but I was one of the nurses in her care, and she felt she should caution me against unwise and excessive emotion. A young woman in her twenties, especially one gently nurtured and still a virgin, had much to lose, she warned.

'I take it you *are* still a virgin?' she suddenly asked me.

'Yes, Matron. Of course.'

'There's no "of course" about it these days, child, but I believe you. And that's why I wish you'd think very carefully, Georgina. I can't instruct you in matters of the heart, but I am concerned. There seems to me no future in this.'

I asked if I could recount Stephen's story, and she nodded. I told her of the reason why he felt he could never go home to his own country and his family because of his wife's plea, and finished by saying that I wished to look after him.

'Why?' she asked.

I began to feel Matron had never known love, or she would not have asked that question. In the end I simply replied that I wanted to do this, because there was no one else who knew or cared about the extent of his deep suffering.

'It's a huge responsibility. I can't imagine how you'll manage it.'

'My father's dead now,' I replied. 'There's only my mother and my elder sister living in our big house, and Stephen and I won't take up much room. We could live quietly up on the attic floor. There's a grand view of the river from there.'

'You've thought a lot about it.'

'Yes. When my time's up and I can leave here, I want to take him with me. He's served his sentence, so he's entitled to be a free man, Matron.'

'He's a sick and disturbed one,' she insisted.

'Not if someone cares for him.' I was equally insistent. 'Like the way I'll care for him. He can't be kept in here against his will, can he?'

'I don't believe so, Georgina. But I think you'll find that he agreed to come here.'

'Because there was nowhere else for him to go. But when I leave here, he wants to go with me. He wants that, and so do I. Can you help us?'

Dear Matron. She did help. We went back to live at the Lodge in the summer of 1930. Stephen was thirty-six years old. Matron Hardy used her influence to have me released from my contract of service a year before it was due to end, and arranged for Stephen to leave the hospital with me. On the money saved from my annual salary of forty pounds, we took the train to London. I bought him some much-needed new clothes, and we posed as husband and wife and shared a room at a small private hotel in Paddington.

A cheap but sweet little hotel, where I gladly lost my virginity, and we happily experimented in the ways of love. One blissful week;

I can still remember every hour of it, they were days and nights of such joy. I never wanted it to end, but when the week was over we went to Epsom where I met father's lawyers, Peacock & Marsh. There I learnt the inheritance from my father's will that had been held in trust for me would produce what seemed like an enormous income of five hundred pounds a year, and Henrietta and I would jointly inherit the Lodge if we survived our mother.

Then I took Stephen home to meet my family. That's when the trouble began, for our arrival was not well received at Leatherhead.

There was an immediate antagonistic reception from my sister; Henrietta was strongly opposed to me bringing home a man with whom I intended to live openly – and a married one at that. She said it would cause gossip in the neighbourhood and create scandal for our family who'd had enough trouble, without inviting more from strangers. Mother agreed, although with some timidity. For several years her time had been spent in solitude in her room, suffering from poor health and mourning her lost sons and our father. She was like a fading shadow now, dominated by my sister.

Things changed, but not for the better. After the first hostility came a different and far more awkward situation, when Henrietta began to realise she might actually have known Stephen from her war service at Netley – that he had been one of thousands who had passed through in her time there. He clearly remembered *her*; there were even references to her in his notebook, and she easily convinced herself that she remembered him. She became possessive in the strangest way. She was forever intruding on us, determinedly reminding him of past events to which I was not privy, like the hated sister they had called Attila the Hun, who was removed from Netley in disgrace, but now lived in luxury on the estate in Monmouthshire she had inherited on the death of her father, the earl. It seemed none of her male cousins survived the war, hence it all came to her, or so my sister informed Stephen.

Daily, Henrietta started raising other subjects that excluded me. They talked of Wilfred Owen and his poetry – Stephen's friend Wilfred – who had gone back to the trenches, and there won a military cross for bravery. Stephen didn't know what had happened to him; he was shattered to learn from her that Wilfred had been killed in the very last week of the war. Such a tragic loss, Henry sympathised; such a fine, talented young man.

The intrusions became relentless. She had no end of news and nostalgia relating back to those days. The Scottish quack, she told him, was now a leading physician in Edinburgh, and it was expected he'd receive a knighthood in the next birthday honours. Henrietta even whispered to him about the patient next door to Stephen in Bed 10, who had once confessed to her that when he masturbated he always liked to pretend he was in her bed making love to her which, while crude and rather disgusting, she supposed was some kind of release. She said she was aware a lot of the poor chaps in wartime had felt like that about her. Poor things, she knew they all lusted after her; knew from their emotional responses they all imagined she wanted to climb into their beds and spend the nights making love to them. And one night she nearly *did* get into bed with one of them. But that, she said, was to remain a secret strictly between her and Stephen. Which meant, of course, he was not to tell me, but naturally he did.

These almost daily excursions into nostalgia started to upset me. I knew Stephen was trying his best to forget the war, while Henry with her endless reminiscences kept prodding at his memory almost every day. I got angry, I admit it. It wasn't jealousy. I knew she had no real affection or desire for Stephen – nor for any of the male sex. It was a way of reliving the war years, which to her were so full of excitement, whereas the decade since had been dull and dutiful, looking after our ageing parents, deprived of the company of nursing friends, and missing the reflected glory of being one of the glamorous Roses. I might even have sympathised - sometimes I did try to make allowances - but this process of constant retrospection meant she was repeatedly unsettling Stephen and excluding me. It led to a monumental row.

One evening when Henrietta was again monopolising the dinner table, reminding Stephen of various doctors and patients who were there in his time, talking of the many chaps who had been so fond of her, I completely lost my temper. I couldn't help it; I asked if any of Henry's so-called 'chaps' ever guessed how expert she was at pretence, and did none of them realise they hadn't the slightest hope of getting her into any bed, because she was a lesbian?

Mother looked rather puzzled by the word; the maid, who was serving soup at the time, dropped the tureen which smashed and spilled its contents all over the Persian rug. The maid fled. Henrietta shouted that it was a lie; I replied that it most certainly wasn't: she'd been a lesbian ever since falling in love with Miss Scott, the English mistress at our boarding school, and everyone knew she was a lez and always would be.

Then I tried to make amends, but too late by far. I said it had never bothered me, I'd known about it for ages, but why did Henry have to bore us rigid with these stupid and fanciful tales about 'her chaps'? She burst into tears, called me an oversexed bitch on heat and swept out in a rage. Mother tottered off to her room, asking aloud what the world was coming to, and my sister and I didn't speak again for years.

After Mother died two years later the ill feeling continued. It even grew worse with our mutual inheritance of the Lodge. I tried to call a truce, but Henrietta would have none of it. She sent for a surveyor who carefully measured the main floor space, and the house was divided into two exact sections. I attempted to tell her it was insane, but that was almost impossible because she pretended to never hear anything I said. So the Lodge became two dwellings, and the connecting door between us was always kept locked.

Perhaps the bizarre living arrangements were for the best. Stephen and I lived in our half of the house in utter harmony. These were the best, the very sweetest years. We loved each other so deeply that we felt no need for any outside company. I did the shopping in the village; I went alone and seldom stayed long. Even an hour was time I begrudged being away from him. As for him, he hardly ever left the grounds. His life was happy and peaceful at last. He spent his days keeping our section of the garden trim, growing vegetables, reading books and listening to the radio, particularly the daily news with great concern as Hitler became the German chancellor and the world again went to war.

Henry, after a series of sexual misadventures, took in a female lover who drove a field ambulance - but to our neighbourhood she was a boarder, and her billet at the Lodge was my sister's contribution to the war effort.

Whenever there was an urgent need to communicate with us, Henry asked the ambulance driver to convey her message to Stephen, who in turn conveyed it to me, and in this way contact was maintained without the stress of proximity. Nobody beyond us four principals and the servants knew of the strange existence inside the walls of the palatial old building. The Lodge had always been such a grand estate, so private from the rest of town, that there was no speculation about the way we lived. It was a traditional case of the Ricksons and the rest of the town, which was how it had always been.

When the Second World War ended in 1945, the ambulance driver departed for a more lively existence in London, and a few years later Henrietta became very ill. It was only then that we were reconciled. I nursed her; Stephen brought her offerings of flowers and fruit from our garden, and in 1956, just when it seemed the nursing and our reconciliation had brought a reprieve, Henry at the age of sixty-two had a massive heart attack and died.

After that, there was just the two us. We had another eight precious years together, then it was Stephen's coffin I followed to the graveyard beside the church. He was sixty-nine, and with all that he had endured it was remarkable he'd lived so long. I was the single mourner there, for we had never tried to acquire local friends, and when it was over I went home and wept with an anguish I had never experienced before. The deaths of my brothers when I was a young impressionable schoolgirl, my parents later, then my sister . . . none had aroused this kind of grief.

Afterwards, months afterwards, I drew comfort from the words Stephen spoke before he died. He said that I'd restored his life. That I'd given him love when he thought he would never experience it again, and he hoped I'd been as happy in our years together as he had. It had been nearly thirty-five years since we met on the wet floor . . . Almost half his life. Often afterwards, I began to think about Jane who had asked him not to come home, as well as the son he never knew, and one day, after a visit to Australia House in London, where I was given an address for Richard Conway, I wrapped Stephen's diary and sent it to him with a rather cautious note.

I kept his own notebook and this, my precious memories of our life together. Dear Stephen, I miss you so much. If I restored your life, you utterly transformed and enriched mine.

Part Four

Patrick

Chapter Twenty-seven

The first trace of sunrise touched the treetops of the Megalong Valley, and lit the sandstone cliffs that enclosed it like ramparts. The scattered towns of the Blue Mountains began to appear, and soon afterwards the plane started its long descent towards Kingsford Smith Airport. The cabin crew were busily collecting breakfast trays and folding away pillows and blankets. A cheerful announcement from the cabin said landing would be in about twenty minutes, and the weather forecast was for a warm and sunny day.

Patrick looked out his window at the pattern of streets and houses below as they reached the western suburbs. The panorama of tiled roofs extended as far as he could see, a drab mosaic only enlivened by splashes of blue from backyard swimming pools. Soon early peak-hour traffic would start to clog the arterial roads, and the day below them would begin.

He and Claire had spent most of his last night in London fully engrossed in Georgina's memoir. Plans for a farewell dinner at their Italian restaurant were cancelled; they paused only for a quick ham sandwich and coffee, as he marvelled at the treasure salvaged by her impulsive visit to Mrs West. Later Patrick re-read it slowly aloud while Claire typed a back-up copy that would be sent to his email address as a safety measure.

They spent much of the night doing this. Both on a high at the discovery, they were too stimulated to consider sleep, and the imminence of his departure seemed to inhibit them from making love. So they had sat by the window and waited for the dawn, neither of them wanting to speculate on the future, watching the streetlights along the river begin to pale while Patrick held her in his arms, trying to forget this was his last day.

His taxi had been late. He'd already persuaded Claire not to accompany him to the airport; it would be a fruitless journey, Heathrow would be packed with queues. He would have to join one as soon as he arrived, then go through security, which meant she'd be left standing in the crowded terminal with nothing achieved, except a distant glimpse of him looking fed-up and vanishing from sight.

The lateness of the taxi created extra tension, prolonging the pressure of their parting. Patrick went out to the balcony to look for it. The morning was overcast and cool; a low grey sky seemed to match his mood, and Claire's, who joined him shivering. She said the change in weather was a hint of what lay ahead. It was all downhill from now on; their Indian summer had been wonderful but winter was imminent. In the parks the leaves were not just falling, they were literally *cascading* off the trees. Soon every branch would be stripped bare. At the weekend the clocks would go back to winter time. It would be dark by four each afternoon. Maybe by three-thirty in the depths of December. That, plus icy winds blowing across Europe from the Russian Steppes to cap it all; she told him he was making his escape just in time.

Normally they would have been laughing at this doleful litany, but it didn't feel like a day for laughter.

'It's not an escape,' Patrick tried to assert. 'I have to go. But you do know I want to come back.'

'Wait till you get home,' Claire insisted vehemently, 'before you decide anything. That's what we agreed.'

'Claire, please . . .'

They'd talked it over while waiting for the dawn. But calmly, not like this. With no sign of the cab, the stress was becoming palpable. Patrick tried vainly to think of something cheerful to say.

'Perhaps you'll have a white Christmas.'

Claire told him that white Christmases were not always that crash-hot. Good for the royalties of the Bing Crosby estate, but not so brilliant when it melted. The last time they'd had a white one in London, it had been horrible. Slush everywhere. Cars skidding. Actually more like a dirty *brown* Christmas, with the streets a lethal mixture of thawing snow and slippery dog shit.

Not knowing what else to do, he put his arms around her and felt her trembling.

It was almost a relief when the taxi finally did arrive. The driver, a cheerful West Indian with a pronounced cockney accent, apologised that he'd got lost, but promised they had heaps of time. He loaded the suitcase and laptop in the cab while Claire and Patrick stood and hugged in mutual misery.

'Take care,' she said, trying to prevent tears that were filling her eyes as she held him tightly and kissed him.

'I'll ring you when we land,' he promised, and looking out the rear window he could see her, shivering in the cold and waving until they reached the end of the street. He wanted to tell the driver to stop, to go back; he had a vivid recollection of Stephen's anguish at having to leave the farm, and how Marie-Louise had stood like this waving to him. He felt the same pain his grandfather had known as the taxi turned the corner and he could no longer see her.

Joanna left Fox Studios and drove home to their new apartment. It had been a long day, her last day, for her director's cut on the picture was complete, and others would finish the sound edit and deliver the film. She parked her Porsche and took the elevator to the penthouse suite.

There were phone messages, one from her father. Was she feeling better, and please ring him? The others could wait, she decided; she and her dad had never fallen out before, and there were some fences to mend. But the phone rang unattended; Carlo did not believe in answering machines. If he was home he picked up the telephone, or the caller could ring again if it was important. This was important.

Dad, she wanted to say, please forgive me . . .

She knew Patrick would be landing tomorrow before breakfast and had sent him the new address, for they preferred taxis to the hassle of picking each other up from the airport. Parking was hell, and the plane was bound to be late. Patrick would not expect her.

She had moved furniture from Neutral Bay and set up a large study with their computers. There was some email for him; two of them contained attachments. The first was labelled 'Treatment' and came with a note hoping he'd had a good trip, to keep in touch and remember they had a deadline for the screenplay at the end of next month. Money for his expenses to date and the script advance had been sent to his bank. It was signed, 'Affectionately, Lottie'. Joanna was intrigued. It was her first indication that a deal had been struck;

their last phone call since her return from America had suggested the opposite.

The second attachment was something different. Headed 'Georgina', it was many closely typed pages and certainly not the project he'd gone overseas to discuss. She scanned the first page. What she saw there made her decide to print it. She went to the fridge and poured herself a glass of wine, then sat down to read it.

It was a surprise to Patrick, being met at the airport. Waiting at the end of a long line for a taxi, he heard his name called and turned to see Joanna waving as she hurried from the direction of the car park. A man near him in the queue gazed at her admiringly, looking envious as Patrick waved a reply and went to meet her. He realised she had caught the attention of other male eyes; her trim figure and good looks always attracted attention.

They met and kissed. 'This is nice,' he said. 'Unexpected.'

'I set the alarm to wake me early. Good trip, darling?' She glanced at him with a grin. 'Or just a long one.'

'Fairly long. Not much leg room at the blunt end. All those extra seats might help the company's bottom line, but don't do much for the travellers' bums.'

She laughed and hugged him. 'Did you manage to sleep?'

'Not a lot. Still, it's only twenty-four hours out of my life, and El Cheapo saves heaps.'

She kissed him again. He smelt her familiar perfume, felt the touch of her lips, and was assailed by memories.

'Never mind, my pet. Next time you can travel up-market in a comfort zone. There's money in overnight from the BBC.'

'Already? Good old Lottie.'

'They seem keen. I'm not surprised.'

'You read the treatment?'

'I sure did,' she agreed. 'Glanced at it, then got hooked. And read the other attachment sent by Claire – whoever she is.'

They reached her Porsche. Brand-new, with the hood down, it looked spectacular. A perfect match for Joanna, he thought, as eye-catching as its owner. They left the airport and headed for the freeway.

'You went to meet on one story, and seem to have sold another,' she observed. 'A better one.'

'I'm glad you like it.' Patrick told her of his encounters with Charlotte Redmond while she drove, sharing her laughter when he related the visit upstairs to God.

'Fabulous!' She eased the car past a line of traffic, then dropped back to the speed limit. 'Sounds like it might actually happen.'

'It *must* happen,' he said, and the new assurance in his voice made her glance thoughtfully at him. 'It's become personal. The unnamed, unknown soldier who was kicked around and ill-treated will have a name at last. And my contract has a clause that says the film will be dedicated to the memory of Stephen Conway.'

Joanna was quiet until they came out of the harbour tunnel, then she turned to him and asked, 'Do you need a director?'

He began to realise there was an agenda behind her meeting him, and felt uncomfortable. He had not anticipated this.

'What about your big movie in the States?'

'Nine months, then I'll be available. It'll take you that long to get up and running.' She sounded buoyant. 'The two of us. It'd be a team effort.'

'Jo, it's not your kind of picture,' he replied carefully. 'And the budget can't afford your kind of money.'

'Put it this way, Patrick. It's clearly important to you, which makes it important to me. I'd do this for whatever the budget can afford.'

'It's not that simple.'

'Why not call your friend Charlotte and ask if they want me? At a bargain price – for one film only. Tell her I'm inspired by the story, and I've never worked with you.'

'Let's talk when I'm over the jet lag.' He was uneasy, for he suspected Lottie would embrace the idea. 'Later today,' Patrick added, 'there's a lot of things we need to talk about.'

They drove the rest of the way to their new home in silence.

The sunlight lit the harbour like a glittering prize. Ferries crossed from Mosman and Cremorne Point, while a sleek hydrofoil slid past on its way to the city. In the distance a fleet of eighteen-footers unfurled sails, and way beyond this activity, off the wooded hillside of Middle Head, a huge container ship stood waiting for its pilot.

A view without parallel, Patrick thought, admiring the vista from the penthouse garden where he stood amid its lush foliage. The photographs she'd emailed him could not do justice to the reality. The glimpse of muddy river from Claire's bathroom, he reflected ruefully, could hardly compete with this astonishing panorama.

'What do you think?' Joanna asked, and he became aware she'd emerged from the living room with a bottle of champagne and two glasses.

'It's sensational,' Patrick said. 'Fantastic.'

'I told my father you'd like it.'

'He approves of it?'

'Darling, he found it.'

'Oh?'

'Raved about it. Declared it ideal for my new status. The kind of high-profile place that'd always bring me home between my work in LA, which would mean we'd never lose touch. And, since it occupies two floors, he pointed out there are enough bedrooms for lots of children.'

'What did you say to that?'

'I said perhaps one child. Maybe another later on . . . I'm afraid he took me literally.'

'He did. So literally that he told my sister you were pregnant. Which is how the news spread to me before you added that postscript to your email.'

'So I gather.' Joanna shrugged. 'I should be angry about it, but I'm determined not to be.'

'About a rumour?'

'No, about Sally voicing a suspicion I might've had an abortion. That my food poisoning might've been a cover. She as good as insinuated so to my face. But we've never exactly been best friends, have we?'

Joanna opened the champagne while Patrick considered how to reply. He watched as she poured each of them a glass, handed him one and smiled. 'Welcome home, darling.'

'Joanna —' he began, but she interrupted.

'The truth is far less dramatic than your drama-queen sister would like it to be. There was no child - and never a pregnancy. I told her if she had trouble believing it, I'd email the Cedars Hospital for my medical records.'

'I'm sure there's no need for that,' Patrick replied. 'But how did Carlo of all people get it so wrong?'

Joanna finished her drink before replying. She put the glass down on the table beside her and spread her hands in what seemed a friendly plea for forgiveness.

'My fault,' she told him. 'When Dad showed me this apartment and wanted me to buy it, I did point out your immediate reaction that it was way beyond us. Which, of course, it was. We'd have been saddled with a mortgage the size of the national debt. But I kind of hinted there might be a grandchild soon . . .' She hesitated, as if that was all she intended to say, then came to stand alongside him at the roof garden railing, her gaze avoiding him and fixed on the sails of the Opera House across the water. 'I might've overdone it. Suggesting I wasn't looking forward to morning sickness, and how we'd stopped bothering with precautions . . . He straight away insisted on helping me pay for the place. When he started planning which room would be the nursery, I realised I'd gone too far and that he'd leapt to the obvious conclusion. That night I had to leave for Los Angeles. By the time I came back he'd spread the news, so I had to lie and tell him it'd been a false alarm.'

'Not very fair to Carlo.'

'No,' she said.

'But I suppose by then he'd paid for all this. Not just "helped", as you'd like me to believe. Paid for the lot. Dug into his deep pockets, because whether you were pregnant or not, you made him believe he was going to be a grandfather.'

She turned and stared at him. 'Whether I was pregnant or not? I made it clear to you I wasn't. Jesus Christ, don't you believe me?'

'What I believe isn't important any longer. I'm just sorry for Carlo, because one way or another, you conned the poor old bugger.'

'Is that a sin, a wealthy father wanting to buy something for his daughter? To protect my future, he said, so I'd always be secure, no matter what lousy tricks life or the film business might decide to play. We all know you can be sky-high one minute and on your arse the next.' She seemed impatient, as if wondering why he couldn't understand. 'Look, I was going to tell you the sordid details, but in my own time. And if it sounds a bit grasping, it really wasn't at all. He wanted this place for me from the moment he saw it.'

How you rationalise so glibly, Patrick thought, gazing at his beautiful and acquisitive wife. He'd never really seen that side of her before. Manipulating her own father, surely unnecessarily, for he would have given her whatever she wanted.

'What's more, I did promise him we'd try for a baby. I'll play fair with him on that, but after I finish this movie.'

'Well, that's something you'll have to sort out with Carlo,' Patrick replied as gently as he could. 'Because fabulous as your new home is, I won't be living here. I'm sorry, Jo, but it's time I told you about Claire.'

Epilogue

The grave looked different now – unlike the disarray they had encountered the first time Claire had brought him here. She had traced it from Georgina's description of the funeral, and soon after his return to London she and Patrick had paid a visit to the tiny churchyard outside the town of Leatherhead. Stephen's name was barely legible; the headstone was thick with lichen and embedded with the grime of years, while surrounding it was a wilderness of straggling dock weeds and blackberry that had grown unchecked, almost obscuring the site. It was clear that for a long time, ever since Georgina had been unable to visit here, no one had cared for this resting place.

Their first task was to restore it. They spent days gouging the algae from the stone, after that using acid to scrub away the dirt until the granite slab looked like new. Then they chopped down the weeds, brought tools to dig out the roots, and sprayed the ground to prevent new growth. Over the earth they laid a cover of ornamental pebbles on a surface of wet concrete. They were both resolved that never again would Stephen's grave be allowed to look derelict.

Patrick watched Claire sitting on the ground with her camera as she took shots to record their progress. Wearing an old pair of jeans and a floppy turtlenecked pullover, her auburn hair tied back and her face bare of makeup, he thought she had never looked lovelier. Except perhaps, on New Year's Eve. He smiled at the memory of it. Arriving at her flat in Ashburton Road, anticipating her surprise when she opened the door to him, the surprise had been his, for he found she was not at home. After repeatedly pressing the bell, he wondered what to do. That was the trouble with surprises: they sometimes rebounded with a clang.

He had telephoned her from Sydney at Christmas to say he was spending a last week with his mother and sister, and was booked on a flight leaving on New Year's Day. When the chance of a business-class seat suddenly came up two days earlier, Patrick took it and enjoyed the thought of startling Claire with an earlier arrival. Which was why, along with his luggage, he was standing outside the entrance to her building, wishing he had accepted her offer of a set of keys and trying to decide whether to find a hotel for the night or sit on his suitcase in the winter dark and wait for her return. In fact he had done neither. When the owner of the downstairs apartment had emerged and recognised him, Patrick asked if he might store his cases inside the building, and had then set off to find a taxi.

He had only been to Claire's office once before, but felt sure that was where he would find her. The building was in Brompton Road, Knightsbridge, not far from Harrods. He arrived as a drunken group emerged from a noisy New Year's Eve party, and he made his way past them towards the elevator in the lobby. Moments later it arrived on the ground floor and the doors slid open to reveal only one occupant, a rather sober one intending to make her way home, who stared at him in delighted amazement.

'Patrick! You're supposed to be in Australia!' Claire exclaimed. 'I thought you were leaving tomorrow.'

'I decided to leave yesterday so we could celebrate the start of a new century,' Patrick told her. 'Don't you realise in an hour it'll be 2001 and the first day of our new life together?'

'You are completely nuts and I absolutely love you,' she told him, putting her arms tightly around him. This prevented them leaving the elevator as the door slid shut, and they were taken rapidly to the top floor and then slowly down again, as drunks from various parties stumbled in at each floor. Many recognised Claire and kept wishing them a happy new year, as well as trying to pronounce 'a smashing new millennium'. Everyone was in a festive mood. It seemed the world was not going to end. Computers would not implode or explode, planes would not fall out of the sky, all predictions of disaster were cancelled. During this slow descent Patrick and Claire were wrapped together in the back of the lift, their lips joined, their hearts beating, hardly able to breathe in the crush that compressed them.

And later, when the old century had gone and they could not hail a cab and no longer cared, they walked arm in arm through Kensington, across Redcliffe Gardens into Fulham Road, then slowly down through the labyrinthine streets of Chelsea, and sometime towards dawn reached home and went to bed.

That was three weeks ago, Patrick recalled, his mind full of how rapidly his life had changed. Joanna was far away in her harbourside penthouse, and there were days when it all seemed like a distant memory. She had been astonished he did not want to remain with her and share the luxurious living; there had been anger and tears before her recognition that their marriage was over. He would never be sure if she had been pregnant and aborted their child, or simply contrived to emotionally blackmail her father into purchasing the apartment. He did realise she would have allowed nothing to stand in the way of her first international movie, and childbirth in the middle of filming on location would've made it impossible. So perhaps Sally was right . . . but there was no point in speculating any more.

He was aware of the irony; if there had been a child it would have brought complications, perhaps jeopardising his return to Claire. Instead he was free, blissful in his liberation and a new life. Like Stephen, he thought, he had found love on the other side of the world. And like his grandfather he would remain here.

A diary that might never have been discovered had sent him on a search into the past and led to Georgina and to Claire. And all because two generations ago a young law student volunteered to go to war, believing he was helping to save his country, unaware his longing for a great adventure would ultimately bring him to this obscure grave in a foreign churchyard.

But at least the grave had now become a fitting memorial. After they had finished clearing the site, Patrick and Claire had turned their attention to the lack of lettering on the tombstone. It bore nothing but Stephen's name and the date of his death. Patrick wanted something more personal. He wondered if he should seek permission from the church warden or the local council, but Claire disuaded him. He knew what he wanted engraved, so all they required was a stonemason. Going cap-in-hand to authority would only lead to an officious bureaucratic nightmare. Hire the best craftsman, she suggested, pay his fee in cash, so as not to create extra work for the Inland Revenue, Britain's tax office, and thus by-pass two bureaucracies.

'I'm a great believer,' she told him, 'in not getting tied up in red tape.'

'That's one of the reasons I love you,' Patrick replied.

When the work was done he took photographs to post to Sally and his mother. Then they lingered at the grave for a time, their arms around each other as they read the new inscription:

IN MEMORY OF STEPHEN CONWAY
A GALLANT AUSTRALIAN SOLDIER
WHO SERVED HIS COUNTRY
IN GALLIPOLI AND FRANCE
BELOVED HUSBAND OF JANE
FATHER OF RICHARD
GRANDFATHER OF PATRICK AND SALLY
DEEPLY LOVED BY GEORGINA RICKSON
1895–1964

Below this, the stonemason had skilfully sculpted a single rose.

[illegible]

[illegible] Great War [illegible]

[illegible]

[illegible] Philip House and Queen's [illegible]

[illegible]

The lecturer was [illegible], with material from the Australian

Acknowledgements

There have been several drafts of this novel since I went to France in 2001 to visit the towns on the Somme. I am particularly grateful to my son Perry Yeldham who suggested I might find a story there. He not only read the first draft but when I was stuck for a title, sent me an email one morning that asked, 'How about *Barbed Wire and Roses*?'

My thanks also to friends Vincent Ball, John and Janet Croyston and Robert Banks Stewart who all read the constantly changing manuscript. John wrote pages of notes on the characters, and yet more pages listing my typing errors. Robert, a British writer and television producer, helped me with reminders of the BBC and its vagaries. My late wife Marjorie was also fully involved, providing her special insight as always.

I am indebted to several published sources: John Laffin's *Guide to Australian Battlefields*; historian Michael McKernan's book *The Australian People and the Great War* with its expert background of the period, plus a reproduction of the Sunlight soap advertisement showing how the Anzacs were commercially exploited; and an article in *The Independent* by Philip Hoare on Queen Victoria's hospital, entitled 'The Netley Experiment'.

The Internet was invaluable, with material from the Australian

War Memorial, and an article 'The Australian Experience' by Dr Peter A. Pedersen on the military death penalty. Most significant was a web site called Shot at Dawn (www.shotatdawn.org.uk), an organisation that ran a campaign to secure pardons for executed British soldiers from the First World War. This was achieved in November 2006, when posthumous pardons were obtained for hundreds of men shot at dawn in the 1914–18 war. On this web site over 1500 military executions are listed. None were Australian.

Finally, my deep appreciation to two people, Saskia Adams and Ali Watts, my editor and publisher at Penguin Group (Australia). With patience and affection they helped me reconstruct this book. It's been a long haul; a difficult time, and without them it might have been impossible. They have my lasting gratitude.

Peter Yeldham
pyeldham@bigpond.net.au

ALSO BY PETER YELDHAM

The Murrumbidgee Kid

Belle Carson was a good-looker, the best looker for miles around; even those who didn't like her (which included most of the women in town and quite a few of the men) had to admit that. But they also agreed she was as nutty as a fruitcake, and the bush telegraph – which spread any gossip the least bit unusual or outrageous – frequently carried news of her.

Belle longs for her young son, Teddy, to achieve the success that eluded her on the stage and screen. Determined to pursue this dream, she abandons her devoted husband and their Murrumbidgee River home for a more vibrant city life. But Belle's obsession leads her and Teddy – whom the press christens 'the Murrumbidgee Kid' – into a world where nothing is safe or familiar. And from her carefully hidden past a threat soon emerges to make their precarious lives even more vulnerable . . .

From rural Gundagai to the bright lights and shady underbelly of 1930s Sydney, this is a beautifully written and absorbing story about an unconventional family's coming-of-age.

Burnt Sunshine

ESTELLE PINNEY

A bet in half-jest, a ruby and a passionate love affair take a man and a woman in an unexpected direction . . .

Sydney, 1936, and the gorgeous Greta Osborne is a burgeoning stage star about to join the famous Palace Theatre in New York. But meeting married British naval officer Andrew Flight at a New Year's Eve party changes everything. Falling recklessly and deeply in love, Greta waives aside any thoughts of New York and Andrew jumps ship. The pair flee to Far North Queensland, where their sudden arrival in a small tobacco town is viewed with raised eyebrows and speculation. Finding themselves caught up in the social unrest and hardship of the Great Depression, the couple is soon pushed further north again to a remote island in Papua New Guinea, where they hope to settle and at last find peace.

A heart-warming and colourful novel, *Burnt Sunshine* traces the testing but joyous journey of Greta and Andrew. Bravely battling disapproval, disappointment and near-tragic loss, together the pair's sustaining love helps them laugh, triumph and take on the world.

An enchanting story of love and adventure that will win your heart.

'I laughed, I cried, but most of all I couldn't put it down.'
Toni Lamond

The Persimmon Tree

BRYCE COURTENAY

The Persimmon Tree is unashamedly a love story. I've always wanted to write one but until now have been afraid to do so. The reason is simple enough: most men in my experience have very little idea of what really goes on in a woman's heart or head. Now, at the age of 74, I just might know enough and have sufficient courage to write on the subject – the way of a man with a woman, of a woman with a man.

My story is set in the Pacific, although not in the paradise we've always been led to believe exists there. It is 1942 in Java and the Japanese are invading the islands like a swarm of locusts.

I have tried to capture the essence of love – how in a world gone mad with malice and hate, it has the ability to forgive and to heal. As it is in this story, love is always hard earned but, in the end, a most wonderful and necessary emotion. Without love, life for most of us would lack true meaning.

'a huge and action-packed saga'
The Age

'brims with drama and tragedy . . . Bryce back to his storytelling best'
Sunday Times